Martina Cole is the No. 1 bestselling author of fifteen hugely successful novels. *The Business* was the No. 1 bestselling hardback fiction title of 2008. *Faces* went straight to No. 1 in both hardback and paperback, and *Close* was a No. 1 hardback and paperback for a record-breaking number of weeks. *The Take* won the British Book Award for Crime Thriller of the Year, and was a No. 1 *Sunday Times* bestseller in hardback, as well as a No. 1 bestseller in paperback. *Martina Cole's Lady Killers*, featuring the stories of notorious female serial killers, was a critically acclaimed hit TV series in autumn 2008 and *The Take* and *The Graft* are currently being adapted for Sky One. *The Know* was selected by Channel 4's *Richard & Judy* as one of the Top Ten Best Reads of 2003. *Maura's Game*, *Faceless* and *The Graft* shot straight to No. 1 on the *Sunday Times* bestseller lists, and total sales of Martina's novels are now at nearly ten million copies. Martina Cole has a son and daughter, and she lives in Kent.

Highly acclaimed for her hard-hitting, uncompromising and haunting writing, as well as her phenomenal success, Martina Cole is the only author who dares to tell it like it really is.

Praise for Martina Cole's bestsellers:

'Cole has the amazing talent of making characters appear larger than life. Another fabulous effort' *Sun*

'Right from the start, she has enjoyed unqualified approval for her distinctive and powerfully written fiction' *The Times*

'The queen of hard-hitting crime fiction' *Bella*

'A blinding good read' Ray Winstone

'Martina Cole pulls no punches, writes as she sees it, refuses to patronise or condescend to either her characters or fans' *Independent on Sunday*

By Martina Cole and available from Headline

Dangerous Lady
The Ladykiller
Goodnight Lady
The Jump
The Runaway
Two Women
Broken
Faceless
Maura's Game
The Know
The Graft
The Take
Close
Faces
The Business

MARTINA COLE

THE BUSINESS

headline

First published in Great Britain in 2008
by HEADLINE PUBLISHING GROUP

First published in paperback in 2009
by HEADLINE PUBLISHING GROUP

3

Cataloguing in Publication Data is available from the British Library

ISBN 978 0 7553 2867 3 (B-format)
ISBN 978 0 7553 4962 3 (A-format)

Typeset in Galliard by Avon DataSet Ltd,
Bidford-on-Avon, Warwickshire

Printed and bound in Great Britain by Clays Ltd, St Ives plc

Headline's policy is to use papers that are natural, renewable and
recyclable products and made from wood grown in sustainable forests.
The logging and manufacturing processes are expected to conform
to the environmental regulations of the country of origin.

HEADLINE PUBLISHING GROUP
An Hachette UK Company
338 Euston Road
London NW1 3BH

www.headline.co.uk
www.hachettelivre.co.uk

For Luke Hubbard.
Gone but never forgotten.

For Tim and Sean.

And Louise Page and her lovely mum.
Thanks, Lou, you're a star.

And Lavinia Warner.
We always get there in the end! Love ya.

And for Sue P. and Elaine.
Great mates and great girls!

For Michael H. and Jordanna – thanks for letting
me use your names!

And for all the people caught up in heroin addiction.
I lost so many friends to it in the 70s and 80s,
I hate that it's coming back again.

Prologue

'Just get her off my doorstep, will you?'

The young woman's whole demeanour was one of controlled anger. Controlled, hard anger. The fact she was acting like this whole scenario was a bad joke spoke volumes in itself. Her deep blue eyes were mocking her protagonist; laughing at her, and telling her she was well able for anything she might have to offer. It was the silent come-on, where actions spoke much louder than words.

The young policeman was nervous; he had never had to attend anything remotely like this before. He had heard about these kind of events, heard how women fighting could be far more intimidating and violent than two men, or even a gang of men come to that. But he had not believed they could be so vicious. So disturbing. Frightening.

The fact that the two protagonists the police were trying to keep apart looked like twins didn't help, especially as apparently they were mother and daughter. But what really threw the policeman was the violence of the language. Not from the lady of the house, but from

1

her so-called mother. From the elder of the two, a good-looker who was well fuckable in his books and who he knew, without any kind of official certificate, was not the full twenty pence. In fact, she was an obvious nut-bag. As her next words proved.

'You fucking lairy little whore, get out here and fight me like a fucking woman. Do you honestly think I am going to swallow that from you, you mad bastard?'

The younger woman grinned, her absolute disgust for her mother written all over her face. Unfortunately this made her look more like her mother than ever. It gave her the same dark expression, the same sinister aura that told anyone who was foolish enough to mess with them that they were both more than capable of taking care of themselves.

The policewoman standing by, waiting to intervene should a fight actually ensue, was impressed with the girl's controlled demeanour. It was obvious that the mother was a headcase, and it was even more obvious that her daughter knew exactly which buttons to press to get a reaction from her. The policewoman also sensed that the daughter was enjoying her mother's discomfort. This was proved when the girl said with practised disdain, 'Listen to yourself, Mum, and then you wonder why I won't have anything to do with you. Why I moved as far away from you as possible. Why I am ashamed to admit you are me flesh and blood. All me life I cared for you, stuck up for you, and you weren't worth it. As everyone always said, you ain't worth a fucking wank.'

The tall woman went in for the attack once more, and PC White again held her back, only this time the job was far more difficult as the woman had the strength of ten men.

As he dragged her physically from the doorstep, a Range Rover pulled up sharply. The noise of it screeching to a halt was louder than the two women's strident voices.

A large, heavy-set man with dark-blue eyes and a determined expression jumped out. He made his way over to them quickly, his powerful body emphasised by the tightness of his sweatshirt. The police realised immediately who he was, and their horror was rapidly replaced with terror. They were in the presence of a local legend, someone they had all heard of, had seen in photographs but who, until now, they had never seen in the flesh. Kenneth Dooley was even more intimidating than they had realised; he was very imposing. And he was not known for having a kindly nature.

Grabbing the older woman roughly from the young policeman he said gruffly, 'Come on, Mum, let's be having you.'

She turned on him then, spitting vitriol. 'I might have known you would be on *her* side as usual, you're like a pair of fucking rednecks . . . duelling banjos you two. Always were.'

He ignored her, dragging her physically away from her daughter's front door. He was rough with her, and it was obvious that this was a regular occurrence.

'Just let it go, eh, she's come back and you will have to get over it,' he shouted to the woman left standing on the doorstep. He was dragging the irate woman towards his Range Rover, but she was determined that she wasn't going anywhere without a fight. He bundled her unceremoniously into the vehicle.

As he pulled away he was aware that the people in the surrounding houses were all watching the proceedings with interest. He had known this would happen eventually, he had just not expected it to happen so quickly.

Jordanna Dooley went back inside her small council house and closed the door on the police and the local onlookers. She had been used to this kind of interest in her family since she was a child. Her mother had developed a habit of making everything in her life public. She was the equivalent to movie royalty where they had lived. Her whole life had been played out to an audience for someone else's benefit. She was the Britney Spears of her generation, and she could have taught that poor whore a few things.

Once inside the house Jordanna found she was shaking, trembling with fear, a fear that was born from memories, not from her mother's actual presence. She had not seen her mother in quite a while and it always amazed her just how lovely she looked at first glance. How young she still seemed, even though the woman had lived at least two lifetimes and had made sure that her children lived them too.

Jordanna had never really known what it was to be a child; all her life she had been nothing more than an appendage, nothing more than her mother's object, her mother's chattel. Her hatred of her mother, like her private thoughts about her, were almost biblical in their outrageousness – she would quite happily send fifty plagues to her if she could. Not locusts or fucking frogs either, she would send that bitch every fatal disease known to man.

So broken had Jordanna been by her mother's disloyalty that she had eventually walked away from not only her, but her whole life. It was the only way she could get some kind of peace. When her mother had hunted her down, Jordanna had retreated into the Bible, into religion, in an effort to make her life mean something, to validate her existence. She had tried to keep her mother away with prayers. God knew, the courts would not help her.

Jordanna instinctively placed her hands across her stomach, feeling the small bump there that she hoped and prayed this time would grow into a full-term baby. Not another sticky mess that she would have to clean up and mourn so painfully like all the others.

That was her mother's fault as well, her inability to keep a child within the confines of a womb that had been sexually invaded much too early, and which now rejected anything that seemed to find comfort inside it. A womb that expelled her offspring before it could even be called a baby, a child, before it had anything even resembling a personality, a life.

It was as if with each of these rejections, Jordanna was being told by nature that anything she produced would not be fit for the company of other human beings, for the real world. That what she was hoping to create was somehow not good enough, was second-best.

And now, seeing what her mother was like once more, she was on the verge of agreeing with that belief. It was getting harder and harder to justify her existence and she knew that was because of her mother's influence. She knew that her early life was still shaping her adult life, even now, no matter how hard she tried to stop it.

But all that still didn't change the fact she wanted a child of her own so badly, so desperately, that she would kill for that chance. She lived for that opportunity, and told herself that it was something she could achieve one day. Without that she would be finished, and she knew it.

Her only real strength was her belief that one day she would carry a child to full term. Would finally hold a baby in her arms and love it unconditionally. She wiped the sweat from her forehead and took a few deep breaths to steady herself.

When she felt calm enough she walked into the small, spotless kitchen and sat down at her new IKEA dining table. She felt the fluttering inside her subside and lit herself a cigarette. The first puff made her feel sick and dizzy, the second draw brought her the comfort she needed.

She was not supposed to smoke, but she needed to now, needed a cigarette desperately. Her mother affected a lot of people like that, she seemed to destroy everyone she came into contact with, and that wasn't an exaggeration, it was a simple fact.

She heard the ringtone of her mobile then, Amy Winehouse singing 'Rehab', and the irony of it suddenly struck her.

She was laughing as she answered the call, but the laughter disappeared when she heard the voice of her grandmother asking belligerently, 'Is it true, has she tracked you down again?'

Kenny Dooley sighed heavily; his mother was now doing her quiet and hurt act. She had a lot of personas but this was the most irritating because it always worked with him. As much as she annoyed him, and she did annoy him, in fact she made him angrier than anyone else in the world, unlike his sister he could still feel a measure of sympathy towards her. It was this that brought on the anger in the first place because she didn't deserve his sympathy, she didn't deserve anyone's. Certainly not her daughter's, who she had bullied and used all her life.

He flipped open the small fridge between the car seats and said gruffly, 'Get yourself a beer, Mum, and stop fucking looking so sorry for yourself. You knew she wasn't going to hang out the fucking flags and kill a fatted calf so why are you acting as if this is a shock to you? If you had waited I would have had a word, tried to get you round there without all this drama.'

He pulled up at the traffic lights and then, looking her in the eye, he said sadly, 'But then drama is what you need, ain't it, Mother? You thrive on it.'

Imelda looked at her only son and said quietly, 'I can't help the way I am. What you see is what you get.'

She was already halfway through the can of lager, and the stench of her breath was filling the car's interior and making her son feel physically ill. She was, as always, stating what she saw as a fact, she thought that expressions like that made her honest, straight. She used them to justify her angry outbursts and her jealous asides. She was one of the most unhappy people he had ever come across, and that hurt him because, when the fancy took her, she could be a diamond. But, unlike most of the people she dealt with, *he* knew that she was hurting inside, had always been hurting inside. He knew that she didn't like herself and did not believe that anyone else could ever like her either. She changed friends often, dropping people on a whim at any slight, real or imagined. She tried her hardest to be what she knew she should be, but inevitably she would lapse back into the person she believed she was really.

'Trouble with Jorge is, she always thought she was better than everyone else, even as a child she looked down her nose at me . . .'

Kenny sighed heavily, he wasn't going to dignify that

shite with an answer. He was too shrewd to get into that conversation.

As he drove along the Whitechapel Road he spied someone he had been looking out for since the previous Christmas. Stopping the Range Rover he leapt out and began to punch the hapless victim of his rage. He battered him mercilessly, far more than was warranted because, deep inside, he really wanted to batter his mother, and this man, this ponce, was available. He was there.

Donny Barker had owed him money for a long time and, to make matters worse, he had disappeared off the face of the earth because of that debt. Now that Kenny could have coped with, understood even, but it was the fucker's reemergence on his old stomping ground that had caused his ire. It was a piss-take – someone on the missing list was to be coped with, their blatant return without the payment of their debt was like a personal insult. And an insult of that magnitude had to be redressed at the earliest opportunity. All in all, the man couldn't have surfaced at a worse time. Kenneth Dooley was a very hard man and, as such, he had a reputation to uphold.

Jordanna Dooley was whacked out. She was over the initial excitement that her mother had caused, and she was tired, seriously tired. As she lay on her bed, she wondered how people coped with the everyday. Most people she knew lived their lives without any kind of real hassle, real aggravation. Whereas her life had been fraught with all kinds of shit since day one.

This baby was her last chance at being normal, being like everyone else, and that was all she had ever really wanted. Normality, that was her only desire, her only dream. Just to be normal, no more and no less. But that was not something she felt was destined to be hers, and that was what terrified her. She was still so young, and yet she felt so fucking old.

Kenny fished a couple of wraps out of his jacket pocket and slipped them into his mother's hand. 'Here you are, go and have a ding-dong, girl.'

Imelda smiled at him then, suddenly aware that they had stopped outside her block of flats.

He opened the glovebox and threw her a wad of money. Then, poking a large finger into her face he said quietly, 'And keep away from her, right? I'll see what I can do in that department, but be warned, Mum, I don't hold out much hope.'

She shrugged then, her face much happier now as it relaxed into a real smile. Money and drugs had always had that effect on her. A couple of grams of coke, an armful of brown and a onner in her purse was her idea of heaven.

As she walked into her block her son watched her sadly; she was like a child, a vain, demanding, selfish child. That's why he felt so sorry for his mum, why he couldn't blank her out, why he accepted her outrageous behaviour and her outbursts. She had always kept one thing quiet, even when she was hurting so bad he could almost feel the pain inside her. She had still kept her trap shut, and he knew better than anyone how hard that must have been for her. Especially when she saw her daughter and was once more rejected without any kind of explanation whatever. But, in fairness, Imelda had always treated her only daughter badly. Jordanna had never known one truly happy day in her life.

Kenny had the key, and he knew he would do anything

to keep the door to the truth bolted whatever happened. Because the truth oftentimes was a hard bastard, the truth more often than not brought nothing but grief and hurt. It didn't bring closure, or decency, or any of the other shit that people who had never been in a position where the truth was a destructive force spouted. The truth was a springboard for many other upsets, bringing them out into the open at last, and then burying the half-truths, the far less painful truths, so deep they were impossible to dig up again.

He knew, and better than anyone, that sometimes, just *sometimes*, the truth could decimate a person and their whole life. It could cause a reaction so devastating it would make Hiroshima look like a playground prank.

Like his mother, he had never trusted the truth, and in their world that wasn't uncommon. He was known for his straight talking, his honesty. He knew that he would never lie about work – it was not feasible. But lying about some things was, in reality, fucking inevitable.

He remembered a priest once telling his class of five year olds that 'The truth will set you free' and the memory made him smile to himself. The truth could be a bigger jailer than most people realised. It was something that a lot of people just couldn't afford. Especially his sister Jordanna, the truth was the last thing she needed to hear. But he also knew that, now she was back in her mother's orbit, it was inevitable, that at some point the truth was likely to come out. Then what?

He didn't know and neither did anyone else. The lies went back to their childhood, and he knew that one day it would all surface, and when that day came, it would blow them all out of the proverbial water.

He also had a feeling that the day he had dreaded his

whole life was near and, in a strange way, he just wanted it over with, wanted it out in the open. Because, God Himself knew, he was sick of keeping it all secret. Sick of living this lie. And living everyone's lie for them.

Book One

All happy families resemble one another, but each unhappy family is unhappy in its own way.

– Leo Tolstoy, 1828–1910
Anna Karenina

If you hate a person, you hate something in him that is part of yourself.
What isn't part of ourselves doesn't disturb us.

– Hermann Hesse, 1877–1962
Demian: The Story of Emil Sinclair's Youth

A child is not a vase to be filled,
but a fire to be lit.

– François Rabelais, 1494–1553

Chapter One

1978

Mary Dooley was cleaning, she cleaned like other people slept; without any thought whatsoever. Her eyes constantly scanned surfaces for dust or smudges. Her mirrors were buffed to a high gloss, and her floors were polished to an almost dangerous sheen. She saw it as her given right, her God-given right, as she was well aware that cleanliness was the nearest she would get to Himself in this life.

When not cleaning, Mary was cooking. Huge, wholesome meals that her family ate without any real regard; after all, they had eaten this way all their lives. She cooked the old way; mashed potatoes dripping with butter and well-cooked joints of meat left to settle into their juices before being hacked apart and placed reverently on to her willow-pattern plates. She made shortcrust pastries and heavy rock cakes bulging with sultanas screaming for thick butter to be spread on them and devoured with a cup of sweet tea. She could do anything with suet and a bit of shin. She could make a cheap cut of meat fit for the Pope himself to devour, as her husband often pointed out when in his cups.

She pooh-poohed his compliments loudly and with her usual ripe language. She disparaged this new talk of salads and the avoidance of animal fats, and all the other crap they talked of that threatened her whole existence. She fed her family and she fed them in the only way she knew how.

Heart attacks indeed. As her own mother always said, sure, everybody had to die of something. Mary couldn't take onboard that you didn't need to die before your time, that she was slowly killing her family with love and good cooking. She saw it as some kind of conspiracy against her and all the other women like herself who had lived through the war and the want and were not going to go back to basic rations for anyone.

Tea was another of her passions. Mary left the big metallic pot on the hob bubbling away all day long until it was stewed black, and that was how she drank it. Black and sickly sweet. She said it gave her energy, and she was correct. It also gave her foetid breath and a furry tongue. This was at odds with her otherwise pristine appearance; like her home she was immaculate. From the tightly rolled French pleat that held in place long, thick, blond hair, coloured now every six weeks while her family were asleep, to well-fitting clothes that wrapped themselves neatly around her perfect size-ten body. For a woman well into her fifties she was still a looker. High cheekbones and deep-set dark-blue eyes saw to that. She had tiny, pretty feet that she was secretly proud of, and which she showed off every summer in cheap but tasteful sandals. They were her only real vanity.

Her hands were rough, well taken care of but still

showing the damage from years of bleach and washing soda. Her skin was assaulted nightly with a good scrubbing of Pears' soap and a thick layer of Pond's cold cream. This seemed to work because she looked much younger than her years and she had the demeanour and carriage of a much younger woman.

Her only vice was smoking; a cigarette was permanently dangling from her cupid-bow lips, and she squinted up her eyes to counteract the constant stream of smoke whenever she had her hands full. Her husband joked it was the secret of her good cooking, the adding of cigarette ash that everyone knew sometimes fell into her batters and her gravies. She laughed as loudly as her family at this, seeing nothing wrong with the occasional lapse of concentration. After all, it wasn't as if it could poison them was it?

Mary folded up her washing, enjoying the feel of its softness and the smell of its cleanliness. She was possessed of a twin tub that she would never part with, for all the new-fangled gadgets they had these days. As she said to Mrs Phillips, her neighbour, what was wrong with these young girls with their constant striving for an easy life, without the chores what the feck was there for a woman to do?

She glanced at the kitchen clock and stopped her folding. It was eight-thirty on a Monday morning, most of the family were away to their works and she was due at the church for nine o'clock Mass. She heard the toilet flush upstairs and sighed heavily. Her only daughter, her late surprise, as she referred to her, as she was over forty when she arrived, was finally up and about.

Pouring the child a cup of tea she took it up with her as she had to get her coat and hat anyway from the wardrobe. She treated this child differently to the boys and, deep down, she knew that, but she would never admit to it of course. She loved them all the same, at least outwardly, though her Imelda was the baby, and that, as she knew very well, was the trouble.

Her daughter got away with murder and, even though Mary knew it was wrong, she couldn't resist her. She was her last one, her baby, and she allowed her more licence than all the others put together.

Mary prayed daily that her trust in her youngest child wouldn't turn out to be misplaced but, in all honesty, she didn't hold out much hope. She had made one too many mistakes with that one, and it looked like they were coming home to roost.

Imelda Dooley was the image of her mother, the only one of the children to have her small build and ability to eat anything without putting on an ounce.

She had the same blond hair and small mouth, but she had her father's large, blue eyes, and they only added to the package, making her look innocent and knowing all at the same time. She had finely arched eyebrows and a small, pointed chin which made her look younger than her years. But the thick make-up that she applied with an expert hand soon put paid to that. Men had been looking at her since she was twelve and her breasts had suddenly appeared overnight. If her father had not been a local Face and her brothers had not been known locally for their short tempers and ability to knock out anyone within two feet of them, she would have been taken down a lot sooner, she knew that much now anyway. She had been such a fool, a silly, childish fool.

She sipped the tea her mother had brought in to her and wondered at how she was going to drop her bombshell, and she knew she needed to do it sooner rather than later. Her mother's personality was not conducive to secrets and if a neighbour sussed it out before her there really would be hell to pay.

Imelda felt sick with apprehension, she had played fast and loose and this was the result; her mother's warnings and advice had fallen on deaf ears. She knew it all, like many a girl before her.

Now she was lumbered, well and truly lumbered, and she knew that this was the one thing her mother would not forgive her.

She was frightened and excited all at the same time, the thought of a baby interrupting her life was more terrifying than the thought of dying. She would actually rather die a thousand deaths than face her mother's wrath and shame. And that was what she would be subjected to, she knew that as well as she knew her own name. Even in this day and age, it wasn't acceptable for Irish Catholic girls to have children out of wedlock, no matter how fashionable it might be for the rest of the country's youth. In this house it might as well be 1900, because those were the values they had to live by.

And as for her father, well, he was her biggest obstacle in all this, because she had no idea how this news would be received, and in what form his anger and his disappoint-ment would take.

She was nearly crying again, and the fear was once more making her feel faint. If it was only her brothers, she would have braved it out, both of whom she knew would see this latest escapade as yet more proof she was a spoiled brat. It was her mother and her father she was frightened of, because they were the ones who would be expected to sort this mess out. And a mess it was.

She put Elvis Costello on her record player and turned the volume up as high as it would go, her mother was at Mass and she had the run of the house. She might as well make the most of it before the balloon went up.

Gerald Dooley was a big man, an even-tempered, large Irishman with hands like bunches of bananas and eyes the colour of wet slate. He was imposing, well muscled, and he had a reputation as a fair-minded man, but not a man to cross. He liked a drink, and could hold it. He went to Mass once a week, as did his children, grown as they were, and he had a little flutter on the horses. He was also in full-time employment with a local Face named Michael Hannon; he collected debts, delivered messages with the minimum of threats and, in general, was what was known as a good all-rounder. This meant he had a wage, paid taxes, and was given a bit on top as a bonus. His family lived well and were respected as was he.

His size and his knowledge of everyone's business were his greatest assets and he had known that since he had been a boy of twelve and he had utilised his strengths from then. In this world he was a big man, outside it he was just another enforcer. He kept on the right side of the law through intimidation and innate cunning. This also held him in good stead with his employer. If he said something couldn't be done then it was a fact. But he would find a way round any obstacles, and that was his forte.

If someone was fool enough not to heed his warnings, always delivered with a friendly smile, then they were mugs, and would be made to pay the price. Rumour had it that a man, missing these many years, had last been seen talking with him. The story had only advanced Gerald

Dooley's fearsome reputation as a man who achieved his objectives through any means necessary.

This truth would be proved once more when he got out of his Jaguar outside a block of flats in Barking. He was dressed casually as usual, but still well put on. Even in his sixties he managed to garner looks from women of all ages. A reputation could do that for a man, especially in an environment like this. On this particular estate a decent car, a nice set of clothes and the ability to fight was a requisite for the women without a man. It screamed a few quid, the end of any aggravation with neighbours or family, and a guaranteed good few nights out.

Gerald was more than aware of this, and even though temptation had always been in his way, he had never succumbed. His wife had always been enough for him, and his family was his life. He had occasionally taken the odd flyer when he had been a young man and he had always found it a rather distasteful business. His guilt had gnawed at him like a priest with a ranter, and he had decided early on that he was happy enough as he was. With the wisdom of age he knew he had made the right decision, because so many of his contemporaries had sacrificed their families for a quick flash and a bacon sandwich. Youth was no substitute for loyalty and time served, even though it had its obvious advantages. No, his Mary had been an exemplary wife, and he appreciated her respect, her kindness and her love for him and their various offspring. For all her religious fervour he knew she would lie on a stack of bibles if the need arose. That was more important to him than anything else.

Today he had brought a new young lad on the job with him, his father was an old friend and the son, though a big lad, was not the sharpest knife in the drawer. But he was willing and that made up for a lot. He had the brawn, and the makings of a good repo man if he was taught properly from the off.

Lads like this made Gerald's life easier, and it worked well for them all. Anyone he trained was guaranteed a good livelihood and was generally regarded as having learnt his trade from the best. Young Declan might not be the most scholarly boy he had ever encountered, but he was willing, with a shrewdness that was paramount in their line of work. Ergo, he got the dosh by whatever means, all he needed was the chance to smooth out a few rough edges and he would be set for life.

When they had reached the required front door, a scruffy-looking flat with dirty nets and scuffed paintwork, Gerald Dooley nodded almost imperceptibly. Instead of knocking politely, young Declan proceeded to kick the door off its hinges. This was not a difficult task and, walking into the warm smell of central heating and cannabis smoke, they saw the occupant of the premises standing in his kitchen with the kettle in one hand and the other hand down the front of his pyjama bottoms.

'Morning, just in time for tea. Only, do me a favour would you?'

The man nodded dumbly, his face devoid of any colour now. Terror was taking over as he felt the trembling that told him he was well and truly fucked.

'Wash your fucking hands first.'

Jason Parks was walking through the spring sunshine like a man who owned the world and, in his case, he believed that to be the truth.

He was a new kid on the block, nineteen years old, and with the world at his feet. He was already responsible for three armed robberies and a Bond Street jewellery heist. His life was a set pattern and he was pleased with its natural progression. A womaniser by instinct and, with a good teacher in the shape of his father, he loved women, money and prestige, in that order. The latter guaranteeing him the former, as he knew from experience. Women had loved him from the tender age of fifteen and, looking twenty, he had been fortunate enough to have the pick of the litters around and about. His first encounter with a thirty-five-year-old French teacher had taught him that most women were as up for it as their male counterparts, they just acted as if they weren't interested because of public censure. In fact, most of the women he had come across would fuck a table leg if it had a nice set of togs and a decent motor. The fact that he was possessed of the gift of the gab was a bonus. He talked a good fuck, and he had found he was capable of delivering one into the bargain. Sex, or more importantly, the promise of the sex act, was his whole life and, unlike most romancers, he loved to pleasure a woman, loved hearing her cry out, watch her enjoy his ministrations; that was as much of a turn-on as the chase itself.

A good-looking boy with an athletic body and fair countenance, he knew he was a babe magnet; women of all ages, sizes, shapes and descriptions loved him. And in all of them he found something to love. He had taken the cherry of more than a few young girls and he had done it with what he considered panache. He saw himself as their teacher in matters of the personal and private. He enjoyed the role of tutor.

He enjoyed both the danger of a married woman and the innocence of a young girl new to the game. Jason liked the knowledge of their bodies, liked the way the experienced women guided him into their bodies all wet and warm and grateful.

Danger appealed to him, and he admitted that to himself.

As Jason snuck into a small, terraced house in Bow he was smiling. The wife of a notorious bank robber lived there and her husband was in court at this very moment for non-payment of fines. That he had been banged up when the fines had been requested was something for the briefs to argue, all Jason knew was that he had a few hours' grace until the man came home, and in that few hours he was going to give his wife the seeing-to of a lifetime.

The woman opened the door with a wide smile and the minimum of clothing and Jason was inside the front door before the two men observing him from the house opposite had time to comment about him to each other. Even though they were shocked at the boy's blatant temerity, to be visiting this particular man's wife on such an auspicious occasion was outrageous to say the least, that they were also impressed with his front, his bravado, was a given. Anyone who would risk their life for a quick feel had their vote, and even though they knew that he was a wrong one, a fucking muppet, they both felt a grudging respect for him, for his guts, for his absolute bottle. Laughing loudly, they shook their heads sagely at one another. He was a lad all right and, as far as they were concerned, he was to be applauded, but they kept that gem of wisdom to themselves.

Gerald Dooley was smiling, and young Declan had the sense to mimic his new boss's behaviour.

Colin Baxter, a junkie with an unfortunate amphetamine habit coupled with a complete inability to pick a winning horse, now owed what amounted to the national debt, not only to his dealer, but also to his bookie, who happened to be one and the same person.

When the kettle finally boiled Gerald took it off the gas and, motioning to Declan, waited patiently until Colin was safely held over the sink, his head about two inches from the china bottom, his arms wrenched painfully behind his back.

Leaning over the whimpering man Gerald said quietly, 'I warned you, Col, and you fucking mugged me off.'

Colin was straining with all the strength he possessed against young Declan's superior strength, terror giving him an extra spurt of energy.

'Please, Mr Dooley, I'll have the money later. I am due a few quid, money I'm owed . . .' His voice was hoarse with fright, with the knowledge that he had finally reached the end of his road.

'Too late, Colin . . .'

As the water gushed from the kettle on to his head and neck Colin screamed, the sound like that of an animal. It was high-pitched and laden with anguish. He fought with every ounce of his strength to avoid the torrent, only making it harder for himself in the long run.

Like Gerald, his captor had no feelings of remorse or sorrow. Young Declan just watched it with a quiet interest, concentrating on holding his prey still while he learnt exactly how these things were done.

He knew he wasn't Einstein, but he also knew he was a quick study, and that meant the difference between a good living and some serious wedge.

He wanted to earn the wedge, and he wanted it sooner rather than later. Gerald Dooley was his ticket to the stars and he felt honoured to have such a teacher.

Gerald winked at him gamely, nothing he did in the pursuit of his occupation was ever done with malice. But it was always done with a certain aplomb. After all, without a decent rep he wouldn't even be employed. He didn't love his job as such, but he knew he was a one-off, knew that he was known as a man who got things done quickly and succinctly. His real forte was that he made sure no one had to clean up after him and in their game that was the main requisite.

If he was asked to demand something, he would get it by any means, and his secret was that he never discussed those means with anyone. He was a hard man, by nature and by reputation, that was his strength.

Imelda could smell the cloying aroma of colcannon, she had loved the smell until her pregnancy. Now the aroma of cabbage and grease made her stomach turn. As she forced herself to take deep breaths, she felt the terror of her situation once more. She knew that she had to get it out in the open, had to tell her mother before she either worked it out for herself or was told by an outsider. Imelda knew in her heart that this was news that was best delivered swiftly, but it was still a terrifying prospect.

As she walked down the stairs, she could hear her mother busying herself cooking the evening meal. She wanted to catch her while she was alone, wanted to spill the news of her downfall in private. Imelda was aware that her mother had a soft spot for her, and she instinctively knew that if she could talk to her alone now, her mother's reaction would be to protect her.

Entering the kitchen she smiled widely. 'That smells lovely, Mum.'

Mary Dooley glanced at her youngest child and

immediately sensed that something was wrong. She had felt that there was something worrying her daughter for a while and now they were alone together she decided to try and find out what was the cause of her youngest child's obvious unhappiness.

'Sit down, child, and I'll make us a nice cup of tea.'

Imelda did as she was bidden. Pulling a chair out from the large Formica table she sat down heavily, her heart aching and her body stiff with nerves.

Mary poured them both a cup of tea and, sitting beside her daughter, she said heavily, 'What's ailing you, child? Are you feeling ill?'

Imelda looked into her mother's face. She was so like her, even she could see that. They were like twins born years apart. In her mother's presence though, she could feel the heaviness of her breasts more acutely for some reason and knew that soon they would betray her. She was as fertile as her mother and she knew that would be her downfall. Because, unlike her mother, she had allowed herself to be used without the safety of a wedding ring.

'Is anything bothering you, child, are you worried about anything?'

Mary was genuine in her distress, was honestly worried about her daughter. It came across in her voice, in her gentleness, and in her expressive eyes. Eyes that seemed to tell her daughter that she was prepared to hear the worst, and unfortunately, the worst was what she was going to get.

Gerald Dooley heard the screeching before he had even entered his house. This was an almost unheard-of occurrence, and his shock was exacerbated by his daughter's language. His Imelda had never uttered a swear word in his presence in her life, so he knew that the harangue he was now party to was serious.

As he opened the front door he kept his movements quiet, listening to his wife and daughter as they went at each other without care.

'You fecking filthy little whore, you'd do this to me and to your poor father? What the fuck have I bred?'

Imelda's voice was as loud and just as angry as her mother's. 'Do you think I fucking planned this then? Do you think I did it to get one over on you? It was an accident, a bloody stupid accident.'

As Gerald went into the kitchen he was amazed to see his little wife with the kettle in her hand, just about to throw it and its contents all over their daughter. It was like déjà vu. Only, he didn't want his daughter scarred for life, no matter what she had done.

Seeing her husband standing there, Mary Dooley immediately stayed her hand, and his daughter looked at him with wide, scared eyes and a defiance that, until then, he had only observed in her brothers.

'What in the name of God is going on here?' His loud voice stayed them both, even more than his actual presence.

'I could hear you two down the street like a pair of fucking old shawlies going at it. What the neighbours must be thinking, I don't know.'

The last few words were enough to quieten down his wife; the neighbours and their opinions were the only thing outside of her family that she cared about. Her reputation was everything to her, and though others might bring their petty squabbles outside the front door, she would normally have died before doing the same thing.

Taking a deep breath his wife looked at him triumphantly and said in a stage whisper, 'Ask your one here. She's pregnant and she won't tell me who the culprit is.'

Imelda and her mother watched as Gerald digested this information. The differing expressions on his face were enough to put the fear of Christ up any man young or old, and his wife and daughter didn't feel any different. As he walked around the table towards his daughter, his hair almost on end and his muscles straining with anger, his wife ran between them both, realising what she had caused. She was a different woman now, a quiet woman, the peacekeeper. The voice of reason. 'Gerry, Gerry, come on now. It's not that bad . . . Calm yourself down, man.'

In that few seconds Mary knew he was capable of killing the child, and the poor child within her. In those few seconds she saw that she had read this situation all wrong. In those few seconds she knew that her doting husband was not above a murder for his daughter's crimes.

Imelda was cowering on the floor now, her face a mask of terror and disbelief. That her father, her dad, could ever turn on her like that was unbelievable. She had thought he would have been the one calming her mother down, which was why she had felt confident enough to argue with her mother in the first place.

She had not expected this reaction towards her. Towards the father maybe, but never towards her. He had stood by her all her life, had been the one she ran to when anything had gone wrong. He was the one who would take her part against her mother, her brothers, even the school. He had been her rock and now she was finally finding out what it was like to live without his blind acceptance. She could see the hatred in his eyes as he looked at her. The disappointment. The absolute disgust.

Gerald was about to attack his daughter physically when he felt his wife's hands on his chest. Felt her shoving him away from his youngest child. Somewhere in the chaos in his mind he knew this was a good thing.

He allowed himself to be pushed from the room, allowed his little wife to steer him towards the dining room and shove him inside. But all the while he could feel his anger and his disappointment getting stronger and stronger. His daughter had lain with someone, and he knew from experience that it wouldn't be anyone they would be pleased to welcome into their home. If that had been the case, she would have had the sense to bring him there. This man was some piece of shit that she had taken up with, because for all her innocence you didn't live in a house like this without picking up a few tips about how the world outside worked.

He pulled out a chair and sank into it, his usual pride in the room was diminished now. Ruined by his daughter's actions. He felt the murderous rage abate just a little and was amazed to find that his wife was still talking to him, still trying to quieten him down. He had heard nothing, not a word of her babbling. It was as if he was on a different planet, a planet where the life he had always known was over. He felt as if he was in a parallel universe, as if he was caught up in an episode of *The Sky at Night*. It was all wrong. Felt wrong. It was out of whack. Someone had taken his baby down and he was going to see that they paid for it. Paid for it dearly.

Even though he cared, cared for all the other people in his orbit, wife, sons, etc., they were really nothing to him. His little girl was the be all and end all of his existence. From her birth, she had stolen his heart. She was the child he had heard about, but had never believed existed. The golden child. The daughter that friends had assured him would mean far more to him than his sons. He had never really believed them.

Until he had looked at his daughter's face, had held her in his arms, he knew that until then, he had not really understood real love. He had not believed that a man could worship a child as he had worshipped her. She had been born at home, like the others, but when he had held her in his arms, he had felt an emotion so strong it had all but broken him. She had amazed him, looking at her was like looking at the world in a new light. Because she was now a part of it. His sons had never had that effect on him, even though he loved them. They would one day be men, grown men. But not this child, she was his late surprise, his baby girl.

He had a daughter, and the knowledge had made him weak, vulnerable. He had looked at her and seen the fall of Adam. He could see why men could destroy another man's property, another man's life, and all for the love of a daughter, a female child. It was such an event in his life he had never really got over it, though he had suppressed it as best he could. He'd never been one to show his emotions to the world and so he had loved her within the confines of his family, and he had loved her with a vengeance, as he had his wife. For the first time in his life, he had known real fear. He had protected her, cared for her, and overlooked her shortcomings. Which were legion, since she had been spoiled by everyone around her since her birth. She had been the one to run to him, climb on his lap, the only one of the children to be wholly his. His sons had always been their mother's boys. And he had accepted that, known that was how it should be. He was, after all, his own mother's son. Sons and mothers had a close relationship, as he knew first-hand, and he also knew that was true of fathers and daughters. As much as he loved his boys, Gerald Junior and Brendan, his daughter was like some kind of unknown entity to him. And he loved her all the more because of that.

Imelda had arrived late in his life and, from day one, she had captured him, and his heart. She had been his reason for living, he had seen her as his bright star, the child who would take him into old age. Her birth had given him the rush he had needed at fifty. He had been blessed with this child. She was like a gift from God Himself, proof of his virility, proof of his loyalty, his love for his wife. She was all he talked about, all he really cared about. And he'd assumed she would have been like the boys, had assumed she would have toed the line, done what was expected of her. So he had not envisaged her being brought down like this, getting laid and left, like any tart around about. She was better than that. She was worth more than that, surely? He had seen her marrying a man who was worthy of her and, more importantly, worthy of him, and the legacy he would leave. He had seen her without stain, had believed she was without anything even remotely sexual. As his baby she had been not only sexless in his eyes, but also without the *want* of sex. He had believed her to be pure. She had acted the good girl, the good daughter.

And he had been fucking wrong. She had been allowed more freedom than her brothers, had been seen by him as a shrewdie, far too clever to be caught like this. He had always known that she was well above her poor brothers when it came to brains, intelligence. The school had said she was a veritable fucking brain-box, that she was destined for great things. Well, if she was such a fucking know-all, how come she was in the club, and how come she had brought this kind on shame on the family? On him?

It was all a fucking lie, a fucking charade. She was no better than the girls he had seen around, the slags, the tarts. She had been like a viper in his breast. Pretending she was something she wasn't. Her innocence was what he cherished, was what he demanded from her. Her innocence was what he held dear to him. What he felt was so special about her.

Now though, she had broken him, she had destroyed all. She was no more than a whore. Even if she had only done it once, he would not feel any different, because once, as far as he was concerned, was once too fucking often in his book. This whore was not a one-time only girl though, he had seen her, heard her arguing with her mother. Gerald knew then that she was far too fucking cocky to have been caught out on the off. The thought of her, his baby, his girl, on the cock was more than he could bear. He was devastated and he was disgusted.

His baby was pregnant and, to make matters worse, he knew that the culprit was not someone she was proud of. If that had been the case, she would have fronted them up, would have argued her end. Would have been woman enough to give them both a piece of her mind. That he could have coped with. Could have understood. Respected even. Because it would have meant she was in love. Would have meant she was adult enough to fight her end. Fight for what she believed in. Instead, she was ashamed, she was cowering from him like the treacherous bastard she was. She was disgusted with herself, so how could she expect him to feel any different?

Never in his life had Gerald felt so let down, so ashamed, so repulsed by someone in his immediate family.

Taking a deep breath he looked at his wife as if he had never seen her before and he asked quietly, 'Find out his name. Find out who he is.'

Mary soothed him as best she could. Of all the things she had expected this day, his reaction was not one of them. She had thought that he would have stood up for this child of his, had believed he would have taken her under his wing. Been the one to bring the family together. But this man before her was like a stranger, like someone she had never seen before, and who she hoped she would never see again. This man was dangerous, extremely dangerous, and for the first time since she had known him he frightened her.

In fact, she was seeing him as others saw him, and it was not a pretty sight. For the first time in her life he didn't make her feel safe and cared for. He just made her feel absolutely terrified and that wasn't a feeling she had ever associated with her husband.

Chapter Two

Jason Parks was lying in his bed, enjoying the softness of the mattress and looking forward to the ministrations he was guaranteed to receive from his mother. She was a real touch in that respect. She cared for him as a whole, from his washing and his ironing, right through to his meals and his penchant for a few cold beers. She took care of him without a care for herself. He was her baby, her little boy. He encouraged her to feel like that, of course. He knew what side his bread was buttered on.

The best thing of all, as far as he was concerned, was that it didn't cost him a penny. The silly old bag did it out of love. Jason was a complete waster, even he had accepted that much. He had no real interest in anything or anyone, unless it would enhance his standing in the community. The community being the people he saw as worth the effort. Worth putting himself out for.

As he lay there in his clean sheets and with his music playing far too loud, he felt his usual smugness. His mother was his biggest critic, but she was also his biggest fan. If he took it into his mind to film himself murdering his family, his mother would still defend him, would never believe that the man on the film was actually her son.

It was one of the reasons he loved her so much. There was literally nothing he could do that would bring down her wrath upon him. She saw him through her special, mother-made, rose-tinted glasses, and he thanked God for that every day of his life. He was sensible enough to know that anyone but her would have aimed him out of the front door years ago.

His father, a cunt of the first order, was also handy, he had a bit of a rep, and a good few quid. His mother kept him in line where Jason was concerned, so that was a touch. His father thought he was a complete muppet, and voiced his opinion of his son at every available opportunity. He called him shiftless, useless, and many other epithets when the fancy was on him. Luckily, his mother was always on hand to stop him before he went too far.

All in all, Jason saw himself as one jammy bastard, an expression he knew was used by more than a few of his so-called mates. He was a charmer, a robber and, on occasions, he was a thief. There was a subtle difference between a robber and a thief; a robber was respected, they robbed banks, building societies or post offices. That was an acceptable occupation in his world. A thief, however, was a completely different entity. A thief was looked down on by everyone, even by the Old Bill. A thief stole from those who couldn't afford it. A thief would scrump anything they came across, a thief was so low they would nick off their own, which was why they were so hated. Thieves were without any kind of conscience, they took what they wanted from anyone in their orbit without any kind of care or distinction. They were vilified by their contemporaries because they were so untrustworthy and so devious.

A thief was the lowest of the low. And young Parks was lower than anyone actually realised. He was a natural-born grifter, if he saw something he liked, he skanked it. A necklace, a ring, a wallet. He would take it without any remorse whatsoever. He was sensible enough, though, to keep his thieving to himself. He was an emerging Face, a robber, and he loved the kudos of that. He saw himself in the future with a good few quid, a decent motor, a few kids, and with a nice bird who was sensible enough to turn a blind eye to his misdemeanours. Life, he decided, was good, and it could only get better.

Imelda Dooley and her predicament was not his problem; she knew the score. She was sensible enough to know that he was not about to hire a fucking dirty great big white charger to gallop round her house so he could offer her any kind of security. No, she needed to get shot of her bellyful of arms and legs, put it down to experience, wipe her mouth, and get on with her life like he intended to get on with his.

She was a fucking mug if she thought he was going to stand by her, she was a lovely little shag granted, but not worth any real upset. He knew her kind, she would be taking on all comers within eighteen months.

He had erased Imelda from his life within minutes, as he had erased many a girl before her. She was a distant memory now, as far as he was concerned, and he trusted her to understand that, and accept it like many another before her.

Sighing happily, he put her out of his mind once more, making a mental note to avoid her mate Belinda like the proverbial plague for a few weeks. What was it with birds?

They always seemed to have a fat, ugly mate to do their dirty work for them. Though he wouldn't kick poor old Belinda out of bed, the ugly ones were always very grateful and they were also more likely to let him have a perve-up. The good-lookers knew their worth and expected to be treated accordingly. The Belindas of this world, however, needed a party piece to make them stand out from the crowd and get a bit of attention now and again, and he knew that Belinda was right up for it, even though she acted like a fucking wilting virgin. Jason grinned, he'd have his hands down her drawers before the month was out.

Imelda and her mother had somehow become conspirators. Since her father's reaction to her pregnancy, they had seen a side to him that neither had known existed. He spoke to no one, he would not sit in the same room as his daughter, and he refused to discuss the situation with his wife. The worst thing of all though, was his insistence that the child be terminated. 'Flush the bastard away', was his only opinion on the subject. To his wife this was worse than anything else, that he wanted them to become party to a mortal sin. The boys as always took his part, took their lead from him. Gerald wanted the name of the father; he wanted to know who had taken his daughter's virginity. Though, in all honesty, Mary wasn't sure that Imelda losing her virginity was something that had happened that recently.

Her husband wanted the name of the man who had brought his family into disrepute, brought shame on them. Because that was how he felt about it all. Ashamed and disgusted. Mary knew him better than anyone. She knew that how people saw him was everything to him. In his world, he had to be seen to be in control, in control not only in his work, the people he employed, but his family set-up too. He was respected because he and his family had always been beyond reproach. Gerald had always lived by a moral code that was only understood by their peer group. By the people who lived by the same code. The rest of the world had their way of living their lives, and that was fine, but they also had their own way of existing, and that was also fine. Until something like this happened. Imelda's situation had thrown Gerald's whole existence into chaos. He saw his family, especially his daughter, as an extension of himself. His children had to be beyond reproach. They had to live within his boundaries and his guidelines. Until Imelda's latest escapade, Mary had never had to deal with a husband who was suffering a major disappointment. He blamed her for this aggravation, she knew that he did. Even though, deep inside, she knew that was not fair, she also knew that he had always brought the money in and left her to bring up the children as she saw fit. Something she had done very well, until now. Until this.

Now she was left to sort it out, make it all better, and she didn't know how the fuck she was supposed to do that, because he could not know who had brought his daughter down, not yet, not until he could be a bit more rational about it and that did not seem as if it was ever going to happen. In fact, he seemed to be getting angrier by the hour. Her husband was like a stranger to her, to them all. He had changed overnight from a caring father and husband to a man who was violent and aggressive. He had been her rock, her man, the guiding light for their family. Now, it was as if she didn't know him any more, didn't know how to talk to him, how to control him. Because until now, she had controlled them all. Her whole family, and her husband had been quite happy for her to do that. It had worked for him, it had saved him from having to actually take part in the whole family set-up. He could stand back and take the credit for his family, he had been happy. Over the fucking moon, in fact. Now though, he was acting like she had brought up some kind of viper, acting as if she had done that deliberately, had set out to destroy him and his perfect life. It didn't seem to occur to him that she might be hurting as well. That she might be as bewildered as he was. That she was as frightened as her daughter was of his reaction to the father's identity was not even an issue with him. He saw Mary as stonewalling him, saw her as a co-conspirator. Felt that she was as disloyal as their youngest child. In short, he saw her as the enemy.

Gerald had always been possessed of a certain paranoia, but that had worked for him, worked for them all over the years. She had never been on the receiving end of it, even though she knew that a lot of people had been. She had never thought she would be the recipient of his anger, of his hate. Until now, though, she had never done anything to bring his wrath down on her, or her children. And, knowing what he was capable of, she was not going to give him the chance now. While he had kept his violence outside of their house she could accept it. Now though, she was seeing the man everyone else saw. The man that everyone else knew so well. She had glimpsed this side of him before they had married, and in her youth had liked it, had seen it as a strength. She had believed, like many a woman before her, that she could control him. Could change him with love, and she had, until now that is. She had never once crossed him, and he had given her complete autonomy over their family and their home. How could she have been such a fool? How could she have allowed herself to believe that she had ever really had any kind of power over her husband or her life?

It had been an elaborate sham that she had unwittingly been a party to.

For all Mary's bravado she knew that he was capable of literally anything when he believed he was within his rights. Overnight, he had become like a stranger to her, to his daughter, who had been the apple of his eye until she had stepped out of line. A line that, until now, had never really been evident to anyone except him.

Gerald was not going to Mass, he was drinking heavily, and he had an air of suppressed rage about him. It was as if her family was dissolving before her eyes. Even the boys were different; the atmosphere in the house was stifling, like a black pall hanging over their very existence.

For the first time in her married life Mary didn't know what to do, didn't know how to make it better. On top of all this was the knowledge that soon her daughter's condition would be evident to the world, to all in their world at least, and the shame would be too much to bear.

How many times had she stood outside the church, how many times had she enjoyed someone else's misery, gossiped about other people's children and their faults, their mistakes. Like her husband she had believed that nothing like that could ever happen to them. She had convinced herself that her daughter would be too bloody shrewd to let that happen to her in the first place. Now they were up shit creek without any kind of paddle whatsoever, and she had no option but to try and protect her daughter as best she could; she had to hope that Gerry came to terms with this sooner rather than later. Even though she didn't hold out much hope.

So many girls had babies now without the benefit of a wedding ring and, while it might be acceptable to the rest of the world, it was still seen as a disgrace by the Catholic community. But even that shame was to be borne, rather that than face the shame of an abortion, the taking of an innocent life. As the priest so rightly said, who knew what God's plan was. One of those poor unfortunate babies might have been the person who discovered a cure for cancer, been a world peace leader. That was a stretch considering where the child was likely to be born, but it was the principle of the thing.

And that whore upstairs wouldn't even let on to Mary who the father was. At one point it had even occurred to her that maybe the bitch didn't know. Imelda insisted that until her father calmed down she would not say a word and, in fairness, she had to admit the girl had a point.

As Mary glanced around her pristine Hygena kitchen with its white melamine doors for easy cleaning, and the pale-green work surfaces, she wondered why they were suddenly incapable of cheering her up. Normally the look of the place eased her tired heart. Normally she felt as if she was in her own personal cocoon of comfort, as if the rest of the world didn't exist outside of her four walls. Now though, it gave her no comfort. Mary's life was suddenly in free fall and she didn't know how to make it stop.

Stoic was usually the word she would use to describe herself, she took whatever life handed out to her and she took it on the chin, whether it was the boys in court, or her husband's questionable career. But she could cope with those things because they were part of her life, and part of the lives of the people around her. Her daughter's wrecking of her young life was different though.

A child was for ever, they were like a constant headache that occasionally brought a smile to your face, or a feeling of pride that washed over you and made it all worthwhile.

There would be no abortion in this house, no murder of an innocent, no matter what her husband said. Fucking King Herod himself would not have been able to get her to do anything so deplorable, even with the threat of death hanging over her.

Mary slipped her beads from her apron pocket, she would say a few decades of the rosary. Mary, her namesake, was a mother like herself. Maybe she might send her the answer to her problems. At this juncture, anything was worth a try.

Gerald was in the pub, and his oldest friend Jackie Martin was watching him warily.

He was like a different person. He was being deliberately obtuse, rude and sarcastic, was argumentative with anyone who came into his orbit, and that was so unlike his old friend that he was at a loss as to how to react to him.

That Jackie was frightened of him was something that had never been said out loud. Gerry Dooley had never been the kind of man who would have exploited that. Gerry had always gone out of his way to make sure that his oldest friend, in many ways his only friend, had never had any reason to feel intimidated by him. Until now.

All Jackie wanted to do was calm him down, get him home. He was worried that Gerry would do something to jeopardise his livelihood, his living. And, in so doing, would nause his up as well. He only earned because this man bankrolled him.

Over the last few weeks Jackie had watched him fuck up everything he had worked for over the last thirty years. Overnight he had become unmanageable, even his sons were giving him the swerve. Not blanking him outright, but keeping their distance when he had a few drinks in him. And who could blame them?

Gerry's behaviour was causing gossip, not that the men involved would have put it quite like that of course. Their wives gossiped, they talked. But it was gossip whatever way you looked at it. Now people were waiting to see what the outcome of Gerry Dooley's latest escapade was going to be. He was supposed to be collecting as usual, only he was out and about, on the piss and, to top it all, he was spending money that was not his to spend. Most collectors would do a drop, collect a wedge, and then demand the money a second time. The people they dealt with would have paid it and all, had he demanded it. But Gerry Dooley had never taken a penny from anyone in his life, had never ever taken advantage of his position, and that was something Jackie had resented over the years because it would have augmented *his* income, it would have made *his* life a lot easier. Other men in his position were guaranteed the extras, but not him. Gerry was as straight as a fucking die, so Jackie had to be too.

Gerry Dooley was not only his mate, his employer, he was also the reason he had never had a serious touch in his life. Who would do something so stupid on Gerry's watch? Other number twos had a private income, had their own little earner, but not him. Gerry prided himself on his honesty, on his integrity. Gerry had given him a good wage, Jackie knew and appreciated that. But he had never had the opportunity to spread his wings, get his own little firm up. That he would have had nothing without his friend's largesse was irrelevant, most people in his position were only there because of who they knew, not because they had any kind of qualifications. He was where he was because Gerry trusted him, and in their world that was more than enough. But it didn't stop him resenting the fact that his hands had been tied for years because of this man, that he had not even been allowed to deal a bit of puff, or a bit of coke because Gerry Dooley didn't agree with it. Even though the people who paid his wages were dealing all sorts to anyone with the poke to purchase it.

And, despite that, here he was, lumbered with a Gerry Dooley who was on a path of destruction and he could do nothing about it. Because everyone knew that when Gerry whistled, Jackie came running. What choice did he have?

It didn't make it any easier though, and when Gerry was on the ball it had been to his advantage. Now though, he wasn't so sure. If Gerry got the bum's rush, where the fuck did that leave him?

Now he was being looked upon to sort Gerry out before he caused any kind of aggravation; it was assumed that he had enough clout with his old friend to be able to talk some kind of sense into him. Walk him out of this pub, and deliver him back home to his wife with the minimum of fuss. No one seemed to allow for the fact that his own sons were within talking range but were giving him a massive swerve, that his own flesh and blood didn't see the need to remove him from the premises so why should he be the one to provoke him even further? Because that is what would happen if he dared to try and make him see sense, make him go home to his wife. In fact, it was home that seemed to be the bugbear, he was avoiding it like the plague.

There was a story there all right, only he knew that, given Gerry Dooley's natural reticence, he would not be getting it any time in the near future.

As Gerry downed another large Scotch and immediately motioned for another, Jackie wished that he had the nerve to remove him from the premises, but he knew he wasn't capable of doing anything like that. Not to Gerry Dooley or to anyone, come to that. He didn't have the bottle to assert himself without a Gerry Dooley beside him, orchestrating the proceedings, and he knew that a lot of their contemporaries were now well aware of that fact. It was one humiliation after another lately, and he didn't know how much more he could take.

The landlord of the pub made eye contact with him then, and he couldn't pretend he hadn't noticed it. Shrugging, Jackie opened his arms in a gesture of supplication, rolling his eyes as if he had no choice in the matter. He could feel the animosity coming off everyone around him, knew that they thought he was a complete ponce for allowing this to carry on as long as it had.

As far as they were concerned, he should be keeping his boss on the straight and narrow, protecting him, ironing out any differences for him until such time as he got his head back to normal, had got over whatever lunacy had overtaken him. This was the first time in living memory that Gerry Dooley had ever stepped out of line, and that just made this all the more conspicuous.

Sighing heavily, Jackie looked meaningfully at Gerald Junior and his brother Brendan and, in fairness to them, he knew that they were pretty much in the same boat as he was. Unable to spread their wings without their father's say-so, and wary of confronting him because they didn't know what would be the outcome. Gerald Dooley, for all his so-called decency and loyalty, was no better, really, than the bullies he despised. Because everyone in his world was only welcome provided they did as he expected, as he saw fit. That fact was becoming more and more obvious as the days wore on.

As Gerry walked out of the pub with his sons in tow, Jackie looked around him, at the people who mattered and, blowing out his lips noisily, he said with a deliberate and theatrical pretence at loyalty, 'What? Can't a man have a few drinks?'

Then, picking up his own drink, he looked around him as if disgusted with the reaction he had encountered, aware that he was not fooling anyone.

He was determined, though, to find out what the big secret was, because he knew that if Gerald Dooley had wanted him to know what was going on, he would have heard about it by now.

Imelda was lying in bed. She could hear her father ranting and raving and, even though she understood how disappointed he was in her, she still couldn't equate that cold-hearted, vicious person with her father. With the man who had brought her up with hardly a raised voice or a cross word. Until now, he had indulged her, not as much as her mother had admittedly, but enough to make her think she was safe, that she was different to the boys. He had let her have more freedom than them because he had believed that his name, his reputation, should have been enough to protect her. That was also the reason why she would not say who the father was to her mother or brothers: until her father calmed down, he was best kept in the dark.

She pulled the sheets over her head, trying in vain to blot out the sound of her father's angry swearing and her mother's pathetic attempts at placating him. Anyone would think she was the only girl in the world to get in the club.

Imelda slipped out of the bed and, standing by her bedroom window, she saw that most of the neighbours were in their back gardens, listening to the furore that was now a common occurrence in the Dooley household.

She knew that most of the women had guessed the cause of Gerald Dooley's sudden lunacy, and she knew it would not be long before everyone knew.

Imelda wondered if Jason's mother had given him the message that she had left with her. Jason knew better than to call her at home, but he could still leave a message with her friend Belinda. In fact, she was actually wondering if Belinda was keeping his message from her. In her more paranoid moments, when she wasn't envisaging Jason under a car, or a bus, she actually wondered if he was just ignoring her. But that couldn't be. He had to know what deep shit she was in. Even though Imelda didn't know what she expected him to do, she wanted him to at least acknowledge her in some way. Even if it was only with a message through Belinda. But she knew in her heart that Belinda had seen him, she knew that she had, and if he hadn't anything to say by now, he wasn't going to say anything at all.

Imelda finally had to admit that she was on her own, that there was no way out. She was trapped in this nightmare for the duration. Trapped with a child that it seemed no one wanted, least of all her. Her mother was more frightened of the priest than she was of her own husband, and after his carry-on that was a serious fear, because her father was terrifying everyone at the moment.

She glanced around her bedroom. A few months ago

this had been like a haven to her, had been where she came to sleep off her excesses. Where her mother brought her cups of tea and bacon rolls, and where her father came to kiss her goodnight, or bung her a few quid. It had been a friendly place, somewhere she had felt safe, had felt loved. Now though, it was a hostile environment, it was suddenly full of dark corners and drab furniture. It was the last place she wanted to be on this earth, but she had nowhere else to go. Had no other option open to her. Imelda had hoped in her heart that Jason might have been moved to offer her somewhere to go. Even though she knew that was ridiculous, it was amazing what the human mind latched on to in times of extreme crisis. That a baby, an innocent child, could have caused all this grief was unbelievable. But she knew it wasn't the child that her father was focusing on, it was the way the child had got there.

She could hear her mother's voice once more, still trying to calm her husband down, trying to quieten him so the neighbours didn't get another earful of his ranting and raving. She could almost feel the spit that she knew he was spraying over anyone within a two-foot radius.

The fear was back again, like a big, black cancer eating away at her. She knew that Jason had abandoned her. All her usual bravado, her loud-mouthed persona that her family's name had always allowed her to get away with, had deserted her.

Even her brothers had no real time for her any more, they just wanted some kind of closure, an end to it all. They saw her as the catalyst for their father's destruction, and she was, she knew she was.

Until now Imelda had not understood just how much she had lost. School had been a breeze thanks to her mother, and her brothers. When she'd been chucked out, her mother had sorted things for her. In fact, until now her whole life had been pretty much as she wanted it. Her father's reaction, his extreme reaction to her latest escapade had thrown her completely. She would have lain money that she could have got away with murder where her father was concerned, and she had a feeling that had she committed a murder it would not have had this much of an effect.

Her father would have moved heaven and earth to help her out then, that was something he could have understood. Anger, violence. In his world they were everyday emotions. But sex, sex or love, he had no real concept of, at least not where his baby was concerned anyway.

Her mother had kept him from her door for weeks, but she knew that was not going to last for ever, he wanted answers, and he wanted them sooner rather than later. A pregnancy did that, time was not on her side, and her mother couldn't keep him from hammering her for much longer.

Imelda could picture the scene outside her bedroom door, knew from the sounds and the scuffling that her mother was holding her father back, was preventing him from bursting in on her. She also knew that her father, until now, had allowed her mother this one thing, to allow Imelda to remain strong about the father's name. Because, like his wife, he didn't want to know really. Because once he pushed it, once he knew, he would have to do something about it. She had relied on that for a good while, but unfortunately no one had come knocking with the offer of a wedding ring. And she had even allowed herself to imagine that happening, had prayed for such a happenstance. And then she had pondered why it was the female who was made to feel as if they were the main culprit when it was the father's fault as much as theirs.

'Would you ever fuck off, woman, and let me sort this once and for all?'

Imelda heard the sound of her mother's body as she was thrown down the stairs, heard her muffled cries as even in her pain she was still too embarrassed to let on to the neighbours what was actually happening.

As her bedroom door slammed against the wall Imelda flinched involuntarily and she automatically tried to protect her baby, a baby she didn't even want. A baby she couldn't even envisage.

Her father grabbed her by her hair, dragged her upright, and she could hear her brother shouting at her, 'Who the fuck is it, Mel? Just give him a fucking name for Christ's sake, before he really hurts you.'

She knew her brothers were more worried about her father than they were about her, didn't want him to get nicked. That was their biggest fear; he was bankrolling the lot of them, and if he didn't get over this latest drama, they would all be left out in the cold. There was a big part of her that understood that, and she wanted to stop it as much as they did, but unfortunately she was too frightened of him.

As her father pushed his huge fist into her face, as she felt the strength of him, she knew that he was capable of killing her. Never in her life had she felt so exposed, so vulnerable.

'Please, Dad, please . . . don't hurt me . . .'

Imelda looked into the face of the man she had loved all her life, and she saw nothing familiar. He was a stranger to her, and she knew then that she was a stranger to him. Since the news of her pregnancy he had taken the time to re-evaluate her status in his community and had decided that she amounted to nothing. His pride was worth much more than her well-being.

It was a real wake-up call and, as always, it had come far too late for her to benefit from it in any way.

'Tell me who the cunt is or I'll break your fucking neck.'

He meant every word, she could hear it in his voice and feel it in his anger. She knew then that he had finally reached the end of his patience, that tonight was her last chance to redeem herself in his eyes.

Her mother was still trying to pull him off her, was attempting to place herself, her own body, between her daughter and her husband.

But Gerald Dooley shrugged her off as if she was a fly, knocking her against the bedroom wall without a second thought. 'I'll fucking stab you, you loose whore you, before I see you make a fucking eejit out of me.'

Imelda saw her brothers standing in the doorway of her bedroom and knew that they were not going to intervene on her behalf. She saw her mother looking at her with fear and she knew that she was finally lost. She knew that Jason had abandoned her, knew that he had left her to her own devices, had so little regard for her and her family that he was confident of her silence. It was then that she knew what she was going to do. Knew then how she would pay him back for her humiliation.

Looking into her father's eyes she said tragically, 'He made me, Dad, he forced me. I didn't want to . . . I couldn't tell you because I didn't know how to. I was scared.'

She was crying now and they were real tears, tears of relief that she had finally found a way out of her dilemma.

Relief that she had finally found the words to stop her father's anger and sense of betrayal. Relief that she had finally found something permanent, had finally found something realistic enough to make her father believe in her once more. Relief that she had finally found a way to make Jason Parks pay for his treatment of her. She was a woman scorned now and she wanted him to know just how fucking hard the last few weeks had been because she had tried to protect him. She had given him plenty of time to step up to the plate and take responsibility for her child, while putting up with her father's wrath, with her father's disappointment in her.

Let him see how far he got now the cat was well and truly out of the bag and she had put the onus on to him. She was almost laughing now at the thought of what Jason was going to have to go through. Let him have a taste of his own medicine. Let him deal with her father and his anger and his hate. She was finally done with it all, she wanted revenge now, nothing more and nothing less. Let that bastard have a taste of her old man and his outdated beliefs. The more she thought about it, the more she warmed to her theme. She was a reckless girl, and she was known for doing reckless things.

Without thinking it through, without understanding the long-term consequences, Imelda decided that this would get her out of this trouble looking like the innocent, would bring her back into her father's good books. The plan was working, her father looked crushed, defeated by the turn of events.

'Who forced you, child, who did this to you?' Already Imelda could feel the difference in her father, she could feel the change in him as he understood what she was telling him. She could see the softening of his features, hear the plea in his voice as he asked her again, gentler this time, 'Give me a name, child, you know his name?'

Imelda nodded, her face a mask of tragedy and pain, throwing herself into the role of the victim as she instinctively saved her own life and her own reputation. 'It was Jason Parks, Dad. He raped me.'

Then he was hugging her to him, his huge arms enveloping her, making her feel safe once more, as he had always made her feel since childhood.

He was weeping now, telling her how sorry he was for the way he had treated her, begging her to forgive him for not realising that she was the innocent party. And, as he hugged her, Imelda saw the way her mother was looking at her, saw the accusation in her eyes and she knew then that this had gone too far. As did her brothers, who were silently watching the little tableau from the landing, both their faces devoid of anything even remotely like an emotion. That she couldn't stop this now, even if she wanted to. It was one lie too many, and she could never take it back.

So, closing her eyes tight, Imelda Dooley cried like a baby, burying her face in her father's shoulder, wondering what her latest outburst was going to cause.

Chapter Three

Mary looked at her daughter for long moments; she was still crying and she was still acting the innocent.

But she was still able to look her mother in the eye, even though she was aware of her mother's scepticism. She was not about to stop the act.

Imelda had always been the one who had caused the most aggravation in this house. The boys had either known better, or had understood that they would not have been given the same back-up as the baby of the family, the only girl. This daughter who looked for all the world like butter wouldn't melt. Mary had given this child a major swerve all her life. She'd lied for her, pretended that she was doing really well to all and sundry, especially her father, when in fact she was not even bothering with her school work. And her husband had believed her because he wanted to believe her, had not wanted to get too involved in the everyday running of this child's life. Of any of his children's lives, for that matter. Though, in fairness, he had done his best with the boys.

But he had left the rearing of this last one to her,

exclusively to her, he had just admired the girl from afar and, if she was really honest, she had loved it. Had loved the power that had given her. Because as much as she loved her husband, she had also resented him at times, resented his utter freedom from them all. And she hated that she had colluded in her own downfall by taking on the mantle of the home and children because she had not known any better.

He had been given the opportunity, like most men, of opting out of his children's lives while still being seen as playing a huge part in it. He had stood back and enjoyed their successes while she had ensured he had never known about their failures, and the failures with this one had been legion. Deep down, his second-hand parenting had annoyed her, had made her feel that the children might, just *might*, have turned out better with more of his time as opposed to his money. Money he had given her with a flourish, money that had somehow bought him his complete and utter neutrality where his offspring were concerned. If they fucked up then she was the culprit because he had trusted her with them. Over the years she had smothered these feelings, had convinced herself that her life was the life she was meant to live. But deep inside, she had known that was wrong. She had always known that he was in reality a waster who had left the brunt of their children's upbringing to his wife, not because he thought she would do a better job, but because he didn't give a flying fuck. But she had never voiced these thoughts out loud until now. She'd pushed them out of her mind because, like most things in her life, if she didn't think about them then they never happened. Until tonight that is.

Now she had to admit that she was partially to blame

for what had happened to her daughter if for no other reason than she had let her have a far looser rein than the others. She had let this last child of hers have the freedom she had never had for herself. She had let Imelda live a life that, in comparison to the others, was outrageously easy, lax even, especially where her father had been concerned. He had been told nothing about his baby or her natural animosity towards the world in general. Mary had made sure of that much herself, personally; she had only ever told him what he wanted to hear, because this last child was his baby girl and he didn't *want* to hear anything detrimental, anything that would give him cause for concern.

Even when Imelda had been expelled from her school Mary had made sure that Gerald had not heard anything about it. Imelda had been a truant, a smoker, a trouble-maker. Like her father and brothers she was a fighter. Always fighting, arguing, and mouthing off to teachers and other pupils alike.

But it was never her fault, it was always someone else's fault. She was her father's daughter all right, he was exactly the same when anything happened that he couldn't cope with, that he knew he had caused.

Mary had done what she had thought was best, had lied and schemed to make sure her husband had never known the whole of anything where his youngest child was concerned. She had made sure he had never known how this daughter of his actually lived, how she really existed in the household where he believed he ruled the fucking roost, where he was the top dog, the main man. It had never occurred to him that his daughter might be a liar, a treacherous whore with no allegiance to anyone unless it benefited her in some way. That she might not see him in the same light as his punters did, as their nemesis, the man who only arrived on their doorsteps when they didn't have the means to pay their debts. Who was all smiles and friendliness until they owed money, then his sociability went straight out the window and they suddenly realised that he had actually been watching them, that his friendship came with strings. Even as all these thoughts were going through Mary's head she felt disloyal, but more than anything, she felt angry, angry and bitter at the girl she had shielded and cared for since her birth all those years before.

Unlike her, Gerry thought his daughter was telling the truth now, was convinced that her silence was because she didn't want to cause any trouble: he was feeling guilty at his treatment of her over the last few weeks. He was ashamed at the way he had assumed she had been fucked and left, the worst thing that could happen to anyone's daughter, let alone his. He was in bits, was convinced that his assumption about his youngest child was a stigma that would now be attached to him, that his instincts had been wrong. Well, his instincts had been spot on, only no one was going to point that out to him in the near future.

Imelda had played him like a con artist would play a mark. Like her old man she had always had a natural instinct for self-preservation and it had always stood her in good stead. Tonight had been no exception.

Mary, however, knew her daughter much better. She knew that Imelda had never told the whole truth about anything in her life, it wasn't in her nature. She was a natural-born liar, she always stretched the truth, forcing home a point, she was willing to look you in the eye even when she knew that *you* knew that she was lying through her teeth. And for years Mary had protected her, had secretly enjoyed knowing something that her husband did not. Namely that his baby, his little darling, was a real piece of work, and she had even loved the fact that they were partners together against him.

Until now that was, because this time her daughter was about to cause fucking murders. Literally.

Gerald Dooley was distraught, he had gravitated from his beloved youngest child being taken down, used and discarded, to her being raped.

A scenario that, in reality, he actually preferred. He had the excuse he needed, the reasoning that would allow him to destroy the person he felt had ruined his little girl. She now had a bellyful of arms and legs, was going to produce a grandchild that was without any kind of substance in his world, that would be born without the benefit of the marital bed. Without a marriage and, ergo, without its father's name. Gerald was not going to swallow that, was not about to give anyone a fucking pass where his daughter, his family and their fucking reputation was concerned. Imelda being raped only convinced him that his initial reactions had been right.

That Jason Parks's father was a local Face was neither here nor there, he knew that once the word was out no one in his locality would hold him in any way responsible for his actions. There were some things that money or prestige could not buy. This was one of them.

They were in the car, driving to Jackie Martin's house. His sons were being unreasonably quiet and this bothered him. It made him feel that they didn't share his enthusiasm for revenge for what had befallen Imelda. It made him feel, and not for the first time, that they were too fucking stupid to appreciate what was actually going down. He was smarting from what had just happened when he had brought them with him to the meet in Canning Town. They were supposed to be his look-outs, his protectors. As Gerald had strolled into the Bridge House pub, he had assumed they had been behind him, had been protecting him. Watching his back, which was what he fucking paid them to do. It was only when he had approached the punter in question that he had realised that he was on his own, that his sons had somehow forgotten to accompany him into the bar. Instead, they had stayed outside, chatting like a pair of fucking drongos. In spite of all his teachings they had not had the sense to cover his back. He had walked in there on his Jack Jones and it was only his rep that had saved him from a tragic end. But it had been a learning curve, not only for his boys but also for him. He had understood that he had raised a pair of fucking imbeciles who had no real conception of the world they now inhabited, the world he had ensured was safe for him and his family with just their name alone. A name that was now tarnished by Jason Parks; with one action Jason Parks had undermined everything that he had achieved over the years.

Gerald had collected the money owed, as always, but the fact that the boys had not even had the fucking brains to actually cover his back had really hit home to him. They had waited outside for him, had waited for him outside a pub that was not only on a busy fucking road, the A13, but was also a road that guaranteed a fucking easy shoot, an easy getaway for anyone in the know.

As he looked around the pub, watched everyone carrying on as if nothing untoward had happened, he wanted to scream out his frustration. He walked out with the envelope of money and felt an anger towards his sons that he knew was born out of his utter disrespect for them and all they stood for. It was a real eye-opener. Somewhere in his drunken brain he knew that there was something radically wrong with them. He knew that they should have been as angry as he was, as offended, and as disgusted. But they weren't.

They were like half men, like a pair of fucking eunuchs. That thought had occurred to him many times before but he had suppressed it. He knew they were not like him, not really. They were only on his firm because they were his flesh and blood. If they were not his sons he would not have given them the time of day. They were a pair of fucking losers, and he knew that deep in his boots. He also knew that he was not the only person who held that opinion where they were concerned. He felt, rightly or wrongly, that these boys of his should have known what was happening with their little sister, should have looked out for her, protected her, but they hadn't. They had not bothered to even oversee their little sister's life, which was something that any Irish Catholic boy would have done without any kind of prompting, would have done because it meant something to them. Because their sister's welfare should have come before their own.

Imelda's predicament had only served to prove something that he had already suspected, that his sons had no fucking real perception of the world that they inhabited. He was still carrying them, and he would always be carrying them because they didn't have the fucking brains to hold their own cocks unless he saw fit to draw them both a fucking detailed map.

Outside in the evening air Gerald Dooley saw them as he had never seen them before, standing by the motor with the usual expectant look on their faces, both waiting for him to tell them what to do. Waiting for him to tell them both what the next step was going to be. They were an embarrassment to him, they were a pair of fucking leeches. He knew they were frightened of him, and until now that had not bothered him. But seeing them, with his world crashing down around his ears, he had to admit the truth to himself. Even now his daughter had more brains in her little toe than this pair shared between them on their best day. Imelda had been taken down by a piece of shit, a piece of shit that her brothers should have been aware of, should have been policing. He had stopped by this pub to collect a debt that was outstanding because he knew that after tonight he could be banged up. Even with all that was going on he still had the sense to do his job, do what he was paid for. Once that was out of the way he could concentrate all his energy on the matter in hand.

'Where the fuck were you two?'

He had thrown the envelope full of cash at his eldest son. 'I was left in there like a fucking spare prick at the proverbial wedding. You two are fucking useless. I can't even fucking sack you, can I?'

He had got into the motor and waited for his sons to do the same. Shaking his head, he had said sadly, 'Drive to Jackie's, at least with him I'll feel like I have a fucking back-up.'

Now when they finally reached Jackie's house Gerry watched the way that they looked at each other; it was a furtive look that he had seen before. A look that had told him that he had stepped on their necks once too often, that he had not allowed either of them to form a real personality of their own. They both always looked to him for direction and, whereas that had once pleased him, all it did now was irritate him.

He had to tell them what to do, when to do it, and how to do it; initiative was not one of their strong points. Even now, at a time like this, when they could see what was important to him, neither of them had the fucking guts to offer any kind of opinion about it all, about their sister's predicament.

They followed him inside quietly, their large bodies and expressionless faces making him feel angrier by the second. As always, they were waiting for him to give them a heads-up, some kind of lead. His big fear was what the fuck they would do when he was inside, or when he finally popped his clogs. Who the fuck would look after them then? When he was gone they would be like a rudderless boat drifting on a sea of ignorance.

Jackie was in bed asleep, but his wife was shrewd enough to notice the demented look in Gerald Dooley's eyes and consequently had the sense not to ask him what he wanted with her husband. Instead, she pointed upstairs before retreating to the kitchen without a word. A small part of her hoped that her husband was about to be disposed of. It was unlikely, but she knew, better than anyone, just what a two-faced, treacherous bastard he could be, and she hoped that this trait had finally caught up with him.

Five minutes later, however, Jackie left the house with a smug look on his face and the assurance that he would see her later. She knew her husband well enough to know that whatever was going down, he was not the cause of it, but he was determined to be part of the cure.

'Stop crying, Mel, you and I both know that this is all a fucking scam.'

Imelda knew from the fear in her mother's voice that

she had gone too far. Though she too was terrified at what she was going to cause, there was still a big part of her inside that was enjoying it all. Was enjoying the drama that she was creating around her.

Despite her shock at her father's reaction, Imelda could not help feeling a deep satisfaction as well. After all, she felt that she was the wronged party in this. Jason had used her, and now he was going to pay for it, and pay dearly. She secretly hoped that her father crippled him, hoped that he was left a shadow of his former self. Was left unable to have sex with another woman as long as he lived. Her jealousy was so raw, so painful, she was willing to do anything she could to see him hurt, see him brought low.

She wanted Jason to know what it was like to be left high and dry, as he had left her. She had banked on him coming through for her, had actually believed that her family would have been enough to make the ponce see sense. But he had blanked her without a second's thought, had not even given her the courtesy of a phone call or a fucking verbal message. He had left her to face this lot alone, and he had to pay for that. He was already on to the next girl, was already fucking someone else. Well, he had made a mistake this time, she was not going to retreat with her tail between her legs. She was not going to give him a free pass, he was going to pay the price for his negligence.

She had lived with this pregnancy and the fear it had engendered for weeks and he had not cared one iota about what she might have been going through. So, if she decided to get her revenge on him, then that was his fucking lookout. See how he felt now the boot was on the other foot and he was the one being harassed and accused. See if he liked being in the frame as the villain of the piece.

Imelda looked at her mother then, saw the way her

mother eyed her with distaste and disbelief and knew she had not conned her as easily as she had her father. So she shrieked with all the hate she could muster, 'Oh, so what's new, eh? You don't believe me, do you? All this time I have kept me mouth shut to avoid all this.' She gestured around her by holding her arms out wide. 'To stop me father from killing someone, and as usual me own mother doesn't believe me, doesn't care about what happened to me. Then you wonder why I didn't tell you about it. But I'll tell you this now. There is a baby, Mum, and it got there somehow, didn't it? I suppose you believe we all arrived with the stork. No dirty, sweaty sex for you, a woman who won't even have the *Sun* newspaper in her house. A house that is so fucking clean and sterile it's like a hospital, a fucking mental hospital. A nut-house and you're the Queen Nutter.'

Imelda was crying now, real tears; she was feeling genuine sorrow for herself and her situation. She was caught up in the lie she had caused, was already half believing it. She was the proud possessor of an audience, and that was all she had ever wanted, had ever needed. She threw herself into the part of the victim, milking it for all that it was worth, while at the same time passing on the blame.

'You knew that I couldn't tell me dad who was responsible without a fucking war starting, you saw what he's done to me over the last weeks, how he's treated me, and you wonder why I kept fucking stumm. Jason used me, and now he has to face the old man.'

Imelda's lovely face was the picture of innocence, her large blue eyes pleading for some kind of understanding. In her bedroom, the bedroom of a typical teenage girl, she looked so young and so vulnerable. To anyone else she would have looked believable but to Mary Dooley, who knew what a gifted liar her daughter was, she looked just how she had always looked to her. Like a vicious, vindictive little mare. It was hard to admit that to herself, but it was the truth. Imelda had always had a dark side to her, had always been capable of causing great disruption to those around her. Imelda lied about the littlest things, it was in her nature. She embellished everything for no other reason than it came naturally to her. She was devoid of any kind of morality. Even as a small child she had schemed and lied to get what she wanted. She would go to extraordinary lengths to get what she saw as revenge for slights real or imagined. Until now Mary had not seen anything sinister in that, but now, now she knew that this child of hers was without *real* emotions, *real* feelings. She knew that Imelda was prepared to offer up Jason Parks like a sacrificial lamb to ensure that she came out of this without a stain on her character, and to ensure that Jason Parks paid the price for not putting his hand up and taking the flak. A small part of her could understand her daughter's hurt, her daughter's need to make him pay for abandoning her. But another part of her, the sensible part of her, knew that this daughter of hers had accused him of rape. Not just of making her pregnant, because that would have insinuated that she was a party to it all, she had accused Jason Parks of the most heinous crime a man could be accused of. And, knowing her daughter like she did, she knew that it was all a fabrication, a lie. A lie that would absolve her of any wrong-doing, a lie that her mother knew would haunt her until the day she died. Would haunt them all. This wasn't just about revenge, this was about destroying one life to save another.

Mary Dooley already knew deep down inside that the

child her daughter was carrying meant nothing to her. It was just a weapon to her daughter, no more and no less. A weapon that her daughter would use as she used anything that she felt might get her what she wanted.

Jason Parks's father believed that he was a real Face, that he was a legend in his own lifetime. He wasn't as well thought of, though, as he believed, but by the same token he wasn't someone to be mugged off. He could have a row, there was no doubt about that. He was a shrewdie in his own way, was a man who saw the big picture. He was also an earner and, as such, he was respected. His only flaw was his over-inflated ego. It was because of this that he didn't have any real friends, and it was why he wasn't on the best terms with his only son.

He earned a wedge that was not only large, but also respectable. In effect that meant he had a legitimate business, a business that was doing exceptionally well and could be used to explain away his affluent lifestyle if ever the need should arise. He also had his other business, the real money spinner, for which, unlike his regular business, he had to share out a large percentage of the profits. And share them he did because he had no choice. Though at times he resented the need to placate those around him.

Timothy Parks felt that he was well past the days of needing any kind of protection, but it galled him that he was still expected to hand out a large percentage of his wedge on a weekly basis to the people he had paid to give him an in all those years ago. He was not the sort of person where this kind of a long-term arrangement was ever going to sit easily on his shoulders. He was more than grateful for the initial introductions, and he had been more than happy to pay the premium for a while, after all, he was not a complete fucking moron. But now he was having serious doubts about the validity of the payments that were still required from him, even though the people involved had no actual involvement any more in his purchase of the products their friends were so willing to supply. Ergo, they were now fucking obsolete as far as he was concerned. They had done what was required and been reimbursed for their troubles. So now he felt that they were taking the piss.

In fact, he was now of the opinion that he might actually be getting ripped off. Royally ripped off, if he was being honest. He had weighed everyone out at the off, so why were they still so sure that he owed them something, that he owed them a large part of his fucking livelihood? He could fucking score off any number of dealers, it wasn't as if they had a unique fucking product. In their world, cocaine, grass or amphetamines was the equivalent of fucking Avon; anyone could get access to it if they really wanted to. He really didn't need such a jealous supplier, especially as nowadays there were so many others to choose from.

That his son was a complete idiot had not escaped him either. He had heard through the grapevine that his boy was now a professional bank robber, and that was fine by him. He saw that as a mug's game himself, it was a lot of bird for what he felt was not enough dough. It was his son's latest foray into the world of dealing that was really getting up his nose, he smiled at the pun. Mainly because he didn't even have the sense to see that he was treading on his own father's toes. Now what did that say about the boy? What kind of fucking idiot shat on his own doorstep?

At the end of the day, he was his son after all. Though, like his mother, Jason was a fucking taker. He took what he wanted and didn't give a fuck who it affected, whose toes it might cause to be trodden on by all and fucking sundry.

But Timmy was being very good about it. He was prepared to give the boy a leg-up, help him get a proper corner for himself, all the little fucker had to do was ask. It wasn't exactly rocket science.

Jason irritated him because he was quite happy to use his family connections to further his career, while at the same time begrudging his father his success. The same success that the little fucker was now trading on to get himself a fucking gee-up in the world of the illegal: the cheap, recreational pharmaceuticals.

In his calmer moments Timmy enjoyed the fact that Jason was a real chip off the old block as far as everyone else was concerned. He admired the fact that his son had the guts to go out on his own, was sensible enough to see that anyone with half a brain used what they could to get on in life. But he only felt like that when he was really mellow, after he had imbibed a few drinks, smoked a few joints. Then, and only then, would he find it in his heart to see the boy as someone to be proud of.

Not that he would ever tell him that, of course, that was something he would one day understand himself through learned wisdom, through his own hard graft; consequently the knowledge would then be far more advantageous because he would have come to that realisation on his own.

As he opened the safe, he was surprised to see Gerald Dooley walk into his office. His office was currently in a rented Portakabin on an industrial estate in South London, an office that he made sure was moved every three weeks to another location so he had a heads-up if anyone decided to flip on him. The appearance of a gang of men was bound to make him feel that something untoward was going down.

'How the fuck did you know where I was?' Timmy was genuinely interested, he really had believed that his constant movement of premises would keep him safe.

Gerald looked around the small space as if he thought the person he was looking for might be hiding under a seat cushion or in the desk drawer. Timmy watched him not only with suspicion, but also with outrage. The people he had been paying the serious bucks to all this time should have ensured that this kind of thing didn't happen.

Gerald Dooley and his crew made the confines of the little cabin seem minuscule, and for the first time Timmy Parks felt a stirring of fear. He knew that this was serious, and he racked his brains for any reason whatsoever why these people should be confronting him like this, in the sanctity of his private offices. He could not come up with anything, he could only assume, which he did, that someone was out to take what was his.

They were blocking the only entrance and the only exit and all Timmy had going for him was his mouth, so he would attempt to try and talk his way out of this situation as best he could. He smiled as if their presence was the most natural thing in the world, as if he was somehow expecting them. Opening his arms wide in a gesture of welcome he said happily, 'Come on, Gerry, don't tell me you've decided to start dealing.'

Gerry was champing at the bit, his anger almost electric in the tiny room. He looked as if he was capable of a murder, and of course he was.

'Where is that cunt of a son?' He was talking through gritted teeth, and his words were almost unintelligible.

Timmy knew then that this was not anything to do directly with him personally, and he felt himself relax, even with Dooley looking like something from a Hammer Horror movie. He was, first and foremost, a man who looked out for number one before he would even consider looking out for anyone or anything else. If he had been on the *Titanic* he would have got into a lifeboat while throwing women and children over his shoulders and kicking the old and the infirm out of his way.

Settling his face into a picture of innocence Timothy Parks said loudly, 'I might have known this was his call, that little fucker is nothing to do with me. You want him, Gerry, you can fucking have him.'

'Where is he?'

'If I know him he'll be out on the nest, then he'll go home to his mother. He is a fucking mummy's boy.' Timmy shrugged then, pleased with himself.

His expensive suit and his cheap shoes were suddenly like a red rag to a bull where Gerald Dooley was concerned. No wonder he had brought up a rapist, a fucking beast. What chance did a kid have with this ponce in the background? He had heard the rumours about this man and his only boy. The boy, rightly or wrongly, bore this ponce's name, and that alone should make him have some kind of care, some kind of pride in what might happen to that name.

Gerald had ensured that his children had good reason to be glad they bore the name Dooley. In his mind, that was why his poor daughter had kept her pregnancy quiet, that was why she had felt unable to tell her family what had happened to her. The shame of being raped was all the more acute as far as she was concerned because of who her father was.

Now this man, this piece of shit standing there like a fucking statue, was acting like his son was nothing in the world. Timothy Parks had brought up a child who had destroyed his baby. He was so fucking indifferent as to what was going on around him that he had not even had the decency to ask why the fuck they were there in the first place. Why they wanted his boy, had not even been curious about what he might have done.

No wonder Jason Parks was a fucking nonce, a fucking molester, a sexual predator; he had been brought up by this fucking moron. Gerald suddenly felt convinced that Timmy and people like him were the reason this fucking country was going to the dogs.

'He raped my baby. She is in the fucking club by that cunt and you don't even care, do you? You have no fucking obligation to me, or her, or your own fucking flesh and blood, do you?'

Jackie Martin saw the look of abject disbelief on Parks's face and knew, like the others in the room knew, that this man had nothing to do with what was going on. But he could do nothing, none of them could do anything without incurring the same wrath.

'He what?'

It was obvious to everyone that even Jason's father, not his biggest fan at any time, had trouble believing that about the boy.

Grabbing him roughly by the throat Gerald Dooley proceeded to slam the man's head onto a heavy oak desk, over and over again. As the man's skull opened up and his blood flowed copiously all over the floor, Gerry began to experience a small modicum of peace.

The desk that was now covered in blood and brains was the only piece of furniture in the place that was worth anything. Like the dead man lying on the navy-blue polyester carpet, it looked completely out of place.

Jackie looked at the two boys and realised that, like him, their breathing was shallow, and their hands were shaking. Like him, they knew that Gerry Dooley was out of control.

Chapter Four

Jason was as happy as a sandboy. He had been well fucked by a well-developed, and very experienced, housewife. He was also well fed thanks to his accommodating mother: he had sated all his appetites bar one. He just needed to get copious amounts of alcohol down his Gregory Peck to round off his day. A day he had really enjoyed, mainly because, unlike most people, he basically did whatever took his fancy. He didn't work a real job, and he saw anyone who did as a fool, a mug. He had a good few quid at his disposal, and he had an active imagination. He filled his days without any bother at all. In fact, he felt as if he was indestructible.

Now, to add the icing on his otherwise pleasant cake, he had been invited into the back room of his favourite pub. That in itself was an honour. It was where people went to do a few deals, but mainly it was somewhere people could go and talk without worrying who might be listening in.

It was a family pub out the front, the barmaids were older and the clientele were basic; men with their wives and older children. They drank together, smiled, and put the appropriate records on the juke boxes. On the surface it was like any other straight pub in the Smoke. Or in any big city or town anywhere in the United Kingdom.

Only those in the business area of the neighbourhood understood that this place was a front. Drinks were cheaper for the regulars, and the Old Bill were not averse to having a swift half when the fancy took them. Afters were the norm, and weekends saw the place rocking with either an Irish band or a local DJ. Kids were often running around the bar, and the atmosphere was friendly, if suspicious of any newcomers.

All in all, it was the perfect front for the owners, it gave them a modicum of security because no one saw it as the real deal. And the people in the know felt safe there. They could drop in and have a drink, and they could also do a few deals, secure in the knowledge that the place was not really seen as anywhere the Filth would be keeping a watch on. The only Filth involved with this pub were the ones whose job it was to protect it. It was a win-win situation for all concerned.

Not that this front came cheap by any means; behind the scenes there was a network of payments and procedures that would make the Inland Revenue ashamed at its complexity. But it worked, and that was all that anyone was interested in. There was a long line of people who earned good money to see this place was left in peace.

So, for someone like young Jason Parks, an invitation into the back room was like a platinum credit card; it meant you had made it. It meant you were seen as someone to be reckoned with; in his case, you were perceived as an up-and-coming potential earner. It was all about the earn; money spoke volumes, and it spoke most languages.

Jason was thrilled with himself and, as he walked through the packed pub, he could feel the eyes of everyone on him and he knew then what made the criminal life so very appealing to young men like him.

He knew he was a showman, knew that would eventually be his downfall. The real Faces were not really known outside of their immediate circles. Not for a long time anyway. It could take the Old Bill ten years before they could even start a real investigation against them because, thanks to the Jason Parkses of the world, they worked young men like him while being far too intelligent to attract any real attention to themselves. They didn't live large, and they didn't attract attention.

Once someone like Jason Parks got an in, they knew they were getting respect, knew that they were classed as all right. And, in their world, that meant more money on the hip, and more kudos on the pavement.

The hallowed back bar, when Jason finally entered it, was a great disappointment to him. He didn't know what he had expected, but it certainly wasn't a nondescript room, full of nondescript people wearing below-average clothes. There was no music, and no bright lights. In fact, it was like his mother's front room. All cheap wallpaper and scuffed furniture. The only thing missing was an underlying smell of cabbage. The bar area itself was small, and manned by a Face called Desmond Pollard. He was big, hairy and he always seemed to be sweating.

There were only five or six other people in there, and Jason didn't really know any of them. He knew *who* they were, of course, but he didn't know them personally. He experienced his first prickle of uneasiness, but shrugged it off. Just because he didn't know them, didn't mean they didn't know him.

That was how this whole world worked, what made it so exciting. You dreamt of something like this happening to you, it was half the reason you grafted. You hoped that the people in the know who were, to all intents and purposes, the business, would notice you. If they did, you were then brought into what was, in their world, a very exclusive club. It meant you had arrived or, at least, worst ways, that you were well on your way.

Des was all smiles and friendly banter and, as he handed him a large Scotch, Jason felt his chest expanding with pride. If only his father could see him now.

Out of the corner of his eye he noticed an open door. It was the original back door of the property, a handy exit if necessary for the majority of the people who frequented this establishment. It led out to the car park, a dark, uninviting area that purposely had no lighting because that, of course, would defeat the object.

'Seen anything of Imelda Dooley?'

Des's voice was neutral, but Jason felt the veiled animosity underneath, sensed the threat that he realised now had been there since he had walked into the room. From the back of the room a small man with a heavy brow and expensive dentistry called out loudly, 'Her father's looking for you, boy. He's out the back and, if I was you, I wouldn't keep the fucker waiting.'

Jason looked around him, saw that he was outnumbered, saw that he had been set up, and saw that he had no escape. For the first time in years he wished that he had a real father, someone he could turn to at a time like this. He had only fucked the girl, and she had been fucked by plenty of blokes before him. She had a reputation as a fucking shagger, it was just his luck that he would be the one to get fucking tugged over it. And he would lay his last penny that it was her grassing him up to her old man for revenge. So he had blanked her? It wasn't like it was the first time that had happened to her, surely? He wasn't going to be the fall guy; her mate had told him the score, if she was in the club the culprit could be anyone in a very long line of candidates.

He felt fear prickle his spine, knew that how he conducted himself tonight would be the yardstick for his whole future. He had to walk away from this stupidity with his head and his pride intact. After all, Gerald Dooley was not a mug, but he was also not in the top echelons of this world. He knew that Imelda was behind this crap, and he also knew that he had asked for it in many respects. He had not even bothered to acknowledge her and that had to hurt. But to bring her old man down on him, what the fuck was all that about? At this moment in time he hated her.

Swallowing his drink Jason placed the glass onto the nearest table and, like the proverbial lamb, he walked out the open back door to what was, in effect, his slaughter. He knew that there would be some kind of welcoming committee, and he knew that it was not going to be made up of people who were exactly his biggest fans. He knew enough to know he was on his own, but he was also confident enough to believe that he could sort this misunderstanding out if he used his loaf. After all, his father was not exactly someone to be ignored.

The only problem was that Jason was hyped up on pharmaceutical cocaine and carrying a weapon, a lethal combination by anyone's standards. Coupled with his fear and boyish pride, it was a recipe for disaster. Jason Parks was not going to go down without a fight. Of that much he was sure.

*

'I don't believe you, Mel, you're lying. If you had been raped you would have said ages ago. Until now he was your fucking boyfriend, so make up your mind.'

Mary Dooley was still unmoved by her daughter's tears, by the girl's hysteria. She could smell a lie from a mile off, especially where her children were concerned.

Imelda was lying on her bed, the picture of tragedy because she knew in her heart that she had been rumbled. But she was not about to let on to her mother that she was aware she had been found out.

She had learnt years before that the only way to survive in this household was never to waver. Never argue unless you had a chance of winning and, most important of all, she knew that her mother would do anything to keep her father from knowing anything about his children that might put his wife in a bad light.

Basically, no matter what happened, her mother would do whatever was needed to stop her husband from knowing the real score where this daughter of his was concerned. That went for the neighbours as well, her mother had a terror of the neighbours that bordered on mania. She was always telling her family the old Irish adage: people only know what you tell them. In their world that was a really good bit of advice. Like most of the Irish families, they knew that the tiniest titbit of information could be someone's downfall. Especially where skulduggery was concerned.

Now that she was cornered, Imelda was determined to keep her story straight, keep her father and brothers on her side. She knew that her being pregnant was bad enough, but if her father thought that she had been an active participant in the pregnancy she would be out in the cold without a second's thought on his part. His behaviour since he had found out about her condition was enough to alert her to just how precarious her position actually was. If she wavered now, her life as she knew it was over.

If she kept up this story she was guaranteed her father's help and goodwill. If she really played her cards right she might even get an abortion; after all, a child that was the product of rape was not a child her father would be welcoming with open arms. Even a devout Catholic like him could be swayed if the circumstances were such that her having the child would be detrimental to her health, her mental health and her peace of mind. All she wanted was shot of this baby, and everything that it entailed.

It was clear to her now that after what she had said about Jason Parks, she had no option but to keep up the lie. What had been, at the time, no more than an angry lie, a way to get her revenge on the man who she saw as the cause of all her problems, had somehow turned into a huge drama, a drama that she didn't know how to step back from. This baby had already destroyed her life, now she knew that her lies would make this child even more unwanted. Not just by her, but by the people she needed to help her get through it all. Her family.

She knew deep inside that if she had not lied, then her father would have come round eventually; after all, a life was a life and, as his flesh and blood, the child would have been accepted eventually. He was too chicken-hearted where she was concerned, and he would have forgiven and forgotten in his new role as a grandfather.

Now though, she had burnt her boats and she knew that the only way out of this was to get shot of the baby, and she could only do that if she could convince her mother that what she had said was true. She also knew from experience that her mother would do whatever was necessary to keep the peace with her husband. She was not as sure, however, about her mother swallowing her having the child terminated; she saw a life as a life. She didn't see the big picture, didn't see that after tonight the child inside her would not be welcomed by anyone. Least of all her. She just wanted her old life back; she had only had a small taste of life as an unmarried mother and it sucked big time, and the fucking child had not even arrived yet.

Imelda could smell the aroma of soap powder as she pushed her face into the pillows on her bed and she wished that her mother would go away and leave her alone.

'Answer me, Mel, and I swear that if you tell me the truth I will stand by you, no matter what. But I have to know what's really going on.'

She kept her face pressed into the pillows, frightened to look her mother in the eye, knowing that she already knew the answer to her question, and also knowing that if she ever admitted her lie she would be finished. She pulled herself up then and, crying noisily and looking for all the world as sad as she possibly could, she said brokenly, 'Please, Mum, leave me alone.'

She *looked* distraught. She *sounded* distraught. But Mary Dooley knew deep inside that this was just another one of her daughter's self-inflicted dramas. Only this time it was really serious, this time she had told a lie that was so heinous and so dangerous it would, without doubt, cause a lot of people a lot of trouble.

'You always think the worst of me, don't you? You always have.'

Mary shook her head sadly. 'Do you realise the trouble you have caused with your accusation, Mel? Do you understand what someone like your father is actually capable of? He'll hammer the life out of the boy and that's fair enough if he did rape you. But if he didn't, then you need to tell me now. If you tell me now I can protect you.'

'Will you leave me alone? I don't *need* this, Mum. I don't need you on my back tonight. I wish you could just for once believe what I tell you.'

Mary sighed heavily, her face a mass of lines, deep, troubled lines that seemed to have appeared over the last few hours.

'I know you better than anyone, lady, and I know exactly what you are capable of. You didn't mention anything about being raped to me. So don't try and pull the wool over my eyes. Because I warn you now, if your father gets nicked over you, I'll fucking brain you meself. As God is my witness, I'll see you pay the price for your antics, if only this once.'

As Mary looked into her daughter's lovely face, saw the crocodile tears and the terror that was there, she knew then, without a doubt, that her daughter was, as usual, starring in her own life story. By the end of the night, Imelda would actually believe her own lies, and so would almost everyone else around her. It was a knack she had, making people believe her, garnering their sympathy and then playing on their kindness until she achieved her ends.

Once she had got what she wanted from people though, she walked away from them without a backward glance. Leaving them wondering what had happened to cause so much aggravation in the first place. Well, this time Mary was not going to let her walk away unscathed, she had a baby on the way and, please God, a child might be just what she needed to calm her down, might curb her behaviour once and for all.

Mary automatically began tidying the room, unwilling to leave the daughter who, from her birth, had caused her nothing but heartache and sorrow. She had colluded in so many of this girl's lies, she was wondering now if she might be partly to blame for this latest upset. She had let her daughter have her freedom because she felt it was a different world now, her daughter lived in a world where she was allowed an opinion, was allowed to choose things for herself. Her own mother had bought her clothes for her right up until she had got married. But Mary also knew that a lot of her parenting with Imelda was sheer laziness on her part. She just didn't have the energy or the inclination needed to keep her in line. Imelda had such a strong personality, was so argumentative it was easier to let her get on with it. Guilt was a terrible thing, Mary knew that better than anyone. She also knew it was something that would never trouble this daughter of hers. Imelda Dooley had never developed a conscience, and she doubted she ever would, especially at this late stage.

Gerry Dooley was more than ready for Jason Parks, and as he watched him come out into the cold night air he felt once more the anger and humiliation wash over him. That his daughter had been taken down by the likes of Jason Parks was too much for him to bear. All night he had hunted this boy down, had searched for him, even though he knew that Jackie and the boys thought he was over-reacting to what had happened. He had got the distinct impression that his own sons did not regard their sister's version of events as wholly honest. Well, she was definitely in the fucking club, so at least a percentage of what she had said had to be true. He had a feeling she was milking the situation, but then that was her, she had always been that way inclined. But then she was a young girl, and young girls were foolish, they were romantic, and, above all, they were vulnerable. Especially where scum-bags like Parks were concerned.

Now the boy was standing before him. Jason Parks had the stance of a boxer, and Gerry knew he was bracing himself for whatever was about to happen. He looked into the young man's handsome face, saw the fear there, and also the determination to face what was coming. Then he gave his colossal anger a free rein.

Jason felt the first punch. It was like being hit by a train, it was so powerful and painful and, as he dropped to the filthy Tarmac, he knew that his only chance of survival was to get back up on to his feet as quickly as possible. He rolled away, grateful for the heavy leather jacket he was wearing. As he got up, he saw the other men around him. He saw Imelda's brothers standing apart from their father and, even in his confusion, he sensed that they were not really a part of what was going down.

Jackie Martin, as always, was waiting to see what happened; he was Gerry's right-hand man though, in reality, he was no more than his Yes Man. He was watching Jason warily and, unlike the brothers, he was willing to do whatever might be needed to bring this to a successful conclusion. As he assessed the situation Jason heard Gerry Dooley's voice, 'You fucking raping piece of dirt.'

Even Gerry Dooley couldn't fail to see the look of absolute shock on Jason Parks's face at his words. Jason was genuinely stunned, so shocked he actually took a step backwards.

Now he understood what was going down, knew then that this man was on a mission. He knew that he was fucked because there was no way he could argue his case with a man who was going to defend his daughter's honour, no matter what.

Jason was shaking his head in denial and Jackie Martin knew then and there that he had not taken Imelda Dooley by force. He was a little fucker, and he was a fucking womaniser. But then he was a young bloke, sex was all he thought about, they had all been there, only they had all had the sense to take their urges out on the girls who were renowned for their generous natures. Girls who did not have fathers who were known for their violence, who earned their very living from violent acts. If this silly sod was guilty of anything, it was bad judgement.

'I did not rape your daughter, Mr Dooley . . .'

Gerald Dooley laughed then and, looking around him at the others, he said angrily, 'Like father like son, scum. You gave her a child, and that's proof enough for me. She's been terrified of telling me who the fucking culprit was and now I know why. She knew that I'd have to fucking kill you, and I will do just that. Make no mistake.'

Gerry advanced towards him once more, his huge shoulders knotted with suppressed rage and his fists clenched ready for another attack. Jason, whose brains were scrambled from the drugs he had taken, and the drink he had imbibed, was a young man who felt that his integrity was being maligned for no real reason, and felt honourbound to defend it. He said quietly and purposefully, 'I never raped your daughter, Mr Dooley, I didn't fucking need to.'

Even as he spoke, he knew he was just making things worse; men like Dooley found it easier to believe their precious daughters had been forced into the sex act. That was far more preferable than believing that their little angels were as up for it as their boyfriends. Jason also knew, somewhere in his drugged and fear-addled mind, that he had gone too far.

As Dooley came at him once again, his animal strength giving him the appearance of a much younger and fitter man, Jason Parks was more than ready for him. He pulled the knife he kept in his jacket pocket out of its hiding place and, as he felt the full weight of Gerald Dooley's anger approaching him once more, he thrust the knife into the man's chest with all the strength he could muster.

It was an odd feeling, almost surreal, as it slipped between the man's ribs and punctured his heart in a split second; he hadn't hit bone, or even the cloth of the man's jacket. The knife, which had a six-inch blade and a carved bone handle, had not encountered any kind of resistance at all. It had entered the man's body silently and slickly. It had achieved its objective though; it had stopped him in his tracks.

Jason couldn't believe how easy it had been. As Dooley dropped on to his knees, clasping his chest with both of his huge rough hands, all Jason Parks could think about was that there was no real blood. Nothing. Yet he knew the man was dying in front of his eyes.

Jason knew that he had delivered a fatal blow, and he was genuinely sorry for that. It was the speed of the action that had thrown him though: with a split second he had taken this man's life.

As Gerald Dooley lay on the filthy ground, the men gathered around stood in silence, all in shock at what had just happened. Each of them was acutely aware that in a few short seconds their lives had been changed irrevocably.

Gerry lay there, his huge bulk completely still now, looking incongruous on the cold ground where only minutes before he had been standing, talking and breathing and alive.

For Jackie Martin and the Dooley brothers, this man's death had left them without a spearhead, without any kind of leadership. Without him to guide them, they were not even sure how they were supposed to react to his death. It was Des Pollard who, with his own interests in mind, took control of the situation.

Des already knew that Jason's father was out of the picture. By all accounts he was as dead as a fucking doornail, and that his death had been hastened somewhat by Gerald Dooley would soon be common knowledge. So the Filth would hear about it sooner rather than later, which was a good thing in some respects as it would stop them all from shoving their noses in where they weren't wanted. So, making a decision that he felt would be the best for all concerned, especially for him and the people who frequented this establishment, he took matters into his own hands.

Taking the knife from Jason Parks, he saw the absolute shock, horror, that this kind of random violence often caused. Unlike professional acts of aggression, for either financial reasons, or for the furtherance of a cause, for example the collection of a gambling debt or such like, this kind of violence caused far more trouble than it was worth. This was wanker's violence, the sort of shite that happened outside cheap nightclubs, where young men with too much drink and not enough brain cells made the biggest mistake of their lives over either a female or pride. This kind of stupidity had no place in their world, where any violence was controlled and was no more than a means to an end.

While Gerald Dooley was still in the land of the living,

his determination to avenge his daughter's rather dubious reputation was acceptable. After all, he had his creds, and he was therefore within his rights to do whatever he felt was necessary to sort out the situation. Now, though, that had changed.

For starters, Des had a dead Face on his premises, and that was something that had to be sorted out, *sooner* rather than *later*.

'Get inside, all of you.'

Des knew that the door to the main bar area was already locked and bolted, so there was no fear of anyone wandering in on top of them all. Two of his own sons were already lifting the huge carcass of Gerald Dooley off the floor and into a nearby van. Des was gutted; the van was nearly new and now it would have to be disposed of at the same time as the body. The clean-up operation was done quickly and quietly, with the minimum of fuss. It wasn't the first time someone had expired on these premises and he had a feeling that it wouldn't be the last. This was more about damage limitation than anything else. He was saving his own arse, and he was also sensible enough to know that all the people involved would be eternally grateful for his ministrations in their time of need.

Des went back inside and poured them all stiff drinks. He saw that the Dooley boys, both of whom were nice kids, though not exactly what could be termed university material, were shaking in shock at their father's untimely death. He also saw that Jason Parks, who he actually quite liked after seeing how he had handled himself, was only a line of snort away from total meltdown. If Jason's old man was still on the scene he would have probably taken his side tonight, but he wasn't. Gerald Dooley worked for some serious people and that was what Des was keeping in mind. They had liked and respected him, and they would also understand his reasons for the night's fucking upsets. Gerry had been looking after his own, and that was something they could all associate with in one way or another.

Des caught Jackie Martin's eye and, shrugging, he walked softly up to Jason Parks, grabbed him tightly by his hair and quickly and cleanly cut the boy's throat. It was a necessary evil. But after the accusations, which like a lot of people he believed were rather exaggerated on Imelda Dooley's part, Jason was already finished in their world. You could live down a lot of things, except grassing or violence against women or children. There were some things that were taboo, and Jason Parks had been accused of rape. As the boy bled out, Desmond was already opening a bottle of industrial strength bleach and telling himself that the place was overdue for a new carpet anyway.

Jackie Martin was saddened at his friend's death, he was on his own now, and he knew that he didn't have the presence of mind or indeed the acumen that was needed for this line of work. Without Gerry he was fucked. He couldn't believe what had happened to his life in the space of a few hours.

Three deaths in one night, the fucking Kray twins had been banged up for less.

Imelda Dooley had watched her mother as she listened politely to the policeman. She had shown no emotion as he had explained to her in a very low and very respectful voice that Gerald Dooley's body had been found on a bit of wasteland, with another man's, and she was now a widow. Imelda had watched in morbid fascination as her mother calmly offered them tea, asked them the appropriate questions and eventually saw them to the door.

In the forty-eight hours since her father and brothers had walked out of the house, the world as she knew it had ended. Three people were dead, and her family had been left without the protection of her father's name.

Her brothers were useless without their father to guide them, even she could see that much, and Jackie Martin, who up until now she had seen as almost her father's equal, seemed to have visibly shrunk before her eyes.

Like her mother, he had aged dramatically over the last couple of days, and she knew that neither he, nor her mother, would ever regain their previous strength. It was as if, with his death, Gerald Dooley had drained the life-force out of his whole family.

As Imelda slipped up to her bedroom, away from the crushing grief that was tainting everything and everyone it came into contact with, she wondered once more at how well her mother had taken her husband's death.

For the first time in her life she felt guilty, felt responsible. It was not a feeling she was used to and definitely not a feeling she ever wanted to experience again. She was the catalyst for everything that had happened, and she would admit that to herself in the dark hours of the night but, Imelda being Imelda, blamed all that had happened on the child she was carrying. A child that had been created without a second's thought by two people who couldn't even look after themselves, let alone a child, and whose existence was the cause of not only its father's death, but of both its grandfathers too. It was a child of pain and suffering and she hated it.

As Imelda sat on the edge of the bed she felt the urge to scream wash over her. She placed a hand firmly across her mouth, convinced that if she didn't then she would start screaming and, once she started, she wasn't sure she would ever be able to stop.

She bent over double then, her free arm hugging her own body, swallowing down the sobs that were fighting to get out. She felt a pain so acute inside her chest she honestly believed the child had finally taken the hint and packed up, ready to vacate her unwilling body. Instead though, she dropped onto the carpeted floor and, rocking backwards and forwards, she cried silent tears. Feeling them gush from her she felt the frustration and the rage building up once more as what she had done, what she had been the cause of, was played out in her mind's eye all over again.

She had always sailed close to the wind, she was the first to admit that, and she had caused her fair share of trouble over the years. But never in her wildest dreams had she ever believed that something so heinous could have befallen her family over something she had done.

Her temper, as always, had been her downfall. Now it had brought the whole family down with her.

As she knelt there, she heard a high-pitched wailing and, for a few seconds, she wondered where it was coming from. It was only when her mother came into the room and pulled her roughly into her arms that she realised the sound was actually emanating from her. For the first time in years she enjoyed her mother's strong embrace, didn't try to shrug her off, or push her away. For once she didn't act as if she was too old and too sophisticated for a mother's love, a mother's gesture of protection.

Instead, she hugged her back, grateful for the contact with another human being, grateful for her mother's familiar smell, a mixture of cigarettes and Ajax toilet cleaner. She needed this woman's support and love badly now. She had not felt this alone, had not felt this kind of abandonment before in her life.

As she cried on her mother's shoulder, Imelda felt her face being touched, felt her mother pulling her face away from the folds of her clothes and, looking into her daughter's empty eyes, she said softly, 'If anything happens to this baby, Mel, I'll hold you responsible, do you understand me? After all you've caused, you had better fucking make sure we have something to show for it. I know you, you have no fucking scruples, you'd flush it down the toilet without a second's thought.'

Looking intently at the woman she had spurned and ridiculed for the best part of her life, Imelda saw something she had never seen before, had never even thought she would see. Her mother had finally been pushed too far. She knew that as she recognised, not only deep dislike in her mother's wide-spaced blue eyes, but also a hardness that had never been there before.

Chapter Five

'We can bury your father at last. The police are releasing his body tomorrow.'

Mary looked at her three children, the boys as always said nothing, they were like a rudderless ship. Drifting from one day to the next. Without their father telling them what to do and how to do it, they had no real sense between them. She was astounded at how dense they actually were, an original thought would die of fucking loneliness.

They now looked to her for their guidance, looked to her for work; she had been forced to pull herself out of her own tragedy to ensure that Jackie Martin gave them a living. And he wasn't much better; without Gerald behind him he was about as much use as a chocolate teapot. It was a fucking joke, except she wasn't laughing. She was doing her best to keep everything going. Money was needed now, more than ever. A lot of people had come through for them, and she was grateful, but those handouts were not going to last for ever. She had to get the boys back in proper work, and thereby get her cut from Jackie Martin, because she wouldn't trust that ponce as far as she could throw him. He was a hanger-on by nature, a number two by chance; Gerald had never wanted anyone he thought might challenge him. Jackie Martin was not cut out for the top job, the mere thought of taking his rightful place terrified him. He was a bully, he liked the kudos of being Gerry Dooley's partner, and he liked the fact that Gerry Dooley hadn't wanted any more from him than that. Gerry had carried Jackie Martin for years, and that was no longer a secret in their world. That the partnership had suited her husband was known and understood. Gerry was a man who would never have relinquished his authority without a fight and he had made damned sure that he did not have a number two, who, at some point in their acquaintance, would suddenly decide he wanted to be the number one.

Jackie Martin had been quite happy to play second fiddle and Gerald had always acted as if they were both the decision makers. But without Gerald's reputation, and without Gerald's brainpower, Jackie Martin was fucked. He did not even know how much was coming in, he had trusted Gerald with everything, and that had suited them all until this had happened.

Now though, with her sons shown up for the retards they actually were, and Jackie Martin acting like he had never collected a debt, or delivered a threat before in his life, things were starting to look decidedly iffy. Mary knew that without her orchestrating their every move, they would all be destroyed and forgotten about in no time. She knew that she had to take over from her old man, and run the business from behind the scenes. She knew that more than a few of the people they dealt with would guess what was going on. After all, Jackie Martin had not exactly come up trumps since his partner's demise. He seemed to have shrunk, physically shrunk. It was odd, but he had somehow lost his swagger, his usual bravado. He was a real disappointment to her. Even though Mary had not expected him to do a Joe Bugner, she *had* expected him to take on some of the day-to-day running of the business.

In fact, he had not even tried. She had sussed early on that it was nothing personal, it wasn't because he was still mourning his best mate, or because he was planning his next move, it was because he didn't have a fucking inkling about any of it. He was coasting, he was playing it all by ear. She had been saddened by his actions, but not really surprised; after all, her husband had confided in her many times over the years, had even respected her advice.

So, she was now the brains of the outfit, and she had to get her head around that fact. It was hard, it was soul-destroying, but it was a fact of life. She had bills to pay and a family to look after. Two huge sons who had good hearts but no initiative, they were nothing more than employees and, as much as she loved them, that was something she had to accept. She had to give Jackie Martin the benefit of the doubt and see that he carried on the business in her husband's name. She could only try her best. She had always been a realist, and she had always been the power behind her husband's throne. She'd long been convinced that her husband's business had not been as difficult as he had made it out to be.

At the moment everything was going their way. As long as they all kept stumm, they were in with a chance. Her daughter, however, was dying to open that big trap of hers, and she knew it was taking all her willpower not to. In the last few months her daughter had gravitated from quiet submission, caused by her guilt, to her usual obstreperous self fighting to break out once more. Imelda had never had what might be termed a long-term outlook on life. She lived for the moment, and that was something that would never change. She was selfish, one of the most selfish people Mary had ever come across. And Imelda being Imelda, it seemed her naturally antagonistic personality was taking over once again. She felt that she had suffered enough, after all, in Imelda's world, everything was about her, never anyone else. As far as Imelda was concerned, her father was dead, as was her baby's father, and there was nothing anyone could do to bring them all back to life. Her attitude now was 'Get over it.'

She had grieved briefly, then it was a matter of keeping the act up for a while. And she'd played her part to a T. In fact, Mary had been more than pleased with her daughter because she had helped with the police and the press. None of them had ever said that she had been raped, it had never been said out loud, but the inference was there all the same. Even the Filth had seen fit to understand how something of that magnitude might cause murders, *literally*.

Mary sighed in despair. Men were strange like that, even the most amenable of men was seen as a titan where their daughters were concerned. The mildest of men would be forgiven a murderous act if he was faced with a similar dilemma. Men, whether they liked it or not, were a bunch of fucking hypocrites. They would shag a table leg, fuck a hunchback if the fancy took them, then laugh about it with their mates. Forgetting, of course, that the girl involved was someone's daughter, someone's sister. Indeed, in a lot of cases, someone's mother. Men just saw it all from a man's point of view, and that meant that even though the majority knew that Imelda had been around the turf more times than a prize-winning greyhound, they still admired and understood Gerald Dooley's reason for doing what he had. He was now a hero in many respects and, even though he was dead, and his family was destroyed beyond repair, even though everyone who knew him felt deep down in their boots that he was a fool, a mug, he had still done what he had done for the right reasons. Ergo, to all the men, bent and straight, he was now an urban hero. After all, Imelda was his baby and, no matter what the truth of it all might be, he had been murdered in the pursuit of his daughter's rapist.

Everyone had given him a free ride because crimes against women were on the increase, in fact, all crime was on the up. It was a dangerous society now, and the advent of punk rock, and high unemployment was not helping matters. The Irish Catholics from the six northern Irish states had brought their grievances to mainland Britain and were determined to be heard and, amid all this chaos and political propaganda, Gerald Dooley had been given a swerve. Suddenly here was a man who was guilty of nothing more than trying to right his daughter's wrong. If he had not died at Jason Parks's hand, had not been stabbed through the heart, Gerry would have been put away for the foreseeable future, most people in the know were aware of that. But as the priest had pointed out to her, Gerald was dead, and dead men couldn't talk. Gerald was suddenly a working-class hero. Amid the complete mayhem that constituted most of the lower-working-classes' lives, Gerald Dooley was a man who had tried to take the law into his own hands. A man who had tried to right a terrible wrong. Most of the people in Britain had no real redress where the courts were concerned, and they knew it. People were fitted up at a whim by the police.

It didn't matter how many times people watched rubbish like *The Sweeney*, the average person understood that, just because someone was a bit of a scallywag, that did not countenance fitting them up for a crime they had no hand in. If the Filth couldn't gather enough evidence against a person they felt was guilty of a crime, then that was their fucking lookout. Fitting people up, like any other scam, had left the judicial system open to all kinds of illicit dealings. Bent Filth were nothing new, but bent Filth who were working the scams themselves were an entirely new entity. The Flying Squad, the Serious Crime Squad, and the average plod were suddenly seen in a new light. All that bad press, coupled with a government who did no more than pay lip-service to the problems that they had caused, didn't help matters. Public morale was at an all-time low: it seemed that everyone was on the grab in some way.

So Gerald Dooley had only been doing what the police should have done: he had been taking care of his own, taking care of family business, and no one was shocked that he had not seen fit to bring the police into it. That he had taken the law into his own hands was not something people questioned. All they had to do was read the papers: every day, it seemed, the world they lived in, believed in, was shrinking beyond recognition. No one would badmouth Gerald Dooley and for that much, Mary would be eternally grateful. Because, like her husband before her, what people thought was of tantamount importance to her. As always, the East End had closed ranks, and the Old Bill had nothing to really go on and, on top of that, they had no real inclination to make this unfortunate set of circumstances more public than it already was. In short, they knew what had gone down and they couldn't do anything about it.

Mary was also aware that her daughter was a scheming whore who, if she didn't watch over her day and night, was capable of blowing the whole fucking shebang. That hard-faced bitch was already champing at the bit, was sick of having to play the victim. She was sick of being pregnant and was fed up with the police and their questions.

Mary knew that though Imelda was wary of her simmering anger, she was not going to keep her equilibrium for much longer. She knew that her daughter's attention span was not something any of them could bank on.

Imelda was bored. She liked things dramatic and passionate and over with as quickly as possible. This was all going on too long for her, and she was now conveniently forgetting why this was happening in the first place.

Mary watched as her daughter bit her bottom lip, saw the bump that was her child, the child she had never once referred to off her own bat. Mary knew, as she looked at her daughter, that she was a strikingly beautiful girl, and that was not just the opinion of a mother, because all mothers were biased, it was no more than a fact. Imelda was a real beauty, and it was that beauty that had enabled her daughter to get away with so much for the best part of her life. She could lie to anyone about anything: she would look into their eyes and tell them exactly what they wanted to hear. And the first few times she did it, they would believe her, because they wanted to believe her and because she was a real beauty, and beautiful people had the edge. But eventually they would be forced to see her for what she was, because Imelda never learnt from her mistakes. She would lie and lie and lie until her lies were discovered. Till she was found out.

Then the teachers, or her friends, or whoever she was scamming at that particular time, would realise how she had played them, would realise that they had been had over, and that they had believed her fabrications without any kind of proof. Her good looks and her natural acting ability had, as always, given her the edge.

Unfortunately, Imelda had never learnt when to step back, had not understood that her lies would eventually be found out. That was her Achilles heel.

But Mary was determined to make her daughter take responsibility for her actions, at least once in her life. She was worried about the baby her daughter was carrying, a grandchild that she herself wanted so desperately, and yet she knew her daughter had no interest in whatsoever. She knew that all the time she was pregnant with the baby, Imelda could just about be controlled. It was after the child's birth that the trouble would start.

At the moment Mary wanted to get her husband's funeral out of the way, then she could start running his business properly. She had Jackie Martin and her boys to use as fronts. But whatever happened, she was determined that she was not going to lose her livelihood.

It occurred to her that she actively disliked her daughter now and, even after all that had happened, that realisation saddened her.

The funeral of Gerald Dooley was much more than his wife had hoped for. It was massive, there were literally hundreds of people in attendance. It was so big that the traffic had to be diverted, and all the radio stations mentioned it in their traffic bulletins. It was a real send-off as far as everyone was concerned.

Cripps Funeral Parlour had done a spectacular job as always. The plumed horses that were pulling the carriage were groomed within an inch of their lives and people lined the roads, their hats removed in reverence.

It was a funeral the likes of which had not been seen for many a year. Young Faces abounded, all thrilled to be there, excited to become a little part of East End folklore. All pleased to have this story for the years to come. They happily mixed with the older Faces, the real criminals. Men who were not inclined to show their faces in public unless they had to. Men who were the movers and shakers of their world, but who had come out of their self-inflicted exiles to pay their respects to one of their own.

Mary watched them: she knew each and every one of them, and their mothers and their wives. She knew that she was respected, knew that she was seen as a good woman. She also knew that the majority of the men there were aware that she was now the main earner for her family. She also knew that, even though they didn't really like that fact, as long as Jackie Martin pretended that he was now the dog's gonads, they would be happy to overlook the truth. Her boys were big lumps, and they could collect a good wedge with the minimum of aggravation, and she knew that was all they would ever do. They were never going to expand of their own volition, between them they were not capable of thinking up even a half-decent scam, or even working out how to *improve* on an old one, bring it up to date.

Even at her husband's funeral, Mary knew she couldn't grieve properly because she knew better than anybody that this day was the only chance she was going to get to push forward her case. She knew that today she had the centre stage because she was burying her husband and, because of that, she was guaranteed an audience with anyone she wanted. She had one chance to prove that she was capable of carrying on her husband's business, to prove that she could be as ruthless as her husband had been, to try and convince the powers-that-be that she had been running the show from the off. She knew she had the sympathy vote, and she also knew that, providing she brought in the money, she would be left alone.

But what Mary really wanted today was not their fucking permission to carry on the earn from her husband; what she wanted, and she was determined to get, was *more* of their goodwill. More money. And she was astute enough to know that today she was liable to get what she asked for.

As they approached the church, Mary looked around the funeral car. She saw her sons in the expensive black suits that she had bought and paid for, their sad faces. The defeated slump of their shoulders and their complete apathy caused her to punch them both angrily in their chests and, as they looked helplessly at her, she whispered with a quiet desperation, 'Will you two stop looking so fucking sorry for yourselves? Get a grip. If nothing else, make your father proud of you both. Act like fucking men, real men. Pull your shoulders back, walk like men. Act like he would have done, but stop acting so fucking weak.'

She was sorry for them, knew that they were hurting, but she also knew that if they didn't grow up, eventually they would be outed. They would end up as someone's gofer. It was on the cards, and she was not going to let that happen to any of them.

Mary looked at her daughter then, saw the arrogance on her face as she looked at her older brothers. She knew that, like herself, Imelda saw them as dead weights, saw them for what they really were.

It grieved her that this daughter of hers had been blessed with not only a serious beauty, but also with all the brains, and it broke her heart that her boys had been blessed with nothing more than their father's brawn. They didn't even have the personality that was required to make them use their strength for their own ends. She had been forced to do to them what Gerry had done: threaten them and bully them into submission.

But she had done that, she had done whatever she felt was needed to keep her family going. She had nearly collapsed in on herself, had nearly let herself succumb to her grief and her sorrow. But in doing that she would have been in danger of abandoning her family in their hour of need. So she had picked herself up, and she had used her grief and her anger, and she had channelled it into something constructive. Women were always the ones who had to make sense of the world around them. Women were always the ones who were left to make the big decisions about the family, the children, the home where they would all reside together in harmony, and from where the children would one day leave without a backward glance as they established their own homes. Women decided what their family ate, what they wore, who they mixed with. Women picked up the pieces, mended their children's broken hearts and broken dreams. And with sons they also sat holding them tightly while they were stitched up or their bones were plastered. Women were the reason for most of the good things in the world. And yet women were classed as beneath men because they were forced by society and nature to depend on men for their money, for their name, for their protection. Well, Mary Dooley had found out the truth of that at long last.

Women were there for their men, they listened to them and they fed them, and they cajoled them when necessary. Women made their men's lives easier, even though a lot of the time it made their own lives harder. Men had no real concept of pain, of love, of loyalty. Why would they, these things were given to them without a second's thought throughout their lives?

It was only now, when Mary was left alone, trying to keep her family together, that it occurred to her just how little her husband had actually mattered in her family's day-to-day life. He had left her alone, and she had found that he was easily replaced. She *could* replace him, and she *had* replaced him. So, what was it all about? What was her life really about? She had married, she had given birth to her children, and she had done everything that had been expected from her. And for what?

Mary had held her emotions inside, she had made a point of overlooking all the gossip about her daughter, had made it her mission in life to make sure that no one around them would ever know the real truth. But this daughter of hers, she was a loose cannon, she was not someone to be trusted. At least with the boys Mary knew she had a modicum of control over them. With this one she knew in her heart that she would not be able to control her for long, there was always going to be a conflict of some kind.

As the Dooley family walked into the church, they gave the impression of a tight-knit, strong family. But Mary Dooley knew it was all an act; she was disappointed in her children and she was disappointed with the way her life had turned out.

When they walked up the aisle of the church and genuflected before the cross of Christ, Mary and Imelda both saw the forlorn figure of Jason Parks's mother; she was to the right of them, kneeling beneath a statue of the Immaculate Conception, her rosary beads already in her hand. She looked deep in prayer.

Mary was strangely cheered when she saw her daughter avert her eyes, knew that even Imelda didn't have the guts to look the poor woman in the face. But then again, neither did she.

That people were already noticing her presence was not lost on Mary, and she knew that how she reacted to Louise Parks being at the funeral was very important; it would be talked about for years and she knew she had to think seriously about the best course of action. This woman had lost her only child, her son, and her son's father, and she was a nice person. It hit Mary for the first time just how terrible it must be for her, to lose your child like that and then be told that he was a rapist into the bargain.

Until now, she had not even thought about how this woman might be feeling, she had not given her a passing thought. The humiliation of Louise Parks's situation washed over her then, the enormity of what had actually happened seemed to hit her like an invisible sledgehammer. She felt her heart constricting, felt the shortness of breath that always accompanied deep shame, and she knew that if her daughter had really been raped she would have chased this woman from the church the second she had clapped eyes on her. But she couldn't do it, she couldn't add to this poor woman's burden.

Mary knelt down in the front pew and blessed herself slowly. Closing her eyes she prayed silently for the repose of her husband's soul, and for forgiveness for her trespasses, which were legion.

Mary knew that she should reach out to touch Imelda in a gesture of support if for no other reason than the sake of appearances, but she still couldn't bring herself to touch her. Instead, she reached out to her sons, and she grabbed hold of their hands so tightly they were forced to move closer to her for comfort's sake.

Then Mary felt herself breaking down, felt the dam of tears that she had been so careful to keep locked inside herself finally erupt. And she cried like she had never cried before and, with the release of all her pent-up emotions, she felt a tiny sliver of relief. She felt like there was a great weight pressing down on her, crushing her, and she also knew that it was never going to go away.

Imelda listened to the Mass, she liked Mass, she always had. She had never seen it as a chore like a lot of friends had, she had always gone to Mass and seen it as a form of escape. Especially at junior school, when they had celebrated Mass every Wednesday at the local church. She liked the calmness of it, liked the continuity of it, the fact that it had been going for two thousand years.

Imelda believed in God because she felt that there had to be something else, something after all this, and also because anyone who was still being worshipped and adored after all that time had to have something going for them. How many people alive today would still be talked about in two thousand years from now?

She sighed heavily, the child was moving sluggishly and her body felt weary.

Imelda looked at the coffin that contained her father's remains and realised that she felt nothing. No remorse, no regrets, nothing. But then, she never really felt anything for long in her life, apart from anger and jealousy. She had felt an occasional twinge of other emotions, but nothing that constituted real, lasting feeling on her part.

She had learnt as a child to mimic the people around her, mimic their reactions to certain situations, and she had found that as long as the situation was about her personally, she could conjure up the necessary emotions, even convince herself that she could really feel them. But she couldn't, not really, she just kidded herself, because if she acted them out, then other people believed in them. It was odd, she had loved her dad, but only because she knew she was *supposed* to love him. She had manipulated him, had convinced herself of her affection for him. But in all honesty, it was another act, like most of her life was an act. Even in the church, watching her father's funeral, seeing the crowds of people who had turned out to pay their respects, she felt nothing.

She glanced at Jason's mum, and felt the anger rising inside her. Now, anger she could understand, she was an angry girl. She always had been, anger was the nearest she had ever really got to a spontaneous human emotion.

In fact, it was her capacity for anger that had made her feel like she fitted in, but even her anger could be manufactured if the need arose. She was capable of great anger, and great resentment, but then she knew that they were one and the same thing.

Resentment was a by-product of anger, anger bred resentment and vice versa. The spawn of those two destructive emotions was the most destructive emotion of them all, *jealousy.*

Imelda Dooley was only really happy when she was feeling anger, hatred or jealousy.

She could hear her mother crying now, could hear the real pain and sorrow in her sobs, knew that she was venting her heartache and Imelda wondered why the sounds didn't have any effect on her.

She knew she made a tragic figure, knew that her swollen belly and angelic face made most of the men, and a big majority of the women present here today, feel the urge to protect her. Her father's funeral was going to go down in East End folklore and she wanted her part in the myth to be about softness and about her youth. She had not bargained for Jason's fucking mother turning up, she knew that much.

She also knew that in the real world, her mother would have wiped the floor with Mrs fucking Parks. But she hadn't, and so she decided that she would treat the woman kindly too, then people would say how generous she was, how kind she was. And then she would drop into the conversation that they had all lost people close to them, and a child needed all the love it could get. She liked that, liked that expression.

Plus she could shove the child on the woman at her whim, which would be a real blow to her mother who thought that the child's birth would be the end of *her* life as she knew it. Just because she had fucked up, didn't mean that she had to pay for it.

She would give this child away without a second's thought, but she knew she would never get away with it. Even a child of a so-called rape, in their community, was still a child. A life. Well, if her mother wanted it then she was welcome to it.

She had felt the rage growing by the day, she had embraced it for the first time ever, she had enjoyed it. Welcomed it. She was never going to live a lie again, not inwardly anyway. She knew she would still have to pretend to the outside world. But she was suddenly caught up in her own world, the world she had inhabited since she had been a small child. A world where no one else mattered, a world where she could relax and not worry about people's reactions to her beliefs or to her feelings.

Now her father was gone, she didn't have to pretend to

herself any more. She was a woman in her own right and she was going to have a child. In their world that gave her a certain kudos, a cachet; she would go overnight from being a miss to a mother; she would have a title.

She wanted to smile, but she didn't. Her father's main boss was going up to give the eulogy. She noticed that Jackie Martin was not asked, even though he and her father were supposed to be best friends, had been partners.

Michael Hannon stood up at the altar and looked out at the sea of faces. He was a nice man, he was also a man who did not suffer fools gladly. He had made his mark many years before, and he had also made a point of keeping a low profile. It was why he was still on the scene when most of his contemporaries were in the nick. He had always believed in delegating, and he had delegated anything and everything he could.

He had only come out today because Gerald Dooley had been his friend since they were children. They had made their first Holy Communion together, and he had the photograph to prove that. As boys, Gerald had always looked out for him, he had been a quiet child, unlike Gerry, who had enjoyed fighting for the sake of it. When they had grown up it had all changed; Michael had been a late bloomer and had suddenly grown up overnight. He had always had a quicker brain, and it was this acumen that had finally separated the two. But he had always made a point of using Gerald over anyone else. He had cared for him deeply, as only a true friend of long-standing could. They had cared about each other, though neither of them would ever have said that out loud of course.

As Michael began to talk, regaling everyone with stories of their childhood and of the scrapes they had got into,

Imelda watched him with interest. He was a good-looking man for his age, and Imelda decided that she might set her cap at him. He had a wife of long-standing, a faded blonde with a permanent scowl and a Rothmans cigarette dangling from her lips. He was known as a ladies' man, with a few girls on the go at any given time, but Imelda decided that she would be the one to win him over; she would have her baby, and then she would go all out to get this man. He would take care of her; like her father, he would make sure she was happy. She felt that he would be prepared to go that extra mile to ensure she was properly taken care of.

It never occurred to her that Michael might not feel the same way, that he might see her as his friend's daughter and therefore not fair game. She only saw him as her salvation, as a way to make herself socially acceptable once more. With him beside her, she would be able to brush off the last few months and start again with a clean slate.

As the Mass ended Imelda was so engrossed in her own little world, she actually forgot why she was there in the first place.

Chapter Six

The atmosphere in the house was getting worse by the day; it was as if a dark cloud of hate was hanging over everything that mattered.

Mary Dooley could not bring herself even to touch her daughter, the daughter she had once adored. The daughter she had trusted to take care of herself, to look after herself. The daughter who had destroyed her whole family with her lies and deception.

The boys rarely came home after their work these days, both preferring the company of anyone else in the world, providing they were not a part of this family. They were finally acting as independent people, since their father's death they were finally coming out of their shells and coming into their own. It still rankled though, their girlfriends were not as quick to come and visit now Mary was widowed. She knew that they had only given her the time of day because her husband was employing his boys. Still, she had not been the nicest of women where her sons and their paramours were concerned, and she admitted that she was still a hard taskmaster in many respects.

Until her husband's death this house had seemed like her whole world, which it had been for a long time. Like many a woman before her, she had done what her own mother had done, had made her home into her own private haven. It was where she had some control over her children and, of course, her husband. While Gerald was alive, she had not needed anything or anyone outside of her little world. The news programmes on the TV showing wars and famines, the soap operas she watched with a frightening regularity, and the documentaries she would force herself to sit through because they were about worthy causes, were about things that were happening in the real world: famine, disease and more bloody wars. In the end, though, it was always about war. Men loved war, and they all looked for one at some point in their lives. Even if it was only with a neighbour, or a workmate they felt was encroaching on their fucking private space. So, like many a woman before her, Mary had created her own little world. A world where she reigned supreme, and she understood the rules and the regulations. As did everyone around her. She would sit through the documentaries and the BBC *News* and the *Panoramas*, because she felt obliged to, felt that was enough to ensure her family's protection. So she would watch them and then relay all her new-found knowledge to her family.

She watched these programmes without any real care, because they didn't really affect her, or her life. She would collect money for the church, try and help the poor unfortunates, as she thought of them. But she had no real feeling for them outside of her initial sorrow at their plight. Once the programme ended she would be hard-pushed to remember John Pilger's name. She had a knack of wiping out the terrible images: children dying, covered in flies and dust and women with dead eyes, nursing babies even though they had no milk left in their sagging breasts. She had felt sorrow for them all, real sadness, and she prayed for them and raised money for their cause. But, deep down, none of it had ever really affected her personally. Because none of those terrible things could *ever* happen to her, or *her* family.

She had always felt *safe*, safe in the little world she had created, and that she had been encouraged to create by her husband. Like her, he had seen the outside world as nothing to do with them personally. As somewhere that didn't overly concern his family. She had existed in that world for many years; her husband, her family, and her religion. In that order. She had always believed that would be her whole life until one day she would finally lie herself down in preparation for the long sleep. And then, and only then, would she be removed from her home. The home she had never spent even one night away from, the home she had been obsessed with since her wedding day. If it wasn't so bloody tragic, she would laugh at it all. Not just at herself, but at her ignorance and her selfishness, for believing that she had something special. For not understanding that there was so much more to life than just living it in such a blinkered and, now she was being honest with herself, such a tedious and fucking mediocre way.

Now that she was venturing outside of her comfort zone on a regular basis, she was enjoying it. She liked the fact that she was finally living a life for herself, even though it caused her such a tremendous feeling of guilt.

For the first time in years she felt alive, really alive, and she knew better than anyone that that alone was enough to unleash all her pent-up Catholic guilt. Now Catholic guilt was a different guilt altogether. It was a guilt that had been established in her as a small child, and that guilt had then grown over the years like a weed, strangling any kind of reason or good sense she might have developed. Catholic guilt was the most destructive sort of guilt because the person that it concerned had no real concept of it. They didn't even realise that it existed. Catholic guilt was something that grew alongside the person, alongside their personality and, in many ways, it did them some good. They felt the need to help the less fortunate, and they felt the urge to make their children better than they were. The person concerned would feel a sense of peace at the knowledge they had helped their fellow man. But the downside was that Catholic guilt also caused heartbreak and hurt because it was passed on and given over to the next generation. Catholic guilt caused families to try to outdo each other. It caused mothers to turn a blind eye to their sons' shenanigans, while they watched their daughters like a hawk. Only, Mary knew, she had *not* watched her daughter at all. She knew she had given her a free pass because she had not had the care, the want, or indeed the energy, to police her while, at the same time, she had not wanted her husband to know just how much freedom his daughter had been allowed. Mary had relied on her husband's reputation, and on her family's standing in their community, to keep her daughter safe from any predators. So her guilt was a hundredfold since her husband's demise. Her world, her perfectly structured and perfectly perfect life was gone. It was over with, and it would never come back again. She had basically blown it. And, to add to all the other guilt she was feeling, she had the added guilt of the thrill she felt at her new-found freedom. At her widowhood. She wondered how many other women must have felt like her. Had felt this strange lightness come over them, as if they were suddenly being given another chance at life.

A life that was not overshadowed and dictated by their husbands. Even though she had still loved and revered Gerry for the man he had been, the provider, the head of the household, her only love, and her only lover. She had been the force inside her house and he had respected her for that. But she also knew that was only while she was doing it as he wanted, as he expected.

Mary knew that she should be mourning her husband, knew that she should still be in the depths of despair, but she wasn't. At least, not about her husband anyway.

Her daughter, though, was another story. She gravitated from wanting to kill her stone dead, with her bare hands, mind, to fantasising about her daughter's demise at the hands of a complete stranger. The atmosphere around her was loaded with sheer malice, and not just from her. Imelda seemed to become more and more morose and aggressive as the days wore on. She never mentioned the baby, or its imminent arrival. She didn't seem to be planning anything on the sly either. She wasn't planning to run away with it, or even give it up for adoption. In fact, she refused to discuss the child at all, in any way, shape or form. Mary suspected she was still drinking, and still smoking. She knew better than anyone that Imelda was not a girl who found it easy to put others first and, in a way, she had admired her for that. But her own *child*, that she could not put her own flesh and blood before her own needs, her own wants. That was something her mother would never understand or forgive.

It just proved to her how selfish this daughter of hers actually was. Proved to her just how her faith and her trust had been abused by her youngest child. A trust that had been the cause of her father's death, the cause of her family's destruction.

On top of all that, Jackie Martin was still on the scene though, in fairness, he was quite happy for her to call the shots, for her to take over the main responsibility of the businesses. He was just glad that she was as astute as her husband when it came to work matters. He was also thrilled that she was quite prepared to let him take the credit for it all. He was good at his job, she would give him that much. As long as Jackie knew where he should be, who he should be with and, most importantly, that he was accompanied by the relevant amount of bone breakers, that is. Mary made sure that her sons were in on the earn. Even though they were still grieving for their father, and were about as much use as a fucking Tampax in a monastery, she had explained to them both in graphic detail what could happen to them all if they didn't pull their weight. Jackie Martin was comfortable with the boys. He knew how to handle them, and they were more than happy to follow his lead. She had a few other employees from her husband's books that she used for the more serious collections and, all in all, it seemed to be working out well for everyone involved.

Michael Hannon was happy enough with how she was running things and, as far as Mary was concerned, that was good enough. After all, it was Hannon who was paying the wages, and she knew that even if he had tossed her work at first because he was sorry for her, he was now giving it to her because she got results.

She had made a point of going after a few debts that she had heard were considered uncollectable. She had researched the people involved and, with a mixture of gentle persuasion combined with more than a few serious threats, she had managed to call them in. She realised that she had something her husband had never had; she took the debts personally. She went after them as if the money that was owed was all that stood between her and penury. She would not swallow, even if the person who owed was well connected. Unlike her husband, Mary didn't understand the delicate balance of the criminal underworld. She explained to the people concerned that a debt was a debt, and that they should pay up if for no other reason than their pride. She told them that the debts they had incurred were well known, and no payment towards them made them look like flakes. Made them look like cheap hustlers. Ergo, they might have swerved the debt but, in doing so, they had only shown themselves to be untrustworthy and, as everyone in their world knew, trust was how they got from one day to the next. She had visited the people concerned personally and she had put her case forward with a quiet voice, but a steely determination, and she had collected the monies. In the meantime she had also garnered herself a rep of sorts.

The people who had written the money off as a bad investment had been reimbursed, though not before she had awarded herself a generous bonus. She explained to them that she had collected their outstanding monies because she wanted them to understand that even though her husband was gone, she was quite capable of taking over from him, and that with Jackie Martin and her sons, they would not have to worry any more that certain people's debts were unobtainable. She guaranteed them that she would personally make sure that nobody would be immune from the payment of a debt again. No matter who they were, or who they might be related to. She didn't tell them that she had gone to the so-called hard-nut relative, the Name who had inadvertently been the reason that a substantial debt had been overlooked. She had explained how the sudden reluctance to pursue the outstanding monies then affected the reputations of all involved, not least them personally. Because it was their name that had stopped the collection of a debt that was owed fair and square. Mary said that her husband, God rest his soul, had explained to her that when he had been advised that a certain debt was to be left, the person owed the money was not only seriously out of pocket, they were also now the bearer of a grudge. A grudge that could only ever have one outcome: the loss of respect and, even more importantly, the loss of loyalty, to the person who had been the cause of the debt's non-payment. That, of course, was themselves. Mary also pointed out that, unlike her husband, as a woman and a mother, she had never owed a penny in her life. She was willing to bring this subject up with the people concerned. She explained that she would understand if they felt that she was undermining them, but she also explained that, as far as she had understood, in their world integrity was often all that any of them had. And, as far as she was concerned, gambling debts especially, were not only money owed, they were also the equivalent to a gentlemen's agreement. Once the shock of her visit, and the reason thereof, had worn off, she then requested their help in her collection of the debt owed. In effect, she asked them respectfully, with raw dignity, to take a step back and allow her to go about her business without the fear of retribution just because a relative or friend of theirs felt that such a connection could actually warrant them being given a fucking swerve of Olympian standards. Mary also pointed out that if they let their family use their name as a reason to do what they wanted, eventually that name would be tarnished for ever. Mary Dooley was so angry, so forthright, and so honest, that she had been assured by each and every one of the people concerned that they would not interfere with her or her collecting of the debt in any way, shape or form.

She had thanked them politely, reiterating that she knew they all understood that a debt was a debt, and that it had to be paid. She had been so frightened the first few times that she had heard nothing but the crashing of her own heartbeat in her ears. Then she had understood that she was being listened to because she had an argument that was without fault. She had given them the opinion of the people outside their own little worlds. And she knew all about living in your own world.

She had proved a good point, and people were now coming to her as a matter of course. She was pleased with how it was working out, but more than anything she was amazed at how much she enjoyed the actual day-to-day running of the business. She had a knack for it, and she was more than surprised at how easy she found it. Unlike her husband, Mary was aware that extreme measures were not to be used lightly. In fact, her mixture of a polite request, followed closely by a vicious demand had proved fruitful. Once the word had spread on the street that they were still in business, that Jackie Martin was more than capable of carrying on the business without his partner and local legend, Gerry Dooley, they had been set. But the real powers-that-be knew that Mary Dooley was the real brains behind the outfit, and they were happy to give her the work. Especially as she delivered.

The fact that Michael Hannon was the silent partner in the business alone was guaranteed to speed up the payment of most of the street debts, and Mary was not averse to a bit of good publicity if it paid dividends. She also knew that the chat on the pavement was already insinuating that she was the new principal of the business, working in conjunction with Michael Hannon.

She neither confirmed nor denied these rumours, as she was more than aware of how beneficial they would eventually be. If Jackie Martin had caught wind of them, he had not mentioned anything to her. But then, he wouldn't. Would he? Jackie was quite happy to let her do the real collar, and he was also happy enough as a figurehead, that was all he wanted out of the partnership. If he heard the rumours concerning her, he had not said a dicky bird.

Mary was enjoying herself for the first time in years; she was using her brain again, and she could feel it kicking back to full throttle as the days turned into weeks and the weeks turned into months. The cleaning of the house was still of tantamount importance where she was concerned, and what she loved most about her new job was that she could do it at her leisure. In her own time. After all, her job did not require her actual presence, all she had to do was research the debtor and find out their local haunts. That was easy, most of the people they wanted were well known to everyone around about, so finding out their daily schedules was not exactly rocket science. It was the more slippery customers that she enjoyed tracking down, and it seemed that she had a natural aptitude for it.

Since she had taken over the business, money was pouring in, and she was determined to keep it that way. Gerald had hidden money all over the place, and she was still trying to locate most of it. It was only now, being left widowed so abruptly, that Mary understood just how much her husband had kept quiet about his business dealings. She also realised just how ignorant she had been about their financial concerns. Gerry had given her a good wage, and she had appreciated that. But he had obviously been salting money away and, unfortunately for her, he had not seen fit to share that information with her.

It galled her, because no matter how she tried to dress it up, or tried to defend his actions, at the end of the day she had to admit to herself that her husband had not held her in high enough esteem. If he had, he would have made a point of telling her where the fucking bulk of their cash was hidden. She wasn't a fool, she knew that the Filth were always on the fucking cadge, loved nothing more than busting someone who worked in a cash-only business so they could have a little dip into what would become known jokingly as the police holiday fund. Gerry paid off a lot of Bill, and he had weighed out a lot of his grasses, as she now did herself but, even taking that into account, and no matter how she tried to dress it up, she came to the same conclusion. Her husband had not seen fit to let her fully into his world. She had asked Jackie Martin if he knew anything about what her husband might have done with his excess monies and she believed him when he had denied all knowledge. She also had a terrible feeling that her husband had not been averse to having his old mate over into the bargain. She just wished she could remember anything he'd said that might give her a hint as to where the money might be hidden. She had even asked the boys, but she had known from the start that would be a fruitless exercise. Gerald would not have told them anything of importance.

After all, Mary now had a daughter who was due to give birth and she needed as much money as she could gather; her grandchild would want for nothing. She hoped the baby was a girl, as the product of a so-called rape she felt that a girl would be easier for people to accept. They had to keep up the rape story, it was what had justified her husband's death, it had also salvaged what was left of her daughter's reputation.

Though from what she could garner, any vestige of a reputation Imelda had possessed, had been destroyed by her early teens. Her daughter disgusted her, she was like a stranger, she didn't know her any more. She actively loathed her, and that broke her heart. It was her fault that they were in such dire straits. Without Michael Hannon's protection they would never have started up the business once more. It would have died with Gerald and the family would have been scratching a living as best they could.

Imelda was now back to her old self with a vengeance; she was argumentative and aggressive and, without her father's calming presence, she was now completely without any kind of stabilising influence.

Mary watched her daughter as she slipped from the room, knew she was going to go upstairs to her bedroom to have a smoke and a couple of drinks. She counted to ten, and then she followed her. It broke her heart that a child she had borne, a child that she had given life to, had seen educated in the Catholic church, and who she had once believed was worthy of her love and her trust, had no care at all for the baby that was growing inside her.

Had no conscience about any of her actions, past or present.

Louise Parks was a broken woman.

Her only son's death had almost turned her mind. The way he had died haunted her every waking moment, even when she fell asleep.

That she loved her son was an understatement; she had

worshipped and adored him. Jason had been her whole life. She had birthed him, cared for him, and looked after him without a second's thought until he had been murdered. Had been butchered.

He was a little fucker, she was the first to admit that. He was a stroppy little bugger too, when the fancy took him, she admitted that, but he was *not* a rapist. She had searched her heart to find the honest answer to that accusation. She had tried her hardest to pinpoint something, *anything*, that might prove her instincts about her only child wrong. She had forced herself to look at her dead boy in that way. Had forced herself to try and find some reason for him to be branded a rapist. But she could not find anything that would make her believe it was true. She could not for the life of her find anything to justify that accusation.

He was not a rapist, he was just a healthy red-blooded boy who slept around and could not connect with the man who had sired him. That was the truth of it; he had been a young man without any kind of paternal influence in his life.

But Jason was not a lad who could have harmed a girl, he never would have hurt a female; he had always had a deep love of women. It was the only thing he had ever had in common with his father; like a mongrel he could smell a bitch on heat from a mile away.

Louise knew that people would think her a fool for what she believed, but she *knew* her son. And she knew that he was not capable of hurting any female in that kind of way. He might have broken their hearts, but that was different. And Imelda Dooley was never off the fucking phone, or the doorstep at one time. But who would believe her if she said that? She would be accused of lying to save her son's reputation. She would be either pitied, or ridiculed.

She had braved the funeral of Gerald Dooley, had seen the girl whose baby her Jason had apparently fathered, had tried to gather up enough courage to ask her if she would please tell the truth. Would please explain that she was lying about her son, because she had to be lying. She had to be making the story up.

But whatever people believed, it was still *her* grandchild inside that girl's belly, and it was well on by the looks of things.

Louise had nothing now, neither chick nor child. But if that Imelda was to be believed, she had a grandchild only a few weeks away from delivery.

Louise would do anything to have a part in its life, to see it grow up, see it bloom. She was so alone that, at times, the pain felt so acute she really believed that it might bring about her demise. She had slipped the girl a note, begging her to let her see her grandchild, assuring her that she would never allude to her son in any way if that was what she wanted. She had put her address and her phone number down, and she had also promised that if Imelda ever needed a friend or a place to go, her home would always be open to her, no matter what. She had felt a need somehow, a need to contact her and establish some kind of common ground with the girl.

It was all she could do, and if seeing her grandchild meant she had to deny her dead son, then she was willing to even do that much. After all, the child was her flesh and blood and, no matter how it was conceived, and she was convinced that it was not through brute force, it was still a part of her family, was still a part of her dead son.

Louise sat on the edge of the sofa; she was so thin the

bones along her spine were visible through her blouse. She had a lovely face, heart shaped and chiselled, with high cheekbones and deep-set blue eyes. She had the look of a twenties flapper about her and, even with her hair scraped back into a ponytail, she still looked much younger than her years. It grieved her that after years of dieting, after all the time she had obsessed about her weight, it had taken her only child's death to achieve her goal weight. She finally understood her mother's old saying, 'Be careful what you ask for, you just might get it.'

What a price she had paid for her new-found svelteness, and even she knew that she was now too thin. She knew that she was far too skinny to be healthy; she looked in the mirror and she didn't recognise herself any more.

She felt the tears welling up inside her once more, felt the tightening across her chest that her son's memory brought on. She wanted to scream at the fates, at God Himself, for taking her boy away from her so violently, and so unexpectedly. For letting her be left alone in this world, bereft of the only thing that had made her life bearable.

Her husband's death had not even really registered, the only time she had even thought about it was when she had been informed by his solicitors that she had been his sole beneficiary, and that was only because she had outlived their son. That her husband had left Jason everything had given her some small consolation. At the end of the day, he had not given him much when he was alive.

She would find herself sitting in Jason's bedroom, burying her face in his clothes, trying to recapture his scent. The smell of him; his sweat, his aftershave, his deodorant. She would feel the terror that the utter emptiness around her would invoke. She would feel the tight band of his loss as it gripped her chest, making her hope that she was at last having a heart attack, or that her heart might actually be breaking in two. But she was still here, she was still alive. It was only her faith and the fear of retribution in the afterlife, fear of being kept away from her son, that kept her from finishing her life. She had to concentrate on the child Jason had given to Imelda Dooley, she had to plan and she had to scheme. Even if all she could do was watch the child from afar, then she would have to make sure that was enough for her.

If she was to be a grandmother, then she had to accept her situation as best she could. She had to keep her head and tell Imelda Dooley whatever she wanted to hear, agree with whatever she said about her son and convince her that she was willing to do whatever she could to make up for her son's actions. She was willing to do just that, she had a lot of money and a lot of what her solicitor called assets. So she knew that she had at least that much going for her. If push came to shove, she would buy her way into the child's affections.

Louise had heard the gossip, knew that Imelda Dooley was not a wilting violet, she also knew deep down that her son had seen a lot of the girl. Louise had spoken to Imelda briefly at the funeral, and she had also seen the mother's reaction to her being there. Imelda had rung this house on many occasions, she had opened the front door to her, and she had also, God forgive her, lied to her for her son on more than one occasion. Jason had not raped the girl, Louise was convinced of that much, and she had searched her heart for even the slightest hint of doubt about her son.

She poured herself another glass of water and, sipping it slowly, she did what she did for most of every day since her son's death.

She prayed.

*

Michael Hannon sat in the back room of his cab rank on Ilford High Road. He was perturbed and not a little annoyed. That Mary Dooley was well able for the debts was not something he really interested himself in, that Jackie Martin was, to all intents and purposes, the new ganger didn't interest him. That he had just been told by an old and trusted friend that the said Jackie Martin was bad-mouthing him because he felt that he was being had over on his percentages of the debts, did interest him. Especially as he was now paying more than he had paid out previously, and also because he hated disloyalty of any kind.

Jackie Martin had fallen into the same trap that all treacherous bastards eventually fell into. He had allowed Gerald Dooley's wife to walk into the top job, and he had thanked God for her doing that. Because Jackie Martin knew that he had no fucking brains at all; he was to brains what Idi Amin was to democracy. Jackie Martin was suffering from an over-inflated ego, coupled with the fact that now Gerry was gone, he had no one to keep him in order. He was an inveterate gambler, everyone knew that, and Gerry had kept a close eye on him and his expenditure. In short, Gerald Dooley had always made sure that Jackie Martin did not end in the same position as the people they were paid to shake down. Gerry had ensured Jackie's debts were paid sooner rather than later. It was something that anyone with half a brain would have understood the logic of.

Without this personal service, it seemed Jackie Boy was suddenly going off the rails, and Michael Hannon had an awful feeling that Mary Dooley was not aware of any of this. Her sons were not exactly the sharpest knives in the fucking drawer and he had a terrible feeling that they would not see the sense in giving their mother a heads-up about this. They were still quite happy to follow Jackie's lead, to do what was requested of them.

Michael sighed heavily – no wonder Gerry Dooley had been paid fortunes to train up other people's fucking idiot kids, after all, he had plenty of experience with his own. Those two fucking morons, plus Jackie Martin, equalled fucking aggravation.

For Michael Hannon though, this was also a bit of a poser, as he was the reason *why* Jackie Martin was even employed and he was the reason Mary Dooley was being taken seriously by those in the know. He was, to all intents and purposes, the business.

He was also not exactly known for having a gentle streak, especially where business or fucking wankers were concerned. So he knew that he had to make sure that Mary Dooley was prepared to go that extra mile, even when it concerned her own workforce. Jackie Martin needed a serious talking-to, and he had to decide whether or not he thought Mary Dooley was capable of delivering it.

Chapter Seven

Gerald Junior and Brendan were both sitting at the kitchen table with their heads bowed low as they experienced their mother's wrath. She was almost in tears as she berated them, as she finally realised that they were never ever going to be any good to her. She knew that she needed to find another number two, needed to replace Jackie Martin sooner rather than later, and she needed to make sure that whoever she chose would have the nous to work with her.

That Jackie could have been such a fool was beyond her comprehension. That she could not give him a second chance was something she had understood very early in the conversation. He had stepped over a very fine line, and she had to make sure that she resolved this terrible situation quickly and cleanly. She would cut that fucker out like a cancer, and she would do it without a second's thought. The real dilemma for her was who she could get to replace him.

Michael Hannon had been very vocal about Jackie Martin's position, and she had understood his point of view. She was more annoyed because she had not heard about Jackie's blatant stupidity earlier; if she had, she might have been able to nip it in the bud. She might have been able to salvage something of their business.

Brendan was his father's double physically, yet he had no real personality to speak of, and his brother was no better. Gerry had forced his opinions and his personality on to these boys with such force that they were incapable of any kind of originality, or indeed, anything even resembling a conscious thought. They waited for someone to tell them what to think and, as she looked at them as they waited for her anger to subside, she felt the full force of her situation. She admitted to herself that never before had she felt so alone, or so isolated. She swallowed down the panic inside her, and forced herself to be calm.

'Didn't either of you think that Jackie's gambling was something that I might have needed to be told about?'

Mary's voice sounded reasonable, even to her, and she marvelled at the difference it made to her two sons' attitudes. They finally looked directly at her, and she could have cried with frustration at their identical expressions of relief.

It was Brendan who answered her. 'Come on, Mum, he's always liked a flutter, you know that. Dad never said anything about it.'

She knew it was the nearest he would ever get to an accusation of any kind. 'Your father monitored his gambling, surely you both knew that? And what about his bad-mouthing of Michael Hannon? Surely that should have been something you felt I needed to know about, after all we are only in business because Hannon has given us his backing.'

She was pleading with them to tell her something of

import, something that she could use for their benefit.

Gerald Junior shrugged. 'Look, Mum, all we have ever done is what the old man, or Jackie, told us to do. We can't be expected to police him, everyone knows what he's like. And he has a point, why should Hannon get the lion's share, when we're the ones who do the fucking dirty work.'

As Mary listened to his voice, heard his words, she accepted then and there that they were never ever going to suddenly come into their own. God help her, they were her sons and she loved them, but they were of no real use to her. If she wasn't careful they would all be scratching a living, and she was determined that was not going to happen.

Taking a deep breath, she steadied the hammering of her heart. The boys were so fucking stupid that they were willing to believe Jackie's rhetoric, they didn't even have the fucking sense to work out the situation for themselves. Why had she never seen just how fucking useless they were before now? Why had she never before seen them for the spineless fucking imbeciles they were? She had single-handedly saved their jobs, their livelihoods, and their reputations. They had then sat back and allowed Jackie Martin to jeopardise all that she had worked for and the worst thing was that they couldn't even see any of that for themselves. She needed to find herself someone with ambition, someone with loyalty, someone who needed the good life as much as she did. That she would be bringing in someone over her sons' heads would be remarked on, she knew that. But after the last few months she had a feeling that no one would be very surprised at her actions. These two boys were never going to be anything more than heavies. That, she knew, was something they were good at.

Smiling gently, Mary said with as much sincerity as she could muster, 'Well, boys, Jackie has burnt his boats. Hannon has more or less insisted that I out him, and that is something we have to do. But we can't just let him go, Hannon needs to be placated. Jackie needs to be taught a lesson, taught that you can't bite the hand that feeds you. Now, you both know that your father, God rest him, would tell you both the same thing if he was here now. So, can I trust you both to do what's necessary, or do I have to go to an outside agency?'

Brendan and Gerald Junior looked at each other then, and Brendan opened his arms wide, as if accepting the inevitable. Then he said with a quiet confidence, 'How badly do you want him hurt, Mum?'

Imelda was listening quietly to her mother's harangue of her brothers; that it had taken her mother all this time to finally realise that they were a couple of fucking morons gave her a small flicker of satisfaction.

As she pulled deeply on her cigarette she felt the child inside her kicking and, rubbing her distended belly, she wished the whole experience was over and done with.

She had decided that once the child was born she would give it to her mother, that way she could get shot of it and, at the same time, she would earn herself a few brownie-points into the bargain.

None of her friends had lasted the course and, even though she consoled herself it was because of her situation, she knew that the reality was because she had treated everyone like dirt.

When her father had been alive, Imelda had not appreciated just how much his name had carried her through her most formative years. She had not understood just how much he had influenced her life, and the way people reacted to her.

That her mother was attempting to re-create that world for them once again, and that she was actually succeeding, annoyed her even though she craved those easy-going days again. Unlike her brothers, Imelda had always known that she had more than her fair share of brains, and she had always used them to her advantage. She had learnt as a small child how to manipulate the people around her. She understood now why her father had always favoured her over her brothers. It was because he had sussed out that they were borderline fucking retards at an early age. In fact, he had been a major factor in the arresting of their developments.

The thought made her smile, and the smile changed her whole face. Imelda looked, as always, like an innocent, her smile was really beautiful. It made her look like an angel, and it belied the anger and the resentment that she nurtured. She held on to every slight, real or imagined, that she felt had been directed her way. She kept a close grip on any insults or any maliciousness that she felt had been directed at her personally and would go over and over in her head what had happened, how she had felt at the time, and what she would do to the person concerned when she was given the chance to repay them for their wickedness.

She felt she had been badly used, not only by her friends, but also by the men she had been foolish enough to fall for. Imelda Dooley saw herself as a victim, and the role of the victim was now something she actually relished, actually enjoyed. That her bitterness was destroying her more and more, she refused to accept. As Imelda's belly grew, so did her discontent, and the depression that washed over her only added to her feelings of persecution and isolation. Her childhood home was now more like a prison, and her father's absence was like a constant reminder of what she had caused, what she had lost. His betrayal when he had found out that she was pregnant had been worse than anything that had ever happened to her before in her life. She had wanted him to make everything all right, instead he had made it worse. She had kept her mouth shut, had waited for Jason to come for her, to make it better. Like her father, he had only succeeded in making it all so much worse. And now she was left with a bellyful of arms and legs, and she was also left with the stigma of her actions, and the devastation they had caused.

She felt the child quickening once more, and as it settled itself into a more comfortable position she pulled back her arm and then she felt the sharp pain and the satisfaction the punch she delivered to her own body engendered.

She had taken to punching the child when it moved inside her because she had a real belief that if she could catch it at the right moment, she would maybe be lucky enough to lose it. She had an image in her mind of her as the poor girl who had lost her child as well as her father, she pictured herself looking forlorn and sad. Then everyone would forgive her because she had suffered such a dreadful loss. But the child seemed immovable.

She read in the papers, and heard stories all the time about women who could not have babies, who could not keep their offspring in the safety of their accommodating wombs. She had seen women who were so desperate for a child of their own that they made a point of being the first in line to hold a newborn baby, believing the old wives' tale that if you were the first to hold someone else's baby, you would be blessed with one of your own. Blessed. What the fuck was that about? Why didn't anyone warn her about just how much a baby interfered with your life, and this was before it was even born. Why was her body swollen and distorted when there were women who would give anything to be in her position and yet they couldn't conceive for love nor money? Who prayed for this to happen to them, who would have seen it as something good, something to celebrate? What woman did not feel complete because they could not do something so fucking easy, so fucking fundamental, that they deemed so fucking necessary to make their lives happier? What was God thinking of to let those women suffer like they did? Then there was her, who was still pregnant after everything that had happened, after all the fucking upset and heartbreak this bloody child had caused.

And her mother, like a bloody vampire, awaiting its arrival, believing that this child would make everything all right, was convinced that this baby was her last chance to do things right.

Imelda felt the familiar terror that accompanied these thoughts and she attempted, as always, to quieten them down. She knew that if she even once gave vent to them, she would not be able to control herself. She knew that she was capable of losing it completely. She knew that if she didn't control her thoughts, and control her reactions to her thoughts, she would lose the last remaining shred of sanity she possessed.

So she took more deep breaths, and she punched herself in the tummy once more. The pain she inflicted on herself felt almost therapeutic, made her feel that she had some control over her body at least. As she heard her mother's heavy footsteps on the landing above her, she sighed and, lighting another joint, she smoked it in silence.

Michael Hannon was very pleased at the quick response to his request. That Jackie Martin had been given a serious hammering in full view of a number of prominent citizens had gone a long way to assuage his anger.

Mary Dooley was a surprise, he had only helped her out at first because he knew that she needed a few quid. After all, it was common knowledge, thanks to Jackie Martin, that she had no idea where her old man had placed his not inconsiderable fortune. Michael had felt sorry for her because, like his own mother, she had been shafted by the one person she should have been able to trust above all others.

Gerald wasn't a slag, he didn't stalk prey, young girls with long legs and the attention span of a gnat. Unlike his own father, who had pursued anything with a pretty face and an accommodating smile. No, Gerald Dooley had done something much worse, he had left his family to wonder where his money was, where he had stashed it in case of emergencies. Michael knew that Mary had, in all probability, like his own mother, been a bigger part of her husband's life and work than anyone realised. She was, he would wager, the real brains of the outfit. So her complete destruction of Jackie Martin was, as far as he was concerned, the only outcome he would have been happy with. She had complied with his wishes, quickly and ruthlessly. Now, though, he knew she would be looking for a new Face to front the business. He also knew that would not be an easy task as her boys were no use, and the men that Gerald Dooley had trained up in the past were not renowned for their brain capacity.

Michael liked that Mary was causing a stir among the

old Faces, liked that she was doing a better job than her old man had and he liked the fact that she was willing to orchestrate everything from behind the scenes, that she didn't feel the need a man would, to make her part in it common knowledge.

He felt that Mary Dooley was going to be an asset, that she was capable of a lot more than she was letting on, and he liked the fact that he knew it before anyone else did. But mostly, he liked the fact that she would be the last person anyone would think of as a partner in his money-lending and money-laundering scam.

She needed someone to front her collecting business, and he needed someone to run his loan-sharking business. He needed somebody who no one would ever suspect in a million years, who the Filth would not even contemplate. Who the people he had to deal with on a daily basis would never suspect of any kind of involvement whatsoever.

Michael felt the excitement that always accompanied a new score. Unlike his contemporaries, he understood that the seventies were almost over, and once the Labour government were out and, thanks to the three-day week and the fucking constant strikes, that would not be too long now, the Conservatives, and their usual promises of borrow, borrow, borrow, would be the catalyst that would enable him to open up a whole new world of skulduggery. Mortgage companies, money-lending disguised as loans, and the inevitable laundering of the profits he had accrued from his other, illicit, ill-gotten gains through such companies.

It was a win-win situation. Mary Dooley was the last person anyone would credit him as employing, and that was exactly what he was banking on.

*

Mary was sensible enough to know that she had a few weeks' grace before she had to replace that fucking eejit Jackie Martin. She was racking her brains trying to think of someone who she could not only trust, but who was in such a position that her proposition would not only be welcomed, but would also be seen for the long-term earner that it was. She didn't want a youngster who saw her as a stepping stone, or an older man who wanted a quiet life until he retired. She wanted someone who could see the big picture, who appreciated the long-term aspects of the business and could see that there was room for expansion. She knew that all the years of helping Gerry were paying off and she also knew that if she didn't get this sorted sooner rather than later, then the business would be taken from under her nose. The frustration that Mary felt at her husband's fucking stupidity still rankled. If she had access to his poke she could call the fucking shots as and when she liked. She sipped her tea, but it was stone cold.

Imelda came into the kitchen then, and Mary looked at her daughter with ill-disguised contempt. She saw the heaviness of her belly, emphasised by the thin cotton dressing gown she was wearing, and saw how emaciated her arms and legs were, and she realised, with horror, just how much weight her daughter had lost. She felt a stab of fear inside her, not for her daughter's plight, but for the child she was carrying.

'Are you eating?'

The question made Imelda laugh. 'Not really, I can't seem to keep anything down.'

They both knew she was lying, but neither wanted to admit to that. This was a game they had played out many times in the last few months.

Mary sighed and, for the first time since her husband's murder, she spoke to her daughter with genuine concern in her voice. 'Look, Mel, are you really all right? You look rough.'

Imelda opened the fridge and took out a bottle of Coke; unscrewing the lid she took a deep draught of the black liquid. 'I'm fine, Mum, I swear. I just feel sick a lot that's all.' She took another deep draught of the Coke and, burping loudly, she smiled that angelic smile of hers. Then, holding up the bottle she said gaily, 'I mean, the vodka helps.'

As she waited for her mother to explode she was disconcerted to see that her mother was just staring at her, her deep-set eyes full of a sadness that was so powerful it was almost tangible.

'I can understand your need to hurt me, Mel, and I can take it, I can take anything you want to dish out to me. But to hurt that child, the child you lay down and conceived without any kind of force whatsoever, that you waited for Jason Parks to acknowledge for weeks in this house, and that you used as a weapon that caused fucking murders, literally. I do not understand your determination to hurt your own child. Your own flesh and blood. Well, fuck you, Mel, drink, smoke, do what you want. It's like you keep telling me, it's *your* baby, not mine. But remember this, at least I wanted it, which is more than its own mother can say.'

Imelda looked into her mother's face and she saw the usual anger, the genuine bafflement that she did not want her baby. She knew that to her mother that was tantamount to a mortal sin. She knew that her mother saw her as unnatural because she couldn't love her baby, because she didn't want it, or anything it might entail. She also saw, for the first time since this had all started, a flicker of compassion, sorrow, for her.

'I'm sorry, Mum, I've tried, but I don't want it, I hate it. It feels like a fucking albatross hanging round my neck. And I know that you don't understand how I can feel like that about my own baby, but I do.'

Imelda was sobbing then, her frail body shuddering with the power of her pain. Getting up from her chair, Mary forced herself to go to her daughter's aid, forced herself to comfort her. And as she felt her girl slip her arms around her waist and hug her with all the strength she could muster, she forced herself to endure her touch. The sadness and the compassion she displayed were for the grandchild she was waiting for, her daughter's touch still made her skin crawl.

If Imelda had not wanted the child, she could have got over that, would have tried to understand that even, but it was her daughter's arrogant disregard for her baby's welfare that had finally finished her where Mel was concerned.

She worried that Imelda's constant drinking and smoking and her refusal to eat the food she prepared for her, might cause some kind of problems for the baby. She had read in the papers about how drinking was not good for the foetus, how the Americans, who were always ten years ahead of everyone else, were now recognising something called Foetal Alcohol Syndrome. And she was worried about drugs. As she saw her daughter's drinking escalate, her dislike and disgust had escalated at a similar rate.

Mary felt Imelda pull away, and waited until she had sat herself down at the kitchen table.

'I don't really drink as much as I let on, I just . . .'

Imelda waved her hands in distress. 'I just feel so horrible inside. I feel trapped, Mum, can't you understand that at all?'

Mary shook her head sadly. 'No, Mel, I can't. The child has done nothing to warrant your treatment of it. The drinking, the smoking and the punching.'

She saw her daughter's eyes widen at her words.

'Oh, I know about your violence towards the poor child. And as God is my witness, how you could even think about such an abomination, let alone carry the thought out, is way beyond my comprehension. I know I let you get away with a lot because I was lazy, but it was also because there was this new world for young women, a world where you could get a good education and a good job. I knew you were a clever girl, knew that you had a bit of fucking intelligence about you. Had you had the wits to make something of yourself, that is. Instead of using that sharp mind you were given, you've fucking wasted it on lies and deceit and your own selfish wants. You can't even see that you have a person inside of you, a real person. And, one day, that person will be an adult, and they will want you to answer their questions, and you will have to do that at some point, whether you want to or not. But I know that my words are wasted, because *you* will never see further than *you*. You've broken my heart, Mel. Even with all the trouble you caused for this family, if you had just once taken the time to consider that poor child, I could have forgiven you eventually. But not now, Mel, you have proved to me the truth of what I had always suspected. You are without any common decency, or any kind of empathy or care for anyone other than yourself. And you know something, Mel, I am actually sorry for you. I am heart-sorry, because you will never know what it is to love somebody more than you love yourself, and you will never ever experience what it's like to be loved in return.'

Imelda shrugged then, and sitting up straight in the chair, she looked into her mother's eyes and said loudly and forcefully, 'And am I to believe that you are speaking from your own experience, Mother? Only, out of your three children, which one of us ever loved you in return and, more to the point, which one of us did *you* ever love more than yourself? Pot, kettle and black springs to mind. You have destroyed us all, one by one, but unlike the boys, I never let you get too close, lady. Your fucking perfect family was only for the benefit of the outside world. For the neighbours, and the people you deemed good enough for your so-called friendship. In reality we knew we were disappointments to you in our own ways. But *my* father loved me, and he was so in love with you that he didn't even see fit to tell you where his fucking poke was.'

She laughed then, at the way her mother had suddenly deflated, seemed to shrink before her eyes. 'I'll tell you something, shall I? I hate you so much it is the only thing keeping me going. I hope you fucking die screaming in pain, alone and unwanted. I pray that you will one day understand the damage you caused us with your self-righteousness, and your greed. I ain't got nothing on my conscience where you're concerned, Mother, but then again, I have no conscience at all.'

The blow, when it landed, was hard and fast, it knocked Imelda off her chair and across the floor. It was powerful enough to draw blood, she could taste it, and as she lay on the floor she could see her mother moving in for the next blow. She instinctively put her hands across her belly, and the gesture was not wasted on either of them.

Pulling herself up from the floor, Imelda leant against

the kitchen table, and shaking her head in exaggerated misery she said, 'I bet you feel much better after that, eh, Mum?'

Mary was ashamed at her actions, at how this daughter could make her want to physically harm her; even pregnant she had still felt an urge to brain her.

'You're like an animal, Mel, but that's a fucking insult to animals, at least they protect their young. You, you couldn't care less about that poor child, you have no soul, you have no fucking care for anyone or anything that matters.'

Imelda laughed then and, wiping the blood from the corner of her mouth, she looked pointedly at the vivid redness that was staining her hand and fingers. Then she said happily, 'Well, be fair, Mum, I've got a fucking good teacher, haven't I?'

Jimmy Bailey was twenty-eight years old, he had thick dark hair, dark-blue eyes and a roman nose that somehow looked good on him personally. He was just over six feet, had an athletic build, and was known as a handful if needed, and a good ally in a crisis. He had made his mark with Michael Hannon over the last eight years, and he knew that if Michael was asking to meet him on the quiet it could mean one of two things. He was either going to be offered a job of some description or, worst-case scenario, he had offended Hannon in some way and was for the fucking chop.

Personally, he favoured the former, he was far too shrewd ever to give an opinion about anyone who mattered. Only a fucking muppet did something that stupid. But there were plenty of them out there, as he had seen himself on more than one occasion. In fact, he was constantly amazed at the fucking sheer stupidity of some of his compatriots. They had a few drinks, a lively bird, and a couple of lines, and suddenly all their carefully created persona was forgotten as they felt an almighty urge to show off.

That was when it tumbled out, who they knew, how they knew them, where the parties being bragged about lived, next, little nuggets of information that they had been told on the quiet were suddenly being repeated as if they were jewels of wisdom.

It was as embarrassing as it was shocking. Jimmy wanted to die of shame for them. But of course he just kept his own counsel. He had only ever tried to step in on one such situation, where the person involved, a mate of long-standing, had, after much cocaine and Jack Daniels, suddenly felt the urge to discuss a recent bank robbery and who also insisted on telling everyone the names of the people involved. Jimmy had stepped in nicely and, after a few bantering jokes about grasses and Bertie Smalls, had managed to get his point across, but the man involved took his meaningful bantering as a blatant accusation that he was a grass. That Jimmy had won the ensuing fight did little to console him because he had lost a good mate who he knew was mortified at his actions, and although he had lost a tooth, he also acquired a scar on his eyebrow that he felt made him look distinguished somehow. He knew he was lucky with his looks; he was possessed of that Gypsy stroke Irish dark skin that, whilst it made him look exotic, also ensured that he had to shave at least twice a day. But women loved him and, as a consequence, he knew that his looks were a magnet for men who were not as well equipped in the looks department. This was usually caused by the said men's wives or girlfriends giving him a blatant once-over.

He had learnt as a young man the power good looks had over women, and he had also learnt of the anger the same good looks could invoke from men. His looks were a double-edged sword and, as his rep as a Face had grown, his need to fight because a woman had tipped him the wink in the full glare of her old man, had dramatically decreased. In fact, he was known in some circles as Handsome Jimmy, as opposed to Ugly Jimmy, who was a mate, and who was ugly.

As Jimmy waited for Michael Hannon to arrive, he felt the first stirrings of excitement inside his breast. He hoped that this was going to be a good earner, with decent hours of employment. He hated early starts, but was obviously not silly enough to say that. If it was a four in the morning gig, then that was that. He would do whatever was necessary to get on in his chosen profession.

Jimmy's own business, and by that he meant his personal business, had not really garnered him any kudos in his world. He had acquired a massage parlour a few years earlier in payment for a debt and had decided to see what it entailed. Now he had six parlours all over the Smoke, and he ran a cab rank that was expressly used by his girls for their home visits. He was earning a fortune and it was more or less legal. He knew that there were still people who looked down on what they would call pimping: it having always been seen as the domain of the Jamaicans or the Maltese. Well, he had been called much worse than that over the years, so he had decided, rather magnanimously he thought, not to let it bother him. He was on a serious wedge, and that was good enough for him. Jimmy had a knack for business and he also had a radar for the type of girls who would be suited to that kind of employment. He only had to get them in there for a few days' graft, and he knew that the money they were collaring would bring them back. They had kids, and they had bills, and none of them were exactly geared up in the education department. If it was a choice between the social security, amply supplemented by a few nights on the batter, he knew the choice they would make. It meant new clothes for their kids, it meant new furniture for their flats, and it meant something that went far deeper than material things. It meant they were financially secure at last, and that was something that these young mums treasured. So, a pimp he might be, but these days, no one was likely to call him that to his boat race. He had come a long way, and he had earned his fucking respect. He knew his own worth, and he never let himself forget it. Plus, he knew that his earning power, and the fact that he had turned a sleazy wank bar into a high-class booking service had forced the respect from even the most severe of his critics.

As Michael Hannon slipped into the passenger seat of his car, Jimmy mentally chalked up one point to Hannon on an imaginary scoreboard. He had not even seen the fucker approach the car, and in broad daylight that was no easy feat. He was impressed, there was no doubt about that.

Chapter Eight

'Look, Mary, I do not want to take over your business. Michael thinks that I will be a good front man for you and, to be perfectly honest, I think he's right. You can still do all the groundwork for the debts, I have no interest in that part of the business. I ain't going to argue with you about this, OK? It's sorted, finished, over.'

Mary knew when she was beaten. But this young man, with his virile good looks and easy-going personality, had thrown her. She had expected someone older, someone she might have had something in common with, someone of her ilk. She had certainly not expected a youngster who had the good looks of a movie star and the reputation of a pimp. That really bothered her, Gerald had always looked down on men who earned their living off women, off girls. Desperate girls, most of them, trying to make ends meet, and finally being reduced to nothing more than animals by sharp-talking clever-clogs like this lad here.

There was something about the business that stuck in her craw. She saw these men as carrion, and her instinct told her that anyone who could send a young girl to a stranger for money was not someone to be trusted. But Jimmy had presented her with a fait accompli: if Michael Hannon wanted him onboard, she had no choice in the matter. But he was first and foremost a pimp, he was a collector on a secondary basis.

Jimmy smiled at her, knowing that his staggering good looks were wasted on Mary Dooley.

'Look, Michael had nothing but praise for the way you can ferret out information about people who owe us. Now, if he says you're a diamond, then I know that has to be the truth. He does not suffer fools gladly, as you know yourself.'

Mary nodded at the logic of what Jimmy was saying.

'So, that works both ways, don't it? I have something to bring to the table as well. But my expertise is in a different field from yours altogether. You find the fuckers, and I will extract the money from them. OK? Now, I know your boys are well known for their aggressive natures and their willingness to smash someone to a pulp. And I believe, most strongly, that with their natural antipathy, and my knack for explaining things to people in a graphic and, shall we say, a violently explicit way, that between us, we have the perfect team. I can do torture, refined, artistic torture if necessary, and I will educate your sons in that. I can also threaten people in such a way that their own mothers could be standing beside them and they would not guess that anything was even slightly amiss. Though the man in question would be at panic stations within seconds of course. So, can we just go for it, Mary, see how it all pans out?'

Mary nodded, as he knew she would, and as she knew she would.

'My boys are good at what they do, you remember that. They were taught by a master, by their father.'

Jimmy Bailey nodded in absolute agreement and, grinning at her with his perfect teeth, he said sadly, 'You must miss him, love, me mum was the same when me old man passed.'

Mary smiled then, a real smile, at his understanding of her situation and at his kindness for mentioning it to her. That he was making a point of offering his condolences.

Jimmy didn't tell her then that he had no family, that his father had been a one-night stand in a succession of one-night stands, or that his mother had abandoned him as a baby only to turn up periodically throughout his childhood, wrecking any chance he had ever had of anything even resembling normality with a woman. He certainly didn't mention that her sons were about as much use as a chocolate fireguard, and were actually bereft of anything even remotely resembling respect.

He had told her what she needed to hear, wanted to hear, and that was something he had learnt many years ago. In care you learnt early on how to manipulate the people around you, it was how you learnt to survive in a system where the odds were constantly stacked against you. A system where you were at the mercy of anyone who was stronger than you, cleverer than you or, in most cases, were running the fucking place, and running it to their advantage. It could be other children but, in most cases, it was the adults you were supposed to trust, who were supposed to be looking out for you. Basically, you were always at some fucker's mercy, and that fucker was very rarely someone of a kind and generous nature.

Jimmy knew the world inside out, and he was pleased with how he had survived within it, and at how he had managed to live to tell the tale in the first place.

Mary Dooley would be easy enough to control. She

wasn't a fool by anyone's standards, and she had a network of people she could call on that guaranteed her the location of anyone they might have the urge to pursue. She was not a push-over as such, but she was like most women of his acquaintance, she would be happy to let him run the show.

As Jimmy looked around her spotlessly clean kitchen, breathed in the smell of Vim, mixed with Pledge, he felt a twinge of regret that he had only ever experienced family life on an occasional basis while in the care system.

He had by then been far too cynical a child to allow himself to be beguiled by it all, knowing that it wouldn't last, and that within a week of his departure the so-called foster parents would be hard-pushed to remember his name. He had therefore only experienced the so-called family situation from afar, as an outsider. It had never occurred to him that it was his aloofness and his fear of getting close to anyone that was the cause of foster parents eventually asking for him to be replaced as their love and understanding kept falling on very stony ground. The very thing Jimmy had used to stop himself from being hurt, was the same thing that had also stopped him from experiencing all the things he had secretly craved, and had led to him being hurt anyway.

He opened his notebook then, and taking a pen out of his jacket inside pocket, he smiled once more, saying, 'So, who owes what, and where can I find the bastards?'

Louise Parks was doing her hand washing, her smalls and what she termed her private and personals, when she heard the doorbell.

Sighing heavily, she wiped her soapy hands on a nearby tea towel and with her usual quiet demeanour she walked through her front room and, once in the hallway, she saw a female shape through the frosted glass of her front door.

She was not expecting anyone, since the death of her husband and son, people had seemed actively to avoid her; those who had braved the consensus of public opinion had not seen fit to return for a second visit. A few, she decided, had come merely to fish for information, most of the others had meant well, but had not known how to comfort her, had not known the appropriate words for such an occasion. Louise had not held that against them, she felt exactly the same way herself.

When she opened the front door and saw Imelda Dooley standing there, she thought for a few seconds that she was hallucinating. She stared at the girl for long moments, still unsure if she was actually seeing her. She could see the dark of the night behind her, could hear the distant hum of the traffic on the Mile End Road and smell Mel's distinct aroma, cheap cigarettes and alcohol.

Imelda looked at her intently, her body tensed and ready for flight at the first sign of any aggravation. 'Can I come in?'

Louise Parks felt her heart lurch inside her breast at this unexpected visitor. Opening the door wide she said quietly, 'Of course.'

As Imelda walked into her home, Louise was suddenly unsure at how she should react. She didn't know how she was supposed to treat this girl. She was desperate to ask about the child inside her but was frightened to allude to it. She felt like a hostage, someone who was devoid of power. Someone who had no real control over her life any more.

Imelda made her way into the kitchen, it was a homely room, but she didn't remember it like this. She remembered the house as always being in uproar, always untidy. Now it looked almost clinical in its cleanliness. She assumed that this was due to the loss of her husband and her son.

Louise spoke then, and her voice was soft. 'It's cold out by the looks of it.'

Imelda nodded. 'It's chilly. Do you mind that I came here?'

Louise smiled then, a real smile that made her look years younger than she was.

' 'Course not, I am thrilled that you found it in your heart to come and visit me. I don't know what to say to you. How to start . . .'

Imelda grabbed at the distraught woman's hands, and she held on to them tightly. 'I felt the need to see you, I felt an urge to come here.'

Louise Parks was astounded at her words and it showed when she whispered sadly, 'Can I make you something to drink? Tea maybe, or cocoa? I craved cocoa when I was carrying Jason.'

Louise stopped herself then, was frightened that she had mentioned his name out loud to this poor girl with the swollen belly and the haunted eyes.

Imelda shook her head slowly. 'I came to see you because I need your help.'

Louise seemed to come to life at her words. Pulling out a chair she said gently, 'Sit down, love. If I can help you I will, darling. I swear that I will do anything within my power to help you out.'

Imelda sat down heavily, playing on the lump she carried, acting as if she was in pain. 'I know that if Jason was alive, and knew what he had done to me, despite everything that had happened between us, he would try and make amends somehow. For the baby's sake.'

Louise nodded in agreement, thrilled at the course the conversation was taking. 'Of course he would, darling, he would be over the moon at me being given the opportunity to help you, to make things right with you . . .'

Imelda nodded almost imperceptibly, her face the picture of tragic innocence. 'That's what I thought. What I hoped you would say.'

'How long have you got to go, until the birth I mean . . .'

'About four weeks, not long now.' Imelda rubbed her belly, caressed it as if in wonderment at the miracle of life.

'Oh, darling, I wish I could do something for you, I don't know what I am supposed to do. I wanted to send you some money, but I was frightened, that's why I gave you me number and that. I was frightened that if I went to your house or approached you in the street you would shout at me to leave you alone. I don't know what I am supposed to do, see, in these circumstances, I don't know how I am supposed to act.' She was crying now, a quiet, subdued crying that was all the more powerful because of its simplicity.

'I will be honest with you, Mrs Parks, I could do with the money, I need to get stuff for the baby and that. I ain't even got a cot, or anything . . . I was hoping that you would see how hard this all is for me, that you would understand how difficult my life is because of this baby. My mum hates it, but she knows that I couldn't give it up . . .'

Louise Parks felt as if all her birthdays and Christmases had arrived at once. Her dream was coming true, her boy's child, her only link with him, was suddenly within her grasp and she was willing to do whatever it took to make sure that she had a part in its life. God was good; he had answered her prayers, and he had brought this child to her door.

'How much do you need, sweetheart, a grand? I can get that for you first thing in the morning.'

Imelda stood up then, and hugging the grieving woman to her tightly, she felt the enormity of the power that she had over her, and would always have over her, because of this child that she was carrying inside her.

She hoped it was a boy, she might even be persuaded to name it Jason, for a price.

Let her mother fucking sweat this one out, if push came to shove she now had another place to go, and she might just do that to teach that old bag a lesson in manners. Louise Parks's sobbing did not touch her in any way. She just saw it as another weakness that she could exploit to her advantage.

But she was sensible enough to keep hold of the woman until her sobs finally subsided. Then she made them both a pot of tea, her face a picture of worry and fear.

As Imelda looked around the house, she knew that this woman was worth more than a few quid. And who else did she have to spend it on, other than her only grandchild of course?

Brendan was in awe of Jimmy Bailey. Whereas they had been used to smashing through someone's front door or, if they were lucky, through their conservatory, he was amazed and impressed at how Jimmy Bailey went about his business.

He knocked quietly on the front door in question and, when it was answered, he asked politely for the man of the house. If he was in, Jimmy asked to speak to him outside, on the pretext of talking business and, once they were out of the family's earshot, he would smile in a friendly manner and then explain in graphic detail what he would do to their wives, sons, daughters, mothers, grannies, fiancées, would threaten whoever he felt was their Achilles heel. He would then proceed to tell them in a low sing-song voice how much he would enjoy removing their eyes, or their fingertips. He would smile happily as he told them about the last man who had forgotten to pay his debts, and how he had waited around for him to come home so he could see his wife, a keen amateur gardener, lose her fingers, one by one, with her own personal pair of secateurs.

After Jimmy chatted to the person in question, he would go inside and talk to their wives and their children, asking their names, what schools they attended, and the kids and the wives, like most people he encountered, would be entranced by his good looks and his sunny smile. They would answer his questions without a second's thought. Jimmy knew that nine times out of ten, the men involved would take the veiled threat onboard. The money would generally be paid within twenty-four hours of the visit.

Gerald Junior didn't like the threats to children and, even though Jimmy assured him that that was all they were, empty threats, he was still not happy about it.

Jimmy said that if they had any problems with the payment, the only person who would be losing a finger or a toe would be the man who owed the money. But Gerald Junior still didn't like the inference, felt that the threats were a bit over the top. But he had to admit, they got results. They had not had to raise a hand to anyone, except of course the coasters: the people who owed a few hundred bar and were loath to pay it. These were obviously seen as fair game. It was the really big debts that were accompanied by the threats towards family and close relatives, and they were the debts that needed seeing to sooner rather than later. Still, they were coining it in, and they were hardly breaking a sweat most days.

Gerald's wife was not a happy bunny though, she felt that since his father's death he had been relegated to no more than a gofer: a go-for this or a go-for that. Gerald resented her inference that he was without any kind of clout any more. And, as he had pointed out on more than one occasion, his mother was the fucking linchpin these days, and Jimmy Bailey answered to her. For some reason this sent his wife off on to an ever louder rant against him and his family. If his mother was the boss, why couldn't she see to it that his job was guaranteed for life?

Poor Brendan was in a similar position, his girlfriend was harassing him for a wedding at some point in the near future, and he was not a man to be rushed. Brendan was not the marrying kind really, his mother and brother knew that and Brendan knew that. The shame was that Brendan's girlfriend of seven years, Tania, couldn't seem to take that fact onboard. She was at the age for marriage and children and Brendan was quite happy to give her a child, it was the marrying part he was not so happy about.

Gerald wondered at how life could change so quickly and so frequently. Less than a year ago he had his father, his family, and a sense of direction, now he had his mother as his boss and Jimmy Bailey calling the shots.

Still, he had no interest in running anything, he knew that he was not cut out for that side of things and, unlike his wife, he had accepted that fact a long time ago.

He tried not to think about his sister and her condition and her lies as well as Brendan did, but they knew they could never say anything to anyone. They had not told their father the truth of it, so they were not about to let that out to anyone else, were they? It was a dangerous thing, knowledge, it made you think about things you would rather forget about. It also made you question things you were better off leaving well alone.

Gerald Junior gulped at his pint of Guinness, and smiling at his brother he asked casually, 'Are you all right there, Brendan, is life treating you well?'

It was a saying of their father's and he said it occasionally to lift his brother's spirits and to keep their father in the forefront of their minds.

Brendan shrugged, and finishing his pint of bitter he said sadly, 'I've had worse days, and I've had better ones.'

It was their father's stock answer and Gerald didn't know how to react to it.

'Where have you been?'

Mary was determined to keep her voice low and calm.

'I was out.'

Mary smiled grimly. 'Have you seen the baby's room? It's beautiful, the decorator finished it today.'

Imelda forced a look of bright interest on to her face and walking up the stairs she went into what was now the *baby*'s bedroom. It was lovely, even she had to admit that. The walls were pale-lemon and the curtains and matching cot cover depicted rainbows. The colours were subtle and the overall effect was one of peace, of calm. The carpet was cream, and the furniture was solid oak.

'It's lovely, Mum.'

And she meant it, it *was* lovely.

Mary smiled then, a real smile that changed her face completely. 'Do you like it, really?'

She needed her daughter's approbation and Imelda felt a small spark of sorrow because of it. She had no care for any of this crap, all she cared about was herself. But she knew how to play the game.

'Honestly, Mum, it's beautiful. If I was going to have this baby for keeps, then I would have this room for it.'

The answer pleased her mother as she knew it would. 'Oh, Mel, can we not try and be friends, at least until the child's here.'

Imelda smiled once more. 'By the way, Mum, what happens to me after the baby comes? I mean, I need to know what's going to happen to me.'

Imelda saw her mother's face settle into its familiar non-committal look and her practised look of feigned interest.

'Well, you aren't going to want to stay here, are you? I mean, with the child here and all. If you wanted the child then it would be different . . . But I think you should move on. Like we said, the sooner you move on, the better, for everyone concerned.'

Imelda nodded. Mary saw the beauty that was her daughter, the face that was so beautiful it could reduce you to tears when you finally understood that the girl you had loved and adored was devoid of anything even remotely resembling a real feeling, an emotion. She had accepted that this girl of hers played at being a fully paid-up member of the human race, but she knew now that she felt nothing for anybody except herself, she only concentrated on what she wanted, on what she desired.

She regretted her outburst, was sorry for striking her daughter while she was pregnant, and knew that she had been foolish to let herself be dragged down to her daughter's level. Dragged into her daughter's drama as per usual. She prayed daily for the child's arrival so that she could finally take it away from her and, by doing so, get her daughter out of her life once and for all. She would never forgive the girl for the lies and the deceit that had culminated in her husband's death. Mary was determined not to let her near the baby, and she knew that would only be achieved with money, and with determination. Both of which she had in abundance.

'So basically, Mum, if I understood you correctly, once the baby's born, I'm homeless. I'm out of the house. Is that what you're trying to tell me, Mum?'

Mary shook her head vigorously, laughing as if she had just heard the funniest joke in the world. 'Don't be so silly. I'll help you get on your feet and get a job. I'll help you to get a flat and some furniture. Christ Himself knows, you're my daughter. I would never see you without.'

Imelda grinned, and it was a grin that seemed to her mother to be drenched in hate, and that made her go cold inside. She had seen that grin before, had finally learnt what it meant to those who were unlucky enough to be on the receiving end of it.

'And just what kind of job would you envisage for me then, Mum? An air hostess, maybe a cleaner, or I know, how about a nanny? I could look after some other fucker's screaming brat, only this time, I would be getting paid for it. I mean, what type of job do you have in mind for me?'

She smiled that wide, toothy smile once more.

'Well, answer me then, I'm genuinely interested in what you've got to say, Mum. I want to picture what I'll be doing while you're looking after my baby. Only I found out that I can get a council flat if I keep this baby, and that I can claim money for it as well. That is without me having to work or anything, you know. Now, I don't know about you, Mum, but I think that sounds like the better end of the deal for me. That appeals to my so-called inherent laziness: apparently the government will even pay my rent for me. Turns out this baby could be quite lucrative.'

Mary had known deep inside that this day would come, knew that this girl would always take the easy option, use whatever, and whoever, she could, for her own advancement, even her own child.

'I'll give you anything you want, but you have to give me the baby, Mel. You don't even want it, why would you hold it over my head like this, Mel? I'll pay you, do anything you want. But you must promise that you won't renege on our deal, that you won't tuck me after all I've done for you?'

'If you can come up with a price that I find acceptable then you have a deal: if not, then me and the baby will be forced to throw ourselves on to the mercy of the council.'

Mary nodded in agreement, terror for the child inside her daughter taking over. 'You name it and, if it's within my power, you will have it. You tell me what you want, that will make it much easier all round.'

Imelda smiled again but she didn't answer the question. 'Nice room, Mum, I just hope that the poor little fucker will finally get to sleep in it.'

Mary was nearly in tears now. 'Oh, Mel, what is wrong with you, why are you so vicious, you don't want that poor baby, you know you don't.'

Imelda shrugged happily. 'No, Mum, you're right, I don't want it. But the whole point is that you do.'

Jimmy Bailey arrived at Mary's house just after eight-fifteen. She was ready for him, as always, and, as always, he was seriously impressed with her almost encyclopaedic knowledge of people's lives. She knew who they were related to, even distantly, she knew where they lived, what they did in their spare time, and she knew who they owed money to and who owed money to them. She could tell Jimmy their parentage back at least three generations and, more to the point, how long it would take them to gather together the money he was after. She could even tell him the people the poor bastard might ask for a loan. She was fucking amazing. No wonder her husband had been such a good collector. With her on the case it must have been easy. Mary Dooley knew everything about everyone. He had asked her how she researched the debts, and she had told him that he wouldn't understand, so he had left it at that. She was a real mine of information though.

He noticed that today she was quieter than usual, and he found himself asking her where the boys were, just to get the conversation going.

'I don't know, they are both grown men.'

Mary was obviously not about to be drawn on anything of a personal nature so he gave up, he had always believed that people had the right to their privacy, and also the right to their own thoughts. Providing they didn't owe *him* money of course. Then, their lives were basically an open book as far as he was concerned, until he got what he wanted, and then he lost all interest in them. He saw the way the big banks repossessed houses for money borrowed against them, saw how the courts took the side of the mortgage companies, the lenders. He knew, like the rest of the country, that people who took out loans were expected to pay them back. It was the law of the fucking land for Christ's sake, only, when people borrowed from him, or people like him, they didn't have the choice of a court case, or bankruptcy, they knew that they had to weigh him out eventually, or they would not have loaned the money to them in the first place. If you borrowed money, you now owed, if you owed, you were vulnerable, if you were vulnerable, then you were going to get hurt. It was almost biblical in its simplicity.

Jimmy also knew that Mary's boys were not possessed of that kind of understanding. But he kept his own counsel, there was plenty of time for personal conversations and opinions in the future.

As he was getting ready to leave, the door opened, and Jimmy Bailey saw a girl who was so lovely she actually took his breath away.

The effect she had on him did not go unnoticed by Mary Dooley, and that was when he saw the similarity between them. Mary must have looked very similar to her daughter when she had been the same age. It was amazing and, as always, his envy of families came to the fore. He was not envious in a nasty way, he was envious in an interested way. He felt his own loss more acutely when he was around people who had real relatives, real family. When people cared about each other, and cared about what happened to them.

He also knew that this was the daughter who had caused more fights than Joe Bugner, and who was pregnant by poor Jason Parks. Jimmy was of the opinion that Jason was not capable of the act of rape, but he also conceded that no one knew the truth of any situation except the people who were there at the time. But he had also heard that this girl had a rep so large it made the Bayeux Tapestry look like a hanky.

But her face, she was like a painting. Her skin was flawless, her eyes were huge and were a deep-blue, so dark they were almost indigo. She was extraordinary-looking and, as she gazed at him with that quiet, steady stare she had, he actually felt himself begin to blush.

She smiled gently. 'Hi. I'm Imelda, Mel.'

Jimmy shook her hand, marvelling at how small and delicate it was.

'Hello. I'm Jimmy, Jimmy Bailey.'

He said his name, as always, with a certain pride because it was now so well known in certain circles.

'I know who you are.'

Then, turning from him as if he had somehow ceased to exist and smiling at her mother she said quietly, 'I need some money.'

Mary looked at Jimmy briefly, then she said quickly, 'Give me a few minutes to see Jimmy out and then we'll talk, OK?'

Imelda grinned then, and Jimmy felt his heart constrict at just how lovely she was.

'I need some money now, Mum, the baby is on its way.'

'Hey, I can drive you to the hospital if you want.' Jimmy felt a real panic at the thought of a baby arriving in the next few minutes.

'I have hours yet, and I would much rather go by myself if you don't mind.'

Jimmy was amazed at her calmness, at how cool she was. He knew that most women were blown away by the imminent arrival of their child, of a real live person. He was not sure how he was supposed to react to her.

He saw how heavy she was, at least her tummy was anyway. Other than that she looked like a little bird. She was wearing a purple smock top, and from the side the child was very apparent; from the front, she looked just like any other young girl. Though he had a feeling that most young girls did not have her eyes; they were almost like an ancient's, as if she knew everything in the world there was to know. He assumed that her predicament might have something to do with that.

Jimmy knew Imelda was classed as second-best now. Like all the girls who had their babies without the benefit of marriage, she would be automatically classed as a second-class citizen. It was unfair really, because if they had an abortion their lives were automatically back on track, and no one would ever know that they had ever been pregnant. They automatically got a second chance at life, at being respectable. He had to admit though, he admired the girls who kept their kids, unless they dumped them, of course, like his fucking mother had him.

'I'll drive you, relax. Get your coat, Mary.'

He felt the tension between the two women, felt the fear that was emanating from Mary, and saw how pale her face had become as she waited for her daughter's permission to accompany her.

'Can I come? Please, Mel.'

She was almost begging and suddenly Jimmy felt as if he was watching something really private and personal, something not quite nice, something reprehensible. He guessed that Mary was being held to ransom somehow.

Imelda shrugged. 'I don't give a fuck, do what you want.'

Jimmy could hear the indifference in the girl's voice, he had only ever heard that kind of vicious indifference in one person's voice once before. His mother's.

His mother had never had any kind of interest in anything or anyone except herself, and *her* life, to his knowledge.

Jimmy felt the same dead vibe from this beautiful girl

that he had felt from his own mother, the few times he had been in her company that is.

Mary was putting on her coat and, smiling in a friendly way, he walked them both through the house and outside to his waiting car. He drove a gold Daimler Sovereign and he was a little bit disappointed that no one acknowledged the beauty of it. But given the daughter's labour, he supposed he could overlook their being underwhelmed just this once.

As Jimmy drove to the hospital he could not help noticing that the two women, who were so alike physically, did not exchange one word during the whole journey.

Now, he was not an expert on female behaviour, and he did not pretend to understand them, but even he thought that the birth of a child should have been greeted with at least a small spurt of excitement.

As he drove to the hospital, the awful silence between them seemed to grow, until when they finally reached the hospital he felt physically relieved to see the back of the pair of them.

Three hours later, after a quick and uneventful labour, Jordanna Dooley entered the world. She was not held by her mother until twenty-four hours after the birth. Imelda had waved the child away, and insisted on being taken to the day room so she could have a cigarette in peace. The day room had a phone, and the phone had guaranteed Imelda the outside world, and the outside world had provided her with the drugs she needed to cope with her new-born baby.

So her grandmother had held Jordanna instead, gently talking to her and falling in love with her. Mary had hugged the child to her, and she had known then that without her in the picture, this poor little girl would be destroyed without a second's thought by her own mother.

Jordanna didn't cry like the other babies, it was as if she already knew, even at such a tender age, that her mother was not really interested in her.

Book Two

But all children matures,
Maybe even yours.

　　　　– Ogden Nash, 1902–1971
　　　　　'Soliloquy in Circles'

A truth that's told with bad intent
Beats all the lies you can invent.

　　　　– William Blake, 1757–1827
　　　　　'Auguries of Innocence'

Who can find a virtuous woman? for her
price is far above rubies.

　　　　　– Proverbs 31:10

Chapter Nine

1981

Mary watched as Jordanna ate her dinner and, as always once the child was within her orbit, she finally relaxed. She saw the bruises on the girl's little arms, knew that she had been picked up bodily by her mother at least once, then thrown violently onto a bed, a sofa or a chair, but that was par for the course where Imelda was concerned. She took all her anger and her frustration out on her little daughter. She did it knowing that there was not a lot anyone could do to stop her. She had the trump card; she was the mother and that meant everything to the people involved in her daughter's shitty life.

Mel was a fucking nightmare, she didn't want the poor child, but she was determined that no one else was going to get her either. She used her as leverage, mostly for money. Imelda *always* needed money; no matter how much money she had, she always needed more.

She was a junkie and that was a junkie's life. The pursuit of money, easy money, so they could begin the pursuit of their drug of choice. Mel also used the child for the guaranteed Social Security money she collected every Monday from her local post office. She also used her daughter for the Family Allowance money she was entitled to, and which she cashed on a regular basis to buy drugs.

Imelda believed the money was hers, for her own personal use whenever she needed an extra hand-out of some kind. Her social worker was so deluded by Imelda's hard-luck stories that she even blagged money off of charities for her, and she also ensured her daughter's utility bills were paid. The social worker had never in her life experienced anyone like Imelda, and it showed. She was so impressed with Mel's hard-luck stories, and the insight into a junkie's lifestyle, that she would forgive her anything.

Any money Imelda accrued from the people she scammed went straight to her dealer. She even entered methadone programmes to keep the social workers happy, make them believe that she was really attempting to sort herself out. She would then sell the methadone around the local pubs, and buy the real deal with the proceeds. It was a cycle of despair, and her little child, her little money cow, was stuck in the middle of it.

Poor Louise Parks was at her wit's end. Mary herself felt such sorrow for her granddaughter's lifestyle, but even more so, at times, for Louise Parks. Imelda would promise Jordanna could stay with her nana Parks, and then Louise would give Imelda the money she required. The little girl would then be delivered, would settle into a routine, would be happy and secure once more. Then Imelda would arrive at some point at Louise's house, with no warning whatsoever, and she would take the screaming child away with her. Mary knew how that felt, because

Imelda did the same thing to her on a regular basis. Sometimes she would have the girl for weeks, months even, and then, in a space of ten minutes, she would be removed from all the safety and regularity that should constitute a small child's life. She would be dragged back to a filthy bed in a filthy flat, and she would be surrounded by people who were not exactly pillars of the community.

Mary would watch from afar as the little girl she loved would gradually disappear further and further into herself, until she stopped talking, or communicating in any way.

Mary would ring the social services and tell them what was happening, and they would tell her the same thing. Jordanna was OK, she was being fed, and she was with her mother. A mother who was trying so hard to get herself together, and who was trying to make a life for herself. The inference being that *she*, Mary, was actually the cause of her daughter's phenomenal hatred, and her daughter's addiction. They would then go on to say that maybe, if she was not so critical of Imelda, she might experience a complete revelation. They told her that a filthy home did not mean that the child was not *loved*. That the absence of clean clothes and regular meals did not constitute a *bad* mother. They asked Mary if maybe she was expecting too much of her daughter, and that it might be her demands that were the cause of her daughter's problems.

It was a fucking *scandal* the way the social services allowed that child to be treated, how they allowed her to live. The little girl was in a constant state of terror, was unable ever to relax, was without any kind of love from her mother. They might tell her that a dirty house was not enough reason to remove a child, that the people who visited the flat were invited there and were her daughter's *guests*. She was told that she should try and build some bridges with her daughter instead of trying to take her child from her. That Mary's repeated accusations of neglect, and criticism of her daughter's parenting skills and her chosen lifestyle, were not doing anything for her daughter's self-esteem. What fucking self-esteem? Mary wanted to ask them. Her daughter would fuck a tramp if it got her enough money for a fix. Her daughter manipulated them all, and they allowed her to, they allowed her to indulge herself on a regular basis. The social workers were the reason her daughter was such a fucking skaghead, they enabled her to do what she wanted and gave her the means to bully her child and her family. Social workers saw Imelda's addictions as an illness. Mary tried to explain that her daughter was a user, a user of people, a user of anyone who she felt might further her career, not just a user of drugs. But it was as if she was talking to a fucking brick wall.

She felt as if *she* was the only person who could see just how withdrawn Jordanna was. Could see how unhappy the little girl was, and how lonely and how distressed she was at her mother's neglect of her, and the viciousness that she had to endure on an almost daily basis from her mother.

What was it with these fucking people? Did they not have qualifications, degrees, did they not see how fucked-up that poor little child was, or how she blossomed when she was away from that fucking leech of a mother and her so-called friends?

Or did they just choose to ignore her dramatic weight loss when she returned to her so-called home, and the sudden fits of shaking when she was forced back there by her mother? When she wasn't even allowed to say a goodbye to her granny, who she had been living with for weeks, sometimes even months.

Jordanna would be dragged out of her bed amid a volley of foul-mouthed accusations. Or taken from the dinner table, dragged and pulled like a doll, her little face terrified and her screams echoing off the walls. Mary herself, the mother of the drugged-up lunatic at her door, would then be forbidden to ever see the child again, she would have to stand there silently as her daughter accused her of everything from sexual assaults on the child to turning her daughter against her.

She saw the drug-crazed eyes and yet she could do nothing about it. If she retaliated, Imelda would just make her wait even longer before she got the call that told her she could visit once more, that told her to bring money. Yet Mary lived for those garbled phone calls, would go to her daughter immediately with whatever amount she demanded from her. And then she would ask her daughter, with all the humility she could muster, if she could maybe take the child home for a day or two, give Imelda a chance to rest, give her a *break* from the relentlessness that was motherhood. And Imelda would play the game, as Mary had known she would. She'd make her wait though, make her work for her granddaughter's little bit of freedom. She enjoyed her power over them all. She'd insist on certain bedtimes, force Mary to agree to impossible timetables that she would not be capable of keeping, but Mary would smile and promise to keep to them, no matter what. Imelda would then tell her that the child was very naughty and very *sneaky* and needed a very firm hand, and she would make Mary promise to smack her if she wet her bed, or didn't finish her dinner.

Mary would agree to everything, as Imelda knew that she would, and she would see her daughter's look of triumph as she once more manipulated everyone around her. She would be forced to agree with Imelda that Jordanna was a drama queen, that she needed taking in hand, and that the child was deceitful and sneaky. It broke Mary's heart to say those ugly things about a child who was so loving and so desperate for affection that she would still run into her mother's arms if she was asked to. That was what the social workers saw, they saw a little child who ran into her mother's open arms and who would hope against hope that this time it would be for ever. Only to be locked back in her dirty bedroom again once the social worker had gone. Who spent hours looking out of her bedroom window, a window devoid even of a curtain. Who slept on a mattress that stank of urine and despair and that had no sheets and no real blankets, that was used by her mother's friends, people who did not feel that it was worth taking care of.

Jordanna's toys were old and dilapidated because the newer ones were sold off, and was denied even the use of the toilet and, when she finally soiled herself, was beaten for being dirty and wilful.

It was a vicious circle, and Mary didn't know how to make it stop. She prayed to God daily that Imelda would accidentally overdose, and yet even as she prayed for it, she felt the guilt of a mother who was wishing her own child dead.

Jordanna was two years old, and she was already wise to the world of junkies and addicts, she already knew how to judge people's moods and how to avoid confrontations.

As Mary smiled at the child she loved so much she saw the grime that was ingrained in her feet and ankles, the matted hair and the nose encrusted with bright-green snot. She knew that the child had been left alone in a cold bedroom for days on end, and that was why her little nose was constantly running.

She would bath her, play with her, dress her in clean pyjamas, and read her a story. She would watch over her as she fell into a fitful sleep where she would jump nervously and moan before waking up in fear, wondering where she was, and Mary would see the relief in her eyes as she realised she was safe. Was with her nana.

Then, after a few days, Mary would see her begin to settle down a bit, start acting like a real child. Unless the doorbell rang, or the phone, or she heard a loud noise. Then she would sit in shock, waiting for her mother to come and start the whole fucking rigmarole all over again.

It was wrong, and the people who gave her daughter this much power over her child should be ashamed of themselves.

'Come here, sweetheart. Let Nanny give you a bath, yeah?'

Jordanna nodded. Her eyes, so like her mother's, were shining with anticipation at the evening ahead. She was still full of trepidation, sure that this little respite from her life would be curtailed at any moment.

Mary hugged the child to her tightly, and wished her daughter dead once more.

Jimmy Bailey was fuming. He had tried to get Michael Hannon to become a silent partner in his new business venture. He had not allowed for the fact that Michael Hannon might turn him down flat, which is exactly what he had done.

Jimmy had explained it to him quietly and succinctly, had emphasised the bonuses that would be guaranteed. He had shown him the figures that had explained how easily they would make their money back. Then he had sat back in his chair, and waited for Michael to agree to his proposal. It would be like printing money, it was such a lucrative proposition.

But Michael Hannon had smiled nicely, then he had said 'thanks', but 'no thanks'. He saw the money that was there to be made, but he had no interest in brothels, or anything that concerned prostitution, period. He had thanked him for his offer, and then they had both had another drink, and parted company no worse off than they had been before the meeting.

But Jimmy had felt Michael's distaste at what he had proposed, saw the slight curling of his lip as he had scanned the projected figures. He knew that even though they were good friends, Michael would always be that little bit wary of his business dealings because, like a lot of the men in their world, prostitution might be the oldest profession in the world, but that did not make it respectable. And this from a man who provided most of the drugs that were sold in the south-east of England.

Jimmy sighed. Well, if Michael wasn't up for it, he would go into this one on his jacksie. He had only wanted Hannon's name on the door anyway, it would guarantee him a free ride from the Filth, and the best behaviour from his clientele, though he was known as a hard man in his own right anyway. So, he was no worse off, it was just that sneer he had detected, that unconscious little look of distaste. It annoyed him that Michael saw him as beneath him and his fucking scams.

As Jimmy sipped his drink, his eyes scanned the pub. As he looked out of the large picture window into the garden, he saw Imelda Dooley and, as always, her face fascinated him. She was a junkie, that much he had already heard.

She was also, apparently, a soft touch for anyone in need of a night's bed and board. She was basically a fucking dog.

Even knowing that about her, he still felt an attraction towards her, and that was unusual for him, he generally liked his women clean and tidy, and without any reputation whatsoever. He liked to know that when he finally fucked them, he was going where no one had ever gone before. At least, not too many anyway. He was not a man who was content to fuck a bird who had been with more men than Catherine the Great, and who was not bothered about it.

Jimmy liked to think of his body as a temple and, even though women like Imelda Dooley were below his radar normally, there was something about her that attracted him. As he watched her, he saw her throw back her head to laugh, and her even white teeth and her high cheekbones were so beautiful that, as always on looking at her, he felt a sudden tightening in his guts.

She was still laughing as she turned to face him and, seeing him watching her, she smiled at him and waved. It was such a girlie gesture, and it made her look so young and carefree that Jimmy found himself waving back at her.

He had seen her intermittently over the years, and the state she was in was generally enough to make him back off as quickly as possible. In fact, he would practically run away rather than even acknowledge her.

But he saw her now, in the winter sunshine, with her twinkling eyes and her tight little body, and he found himself miming a drinking motion with his hand. She nodded her agreement and he watched her come into the warmth of the pub. As she approached him, he saw the effect she had on most of the men around him.

She had an almost feral sexuality about her that was so blatant, and so powerful, it was almost physical in its intensity. She seemed to have no knowledge of the effect she created, but Jimmy had a feeling that she was more aware of her sexuality than she let on. She smiled at him as she sat down opposite; her long legs were encased in sheer black tights and she had on a short denim skirt. Her boots were high-heeled and they were so tight she wore them like a second skin. She had on a punk rock T-shirt, and a tiny cropped jacket. She had to be freezing, but Jimmy didn't mention that of course. Instead, he went to the bar and got them both a drink. He made sure that Imelda's was a large one, he had a feeling that she would expect that from him.

She took the Jack Daniels and Coke and swallowed half of it before she even spoke to him. 'How did you know I drank Jack Daniels?'

Jimmy smiled then, and said with mock guilt, 'I've seen you out plenty of times, and noticed you were on the Jacky D. It ain't exactly rocket science, is it?'

She didn't smile back, she thought he was alluding to her taking heroin. Most people who used heroin drank strong alcohol while they were waiting to score; it took the edge off. But he wasn't alluding to anything, and she realised that when he said sincerely, 'I have to be honest, it's not a drink I have ever seen many women favour. So that was why I remembered it so well.'

She finished the rest of her drink in one swallow, then, holding the empty glass out, she raised her eyebrows in a questioning motion.

Jimmy took the glass and went to the bar. He got her a triple this time and, taking it back to her, he watched as she supped half of the drink in two large swallows. She was a real drinker, and obviously she drank large quantities on a regular basis.

'Oi, relax. If you keep sinking them like that you'll be on your back in no time.'

Imelda laughed. Then, swallowing the remainder of the drink down, she said huskily, 'Well, I'm game if you are.'

He was startled at the effect her words had on him. He felt a stirring in his groin and, as if she had read his mind, she leant forward and whispered, 'I can feel it too, shall we go?'

He looked into her eyes, and they were so open, and so honest, that he was once more mesmerised by her. If any other woman but her had propositioned him as she had, he would have fucked her off with a very loud and expletive-strewn tirade. But he found himself following her out into the cold night air and, when they were seated comfortably in his very expensive and very clean Mercedes Sport, she lay back against the black leather seat and closing her eyes she asked him politely, 'Can we go to yours? My flat is like a bomb site.'

As Jimmy pulled out of the Prospect of Whitby public house he caught a trace of her body odour – she had a deep muskiness that was apparent even over the cheap perfume she had obviously drenched herself in.

When they got to his flat in Kensington, they had still not spoken a word to each other and, when he opened the front door, and motioned for her to precede him, she smiled happily at his good manners. Once inside, he saw her looking around in amazement at his home and he felt once more the pride that this flat gave him.

It was absolutely stunning, and he had got it on the cheap, with all the furniture already *in situ*; a professional gambler had made the mistake of coming to him for a rather hefty loan. Jimmy had given him the loan without a thought, and he had also given him a second and, eventually, a third loan. The man concerned had been given every chance in life: private school, the works, yet he was still a fucking loser, a gambler who lived off his family. Jimmy had then called all the debts in simultaneously.

The man in question had brought him to this flat only once, very early in their acquaintance, it had been the prat's way of showing him that he was a man of means, had a few quid in the pipeline. A way of proving he was more than capable of paying any debts that he might incur. But Jimmy had known it was a scam from the off. He was the usual Hooray Henry, all weak chin and no real bank balance. Jimmy had wanted this place from the off, and he had been determined to get it. Thanks to the bloke's addiction to the horses and the roulette wheel, he had not had to wait long before he had got it. Fair and square.

Now he loved the look on people's faces when they entered it, it was pure class, and you could not buy class. The ponce who had lost the place to him had that much going for him anyway, even if he didn't have a lot else these days. Why people gambled, Jimmy did not know, it was a real mug's game.

'Like it?'

Imelda nodded, her face suddenly serious and reflective. She felt out of her depth and they both knew it. 'It's lovely, Jimmy. Can I use your john?'

He laughed at her earnest little expression, she was really sweet when she wanted to be. It was a side of her he had never experienced before. He decided that he liked it.

He walked her to the bathroom and opened the door for her, as always the gentleman. He went into the lounge and put on Elton John's *Goodbye Yellow Brick Road* album and then, as he walked out into the hallway again on a quest for ice cubes, he saw that the bathroom door was ajar. Against his better judgement, he could not resist popping his head inside and, as he went to say something funny, he saw her as she was pushing a needle into her groin. She looked what she was then. It was amazing how she had gone from a natural beauty to a filthy skaghead in seconds. Suddenly he noticed the greasy shine on her hair, and the grime under her fingernails. He saw the yellow tinge to her skin that all junkies acquired eventually, and he saw the scuffed and run-down heels of her boots as she lay sprawled across his toilet. He felt physically sick that he had even contemplated fucking her. She was rank, fucking scum.

She was nodding now, was away with the fucking fairies, and he knew that she would be like that for at least the next ten minutes. So he went back into the lounge and, pouring himself a large brandy, he wondered at how he had nearly succumbed to shagging someone who had such a low opinion of themselves they were willing to dice with death on a daily basis just for a high. He felt that she had tainted this flat, that she had brought the putrid mess that passed as a life right into his home. He was absolutely gutted.

Fifteen minutes later she came creeping into the room, and he could see the wasted look on her face and smell the stench of fucking loser all over her.

She smiled timidly. 'I needed that, it was so freaky coming here and seeing you, but I wanted to ask you a favour, see. I hope you won't do your nut like, because I know you and me mum are quite tight.'

Jimmy was astonished that Imelda had no shame at what she had done. That Imelda did not feel that she had even *done* anything wrong, yet she had jacked up in his home without even asking him if he minded. Without even *caring* about how her actions might affect him.

'What, Mel, what do you want to ask me?' He was barely keeping a lid on his anger now.

'Well, I was going to give you a freebie anyway like, but basically I want a job in one of your houses. I am *great* at fucking, always was, even as a kid.'

She was suddenly aware of the atmosphere in the room. And, grinning apologetically, she said seriously, 'And I promise you faithfully that I won't ever bring any gear with me again, I can see you don't like it.'

He knew that *she* knew that *she* had fucked it all up for herself. She knew that he was now desperate to get her out of his flat, and out of his life as quickly as possible and with the least amount of ag possible. She was like a fucking leper to him now, standing there in his home, and she was obviously too embarrassed now even to sit down without a gold-engraved invitation, because she knew she had done a fucking wrong one.

'Get yourself sorted, I'll weigh you out for a cab home, all right?'

She nodded slowly then, as she watched him finish his brandy, and search through his pockets for a five-pound note, she felt the anger that was always bubbling away under the surface. He was blanking her, and she knew it. She also knew it was because she had jacked up in his fucking toilet. In his so-called personal space. Well, fuck him.

'So, what about the job, Jimmy? Am I in or what?'

He shook his head. 'No way, I don't have fucking junkies working for me.'

Imelda laughed then, at his total hypocrisy. 'Oh, I see,

so a prostitute who is clean drugwise is perfectly acceptable, but a prostitute who takes drugs is not acceptable. I
can't really grasp that logic, Jimmy, care to fill in the
fucking blanks for me?'

Jimmy threw the fiver at her and said loudly, 'Get out
of my sight, you cunt. Get a cab home, or go and score,
or whatever you fucking people do when you are lucky
enough to come across paper money. But whatever you
decide to do, just get yourself out of my home now.'

She picked up the money and, pushing it into her skirt
pocket, she held up the tin that contained her works and
used it to point at him menacingly. 'I might be a fucking
junkie, but I am a junkie through choice. You will always
be no more than a fucking pimp, a purveyor of women's
flesh. So, don't you come the high and mighty with me,
boy. On a scale of one to ten, you don't rate much higher
than me, and don't you ever fucking forget that.'

With that she wiped her arm across a nearby table and
laughed as all the ornaments smashed loudly on to the
floor. Then she walked from the room with as much
dignity as she could muster.

Jimmy waited until he heard her slam the front door
behind her. Then he looked at the broken pottery, the
broken ashtrays on his lovely wooden floor, he looked
around him and he saw her fucking diseased and scrawny
body everywhere. That he had actually fallen for her
charms, knowing what he knew about her and then, worst
of all, he had brought her back here, to his *home*. To where
he *lived*, and she had desecrated it with her fucking junk.
But, even more than that, he was disgusted with himself
because he had actually entertained the notion of sleeping
with her. What the fuck was *he* on?

He showered twice, and then he cleaned up the mess

she had made. But the place still felt wrong to him. He felt filthy, he felt violated. And the fact that she had only come home with him in the first place to try and get a job as a fucking brass was rankling him more than he would ever have admitted to anyone, least of all himself.

'Come on, Jordanna, give your nana a big hug.'

Mary felt the little arms as they circled her neck, and she kissed the child's upturned face over and over again, enjoying the clean smell of her, and enjoying the feel of her fragile body as she hugged her tightly against her. This girl was her life, and she knew that, no matter how often her daughter abused her, or how much she charged her for this little one's company, she would pay it gladly. She was like an angel, a little blond-haired angel.

As she settled Jordanna down on the sofa, she heard a gentle tapping on her front door. She opened it without a second's thought, and there was her daughter, drugged out of her head, and almost incoherent with rage.

'Oh no. Come on, Mel. Let her alone tonight, eh, she's just fallen asleep.'

As Mary spoke she saw the child sitting bolt upright on the sofa, her eyes wide open with fright, and her little hands clenched into fists of terror.

Jordanna started crying then, calling for her nana, hoping that just once, she might be able to keep her there somehow.

'Look, Mel, I've got a onner in the kitchen, take that. Go out and have a good time, you look like you could do with one.'

'Fuck off, Mother. You're a *cunt* and so is your fucking scum-bag of a partner, Jimmy.'

Hearing Jimmy's name along with hers was so

unexpected that Mary wondered if she had imagined it.

Imelda picked her daughter up roughly and wrapped her in a blanket.

'Please, Mel, don't take her, leave her here. I'll go and get the money for you, shall I?'

'Stick it up your arse, and you tell your mate Jimmy that no one fucking treats me like shit and gets away with it.'

'What are you talking about, Mel? What has Jimmy Bailey got to do with anything?'

She was trying to stop her daughter from leaving her house with the child.

Imelda pushed her mother roughly out of her way. 'I have a cab outside, and my baby is coming home with me. You want her, you fucking bitch, well, you can thank your mate Jimmy for cutting your little holiday short. I know that you've run me down to him, that's why he treated me like dirt. But that's you all over ain't it, eh? I bet you have fucking slagged me into the ground to him. Fucking putting me down all the time. Well, no more, and you ain't doing that to my daughter either.'

Imelda was already halfway up the garden path, and as Mary watched them drive away from her she felt the useless tears of frustration and rage that always accompanied a late night visit from her only daughter.

She picked up the teddy bear that Jordanna always slept with when she stayed at her nana's and, hugging it to her chest tightly, she sobbed as if her heart was going to break.

Lance Bradford was a bully. He had always been a bully, even as a small child he had developed the knack of bullying and at the same time he had also found out that he actually *enjoyed* the experience very much.

As he sat in Imelda's flat, he was now enjoying seeing her anger and her hatred as she shouted and railed at the world in general. He didn't know who had rattled her cage, but whoever it was had done a fucking brilliant job of it. She was almost beside herself with rage.

The kid was petrified, she was sitting on the cold floor and her face was white with fear. The pretty little thing was shrewd enough not to move a muscle, she sensed that her mother was just looking for an excuse to let rip. Lance knew that Mel was enjoying the poor little mare's terror almost as much as he was enjoying her anger. She was like a mad woman, and after a while he decided that he would wind her up a bit. Find out what had caused this latest psychotic break of hers, and then keep on about it until she snapped again.

As Imelda picked the kid up roughly by her arms and laid her none too gently on the sofa, he was amazed when she actually took the time to cover the child with a blanket. The place was filthy, as always, and the newly scrubbed Jordanna stood out like a sore thumb. He watched as the little girl closed her eyes and attempted to lose herself in the oblivion that was sleep. Imelda was still angry, but she was slowly calming herself down. As she poured herself a large vodka, she said seriously, 'Where's my fucking money?'

Lance had forgotten that he had used it to score for them, and he said gaily, 'I got us some gear with it. I got us a Henry, an eighth.' He then pulled a plastic bag from his jeans pocket.

Imelda stood there, staring at him as if she had never seen him before, and Lance knew that look of hers. She even frightened him when she was like this.

'Are you telling me that you *stole* my money and

fucking scored *drugs* with it? You actually *stole* my fucking cash, the money I had saved to buy food for *my* baby, and you bought fucking *drugs* with it?' She was seriously on her dignity now, full of self-righteous indignation, and spoiling for a proper fight.

'Are you taking the fucking piss out of me or what? Have I got cunt tattooed on my forehead or something, is that it?'

Lance started to laugh. He was a fairly big lad, and he knew that once he started to burn the brown she would not be able to resist it. He set about the business of preparing them both a nice little armful, confident that she would not be able to refuse it once it was in front of her.

Imelda watched him as he began his preparations, and as he opened the plastic bag to measure out the heroin, her booted leg caught him and the bag of smack at the same time. She watched his face as he saw the pale-brown granules go up into the air like a minute atomic bomb. When it finally began to fall towards the floor it was everywhere, all over his jacket, all over the filthy carpet, and all over the coffee table that was littered with everything from overflowing ashtrays to mouldy tea cups.

Lance was in shock at what she had done. She had just wasted a serious amount of gear, and she did not seem to give a flying fuck. The majority of it was ruined, was unsalvageable.

'You stupid fucking whore, what are you doing?'

Imelda was already too far off her face to care about anything except the next fight she was determined to have. Jimmy and his reaction to her had destroyed her, had shown her up for what she really was. She was out of her brains, but she was also acutely aware that her life was once more spiralling out of control, and she knew that she was not interested enough in her own existence to understand why it was happening to her once again. She believed it was this man's fault, believed he was the cause of her unhappiness, of her despair.

'Get out of my flat, Lance, and get out now.'

She was so still and so insistent that he knew she was serious, and as he looked around him at the waste of their gear, and as he looked at her, and saw the triumph in her eyes, he felt a rage overtake him. She treated everyone like dirt, treated everyone like shit. He was suddenly sick of her, of her arrogance and her disloyalty.

Jumping up from the sofa he smashed his fist into her face with all the strength he could muster. She crumpled beneath his strength, beneath his anger. Then she saw the hatred that he normally kept hidden inside. He punched her again, harder this time. Determined to make her understand the error of her ways.

'You fucking slag, you think you can fucking treat me like a cunt, do you? Well, I'm going to fucking teach you a bastarding lesson in etiquette.'

As he began to lay into her, his fists flying and his anger given free rein, Jordanna started screaming in fear. She was attuned to people's moods, it was the only way she could survive in this house, and she sensed that her mummy's friend was so angry that he might hurt them both really badly. After all, he'd done it before.

As Lance battered her mother's face and body over and over again, Jordanna slipped off the sofa and ran into the kitchen. Opening the cupboard under the sink she got the big gun that her mummy's other friend Georgie always kept there. She held the gun tightly to her breast, and she waited until the noise and the violence died down.

She finally looked into the front room, keeping as quiet as possible. It was very still. Very silent. But she could feel the heat of their anger, feel the hate that seemed to follow her mother around like a bad smell.

She saw that Lance had stopped hitting her mummy, he was now busy trying to salvage some of the brown, trying to scrape it off the carpet, off the furniture, and she could see her mummy lying on the floor bleeding and bloody, her face swelling.

Jordanna waited patiently in the kitchen, the freezing cold of the floor tiles making her shiver, until her mummy finally crawled out to her. She was bleeding from her nose and her mouth, and she looked like a ghost lady. As she looked at her little daughter she grinned, and the blood and the snot that was mingling together made her look even scarier.

'Good girl, Jorge. You are a good girl.' Taking the gun from the child, Imelda pulled herself up from the floor and, walking back into the front room, she pointed the gun at Lance.

Lance sighed in annoyance. He was still attempting to recover their stash, still trying to salvage their score. His physical attack on Imelda meant nothing to him, he saw it as her punishment, as something she had deserved. He certainly didn't see it as anything serious, as anything the child might find frightening, might see as threatening not only to her, but also to her mother. Lance was angry, angry and uncaring. He had no interest in the woman he had beaten, or the child who had witnessed it.

'Oh, give it a fucking rest, Mel. Like that fucking thing's loaded and, even if it was, you ain't got the fucking guts to shoot anyone. You are a fucking drama queen.'

As he spoke the last two words Imelda pulled the

trigger, the sound was so loud in the quiet of the room that she actually jumped with fright.

Lance was lying back on her sofa, and half of his head seemed to be gone. In fact, Imelda was in total shock at what she had done. She had wanted to shoot him so badly, and she had done just that. Her temper was such that she had shot him without any thought for the consequences of her actions. She saw him lying on the chair and she knew he was dead. She was glad he was dead. She was pleased that he had paid the ultimate price for his disrespect of her, for his arrogance. Then she heard her neighbours calling out to each other, and she realised that a gunshot was bound to get their attention. She knew that she had to use her head, had to find a way out of this situation. She wiped the gun clean with a cloth, and holding it carefully she went back out to the kitchen and placed the gun once more in the child's hands. 'Look after that for your mummy, yeah?' Then she manipulated her daughter's little fingers so her fingerprints were on the trigger and on the handle. She made sure that they were everywhere.

The gun had fired easily, without any need for her to really squeeze the trigger. The gun was so well looked after that anyone could have fired it.

She scrubbed her hands with bleach while waiting for the police to arrive. As anticipated, she did not have to wait very long.

Jordanna held onto the gun as her mother had requested, she always did what Mummy said, it made her life so much easier. She was still clutching the gun to her chest when the police came crashing through the front door.

Chapter Ten

Jordanna was quiet; as always she was waiting to see how the land lay before she made the mistake of opening up her little heart and allowing any kind of reaction to the manufactured affection of her new foster parents. Unknown to her, her nanny Mary was still trying to get custody of her, but until her mother was either bailed out, or sentenced to a prison term, she was in the care of the Baker family.

Emily Baker was a nice lady, she went to church regularly, and she tried as hard as she could to think the best of people but sometimes, she had to admit, she found that very difficult. As a person of faith, she sometimes found the world around her very hard to comprehend and, even though she knew it was wrong, she could not stop herself from judging people and finding the majority of them wanting.

Her local vicar was a very easy-going type of man, and she knew that he felt she was severely critical of the people around her. But she could not help it.

Like this little girl with her big blue eyes and her thick blond hair, who was absolutely beautiful. She looked like the children in adverts. Perfect in every way, and yet this child was suspected of a murder, was suspected of picking up a gun and shooting her mother's lover. It was scandalous. And, also, Emily Baker had to admit, quite exciting.

Unable to produce any children herself, she had persuaded her husband that they should foster, to give poor unfortunate children a few weeks, or months of happiness, show them what a real home should be.

Unfortunately, she had not allowed for the hard work that most of the children who were taken into care actually needed. They were often broken both mentally and physically, were fractured somehow, and they were usually very quiet and unable to respond to her immediate loving advances.

In fact, she got the distinct impression that, more often than not, they did not even *like* her very much. She had tried, and she had tried again. But she had never understood how hard it was for these kids to bond with people, how cynical they had become because of their upbringings, their environments, and how distrusting they *had* to be to survive.

Emily Baker knew that the children had often been the recipients of terrible treatment, neglected or uncared for, even abused. Yet she still could never forgive them for their ungratefulness, for their refusal to respond to her overtures of friendship. It had not occurred to her that the children she was asked to care for had never had a healthy relationship with an adult before, that they were expecting to be treated with contempt, to have their personal wants disregarded as a matter of course. She didn't realise that it might take time to gain their trust and their affection.

Emily Baker saw them as evil little sods who threw her kindness back in her face, and who saw their aim in life as making as much mess as possible. That was again seen by her as another kick in the teeth, another insult from these children who, she felt, were far beneath her, and who still felt the need to go against her every directive.

She hated to see her perfect home messed up by them, hated watching as her well-cooked food was eaten as fast as possible without any appreciation whatsoever for the time she had invested in its creation.

She knew that her husband did not want any of these children for the long term, did not want to adopt, and had only agreed to the fostering because it would bring in a few extra pounds and keep her occupied while he was at work.

She still felt that she should be achieving something though, but what that might be, she was not sure of. She had assumed that the children she was asked to care for would be eternally grateful for the opportunity to experience such a nice, clean house, and such a nice set of parents. After all, these children were mostly produced by people who had nothing more going for them than the fact that they *could* produce children. They seemed to produce them regularly, and at an alarming rate. She had watched and learnt over the years, and she had accepted that the children who came into her orbit were already without any kind of hope or any kind of expectation for the future.

Jordanna watched the woman's every move, and knew that the woman was also watching her every move. She knew that this heavy-set lady with her cross-looking mouth and tired eyes was not exactly overjoyed at her presence.

She wanted her nana, her nana Mary was the only person in her world who really cared about her, who really loved her. Her nana Louise did, but she was often absent from her life, sometimes for months on end; she knew that her mother hated her even more than she hated nana Mary. She also knew that unlike nana Mary, nana Louise was much easier to frighten off. It was hard for Jordanna to comprehend the politics and the intricate relationships of her mother and the people on the outside of their world; she was never sure who was actually classed as socially acceptable at any given time.

So, she did what she had found was always her best bet, she watched and she waited, and she kept as low a profile as possible until she could gauge the temperaments of the people around her.

It was these self-defence mechanisms of Jordanna's that were now making Emily Baker so annoyed with her. She was not experienced enough to understand how damaged this lovely little girl actually was. So consequently she took the child's natural reticence as a personal affront, felt that her offers of love and caring were unwanted and, worst of all, unneeded. She had not yet worked out that it was not about her and her dreams and wants, it was about the children she was taking into her home.

So little Jordanna, at two years and eight months old, had inadvertently been thrown from the proverbial frying pan into the heart of a roaring fire.

Imelda was still trying to convince anyone who would listen that Lance had been the love of her life, that he had attacked her in a jealous rage, and that her daughter had inadvertently shot him by accident, determined to protect her mummy. It sounded like shit even to her ears. But it was all she had to use. She knew that the Filth could not prove her part in Lance's demise, no matter how much they might suspect her involvement.

All they knew for sure was that he was *dead*, and no one knew what exactly had happened except herself and her little daughter. And her little daughter, as usual, had nothing to say to anyone. Imelda had already briefed Jordanna on how important it was to keep her mouth *shut*. Jordanna was a fucking pain anyway. She didn't have the brains of a wood louse and, at the end of the day, she was hardly what anyone would class a great conversationalist.

Imelda knew that she might get a tug for having a gun in the house, a gun she had assured the police had been Lance's, but she knew that whatever she might be sentenced to for possession of a firearm, it would be fuck all in comparison to a murder charge.

She could quite easily cry with laughter, but she knew she would be much better off if she didn't succumb to that at this particular moment in time. But every time she thought of Lance's face when she pulled the trigger, she felt an awful urge to laugh out loud. He had not believed that she was capable of shooting him but, as she had found out alongside him, she fucking well was.

As he had sat there, smug and bursting with self-assurance, happily assuming that a nice big fix, paid for with *her* money, would be enough to bring her to heel, make her toe the fucking line, she had felt such a rage and a hatred for him. She knew that not only did Jimmy Bailey think she was a fucking loser, a fucking skagheaded idiot, even a piece of shite like Lance saw himself as far superior to her.

It had been a learning curve all right, seeing him as he really was, finally understanding that he was just using her and her flat, even her money, without having the decency to at least pretend that he respected her and everything she was providing. He had the fucking brass neck to laugh at her, to treat *her* like a fucking dolt, a fucking *imbecile*. Well, she had finally had the last laugh, and it felt good.

She was finished with people using her, imposing on her good nature, making her feel that she was second-rate, even though they were depending on her to supply them with whatever they needed.

Imelda was absolutely mortified at the abuse she had been shown by Lance for her generosity of spirit, and for her faith in people in general. No matter how much she wanted to believe that the people she mixed with were honest and true, it was always proven to be nothing more than a sham, a terrible pretence. Imelda was really getting into her part now: she was the wronged woman, the fool in love.

She was also in dire need of something of a chemical nature and she needed it soon. The methadone she had been given by the police doctor had ensured that she remained more or less lucid. But she would need something a bit more powerful than that shite to get her over the next few days.

As long as Jordanna kept her trap shut she should be home and dry and, even if the girl did spill the beans, who would take the word of a child anyway? Imelda was in a win-win situation.

Still, she was tired, and she was aching, and she hoped that the doctor was as liberal with his sleeping pills as he was with the methadone.

To have asked where her daughter had been taken had not even occurred to her, and that fact was not lost on the policemen concerned. She had not once expressed any interest in the child's welfare or whereabouts since she had been taken into custody. A child that apparently she worshipped and adored, and yet whose date of birth had somehow escaped her memory for the time being.

Imelda Dooley was as guilty as a monk in a brothel, but the police could not prove it. She was well known as a junkie and a troublemaker; she had a reputation for violent and aggressive behaviour, and she was an accident that had been waiting to happen for years. She was already seen as a major influence in two other murders. Her own father, and the father of her child, had both died because of her.

But, even knowing all that, with only a small, silent child as a witness they knew they could prove nothing against her. That the murder victim was Lance Bradford was not helping matters either. If his rap sheet was read out at the trial, there would be a good chance that Imelda Dooley might be put forward for a commendation of some sort. He had been nicked for everything from burglary to attempted rape and he was not exactly what they would term a sympathetic victim. He was the child of wealthy parents, who had indulged him all his life, and who had created a monster that they had finally unleashed on to an unsuspecting world when he had become too much for them to handle. He had been afforded every opportunity, and he had still chosen to spend his life on the needle.

But even with that, the police strongly suspected that Imelda Dooley had shot him in cold blood, that she had murdered him without a second's thought. Even the bruises and cuts she had accumulated did not move them in any way. Imelda Dooley was known as being capable of causing the Lord himself to lash out at her. She was not a battered wife, or a victim of any kind. She was not even seen by them in any way other than as a predatory junkie. The wounds she had could have been delivered by anybody; after all, she seemed to make people want to smack her one.

But she knew how to play the game, she knew how to

make herself look like the real victim in all of this. She knew how to play the bystanders, and she knew how important the innocents were to her case, and how easy she could hoodwink them. The police knew she was a real handful, and they accepted that.

She knew more about the law than most of the CID put together. She was very clever and she was also very dangerous because she had no real fear of the law, or of its consequences.

In reality, the police involved knew that once the social workers and the probation officers got involved, they would be lucky to charge her with possession of a firearm. After all, she claimed that the gun in question had been owned by the victim. He had been shot by a little girl who was not inclined to discuss the ins and outs of the night in question. She was two; she would be hard-pushed to discuss the latest nursery rhyme she had heard. Her prints were on the gun, and the gun was easily fired, it needed no real pressure to release the ammunition inside of it. A child was capable of using it, and quite capable of accidentally killing somebody with it. Especially someone who was hurting their mummy. But it felt wrong, it felt too manufactured. They knew when they were beaten, but it still rankled.

Jimmy Bailey felt guilty, he had a feeling that his reaction to Imelda and her lifestyle just might have had a bearing on what had happened to Lance Bradford. He was a realist, he could add two and two and make a resounding four.

As Mary explained to him how her daughter had come into her home ranting and raving about him and his disrespect for her, and had then taken the child from her as a punishment for what she believed was a conspiracy of some sort, he had feigned surprise and he had hoped against hope that she would fall for his innocent act.

She had. Mary was a nice lady, it would not occur to her that he could have actually been a part of her daughter's daily madness. She would not even consider him and her daughter together in any way, shape or form.

Yet Jimmy Bailey knew without a doubt that it was his actions that had brought about Imelda's latest escapade. Once again her anger and spite had resulted in a death, only this time her daughter was implicated, and he had a feeling that Imelda would guarantee that the child would be held responsible. It was an abortion from start to finish.

'Mary, love, relax, eh? Sit down and I'll get you a drink.'

He had brought a bottle of brandy with him and, opening it, he poured a generous measure into a tea cup that had been left to drain by the sink.

Sitting her down in a kitchen chair, he pushed the cup into her hands and waited while she took a few deep gulps.

It seemed to steady her, because she stopped trembling and, taking a few more deep breaths, she said sadly, 'She did it, Jimmy, and I know that for a fact. She is blaming the child because she knows that little girl would never talk against her, she would be too terrified. Jordanna is petrified of her mother, Imelda treats that girl like a fucking animal.'

Mary had never before admitted to anyone outside of the social services that her daughter was mistreating her own child. Jimmy was shocked at the admission: over the last couple of years he had never once heard Mary say anything detrimental about her daughter's parenting skills.

He sighed heavily, his handsome face was closed and

wary as he decided how best to cope with this new development. 'Come on, Mary, you don't mean that.'

He was giving her an out, a chance to take back her accusation and with her denial of the said accusation he could once more pretend that he was completely devoid of any kind of involvement in Imelda's latest catastrophe.

But Mary nodded her head with a violence born out of frustration. 'It's true, Jimmy, she treats Jordanna like a fucking household pet. Actually, a pet would be treated better. She uses that little child like a weapon to make me do whatever she wants. She uses her to get money from me for drugs, if I pay her enough she'll grant me some access. But I always know that at some point she'll arrive at my door and take her away, accusing me of all sorts, but really it's only because she needs to produce her daughter to guarantee her Social Security money, her Family Allowance, and prove to the social services that the child is actually resident at her address. I know that I should not say this, but I hate my daughter with all my heart and soul. I can't look after my own grandchild, and I don't know where to go next.'

Jimmy put his arm around Mary's shoulders, he was genuinely sorry for her and her situation. He knew that her granddaughter was everything to her, and he wished that he had left the fucking Prospect of Whitby alone.

'Look, Mary, I'll talk to Michael Hannon, he will know how to find a brief who specialises in children's welfare. That is what you need now, someone who knows the law, and who is on your side. You and I both know that a good brief is worth his weight in gold, even if we also know that he will probably charge as much by the hour. So don't let this get on top of you, get you down. You took over a fucking serious bit of business after your old man died, and I rely on you these days because you are so good at tracking people down. So bear that in mind. Imelda is a shit-bag, but you have me and Michael behind you so you are in with a good chance. Now, please stop crying, and let me get us both another drink.'

Mary was cheered by his words, she had needed someone else to back her up, believe in her, and Jimmy Bailey was the last person she would have expected to do that for her. Life was strange, you found comfort in the oddest of places.

'Thanks, Jimmy, I know this is way over your head, and I'm sorry for unloading it on you. But I don't know what else to do, the boys are useless and they have no care or interest in Imelda or the child, and I am terrified that she'll be put into care full-time, into a home or something. Jordanna is a lovely girl, but she will only open up with the right people; if you don't know her like I do, she can come across as being a bit simple. But it's just a self-defence mechanism against her mother's anger and spite.'

Jimmy Bailey was unsure what he should say to make things better. He had been brought up in the care system and the knowledge he had of the reality of it was not something he felt he should share with Mary Dooley at this particular moment in time. In care, he had personally experienced violence, disgust, brutality of both a physical and a sexual nature, but the worst thing was that he had also been on the receiving end of the worst cruelty of them all: indifference.

To be ignored as if you did not actually exist was worse than any physical abuse, because eventually you began to believe that you were so useless and so uninteresting that you might as well have been invisible. It was made even worse because if the powers-that-be saw fit to overlook you, then the other kids saw their chance at having someone to look down on too.

Jimmy knew exactly how it felt to be ostracised for no other reason than that you were the new kid on the block, and the previous new kid was looking forward to persecuting the new guy with all the enthusiasm he could muster.

But it was the adults' indifference that really left a scar; when you tried to confide in them about what was happening to you after lights out in the dorm, how the bigger lads were using the younger boys as their personal slaves, and knowing that the person you were trying to alert to your plight was already more than aware of what was happening and still did not give a flying fuck for you or your welfare. It was then, when you suddenly realised that you were on your own, that nobody in the world cared about what happened to you, and that the only person you would ever really be able to count on was yourself. It hit you harder than a breeze block dropped from a tower block. So you either accepted your fate, or you made up your mind to fight against it with everything you could muster.

Jimmy had chosen the latter and, after going to bed with a couple of large builders' bricks that he had secreted inside his pillowcase, he had proceeded physically to take out a tall, heavy-set and arrogant fifteen-year-old boy called Dennis Crosby, by smashing him over the head repeatedly with his home-made weapon until he stopped moving. Crosby was after him for sexual reasons and he somehow knew that. Jimmy also knew that if he had not taken him out once and for all, he would have been destroyed on a nightly basis.

He had then taken Mr Crosby's booty from his bedside cabinet. It had consisted of contraband, primarily cigarettes, money and drugs. The drugs were mainly sleeping pills and Valium. There were a few purple hearts and a few other stimulants for the older kids, the kids who were too old or too big to be preyed on any more. But in the care system, most of the kids just wanted oblivion. Sleep, that was the main thing they all yearned for. Deep, undisturbed sleep.

Jimmy had learnt a valuable lesson, that the strongest was not always the biggest. That, if you needed to, a weapon was a good way of putting your feelings across, especially to certain people who only understood a stronger will than their own.

After that night, he had been left in peace, but it had been a real learning curve, and he had never dropped his guard again. He had learnt how to defend himself, and he had finally understood how important your reputation as a hard man could be.

But he also heard stories about how the girls were invaded, and the thought of that little child having to endure what he knew a lot of the men who worked in the care system thought of as a bit of *fun*, was too much for him to contemplate.

Jordanna was her mother's double, from the deep-blue eyes to her well-sculpted cheekbones. He knew from experience that she was exactly what those fucking nonces dreamt about and looked for. And he wished that he had kept his fucking distance from it all, because now he would have to do something about it. He knew better than anyone what the care system did to the kids who were unfortunate enough to have to live in their family's shadows.

*

'I don't want her any more, and I know that you won't have any kind of opinion about her personally, because you never do. But I think she is another one of those children who are *too* disturbed for anyone to reach. She doesn't talk, or move, she does nothing. She is so pretty as well, like a little doll, but she has not even blinked in my presence. I want a child I can at least communicate with, who can react physically with a hug, or a kiss. I want them just once to give me a baby I can actually baby.'

Emily knew that her husband was not really listening to her, and she was fine with that. All she really needed was someone within her vicinity who looked as if they were interested.

'She has only been here a little while, give her a chance, Em. After what she has been through I ain't surprised she doesn't talk. She seems like a nice kid, even I can see that she is very pretty.'

It was the first time her husband had ever made a remark about any of the children that had passed through their home and Emily felt quite excited at this new development on her husband's part. Emily was suddenly overwhelmed with emotion for the little girl with the long hair and the empty eyes, seeing her for the first time as a real person, not as another child who was not ready for her hugs and kisses within the first two hours of her arrival. Another child who was unappreciative of the home comforts she was desperate to give them.

'You're right. She is a little dear and I expect too much too soon.'

She smiled then, and her husband smiled back, hoping that this time she gave the kid time to adjust to the new environment.

Jordanna listened to the conversation with her usual blank expression, she was not yet three, but she understood everything that was being said around her. As she saw the lady smile properly for the first time since she had arrived in the house, she decided how best to cope with this new scenario. How she should act to make sure she was not going to get beaten or starved; both of which punishments her mother had used to keep her in line, to make her do what she wanted her to do.

'Drink please.'

Her voice was soft and hesitant, and Emily was so thrilled at those two words that she felt as if her chest would explode with pride.

She saw her husband grin, and raise his eyebrows in a gesture of amazement at her request.

Emily was thrilled at the little girl's sudden interest in her surroundings. 'Orange juice?'

Jordanna could see the kindness and the gratitude on the woman's face, and knew that she had done the right thing. It might not last long here, but she was determined to make her stay as easy as possible.

She nodded her assent, and smiled widely, with all her energy. She had perfected this smile a long time ago to make her mother believe that she was thrilled by her attention, to make her mother think that she was happy in her company. She could feel the tight movement of her face, her cheeks, even her ears. As she attempted to please the two people in the room with her Jordanna wondered, in her own bewildered way, what was going to happen to her next. She hoped against hope that whatever it was, it would not involve her mummy.

As she was crushed against the lady's enormous chest she smelt her peculiar aroma, stale sweat and perfume. But she knew better than to pull away from her, after all her mother and her cronies had smelt much worse.

Michael Hannon was nonplussed, for the first time in his life he did not know what to do. Mary Dooley was a star of stars, but her daughter's shit was not his concern, and yet Jimmy Bailey was standing in his office expecting him to reel off the names of people who could help her.

'I don't have anyone on my books who deals with fucking children's rights, have they even got any?' Michael smiled in consternation, showing his immaculate white teeth, and knowing that Jimmy was not impressed by his pristine white railings or the answer to his question.

But he was being honest, he didn't know a brief who could sort out children's issues and he was not in a fucking tearing hurry to meet one personally either. It was so fucking annoying, people fucked up, and then they all descended on you, expecting you to be the jewel of wisdom.

Well, he was not that conversant with the law anyway, unless it pertained to him personally, and this quite obviously did not.

'Well you must know somebody who could recommend someone, that's all I am asking of you. Mary needs the best of the best, and you are known around the law courts, I just hoped you would ask about, that's all. For fuck's sake, she is a mate and she is a valued fucking worker.'

Michael Hannon smiled then. He felt bad for a few seconds, he knew he should have been doing this for Mary Dooley, not Jimmy Bailey.

' 'Course I will. I'll ring my barrister and get a few numbers. What's the chat about Imelda anyway? Is she going to be bailed or what?'

Jimmy shrugged with exaggerated indifference. 'I could not give a fuck, to be honest. Mary is my priority at the moment and that little child.'

Michael Hannon smiled in wonderment. 'Why are you so bothered about her?'

Jimmy looked into his friend's face and, searching his eyes for some kind of understanding, he said sadly, 'I was brought up by paid parents, remember, that's when I wasn't in a home, of course. So, unlike you, Michael, I have a working knowledge of how the care system actually works, and I wouldn't wish it on my worst enemy, let alone a two-year-old child.'

Michael had the grace to look ashamed. 'I'll get the numbers for you now then, shall I?'

Jimmy wanted to hammer him until he couldn't walk. Instead he said quietly, 'Good man.'

Three days later Imelda was bailed out to her mother, on the proviso that she resided at her mother's address, and that she attended a methadone programme to be determined by her social worker. She was also told that her daughter would be returned to her care within the next twenty-four hours.

Mary was not thrilled at having her daughter under her roof, but she would put up with anything to get the little one back home with her. She felt, deep down in her boots, that Imelda would not be brought to book for Lance's murder. She knew that her daughter had shot him, knew how angry and vicious her daughter had been that night. After all, she had seen her first-hand herself when she had come to take Jordanna away from her.

Mel was still insisting that her daughter had shot Lance accidentally, while trying to defend her mother from his violent temper. Accidentally was meant to mean that, as a child, she did not know what she was doing. Jordanna was supposed to have seen her mum being beaten and gone to get the gun that was kept under the sink in the kitchen, and then shot Lance to stop him from hurting her mummy any more. Mel had the bruises to prove he had attacked her that night, and her daughter being so cute, no one was willing to bring any charges that might involve the little girl.

Though Mary had heard through the grapevine that the Old Bill were doing everything in their power to build a case against her daughter, she also knew that, with the circumstances being so unusual, and the victim in the case being such a dirt-bag, there was not much chance of the truth ever coming out.

She would attempt to get what she could from little Jordanna, but she knew already from the local CID that Jordanna would not even acknowledge any questions that pertained to the events of that night, let alone enlarge on them, or give some kind of answers. She was not yet three, and she was already shrewd enough to keep quiet around the Filth.

It was so annoying for Mary that she was back to square one, her daughter once more ensconced in her old bedroom and her baby girl being ignored by her mother, though she was completely loved by her nana.

And the worst of it was that she had seen the frown that crossed little Jordanna's face when she had realised that her mother was staying at her nana's house too. Mary wondered at how her Imelda, her own baby, could have turned out to be such a lying mare and, even worse than that, how she had been born such a crap mother. Even a stray dog would have done more for its pups than her child had done for her baby. She'd wondered occasionally, in her darker moments, if she had made her daughter like she was. If she had done something without realising it, and that whatever it was, it had made her daughter into the selfish, useless ponce she had become. But she could never think of anything specific or otherwise that could account for her daughter's behaviour. She had ruined her, but even that had been in a good way. She guessed it was the drugs, she always blamed the drugs, there was no other reason she could come up with.

As Mary hugged little Jordanna to her tightly, she saw Imelda watching them both from the corner of her eye. Mary was thrilled at Jordanna's return and, as she hugged her, she talked to her in her usual baby talk. Jordanna loved it, she liked the sound of the words and she tried to repeat them as often as she could. But her attention span was short and her eyes were always watching to see what her mother might be doing; she was naturally subdued by her mother's presence in the house. But there was not much that she could do to change that.

Imelda walked towards her daughter and said loudly, 'Bad baby.'

Jordanna did not move an inch. Instead, she stared her mother down and, as she walked away on her little legs she said loudly, 'Mummy bad.'

Mary grinned with pleasure, she was not about to disagree with that diagnosis, the child had a valid point. Her mummy was a bad girl.

Imelda was already on her way out of the house, and smiling at her little daughter she said gaily, 'Mummy good, Jordanna bad. Jordanna horrible little bastard.'

Mary pulled the child's head into her bosom in an attempt to stop her hearing what her mother was saying to her. 'Don't say that to the child, what the hell is it with you, why can't you just for once be like everyone else?'

Imelda laughed as if what she had just heard was so lame it was not even worthy of an answer.

So Mary grabbed her daughter's arm, and turning her round none too gently she asked her again why she had to be so wicked to her own child.

Imelda pulled herself away from her mother's grip and, wiping her arm clean of imaginary filth, she said sarcastically, 'Hasn't the lawyer told you? I'm having another one. I'm pregnant, Mum. Lance was the father. Maybe I'll like this one.'

As she watched her daughter disappear down the path Mary felt an overwhelming urge to fell her bodily to the ground. To attack her, and hurt her like she hurt everyone around her.

But she didn't, she knew that was exactly the type of behaviour that Imelda would be hoping for. It would just garner her more sympathy, and give her more reason to stop her access to the child.

As Mary closed the door to make sure her daughter had actually departed, she looked at her little granddaughter and sighing heavily she said softly, 'Jesus Christ, that's all I need, another bloody child to fight over.'

The charges against Imelda were dismissed a few weeks later, and she took up residence once more in her council flat. That it had been the scene of a horrific death was not something she was that bothered about, in fact she seemed to revel in her new-found notoriety.

And, as her belly grew, her interest in her daughter diminished even further. The new child was her only real interest, but the pregnancy did not do anything to stop her lifestyle in any way. If anything, it just seemed to increase her capacity for self-destruction.

Mary had Jordanna to herself at last, but that did not settle her mind, because she now had the new child to worry about, and she had to wonder at how this new little grandchild of hers would fare under its mother's tutelage.

Chapter Eleven

Kenneth Dooley was a lovely child, and his mother seemed actually to like him in her own haphazard way. She seemed interested in him, at least as much as she could be. In comparison to how she felt about her daughter, her interest in her son could be construed as over the top. She had no real interest in the children's day-to-day lives, in fact she was so self-obsessed and disinterested in Jordanna that the fuss she made of her son was so unusual it was seen as her only saving grace. It made people believe that she could not be all bad, after all, she *loved* her son. The fact that she had no time for her daughter, and that her children lived with their grandmother because she was not deemed fit enough to take care of them, and that she had no intention of caring for her kids anyway, was miraculously forgotten about. Kenneth was the love of her life, and because of her feelings towards him, her sins were nearly forgotten.

Imelda was surprised but she actually did feel some real emotion towards her son. He was big, and he was handsome, and he attracted people's attention on the rare occasions she went out with him in public. He had a head of thick, curly blond hair and long, powerful-looking legs; he would be tall, that much was obvious, and he was a sunny-natured child who smiled at everyone who came into his little world.

Mary Dooley felt such love for her grandson that it amazed her; with Imelda as his mother he would need all the love and help that he could get. Jordanna had known from day one that Imelda was not to be trusted, and she had had every reason to think that, but Kenneth had not been on the receiving end of his mother's frustration, or her phenomenal anger yet. So he had not seen her as she really was, he had not yet wondered why she didn't live with him, or look after him, like other mothers did their children. He had all that to come, and Mary hoped that, like his sister, when it did become clear to him, he would understand that it was not about him, or Jordanna, it was about her, their mother, Imelda, and the abortion that was her life.

Jimmy Bailey was good, he always asked after the children and Mary appreciated that. He had also taken over the role of surrogate uncle to them both.

When her two sons had informed her one afternoon that they were going into partnership together in a scrap yard she had been both upset and hurt at their obvious defection from the family unit. She was shocked by their announcement but, after Jimmy had reminded her that they would never be an asset to her, or anyone else for that matter, she had got over her initial annoyance and given them both her blessing. She had done that because she knew that nothing she could say would change their minds or make them stay in her life. She accepted that they were distancing themselves, not only from Imelda, but from her as well and from the kids, and she loathed them for that, even as she understood the reasoning behind it.

Neither of the boys seemed in the least bit inclined to give her a few quid, help her out financially; not that she needed it, but it was the principle. They were quite willing to take from her, on the other hand, as and when they felt the need to.

But, more to the point, neither of them even bothered to seek out her company any more, and that hurt her, that had really cut deep. Even though she understood their actions to an extent, she could not forgive them their treachery. They were both snides, were both fucking useless.

She had no one to rely on, and they had made it more than plain that she never would. It was a real eye-opener for her, their father's death had left them all adrift. But instead of feeling a measure of loyalty towards her, they had both taken a step back. They had not felt even an iota of loyalty towards her personally, their own mother, the woman who had birthed them, who had raised them, fed them and wiped their arses.

That she could take on both of Imelda's kids was way beyond their comprehension but, as she reassured herself, where those two treacherous bastards were concerned, so was long division. They were not exactly the most intelligent of lads, or in any way the most caring, they had not even offered her a shoulder to cry on since the death of her husband, their father.

So she was content to throw herself into her new family. She knew these children needed her and, more to the point, she needed them.

So she waved them off, her sons, with the warning that she expected to see them at least once a month, and to her sorrow they were quite happy with that. It suited them all, they kept up the appearance of a united family, but did not have to put up with each other on a daily basis, and Mary could concentrate on the two children her daughter had produced, and their immediate needs.

Imelda was the only fly in an otherwise perfect ointment. She did not want the children at all, not on a permanent basis anyway, but she would turn up on a semi-regular basis and make herself busy with them for appearances' sake. Imelda no longer tried to take the children away from their nana by brute force, though she was still capable of delivering the threat when the fancy took her. But Mary now knew that the threats were as empty as her daughter's purse, as she knew that if she gave her some money she would bugger off once more and leave them alone.

Mary was still tracking down people who owed money around and about, and she was still doing it without any real effort; her network of women was large, and it was reliable and growing by the year. They could track down anyone within days, and Mary paid the women well for their information. She knew that was enough to ensure their loyalty and their continuing support; Mary was the equivalent of a pension plan for many of the women she dealt with. Thanks to her, they had a few quid in reserve and were able to see themselves through the seasons. They did not have to rely on their children for handouts then, because as they had all eventually realised, their kids were no better off than they were. It was a different world now, and even though they had all looked after *their* parents, they soon came to understand that the same courtesy was not going to be extended to them. Mary was their lifeline, and the reason they still had a modicum of self-respect.

For Mary Dooley, life was good in many respects, and though she was lonely sometimes, she knew that her grandchildren had to be her main priority. The boys came every month, and she enjoyed their visits, but she was always glad to wave them off. They usually came with a catalogue of disasters, and with the want of more money to tide them over. They were not what she would call businessmen. She would weigh them out, and when they left she would heave a secret sigh of relief that she was once more left with her surrogate babies; the children she loved more than she had ever loved any of her own.

Little Kenneth was as bright as a button, and twice as handsome. Whereas Jordanna was a tiny thing who loved her brother with a passion.

But the only worry for Mary was that while Jordanna was not enamoured of her mother, and that was something anyone would understand, considering how she had been treated by her, Kenny Boy, as they called him, seemed to adore her.

Jordanna had never spoken to anyone about the fateful night that had culminated in Lance's death, and Mary wondered sometimes at how Kenny would react when he heard, as he surely would, that his sister had shot his father and killed him stone dead. Even though that was something no one in their right mind would believe.

Mary would watch Jordanna sometimes as she slept, and she would try to picture her with a gun in her little hands, but she just couldn't envisage it somehow. She had a problem seeing that poor little child defending her mother, the mother who had done nothing all her life except use her as a convenient stick to beat everyone around her with. But the police had been forced to accept her daughter's statement as fact, because they had no other statement to use against her. Like Mary, they knew there was something seriously wrong about it, but like her, they had no way of proving it. Mary would watch her granddaughter as she slept, would watch her as she tossed and turned, as she moaned in pain and terror, and she prayed then to the Holy Mother that the child would find some kind of peace, would find some kind of happiness.

Imelda still stuck to her story that Jordanna had been the culprit and, as everyone now knew that Lance had fathered Kenny Boy, it was well known that Jordanna had killed her brother's daddy. It was something the child would one day have to live with. The children would both have to live with it, and as they were so close, as Mary was determined to make sure that they were, she hoped they would be able to cope with it, would love each other enough to understand that they were nothing more than victims of their mother's lifestyle, their mother's neglect and her selfishness. It was a terrible situation for everyone involved. But, like everything else that had happened where her daughter was involved, Mary tried not to dwell on it too much because if she did, it just broke her heart all over again. But she still wondered at what the future had in store for these two children, and she worried about how they would cope with what had happened on that fateful night so long ago, and if the bond they shared would be strong enough to keep them together once the truth was finally out.

Imelda was looking good, and she knew that. It was strange how, even though she was now on the skag, she still did not look that rough. She had a natural glow to her skin and bone structure to die for, so her beauty was always protected somehow. Even she knew that much, and she was just pleased that nature had seen fit to give her an edge over most people.

She was wearing a short black leather skirt, a matching waistcoat with a sheer top underneath it, and her trademark high-heeled black boots. She was every inch the sexy babe, and she was charging for her services accordingly. She had been on the bash for a good while now, and she found that the life suited her disposition. She liked the money, the hours and, best of all, she liked the fact that she could score all over the Smoke as she was cabbed to her different destinations.

She had no qualms about her customers, they were so under her radar as to be almost invisible. But she smiled in the right places, pretended that they were the best fuck she had ever had, and she made sure that they wore a condom. If they wanted to ride her bareback then she charged them extra. It always amazed her that there were men who were quite happy to put their lives and their marriages on the line for a naked fuck. She never injected herself in her arms, she had learnt many years before that track marks made you a target, for the Filth, for bullies; they showed you up for what you really were. She had always made a point of injecting herself in her groin area, her ankles, anywhere that was not visible to the average person, or could not be hidden from view, hence her trademark boots. Men did not pay out for junkies and they did not pay extra for bareback from anyone they thought might be diseased. Imelda had never shared a needle in her life, not since her initial introduction into the world of heroin, anyway. She might be a stoner, but she was still sensible enough to know that you had to keep yourself to yourself; it was about self-preservation, no more, no less. She had altered her behaviour to make sure she could earn the most money. And she did earn it, and she intended to carry on earning it.

She had a good few quid, a nice supply of the brown, and she had a reputation that preceded her wherever she went. And she liked that, she liked being notorious, she loved that people talked about her, and pointed her out.

She played up to it and, with a few drinks in her, would sometimes re-live the night her daughter had killed her own brother's father. Sometimes she embellished the story so that Jordanna came out a little heroine who had stopped her mother from being beaten to death, other times she would describe a tragic accident that had deprived her of the love of her life and her son of his father.

Either way, she was not about to tell the truth, and though more than a few people had their own version of events, they were sensible enough to keep them to themselves. After all, Imelda Dooley was not someone you would deliberately pick a fight with; she was more than capable of looking after herself if the need arose, as had been proven.

Imelda liked the cabbing around town, she liked the feel of travelling to an unknown destination and, as she was a real looker, she was often asked for by name so she had a lot of regulars and a lot of money. Unfortunately, like most women of her persuasion, she spent her money without much thought, always with the belief that it would be there again the next day. Which it was, only inevitably the day would come when her youth and her wide-eyed beauty would start to wither and fade, and that was when she would wish that she had been a bit wiser with her money when she had been earning it in large amounts. Then she would understand how hard the business was for the women who were getting older, and she would suddenly notice that every few months a whole new batch of young girls would emerge on the scene. Then she'd wish that she had put a few quid away for the inevitable rainy day.

But, for the moment, Imelda was on a roll, was loving it, and she was still frightened enough about what had happened to Lance to guarantee that she would keep a lid on that famous temper of hers for the time being.

She had once done nearly three months on remand for a GBH charge, and that had been enough for her, she was not about to make that mistake ever again. She had got away with murder, and then nearly been sent down for a fight with a fellow worker. It was bloody laughable.

Imelda often wondered if Lance was actually Kenny's father. She knew that it was not something she would ever know for sure, not that she was going to admit that out loud of course, but sometimes she looked at little Kenny and saw Georgie Boy, the owner of the gun that had been used against Lance because of his stupid fucking antics. Lance had asked for everything he had got, she was convinced about that much. No one spoke to her like that and got away with it. But when she looked at her Kenny, she saw Georgie Boy, not Lance. He was like the spit out of Georgie's mouth as they said in East London society.

Imelda felt no regret; in fact, she would do it all again if she felt the need to, and she was happy about that as well. She felt that people were too quick to swallow in this day and age, and if they had any real sense they would know that some people needed taking out, and for their own good at that. She also knew deep inside that she was not like other people, that she was in a different league. Imelda Dooley felt that she did not have to live by other people's standards because, after all, she had literally got away with murder. That thought made her smile and, as always, her smile made her look like a young girl, not someone who had produced two children and who had a heroin habit so big and of such duration that anyone else would have been dead long ago.

The cab driver was a married man called Arnold Dukes and he was in his early sixties; he had taken to cabbing after he had taken his retirement from the docks. He was watching the girl in his rear mirror, and her beauty had captured his imagination. She looked new to the game, and that, as always, was her greatest asset. She did not look battered yet, she did not look what she was: a junkie, a whore. She still looked fresh faced; she was one of the few people who could abuse their bodies with drink and drugs, yet it didn't seem to leave a mark on them. She looked like any other young girl; her skin was bright, and her body taut. She offered the men that she serviced the illusion of extreme youth, and that alone was enough to make them believe that she was still new to it all. She knew that and she played on it, used it to her advantage when necessary.

Arnold was the possessor of a grey comb-over, and a spectacular set of rapidly decaying teeth, and his idea of personal hygiene consisted of a bath every couple of weeks and the daily changing of his socks, though that was actually a necessity because the cab was so confined. He had been pulled up over the stench on more than one occasion.

He smoked Capstan Full Strength, and he had a penchant for hand-knitted cardigans and Ben Sherman shirts. He had all but given up on the sexual side of his life until now, until he had seen this girl. He knew she was a brass, but she was stunning. She was built like the movie stars of the forties, big-breasted and possessed of a certain innocence that he was attracted to. He wanted her desperately, and as he knew that she was for sale anyway, unlike most of the women who might have frequented his taxi, he felt that she could be within his reach.

Imelda saw Arnold Dukes looking at her in the mirror, and she smiled seductively, opening her legs slightly so he could get a quick glimpse of what she had to offer. Arnold was over the moon at the way she was coming on to him. He actually thought that she might even fancy him.

'How much do you charge, love?'

She grinned at him then, and laughing huskily she answered him in such a way it could almost have been mistaken for embarrassment at his cheeky question. In that moment she made him believe that he was the only man she had ever wanted in the world, and he swallowed it hook, line and sinker.

'Twenty quid to you.'

He knew she charged forty quid a time, knew that all the girls did. Twenty quid was cheap and he knew that. But it was still a lot of money to him. He had it though, and he was willing to weigh it out to feel her firm tits, her soft flesh, and explore her tight little pussy.

Ten minutes later they were parked up in a deserted side street and he was already gasping for air and fumbling with excitement as she climbed on to his lap. As he spewed his particular brand of pornographic filth into her ear Imelda was already planning her next score.

Arnold was just another man in a long line of men who she saw as weak, as fools, and who saw her as young and innocent. Even her reputation and the stories about her didn't stop men from wanting her, she knew that she had that edge, knew that her notoriety just added to her allure for some of her punters and, consequently, added to her earnings. Unlike most of the girls, she didn't have a pimp as such, she looked out for herself. But unlike most of the girls in her business, she had no qualms about people knowing about what she did for a living. She was proud of it.

Twenty minutes later she was knocking on a door in Hammersmith. A retired teacher with a bad back, bad breath, and a wife who was away for the night in Slough, visiting their first grandchild, ushered her into his home with a nervous smile and the guilty hope that she would make him feel twenty-one again. He had one eye on her, and one eye on what he saw as his valuables and, to make the night even worse, he was listening out for the phone call that would tell him his wife had arrived safely, and that his new grandchild had a look of him. He was like the majority of the men who asked for home visits, he had thought about it for so long, and dreamt about it for even longer, that when it finally happened he had not allowed for the guilt and the disgust at himself for bringing an actual prostitute into his own home. He would then worry that the woman he had fantasised about for so long now knew his address, knew where he lived. That she could come back at any moment, and blow his little world apart.

It never occurred to the men that the girls concerned went to so many addresses around the Smoke that they didn't take any notice of their surroundings any more. Didn't realise that the man in question was of as much interest to them as a political debate on the health service and that all they wanted was to get it over with as quickly as possible so they could go on to the next punter, and the next, and the next, until they all merged into the same person. Guilt was a wonderful thing for prostitutes, it made their lives so much easier. That was always the problem with the cheaper end of the market.

Michael Hannon was annoyed, really annoyed. He was not given to grandiose displays of anger or temper but, for the first time ever, he was very close to that now.

Jimmy Bailey had offered him an in on a new business venture a while ago. He was a man of liberal tastes and he was willing to listen to anything that might afford him the opportunity to earn a crust but Michael had blanked him then, when he had asked him to front a brothel with him, because he was old-style and saw the procuring of women and girls as the domain of the foreigners, the Maltese, the Spanish, even the Jamaicans.

But he had found out that, to his detriment, Jimmy's brothel was now raking in fucking serious fortunes. So, in fairness, Michael Hannon felt he had the right to be gutted. To be wound up, to be aggravated and aggrieved.

Now Jimmy was asking him, once more, if he wanted an in to his new business, and he knew that Jimmy Bailey, a lovely bloke when all was said and done, was relying on him to say as he always had, a resounding *no*. He was only asking him out of respect, and once he said 'no', as was expected, Jimmy would then be free to go to whoever he felt was up for his kind of business.

Unfortunately for Jimmy Bailey, Michael had recently realised the error of his ways, had seen for himself how the eighties were turning out to be the new golden era for the oldest profession in the world. It had somehow been catapulted to the forefront of everyone's minds and had been seen for the earner it really was. There was no stigma attached to it any more, people were realising that the money from it could be used for other things, to finance other businesses. Even hostess clubs were back in the running again, as were other aspects of the business.

Thanks to new legislation, and some very old laws, as long as a woman did not solicit for sex on the actual pavement itself, and as long as she cabbed it to an address, she was not, in effect, breaking any laws at all. Once inside private property she was free to ply her trade, and there was nothing anyone could do about it.

The laws of this land had never seen fit to bring the *buyer* of sexual favours into a court of law and, providing the woman concerned did not solicit on a public highway, she was as safe as fucking houses. Bailey's cab ranks were the tools that guaranteed him a serious wedge. And that wedge was now being talked about and discussed at length, by all the people in the know.

So now Michael Hannon had decided that he wanted an in, and he wanted a serious in at that. He wanted it all, as was his prerogative. He would just take what he wanted in the end if that was what he felt was his only viable option.

But at least he had the grace to admit to himself that he had been wrong in his previous assumptions, and that he had looked down on Jimmy and his selling of the female form, had seen it as a big negative. He'd seen the venture as something that was not an option for him, as something he had believed was only for men of a certain ilk, who had no respect for themselves, or the people around them. That was the old way of thinking though, he knew that now. That was for the old boys, the moustache Petes. They saw pimping as beneath them, and it was in their day.

But Michael now saw the potential of it, saw that it was the best way of making serious money in the short term, and that he could carry on making it in the long term. It was the perfect way to earn a real wage, and he was then going to use that wage for other purposes.

And, even though he still had a genuine distaste for it all, he was shrewd enough to know that if he didn't jump on this particular bandwagon there were plenty of other people who would.

As Jimmy Bailey sat opposite him, Michael smiled what he hoped was a real friendly smile, and he wondered at how Jimmy was going to react to his complete turn-around. Because he knew who Jimmy was going to offer the in to next, even though the man had turned him down before, and Graham Parker already had too much power as it was. Michael also knew that Parker was going to snatch Jimmy's hand off this time.

So Michael Hannon knew that he had to make it clear to everyone involved that he had been the recipient of a complete change of heart, and that he was now willing to go into this new enterprise with all his considerable strength behind him.

He knew that Jimmy Bailey was expecting his usual 'thanks', but 'no thanks', and that Jimmy might not be that enamoured of his sudden agreement to the deal. He also knew that Jimmy Bailey was shrewd enough not to let his disappointment show. So, providing they played their parts properly, everything should be hunky-dory.

Imelda was gone, she was so out of it she was unaware of where she was, how she had arrived there, and who she was supposed to be with.

As she looked around her at the flickering darkness of the discotheque, she could feel the music washing over her, it was loud and it was funky, and she was rocking along with its beat. The flashing lights were really making her feel a part of it all; as she watched them change colour and sequence she felt as if she had been born for this moment. It was always the same with her, she lived from one day to the next, one experience to another and she had never once thought about the future. Drugs were the only reason she felt capable of joining in anything that consisted of people. Without the drugs she knew she wasn't capable of connecting with others. She liked the heroin because with it she could just drift out of the world around her, and she had a bona fide reason to be alone with herself and her thoughts. With LSD though, she could do what she was doing now, she could actually enjoy being with like-minded people. She could experience being in a crowd without her usual feeling of detachment. Imelda liked hallucinating, liked the whole concept of it, liked the knowledge that the other people around her were feeling the same thing. It was the only time in her life that she felt she belonged. That she felt she was a part of something bigger than her.

As she pulled herself together, she looked at the people she was with and, sighing heavily, she was pleased to note that she knew the majority of them. She was also a teeny bit disappointed that they were all people she knew only on a peripheral level, knew them only through other people.

They were youngsters who, unlike her, were not really that experienced where tripping was concerned. But she was OK with that, she had accepted many years before that, unlike her, most people went home at some point. Had accepted that most people had jobs and lives that they returned to at regular intervals. That, unlike her, they didn't see their world in all its terrifying reality from their drug-induced haze and, unlike her, they couldn't function in that world in a drug-induced haze.

But she *could*, she functioned better in fact, because she could see the world as it really was, she saw the real world, and she knew that the people around her took drugs to access a pretend world that they enjoyed for a short while, and then exited. She didn't do that though, she only really felt normal when she was out of it, then she felt as if she had come home, felt that she understood the people around her.

Without the chemicals, she had nothing to offer anyone, she had no feelings or care for anyone else. But with the opiates, or the LSD, whether it was Californian Sunshine or the real thing, Microdot, which was getting harder and harder to come by thanks to the advent of blotting paper and its obvious merit where sales were concerned, she always felt that she was coming to life at last. She had tried to explain it to the psychiatrist when she had been in prison, had tried to make him understand why she needed the drugs and how they made her finally feel something.

But it had been a waste of time. Even though he had wanted to understand her, had been fascinated by her. In fact, she had known that long before he had. It was her looks, no one ever wanted to believe that someone who looked like her could really be bad, could truly be devoid of any emotions or feeling.

Imelda knew that even the judge at Snaresbrook Crown Court had been dazzled by her beautiful face and her wonderful body.

A few days in her company and they would realise that she was a few paving slabs short of a patio. But, where first impressions were concerned, she always had the edge.

She had been put into Holloway Prison after Lance's death, and she had been approached by all and sundry within hours. Her looks always guaranteed her people's interest, and she knew that better than anyone. When it was necessary, she was sensible enough to gauge the mindset of whoever she was with at any particular time, and she would then become the person they wanted her to be. She knew that about herself. Had known it for years. She knew that she *pretended* to feel things, that she copied emotions from the people around her, copied their reactions and their feelings so that she could blend in. She had learnt what the appropriate reactions were to certain situations and had learnt that her instinct to obliterate anyone who stood in her path would only get her into trouble. She knew that she did not have any feelings for her family, even her own children. She liked Kenny Boy because he was a male, and she had only ever really got on with men. She had something they wanted, and she was quite willing to let them have it for a price. She understood now that her way of living was not the norm, but she didn't care about that as such, she cared about nothing.

As Imelda picked up a vodka and tonic from a nearby table, she knew without any doubt that it was her drink. She didn't know how she knew that, but she knew it was true. She loved the feeling of being completely out of the game, yet knowing what was going on around her at the same time. Gulping the drink down quickly, she felt the first initial rush of the LSD slipping away from her. She was now just entering the tripping stage, she felt the chemically induced heaviness envelop her as it attacked her body, and then five minutes later she felt the explosion of colours and sound that heralded what was, to her, the best twenty minutes of the whole experience. After this, it was still a great feeling, but it wasn't as intense, didn't have the same resonance. It was like anything in life: once the initial feeling was over with, it was never the same again.

She closed her eyes and let the feelings overwhelm her, she could really feel the music now, as if it was emanating from her skin. As the DJ put on Average White Band's 'Play That Funky Music, White Boy', Imelda felt as if all her Christmases and birthdays had arrived at once. As she danced to the music alone, in her own private world, she was unaware of the two men watching her closely. The people she had attached herself to earlier in the evening were quite happy to revel in her company. She afforded them a measure of respect that, as youngsters, they had not yet garnered for themselves. They made sure she had a fresh drink when she needed one, and were thrilled if she acknowledged them in any way, shape or form. They were still so young and naïve they thought that Imelda Dooley was someone of note, of renown. Her reputation was seen by these children as something to admire, and they were still stupid enough to be thrilled to be seen in her company.

Imelda knew all of this on some unconscious level and, like most people with an ounce of brains inside their heads, she was also baffled by their complete admiration of her. All she was ever interested in was getting wasted, she had only hooked on to this lot because she needed people to hang out with. She was quite capable of getting off her face alone, but experience had taught her that, like animals in the wild, she was much better off if she was seen to be part of a crowd.

Imelda was over the best of her trip within the hour, and she made her way towards the exit. As she walked out into the cold night air and hailed a black cab, she was already more than aware of the two men who had been watching her for most of the night. When she drove away she stared at them both so she could file them away for future reference. Still tripping, that might be harder than she thought.

Chapter Twelve

Jimmy Bailey could not believe what he was hearing. He had been royally blanked by Michael Hannon when he had offered him an interest in his business months before and, truth be told, it had fucking smarted, it had really hurt him that Hannon had all but dismissed him and his seriously lucrative and constantly expanding businesses out of hand. He would never have admitted that out loud, of course, but because of Michael Hannon's refusal the last time and, let's face it, that refusal had been quick and abrupt, he had been pissed off. It had been a calculated refusal, it had been delivered in such a way as to let him know that, even though Michael might like him, and work with him on other interests, where Jimmy's personal businesses were concerned, he had no interest whatsoever as he saw them as beneath him.

Because he was involved in prostitution Michael Hannon had more or less insinuated that Jimmy was beneath his fucking contempt. He had not said anything like that outright, of course, he had not wanted to cause a rift between them, but Jimmy had sussed out the gist of what was going down. Hannon thought he was above the skin game, saw it as something to be ashamed of. Something to be looked down on.

Well, for Jimmy, that had been a real learning curve, one of many he had experienced over the years. He had swallowed the veiled insults and the outright jokes about his chosen profession, mainly from his peer group. He had made a point of laughing harder than any of them at their jokes. In effect, he had swallowed their derision, but at the same time he had also expanded his empire quietly and confidently, and he had always offered his boss an in. His boss had refused, but at the same time, he had given Jimmy his personal permission to expand and was always appreciative that Jimmy saw fit to let him know what was going on. Jimmy was not a fool, he was a realist, and that was why he was now in a position to buy and sell the fucking lot of them if he needed to. And why Graham was so eager to join forces with him.

Now, when Jimmy had gone to Michael with his latest plans for expansion, as a courtesy, and also as a necessary formality, he had expected the big 'no' as per usual, and he would have smiled and acted as if he understood Michael Hannon's reticence at what he was doing, and that should have been that. But that had not happened this time around.

Michael Hannon had informed him that he was sorry for his earlier refusals and, on reflection, he was willing to become his partner. Not a silent partner either, even though that was all Jimmy had ever wanted from anyone. Oh no, Hannon wanted to be a full-blown part of his business. In effect, Michael wanted to come in as his boss. The business he had built up all on his Jack Jones, because no one wanted to get involved with brasses, toms. After the sixties, and the decline of the clubs, the skin business had become the domain of the foreigners, mainly the Maltese and the West Indians, and as such, it was still seen by many of the men he dealt with on a daily basis as beneath them.

Jimmy had shrugged his shoulders at their apathy, as he had shrugged off the opinions of the people around him for years, and he had kept his dealings quiet and very confidential. He had eventually earned the respect of his peers and he had also pocketed a large and regular wedge of Herculean proportions. It meant that he was earning too much for his own good, and that Michael Hannon, albeit a good mate when needed, now saw his success as a threat to him personally.

Jimmy knew that his purse was filling up faster than anyone's because he had tapped into a business that was not only classed as the oldest profession in the world, it was also the only business that was not affected by recessions, trends, fashions or anything external. It was a business that was always in demand because the people who used the services provided had always used them. Would always use them because they always had to explain away the money they spent on their entertainment anyway. He was dealing in what was, in effect, dead money, it was all in cash. Jimmy was more than aware that prostitution was the only industry that was *always* in demand, no matter what was happening in the real world.

The only people in the flesh business who felt the bite of a recession were the hostess clubs, they were hard pressed to get punters in because it cost the punter a fortune in drinks and extras before he could even think about taking the girl away with him.

Jimmy had made a point of taking out the middle man

and he had cut the overheads because his punters did not have to pay for the premises if they were in their own homes.

Jimmy's brothels were all private addresses, and as he owned the houses concerned, they were also good investments in themselves. His brothels were well run, spotlessly clean and well decorated. They catered for every taste and for every pocket, and they were also very discreet and possessed of a really good bar area where the girls were open to negotiation, and were looked after by huge, muscle-bound doormen who were paid to keep the rabble element out. They also made sure that the girls who worked there were treated fairly and decently. If any of the girls were abused, either verbally or physically, they knew that they would be protected.

Jimmy might be a pimp, but he made a point of ensuring that anyone who worked for him was afforded a measure of protection they could never guarantee for themselves on the streets, or in the hostess clubs for that matter. Once a girl left a hostess club with their punter for a hotel, they were on their own. Even Jimmy's cab drivers were expected to wait for the girls after they had dropped them off. And, if they were still there after their allotted time, they were expected to go to the front door and knock, and wait there until they were assured the woman concerned was all right. If they were requested to stay longer, the cabbie was to stay as well, wait until they finally emerged. Jimmy's cabs also catered for the men who did not want to be seen in a brothel, no matter how discreet. Jimmy understood and respected that. His brothels, on the other hand, were frequented by men who liked to socialise with desirable and willing young women, who also enjoyed the company of other, like-minded men.

Show-offs liked brothels. The kind of men who enjoyed hunting in packs, who needed the bravado of their friends before they could perform, needed brothers. Jimmy understood the psychology of his customers, understood that they were all different, yet basically the same. The men he catered for were fucking users. They saw the women they were purchasing as nothing more than a hole. Jimmy despised them, but he made sure they were all welcomed and treated like valued friends. It was why he was the most influential and the most desired pimp in the Smoke.

The girls flocked to him, even Imelda Dooley, and he made sure that they were taken care of, and that guaranteed him their loyalty as well as sixty per cent of their earnings.

And now, after all that hard work, and after all his investments, he was expected to smile happily and hand everything he had built up over to Michael Hannon. On a fucking whim. That was never going to happen, not in his fucking lifetime anyway, and certainly not in Michael Hannon's. But he hoped it didn't come to that. But Jimmy knew he needed to be shrewd, crafty, he had to find a way out of this that would leave them both with their egos intact and their friendship still strong.

Imelda woke up to no one and nothing, and that was just how she liked it.

The radio was on, as always, she kept it on twenty-four hours a day, seven days a week. She liked the sound of voices in the background, she liked the sound of other people's lives, she always had.

As she slipped on her dressing gown she caught a glimpse of herself in the mirrored wardrobes opposite her bed. She looked at herself as always, as if she was observing a total stranger. She marvelled that, even after two children, she had hardly a mark on her skin. But then she saw the condition of her legs and her feet, and knew that soon she would be unable to find anywhere to inject herself. She used her groin most often, and she had also used her neck on occasion. But she was too sensible to use the obvious, her arms. In her boots she could hide a multitude of sins. She always kept her boots on, and she knew that the men she was with were quite happy for her to do so. She also knew that if they found out she was a junkie they would be mortified. They paid her to perform sex acts, but her drug-taking would be seen by these same men as something abhorrent. The hypocrisy was not lost on her.

Imelda went through to her kitchen and began the daily ritual of burning her first hit; she loved the first hit of the day. It was always the most intense, and as she backed it on the spoon and watched it bubbling, she felt the familiar excitement inside her that heralded her first high. The whole process reminded her that she was on her way to oblivion, and it also reminded her that she had loads of gear, had bags and bags of brown so, unlike most junkies, she wasn't burning one armful while simultaneously worrying about where the next one was going to come from. She was always in possession of more than enough for her needs. She made sure of that.

It was a great feeling for her, the knowledge that she had plenty of the only thing she had ever really cared about. That was what money did for you; after all, rich people never had to scratch around for a wrap. That was why they never got found out like everyone else, their habit could be hidden away, like alcoholism. In a nice flat, with plenty of money, they could function quite happily when it was necessary. It was only the poor who got found out; they thieved, lied and even robbed their own to satisfy their cravings. Imelda knew she was what was classed as a functioning addict, she had learnt all about it while on remand. She also knew that, like functioning alcoholics, she was capable of fooling everyone around her, and she did just that.

She looked at the kitchen, it was filthy as usual, but she didn't see that. As she pushed the needle into her groin she sighed deeply and blissfully. She felt the rush as the drug reached her brain and exploded silently, once more numbing her to the world as everyone else knew it. She slumped back in the chair to enjoy her first taste of utter oblivion and, like all addicts, she was already thinking about the next one.

As she sat there, half-naked, her legs spread apart, her innermost body exposed without any kind of care, for herself or anyone else in the world, she smiled widely, finally she was at peace. She was at one with her environment.

Ten minutes later she was up enough to make herself a coffee, and she counted the money she had stuffed into her bag the day before, and then she planned the new day ahead with a meticulousness that even General MacArthur would have approved of.

Mary Dooley was worried, but then she was always worried about something. She was convinced that she was being watched, and even as she let the thought go through her mind, she was telling herself she was being silly.

As Jordanna ate her breakfast, she felt the urge to cry because, as always, that little child left her own food to go cold as she proceeded to make sure that her brother ate his.

Kenneth loved Jordanna, he knew instinctively that she had his best interests at heart. As he grinned at her, his whole face lighting up with happiness, Mary once more felt the urge to break down and weep.

But she didn't, of course, she never cried, at least not in front of people, not any more. She was strong, and she needed to be strong, these two needed her and they *needed* her to be normal, she was the only stable thing in their lives, the only person who they had ever been able to rely on.

Mary walked to the window once more and peered through the nets; the two men she had noticed hanging around over the last few days were now nowhere to be seen. But she knew that they were watching her. She didn't know how she knew that, all she knew for sure was they were watching her every move.

She had already ruled out the Filth, they were not about to let themselves be seen so easily, also, she had done nothing wrong in any way, other than finding people. She was as clean as the proverbial whistle. In fact, the Filth had approached her on more than one occasion to ask her politely if she could locate certain individuals for *them*.

Mary had looked for the people in question, and if they were wanted for sexual crimes, or were known as wife beaters, or if they had left a family behind to fend for themselves, she had served them up. Her little contribution ensured her an easy ride for the future where the Old Bill were concerned. If they asked her to find someone who was what she termed one of her own, she apologised and said that all she could find out about them was that they were believed to have left the country.

She then made a point of alerting the people involved, and they were always effusive in their gratitude. Mary worked in a business where trust and honesty were the main ingredients. The people she would tip the wink to were often more than happy to repay her with the current address for one of her errant customers.

So, being on the ball as she was, Mary knew that if she thought she was being watched, then the chances were that she was. She had already dismissed them as people who owed money to someone heavy, and who knew she would be approached at some point to locate them. They would not have waited so long before confronting her. She had been in that position twice before, and she had talked both of the men down within seconds, pointing out that she was a symptom of their problems, not the cure. She had also had the front to inform them that if anything happened to her, the person concerned would be hunted down like a dog. She knew that she had a good reputation, people came from far and wide for her expertise, and she knew that all the time she could deliver, she was guaranteed a good income.

So these two men, who she knew were watching her, intrigued her as much as anything else. She was now watching out for them in the same way that they were watching her.

Mary poured herself another cup of tea and, smiling widely at the children, she went back to the window to resume her sentry duty.

Michael Hannon was watching Jimmy Bailey as he struggled to find the necessary words needed to out him from his business proposition once and for all.

It was early for Jimmy, just after ten-thirty in the

morning, and he had arrived at Michael's house all smiles and camaraderie. Michael had expected this visit, had been readying himself for it in fact.

He liked Bailey, he was a nice enough bloke and he didn't want to fall out with him unless he had to. Then, of course, he would be forced to fall out with him big time. Apparently Jimmy still couldn't comprehend that he was the alpha male here. Jimmy clearly needed to be reminded that he could only work his businesses with Michael's goodwill and his permission. He had been bloody good to Jimmy over the years and, even though he had looked down his nose at what he had seen as Jimmy's obsession with prostitution, he had been tipped a very serious wink about just how lucrative that business was.

Jimmy Bailey was really raking it in, and that was not something Michael Hannon could let go. If he was scrumping a fucking considerable amount and, from what he had heard, it was fucking fortunes, then he wanted an in. Even though Jimmy had observed all the formalities, for example, offering him the in from the off, Michael had not wanted any part of it, but the problem was that Bailey would now soon be in a much better financial situation than he was, if he wasn't already, and the fact that he was considering going into partnership with Graham Parker was another consideration. Together they would make a formidable team.

Michael trusted Jimmy Bailey, but that did not mean he would still trust him two years down the line. Money, especially large amounts of it, changed people, whether they liked it or not. Money really was the root of all evil. Especially in their game.

So, sipping at his coffee Michael leant against the work

surface and smiling in a friendly way he said gently, 'So, what's the problem, then?'

Jimmy sighed. His dark features were closed now, his face devoid of any kind of expression. 'I don't know how to say this to you, Michael, so I'll just come right out with it.'

Michael didn't move or react in any way at all, he just waited patiently for Jimmy to speak.

'I want a partner, but I want a sleeping partner, I want my partner to be in a fucking coma. I have built this up by myself, right from the off, and I don't know if I can take someone else suddenly having an opinion on it all. Can you understand that, Michael?'

Michael Hannon didn't say a word for a few moments; he knew that whatever he said now would be the yardstick that would be used between them in the future. He knew that he had to think clearly and succinctly before he answered Jimmy, because this man had not asked politely for him to take a back seat, he had just declared outright that he was not willing to share the day-to-day running of the business in question with anyone at all. He therefore had to be very careful as to how he reacted to this state-ment. He weighed up the pros and cons in nanoseconds and, sighing heavily, he opened his arms out wide in a gesture of disbelief and sorrow. 'I don't want to walk into something that you have built up by yourself. You wanted a partner and I am willing to be that partner. If you don't want me to give any input, then I will respect your wishes. All I want is a slice of the pie, that's all, mate.'

Jimmy Bailey felt his body relax, he had not realised just how tense he had been. He knew that Michael had expected to walk in and take over, and he also knew that he had only staved him off for the present. It was not in

Michael Hannon's nature to be a part of anything without at some point trying to take the lion's share. It was the nature of the beast, it was the survival of the fittest. It was also not going to happen, not in his lifetime anyway.

Well, he had managed to calm him down this time, but he knew it was early days yet. At some point Michael Hannon was not going to be so easily placated and that was when the trouble was really going to start.

Imelda was watching her two children with what her mother always described to herself as an unhealthy disinterest. Mary would observe her daughter as she looked at the children she had produced from her own body, and see the complete and utter bewilderment in her eyes. It was as if Imelda had no recollection of carrying them inside her, or the pain of giving birth to them. She had no real care for them at all. She liked to show Kenny Boy off, but that was because he was a big lad, a handsome lad, and Imelda could only ever really bond with males. Poor Jordanna was seen by her mother as a threat, all females were seen as a threat to Imelda. Jordanna was already a beauty, and that was not just the proud granny talking either. Jordanna was stunning, she was her mother's double in many respects. But thank Christ she had not inherited any of her mother's personality. Jordanna was a kind, generous and giving person, and she found it inside her to forgive her mother time and time again for her wanton neglect and for her vicious remarks.

She herself would police her daughter when she visited her children, unable to cut her daughter completely out of her life because Imelda had custody of the children and therefore she only had them because Imelda said so.

Mary didn't think that Imelda would bother with all

that drama again, would probably not try and take them away from her out of spite, she was older and wiser these days, but she was still capable of using them to get what she wanted if the need ever arose.

On the plus side, however, Mary was also well aware that Lance's death was still an open case where a lot of people were concerned, especially the Filth. So she knew that Imelda had to toe the line in many respects because of that, and she was confident that Imelda was not about to have her life turned upside down by two little kids, kids whose lives were monitored by social workers and probation officers. Not that they had been any use the last time. They were fucking useless, all they did was spout shite. If Imelda burnt the poor little fuckers alive they would still try and find the good in her.

But, even knowing that, Mary also reminded herself that Imelda, when thwarted, was capable of anything, would use anything or anyone to make her point, or to force the issue. She was a wild card, and as such she had to be kept close. Like any good enemy she needed to be watched, and watched over carefully.

'Ain't she got weird legs?'

Mary looked at her daughter and, frowning slightly, she looked once more at the television in the corner of the room. It was never turned off, and Mary stared at it for a few seconds trying to work out who her daughter was referring to. All she could see was three men discussing the latest world events.

'What are you on about?'

Imelda pointed at her daughter and said loudly, 'Her, Jordanna, she's fucking weird. Look at her legs, they are two minutes off bandy. I never noticed that before, did you?'

Mary saw the hurt on Jordanna's face and, shaking her

head slowly, she looked at her daughter and said snidely, 'Had a fucking good look at yourself lately? That child is your double, lady, so if she has got bandy legs, then she inherited them from you.'

Imelda laughed at her mother's indignation. 'She's fucking bandy, Mother, you could drive a number nine bus between her legs.'

Kenneth was now watching the two women, he sensed their antagonism, their mutual dislike, and he felt Jordanna's nervousness as if it was his own. He moved instinctively towards his sister, Jordanna opened her arms to receive him, and she pulled him into her arms. They stood together as if they were one, and Mary saw the anger that simple action caused by the sudden dislike in her daughter's eyes.

She hated Imelda when she was like this: petty, hateful, vindictive. She wished her daughter dead at times, and the guilt she felt for those thoughts was terrible, yet she still wished for it on a daily basis.

Imelda was wearing a beautiful navy-blue wrap dress; it was very plain, and it looked wonderful on her slim frame. Her hair was perfect as always, as was her make-up. She wore her trademark boots, but they looked good with the dress; her long slim legs made it possible for her to wear what she wanted and still look good. Her Imelda, her junkie daughter Imelda, unlike others of her ilk, looked as far from an addict as you could possibly get. She was such a strong personality that, even though her life revolved around drugs, she still had the determination and the energy to make sure she was well turned-out.

Mary had to admire her at times, she knew how to fucking con everyone; she looked for all the world like a young girl on her way to work.

'Come here, Kenny, come to Mummy . . .' Imelda was holding out her hand towards him, her whole body stiff with annoyance, and Mary saw the bewilderment on the boy's face.

'I said come here, Kenny. I'm your fucking mother, whatever *she* might try and tell you. Now, come to me this minute.'

She was still holding out her hand, and Kenneth was still standing with his sister wondering what he was supposed to do for the best.

Mary pushed her daughter towards the kitchen. 'Stop it, Mel, I ain't having it any more, I told you that the last time.'

She was still pushing Imelda away from the kids and, as she approached the door that led into the kitchen, she pushed her daughter through it with all the strength that she could muster.

As Imelda stumbled out of the room, Mary looked at the two dumbstruck children and gesturing with her eyes towards the ceiling, they both took the hint and went up to their bedrooms. Jordanna was visibly shaking at her mother's presence, and Kenny was, as always, unsure about who he was supposed to be pleasing this time round.

Imelda, however, was fuming now. 'Fucking push me like that, you're lucky I don't fucking lay you out, you old bag.'

Mary ignored her words, she was used to her daughter's vitriol and she sighed heavily before saying sadly, 'Leave the girl alone, Mel, what has she ever done to you, eh?'

Imelda lit herself a cigarette slowly and with exaggerated nonchalance, before saying loudly, 'What has she ever done to *me*? You ask me *that*, after what she did, after what she caused . . .'

Mary had listened to this same harangue about the child so many times before, and today she threw all caution to the wind as she shrieked in anger and frustration, 'Oh fuck off, Mel, no one believes that she did it, only the fucking no-necks you slob around with. She kept you from getting a fucking serious lump, because I know in my heart that you shot him. I also know that if it had not been him you would have killed someone eventually. You are a great big fucking accident waiting to happen; you caused your father's death, and Jordanna's dad's as well. You cause trouble without any thought for who might be caught up in the abortion that you call a life. That little child, that lovely, dear little girl, has never done anything to hurt anyone in her life. And I swallowed you blaming her for Lance because I'm your mother, and I didn't want to see you go down for years and years. But I tell you now, I wish they had banged you up. Because at least then I would have been spared the knowledge and the public humiliation of you being on the fucking bash, on the game. You leave her alone in future, Mel, or me and you will really fall out. I know you fucking think you can treat people however you want, well, you can't.'

Imelda was, as usual, completely unfazed at her mother's words: nothing affected her unless she chose to allow herself to be affected by it all and then she would act either outraged, deeply angered or, at a push, she was also capable of acting out being desperately hurt.

Mary likened her daughter to a robot; she had no genuine feelings at all, and where that knowledge used to worry her, now she just saw it for what it was. Her daughter's natural personality, if you could call it that. She was a strange girl, and she lived a strange life that consisted of her, and her alone.

Mary had stopped caring about that a long time ago. She loved her, but she had never really liked her. But she was lumbered with her, and she had to accept that.

Imelda was in her outraged mode today, and Mary watched her daughter as she pretended to feel emotions she knew deep inside she was incapable of really feeling. It was all an act, her whole life had been an act of some sort.

'I hate you, and I hate her. You two are so alike, Mother. She might look like me on the outside but inside she's just like you, a bitter and twisted old fucking witch.'

Mary laughed at her daughter's choice of words, she never ceased to amaze her.

'Oh, Mel, I wish you would listen to yourself sometimes so you could see what a fucking eejit you really are!'

Imelda was laughing with her now, and Mary knew that once more her daughter had experienced another of her lightning changes of mood.

Mary shook her head in despair, why did no one else see her daughter for the fucking maniac she was? Why did they always fall for her lovely face, and for the act she would put on for them all? She remembered the psychiatrist in Holloway, he had been deceived within minutes of meeting her daughter, and she had sat back and watched it happen, powerless to do anything about it. She had watched her daughter as she played the victim, then the coquette, and finally, she had played the innocent who was openly enamoured of the man sitting before her. He had not had a cat in hell's chance, and she knew that he probably still patted himself on the back at his success with Melly, as he called her.

'Oh come on, Mum, let's not row any more, eh?' Imelda was almost pleading with her now, beseeching her mother to let it go.

Mary shook her head again slowly, her troubled face showing her absolute incredulity at her daughter's utter disregard for morality, for decency. She put the kettle on and then, sitting at the kitchen table, she opened the paper and concentrated on the crossword.

Imelda chain-smoked and sat casually beside her, giving her the answers to some of the clues as if nothing had happened.

Jimmy Bailey was sitting in the Crown and Two Chairmen pub in Dean Street. He had a large Scotch on the rocks, and he was nursing it with more care than Florence Nightingale. He liked this pub; like a lot of the places in Soho it had a nice atmosphere about it, but then he also knew that unless you were a Soho person, these places could seem like the arse end of the world. It was about knowing where you were, and who was who. As he sipped his drink, his eyes were watching the door. Every time it opened he felt his heart stop in his chest, and when it wasn't Imelda coming inside he would relax once more. He annoyed himself when he waited for her like this, for just a glimpse of her, just to satisfy his need. He just had to see her sometimes, not to touch her, or talk to her even, just see her face, nothing more.

Jimmy knew that if he wanted her, he could line up with the rest of them and pay her, and he knew that she would give him the same service she gave everyone else. But he also knew that she had somehow got under his skin and, even knowing everything that he knew about her, he still couldn't shake her off. So periodically he did this, he sat and waited in one of her regular haunts, just so he could look at her.

He knew that his obsession with her was not healthy in

the least. But he also knew that he could not do anything about it. He would look at her for a few minutes
and then he would leave, his thirst for her slaked for a
short while.

Jimmy loved Imelda in a strange way, not her as such,
but the image he had always had of her, the image that she
represented to him, and to everyone else for that matter.

With her long, blond hair and her wide-spaced blue
eyes, she looked like the girl next door, only she was a
better, newer, more improved model. And he wondered
over and over again why she was the only person ever to
make him feel like this. Why it took a whore, and a dangerous whore at that, to make him understand what real love
felt like. He hated her for what she was, and hated himself
for still wanting her, even though he knew she had been
under more men than a public latrine. But no matter what
he told himself, the fact remained that he still wanted her,
ached for her, in fact.

As he was drinking the last of his Scotch she came
through the door. She was alone, as always, and she was
already well gone, her eyes told him that much, though to
the layman she just looked sexy. Her stoned eyes just made
her look even more desirable, they were softer somehow, a
much deeper blue. It was the dilation of her pupils, they
gave her the look of innocence.

Jimmy saw every man in the place give her a once-over,
and he chastised himself for the spurt of jealousy that
coursed through him, and reminded himself that any one
of the men in here could possess her body if they paid the
price required. And he even got a cut when they did. She
would do whatever they wanted, and she would do it
willingly, and with a good measure of experience; she
would see that they had the time of their life.

He hated himself for waiting to see her, for being reminded that she was only in here between jobs, and that at any moment one of his cab drivers would pop his head round the door and beckon her outside to take her to her next punter.

As Jimmy placed his glass on the table he saw that she was watching him now and, sauntering over to where he was sitting, she lowered herself into the chair opposite him. 'Long time, no see. How are you, Jimmy?'

He smiled then, and Imelda saw how good-looking he actually was when he wasn't scowling. 'I'm all right, and yourself?'

She shrugged. 'I'm always all right. I am lucky really, I take every day as it comes. I just go with the flow.'

She was laughing at her own wit. 'What you drinking, Jimmy? I'm buying.'

Jimmy watched her as she got the drinks in, saw her natural femininity at work. She had been graced with a poise and a dignity that was somehow all her own. Providing she didn't open her big trap, of course, then the whole illusion disappeared in seconds.

But as she was now, he saw only perfection. Her long, slender hands, her wonderful bone structure, her lightness of movement, the fluidity of her limbs as she walked back towards him. Placing the whisky down on the table, she raised her own glass at him as if in a toast. 'I knocked the Jack Daniels on the head. I drink vodka these days.'

He nodded at her, unsure how he was supposed to answer, like her he was remembering their last encounter. Which was why she had felt the need to bring up about the Jacky D.

'I feel awful about that time, you know, when we went to your flat.'

Jimmy shrugged dismissively. 'It's in the past, forget about it. I have.'

She grinned then. 'I wish I had forgotten it. Fucking hell, you aimed me out that door so fast it's a wonder I never burnt a hole in your carpets.'

'Look, Mel, I was out of order that night, I was rude and a bully, but it had been a bad day all round, you know. And you fucking skagging in me toilet didn't help.'

Jimmy gulped at his drink, feeling the burn as it went down his throat, wishing he was meeting her for the first time ever, wishing that she was just a girl, a normal girl.

Imelda was laughing now. Her nasty side was always there, underneath the surface, waiting to come out. 'Your face! It was a fucking picture. But I was so nervous I needed something to calm me down. You know, I actually believed, right, that *we* were on a date or something. How fucking mad is *that*? I went into the john to sort me head out. Because in your car, as we drove to your place, it all went quiet, do you remember? And I felt as if we were, I don't know how to explain it, I felt as if we were, you know, like a proper couple or something. I don't know why I'm telling you all this, but I just wanted you to know that I understand why you lost the plot with me. And of course, if you remember properly, that was the night Lance died, wasn't it?'

Suddenly Jimmy had the distinct impression that what Imelda was saying to him was somehow loaded, like she was accusing him of something. She was still smiling at him with that wide open smile of hers, the smile that made her look like a normal person. Like a nice girl. A girl you would be proud to bring home to meet your mum and dad. But he knew that the smile was like everything else about her, a sham. The smile was not even real, she used it for her own ends. He was heart-sorry for her then, sorry that her life consisted of sly digs, innuendos and the constant pursuit of drugs. He was wondering why he had made the mistake of talking to her, why couldn't he just be content with looking at her? It was so much easier if she didn't get the opportunity to actually open her mouth, or air her opinions.

'I can't help wondering at times, you know what I mean, Jimmy? I wonder sometimes, especially late at night when I'm on me own, that if you had not lost it like you did, and if you hadn't dinged me out on to the street like you did, I wonder if maybe, just *maybe*, poor Lance might still be alive.'

Jimmy felt his face freeze, felt the controlled hatred that was the real Imelda, and he knew that she had enjoyed every second of his attention, and was revelling in the obvious discomfort that her words had caused him.

Pulling himself together, he smiled lazily and, picking up his drink once more, he said with as much revulsion in his voice as he could muster, 'Correct me if I am wrong, but are you saying it was you who topped him then, and not your little girl? That if I hadn't slung you out like I did, but decided to go *slumming* for the first and only time in me life, are you saying you would not have gone home and, ergo, Lance would still be in the land of the living instead of being well planted?'

Jimmy could see how the pupils of her eyes had widened, and he knew that was caused by fear this time, he saw the way her jaw tightened as she gritted her teeth. He knew that he had struck a chord somewhere inside her, and he also knew that whatever thoughts he might have harboured towards this woman, they were gone now. Were over with. Finished.

Imelda Dooley was fucking poison, and a dangerous poison at that. But he was well able for her, and she knew that now almost as well as he did.

'I knew you were fucking lying all along, knew that only you would have been cunt enough to blame your baby, a little child for crying out loud, for your mistakes. Even the Filth had their suspicions, didn't they? Your mother told me that herself.'

Jimmy shook his head dramatically, laughing at her with a mixture of derision and disgust. 'You are scum, and even though I've always known that, until now I had always tried to give you the benefit of the doubt.'

He leant forward in his chair until his face was inches from hers. 'Now, fuck off. You're a fucking slag, and if you ever approach me again in a public place, I'll break your fucking neck, lady.'

Imelda knew that she had done a wrong one, knew that Jimmy was not as soft as she had believed, that he did not have a secret crush on her any more and, worst of all, she knew that he was capable of doing exactly what he had promised.

She saw the naked hatred in his eyes and knew that he saw the truth of the situation with Lance as if he had been present in the room with them. It wasn't often that her instincts were wrong, but it seemed that this time they had been seriously wide of the mark.

As she was attempting to rise from her seat Jimmy grabbed her arm roughly. 'And, by the way, you are out of the business. If all my girls came down with fucking galloping crutch rot overnight, I still wouldn't give you the time of fucking day. You treacherous fucking whore.'

He slammed her back into her chair with as much force as he could muster, then standing up, he looked her over once more as if she was so much dirt.

Then he walked out of the pub, his back straight and his head finally clear. She was like a fucking disease, and he had cured himself of her at last. He felt a lightness come over him as if he had just been let out of prison.

And it felt good.

Really good.

Chapter Thirteen

'I used to worry about you at one time, did you know that?'

Jimmy Bailey laughed at Mary's seriousness. 'What on earth for?'

Mary felt embarrassed suddenly, but she knew she had to finish what she had started. So, taking a deep breath she said quietly, 'I honestly believed that you had a soft spot for my Mel. I know it sounds mad but I really did believe that for a long time. I hoped you might have been the man to sort her out, even while I worried that she would destroy you.'

Jimmy felt himself starting to flush, knew that Mary was more than aware that she had guessed rightly and he also knew that she was aware that somewhere along the line, Imelda had fucked it up for herself as usual.

'Me and Imelda? Are you fucking sure?' He was laughing, was pleased that the laughter sounded genuine. Wondered at who else might have sussed out his secret. 'No disrespect, Mary, but I ain't that fucking hard up.'

Mary didn't answer him. She just looked at him with

those deep-blue eyes that seemed to have been passed down to all her children, and her grandchildren. He wondered briefly if she ever saw her own eyes looking back at her, if she noticed that she had given them all her finest feature.

'I don't know where you get some of your stories from, girl. But I can tell you this much, Imelda and me have more chance of getting a dose of clap off the fucking Pope than even sitting in the same room together without fighting.'

Mary smiled, but she was sad at his vitriol and she could not disguise that fact. She also knew that it was pointless trying to make anything even remotely sensible come from this conversation. So she took a mental step back, and sighed knowingly; still, she knew that she had to let him realise that she knew the score, no matter what he might say to the contrary. 'Well, I'm glad we got that sorted out anyway.'

He didn't laugh as she had intended him to, and she didn't laugh about it either. In fact, they were both left out on a limb. They were both embarrassed by her words, and even more so by the truth that lay behind them.

Jimmy wished he knew how to make everything better for Mary. He wished he could take her in his arms and comfort her for all the losses she had endured, and for all the sadness she had been forced to confront. She had started swearing like a merchant seaman these days, curses speckled even her most mundane of conversations and he knew her bad language was nothing more than a form of self-preservation. She used the foul language that she hated as a way of keeping people at arm's length. She had a cross to bear that Jesus himself would have been hard put to carry for as long as she had been forced to.

He admired her, he really did admire her. She was just an old dear to most people, and to the majority of men he knew that meant she was beneath their radar. Once a woman reached a certain age they became invisible to the male population. What they didn't know was that Mary Dooley had the knack for finding people who did not want to be found. She was fucking phenomenal, she had a network of old dears who she had known for years. She knew the mothers of every major Face in the Smoke and beyond and she would find out from them where their sons were, who they were working for, and then she would casually sneak in the name of interest to him or his associates and, if the name was someone they knew, she would be given the full SP on them. She never wrote anything down either, kept it all in her head, even the phone numbers that she procured for him. She knew she could be raided at any time, and she made sure that the Filth would find nothing at all, not a fucking brass razoo. So when Jimmy saw some of the newer, younger Faces unwilling to even give her the courtesy of a nod, he would feel his blood boil, and he would then take it upon himself to give the little bastards a lesson in criminal etiquette. Namely, that she was not only the widow of a man who they would all aspire to be, but she was also one of their most respected and distinguished collectors of interesting information. He would then ram home how she was respected by the hardest of men and that she was on an earn of Olympian standards. He loved to see the looks on their faces when he revealed that to them. He would watch the recipient of his wrath as they digested his information, and if they were shrewd enough to listen carefully, and change their attitude, he knew he would keep them on. If, on the other hand, they looked at him as if he had just shagged a fence panel in broad daylight, he knew they were not worth a wank. Then he knew that they were just biding their time till they saw what they would eventually perceive as the big time. That consisted of either drug-dealing or bank-robbing, neither of which they would go into with any kind of finesse at all, therefore guaranteeing that their eventual capture would be sooner rather than later. He was sorry to see a good lad go to the bad because they were too stupid to see that respect had to be earned and that the game they were in would not be learnt overnight. But a lot of lads were susceptible to quick earners.

Jimmy hated to point out that the really good drug-dealers had been at it from their teens, and good bank-robbers, who were rarely caught, were only so good because, like doctors, teachers and nuns, real bank-robbing was almost a fucking vocation. It was something that was inherent in the person concerned from their childhood, was almost like a talent. It was something they had inherited and understood as their future, their only real interest in life. Anyone who was willing to spend months casing a joint, watching its daily grind, and planning how to exploit its many weaknesses, was capable of getting away with it. Unlike the robbers who went into their local post office with a sawn-off and the unfortunate belief that the gun alone would ensure the cooperation of the people involved and who, through bad planning and bad timing, were captured within hours or days, and who were suddenly looking at a twelve-stretch.

The real bank-robbers, who were naturally good at it, were well able for the trials and tribulations that being on the rob often ensured. They kept a low profile and didn't even attempt to use the money they had amassed for at least eighteen months. By that time they had made a point of distributing it to as many different locations as possible. Real robbers enjoyed the chase, enjoyed the planning, and knew that the outcome would be to their advantage.

The other side of this coin though, were the young men he tried to mould, who if they had been of the real robbing persuasion, would have already knocked off their first bank job long before they came to his notice. He was given their names and their CVs by their fathers, who all saw him as someone who might just be able to mould their boys into half-decent debt collectors, and with that in mind hoped he would then turn them off the rob. The men saw him as someone who would at least give their sons a grounding of sorts, and the opportunity to make themselves a living that was not going to get them an eighteen-year sentence. A sentence that they were ill equipped to cope with, as they had not even been on holiday without their parents, let alone banged up in a nick.

When Jimmy sent the majority of these boys packing, they didn't even have the brains to realise that, from their fathers' point of view, he was the last-chance saloon. They were the ones who would mention their fathers' names at every available opportunity, and that always grieved him, because they were so fucking dense they didn't even have the nous to get on in life by their own ticket. They saw their fathers' names as enough for them to get what they wanted from life. How sad was that?

In fairness, he was pretty easy-going in many respects, but if they didn't have the brain capacity or the good manners to know that someone like Mary Dooley was deserving of not only their respect, but also their time, then they were no good to him. A real debt-collector had wonderful manners, was capable of charming a mother out of her house so they could get access to her son, or talk a dutiful wife into giving them her husband's whereabouts. A debt-collector would use his deference and his humility without question, and would only use violence as a last resort. They would only harm someone if that person was fool enough to disregard their veiled threats, and their attempts at civility. Once that was gone, the person involved deserved all they fucking got. It would then be open season; after all, he had a living to make like everyone else. And, under his personal tuition, the violence, when it did finally arrive on the said borrower's doorstep, would be of such outrageousness and of such controlled hatred that the person concerned would think very carefully before he would chance getting a second instalment.

Jimmy mentally shook his head at the stupidity and arrogance of the majority of the male population. They were so foolish, they never believed that anything bad could happen to them. When it did, they acted like fucking teenage girls, complaining and moaning.

Mary was smiling at him again, a real smile this time, and he understood that their contretemps was over and done with.

'Did you find Dicky Mullen?'

She grinned then. ' 'Course I did, but I also found out that he ain't being hunted for a debt. He is being located for a *grudge*. So you tell *whoever* it is that wants him I expect a fucking decent drink on top of me usual before I open my trap.'

Jimmy laughed at her, as he always laughed when she took it into her head that she was not being paid enough for her information which, of course, she wasn't.

She was right though, he had to admit that to himself. A grudge was completely different to a debt. A grudge was personal, and that meant the person being hunted was aware of his situation. Also, if a grudge was brought to them, it meant that the people involved had exhausted every other avenue known to them. She was literally their last resort.

So she was right to demand a decent wage; after all, she had achieved in twenty-four hours what they had not managed to achieve in months or, in some cases, years.

'I'll sort it out, Mary, don't worry, mate.'

She shrugged nonchalantly. 'I ain't being funny, Jimmy, but I know me worth, mate. Unlike that daughter of mine, I have always known me worth and it has always been far more than anyone has been willing to pay, even my old man. The father of my children. And that is why I fucking hold the bastards to ransom. I get my due in the long run, and I make sure that I get it and all.'

Mary was suddenly on the verge of tears, and he knew that she was lonely and frightened and still unable to comprehend how her life had been ripped apart overnight.

'I look at my Mel, and I wonder what happened to make her like she is? What the fuck did I do to make her into a fucking junkie? And, as if that ain't bad enough, she's a cold-blooded, vicious, treacherous fucking whore. She breezes in and out of the kids' lives, and she hates little Jordanna whereas Kenny Boy, well. He's like her personal little boyfriend, and poor Kenneth, God love him, is about as much use as a chocolate fucking teapot. He lets her do whatever she wants with him, he is so scared of offending anyone, God love him. He doesn't see her as everyone else does, he only sees the gifts she brings him and the sadness inside her. She is so good at the sadness bit, Jimmy, I mean, in all honesty it's fascinating to watch her work.

Even I fall for it, and I, better than anyone, know what she is capable of.'

Jimmy was sorry for her, and he also knew that she understood his attraction to her daughter better than he did. He also knew that she had hoped that he would take Imelda in hand and make her into a nice person somehow. Never mind that Jesus Christ himself would be hard-pushed to perform a miracle of that immensity.

'Look, Mary, you have two choices as far as I can see: you either swallow your knob and accept Imelda warts and all, or you do what we both know is right. You cut her out of your life like you would a fucking cancer, and in doing so, you can give those poor kids a chance at a decent upbringing. She will taint them, and you know that's true. She taints everything that she touches. She is a junkie, and if that was the extent of her fucking problems we could all cope with her. But she is a fucking Looney Tunes into the bargain, and you know that as well as I do, Mary. She is a wicked, vindictive piece of shite who relies on you to make sure she has a home of some description to return to when the fancy takes her and when the people in her world have had enough of her, have had enough of her hatred and her underhandedness. Look on her as the treacherous cunt all druggies are deep down inside. She would sell her kids at the drop of a hat if it meant getting what she wanted. You know that.'

Mary knew Jimmy was referring to Jordanna's part in the shooting now, knew that he had the same thoughts as her about what had actually happened that night.

Jimmy watched the changing expressions on her face and knew that Mary would never be the same kind and generous person she had once been. It was too late for all that now. Circumstances had dictated otherwise. He sighed then, sorry for his words, sorry to have hurt her feelings.

Mary nodded her head slowly, aware that everything he had said to her was the truth. Over the years she had become very close to Jimmy Bailey, and she knew that those feelings were reciprocated. He looked on her as an honorary mother, and she saw him as her honorary son. In fact, she thought more of him than she did of her own sons. They were a pair of fucking idiots, her so-called sons. Both were pussy whipped by their wives, and as for the fucking wives! Well, she had to say, in all honesty, that if her sons' idea of marital bliss was being dictated to by a couple of screeching harridans then they had achieved their objectives. And Brendan had only agreed to get married to keep that woman quiet. She could have understood it if they were a pair of good-looking babes, but the beauty gene in their families had obviously skipped a generation or two. And, worst of all was that they were bosom buddies; the wives were like clones. But then she understood that much at least, birds of a feather and all that. These days she only saw them when they needed money, and that was far too often for her liking.

Jimmy Bailey smiled at her gently and said sadly, 'What a pair we are, eh, Mares? But, on the bright side, at least we are in a good position. We earn a decent crust and we don't owe fuck all to anyone.'

Mary laughed then, her face shining with delight as she answered him with another old East End saying. 'My old man always said, you can pick your friends, boy, but unfortunately you can't pick your family.'

'If you could, Mary, would you be content with your lot or would you trade them all in for some newer versions?'

Mary stopped laughing then, and looking him directly in the eyes she said honestly, 'I'd trade all mine in a heartbeat, except for the grandkids of course.' Then, after a few minutes of silence she said honestly, 'But then again they are still babies, aren't they? Who knows what the future will bring for me or for them? One thing I do know, though, with my Imelda as their mother they had better learn to develop a thick skin. She is bad enough on her own, but once the kids at school find out about her those two will be like lambs to the slaughter. Especially little Jordanna.'

'At least they have got something going for them, Mary. You. And, if push ever comes to shove, they know that you will always be there for them.'

'We'll see. All I know for sure is that I am frightened for them. I know that they will never be given an easy ride.'

Jimmy shrugged then, annoyed at her defeatist attitude. 'Whoever got an easy ride? What can't kill you makes you stronger, and me and you both know the truth of that fucking old chestnut.'

Mary laughed once more, but her heart was already broken by the cross those two little children were going to have to bear for the remainder of their lives, especially Jordanna. If only her Imelda would leave, would go to another part of the country or, even better, go to a completely *new* country. And, while she was there, she hoped against hope that her daughter would somehow meet with a fatal accident. She hated that she often fantasised about her daughter's death, but it kept her sane, and she also believed that the fantasy would make the girl's demise much easier when it finally happened. Because she knew her daughter would not make old bones. Her lifestyle would see to that.

*

Imelda was sitting with two girls of indeterminate age, who were both blessed by mother nature with overly large bosoms.

Imelda was genuinely impressed, she knew that God was good, and that when He had endowed these two with their enormous knockers, He had only done so to ensure that the humongous tits supplied would be guaranteed to stop people from looking at their ugly faces. She was laughing to herself at her own wit.

The elder of the two girls, Jacqueline Basin, was watching Imelda warily, everyone knew that she was a fucking nut-bag. She was capable of anything, capable of picking a fight with her own elbows if the fancy took her, and she was more than capable of winning the fight, of course. She was a real loose cannon, and she was also capable of extreme viciousness if she felt she was being disrespected in any way, shape, or form.

As they waited for their next customers to arrive they sipped cheap wine and chain-smoked cigarettes. The room they were in was small, decorated with deep-red paint, the walls, the ceiling, even the doors. The air was heavy with the scent of cheap perfume and cigarette smoke, the only light came from a lava lamp that was placed on the floor by the window, and the only noise was from a portable TV that was rarely tuned into any of the stations for any length of time. It was like watching the programmes through a snowstorm, but no one really minded. The chairs they were settled into were plastic, cheap, and very uncomfortable. It was a miracle that Imelda was willing to sit there for any length of time, at least that was the private opinion of Miss Basin and her friend.

They were at the lowest end of the market, and she

knew that for a fact. The massage parlour where Jacqueline had worked before coming here had more class about it, this place catered to the lower echelons of their society. This was strictly a quick fuck and home to the old woman kind of establishment. Imelda Dooley was far too good-looking for somewhere like this really. She should be out on a real earn, and if Jacqueline had been blessed with her looks she knew that was exactly where she would be.

Caroline Jones was short, dumpy, and devoid of any-thing even remotely pertaining to an IQ. She was a really nice person though, devoid of any kind of jealousy or bitchiness, and she was always ready for new people, new friendships, or for just plain chatting. As she looked over at Imelda Dooley, saw her smart clothes, her lovely hair and her perfect make-up, she finally found the courage to ask her outright the question that had been plaguing her since she had started work here. 'Why on earth are you working here, Imelda?'

Jacqueline Basin nearly passed out with fright at her friend's inquisitiveness.

Finally, Imelda grinned and, making a face that said very plainly to anyone who could see it, *Are you stupid or what?*, she said gently, 'Why do *you* work here?'

Imelda seemed genuinely interested in the girl's answer. Caroline smiled, and answered her question honestly and without any inkling of the danger she was actually in. 'I work here because it's local for me, I only live down the road, it's warm, and I'd had enough of standing around Shepherd's Market last winter. Fucking freeze your drawers off there, mate. But by the same token, *you* can pick and choose where you want to work, surely? You're lovely, and you still got that fresh skin that men like, and your legs are fucking fantastic. If I looked like you I'd be straight up the West End, mate, on a proper few quid, not fucking dossing down here with these low-lifes.'

Imelda thought about what the girl had just said to her, and she knew she was just putting her wise. She knew herself that she should have more fucking respect for herself than to work in a cheap creamery like this place. Most of the clientele only had the money for a wank.

But then, to her, money was money, and a punter was a punter. She had no care for what they looked like, smelt like, or dressed like. Prince of the realm or a fucking tramp, they were all the same to her. As long as they had the money agreed, she did not give a flying fuck. But she knew that if she wasn't careful, she would end up selling herself short once too often.

She had lost out on fucking Bailey's cabs, they had been told that she was now *persona non grata*, she had been well fucking eradicated from Bailey's hit parade. Even though she had been one of his most popular girls, had been requested over and over again, he had still aimed her out of it. And she knew it was because of her big fucking trap. But she had really believed that he had a thing for her, when he had fucked her off that day she had decided that it was because he fancied her, but had lost his guts at the last minute.

She had been well up for him as well, after all she had wanted the bloody job. He had threatened to blackball her then, but she had not believed him capable of it. She had thought he was just using empty threats.

Well, she knew different now. Jimmy Bailey had turned out to be a vindictive little fucker. But she knew she could work a lot of better places than this if she wanted to. The big hostess clubs would kill for her, she knew that. But she didn't want to waste half the night talking to a fucking punter, making sure he bought the requisite two bottles of champagne and the pack of fifty cigarettes, and only then could she get him off out of it into a hotel somewhere. It was too much like hard work. And for what, a hundred quid? She would rather do five blokes quickly at twenty each than spend hours making conversation with a complete fucking oink, and even then she had no guarantee they would cough up the readies, nine times out of ten the poor sap had already been fleeced of most of his earnings. By then the fright at his predicament would kick in, and that was what would leave her with nothing more than a paltry hostess fee. No way was she going to chance that.

She *chose* to work in this place because, like little fatty here, it was convenient for her. She was not like the other girls, she saw what she did from a purely monetary level. As far as she was concerned, a punter was a punter, she did not care either way.

But the girl's question had caused her to question the logic of her situation. After all, she *was* a very good-looking girl, and she knew that was true without a shred of vanity. She knew she was really good-looking, beautiful even.

Her looks meant nothing to her on a personal level, and she knew that sometimes when she took on certain punters they were amazed at the fact that she was willing to fuck them at all. Let alone for a measly twenty quid, or thirty quid if she felt so inclined.

Imelda found that she was suddenly mulling over the girl's query, was straight enough this night to see the logic of what was being said to her. Deep inside herself, she knew that she was worth much more than this, had the means to make *real* dough from her looks.

Smiling widely, she said to Caroline, 'I think you're

right, you know. I should get meself into a club of some sort. But I hate the idea of hostessing, all that energy you have to expend, and you still don't know if the cunt will weigh out for a fuck at the end of it all, and you can sit there for three hours for nothing more than a fucking hostess fee. Do you know of anywhere else that's a guaranteed earner?'

Jacqueline was nervous of talking to Imelda on a one-to-one basis, but tonight she seemed so nice and so friendly that she said timidly, 'Have you tried Basil's cabs in Soho?'

'Who's this Basil then?' Imelda sounded intrigued, but also she sounded bored, disinterested; it was how she communicated with other females. She didn't know how to be genuine with women, she had no real rapport with them. She only knew how to connect with men. Males. Punters.

Jacqueline laughed in abject disbelief. 'You telling me you never met Basil? He runs loads of women, but he does his real earners out of his cab office. He would fucking love you, girl, and I ain't just saying that either. He can be a nasty bastard, but he lets you earn, you know. I know a girl who works for him, she is really young and really pretty and he sort of handles her personally. He has a good few of his own personal earners, girls he takes a special interest in, until they lose the first flush of youth that is.' She was obviously speaking from her own bitter experience.

'Is he a pimp then, by any chance?'

Jackie and Caroline nodded their heads, completely unaware of the sarcasm directed towards them both. They nodded in a sad and defeated unison, trying to help her in their own way, even though they could not help themselves.

'But that's the strange thing with Basil, you don't have to go with him sexually in any way, he is happy enough to get a cut from your wedge. He supplies the punter, and the cabs.'

Imelda nodded, finally interested in what they were telling her. 'I like the cabs, I like that whole fucking set-up. I was really fucking stupid, I only went and picked a fight with Jimmy Bailey. I was on a real good earn with him and all. But he is a right fucking tart. He didn't have to fucking out me from the workplace, but he did. The piece of shit. But I like the sound of this Basil, he sounds more like my cup of tea. Do you have a phone number for him or anything?'

They gave her his address and his numbers happily, both relieved to think that she was not going to be competition for them in the future.

'Just be careful how you treat him, he comes across as a pussy cat, but he can be a ruthless bastard if the fancy takes him.'

As Jacqueline finished speaking, a young man came into the room and he smiled widely at Imelda, as they all knew he would. He had what was commonly referred to in East London society as a mouth full of dog ends. His teeth were literally rotting in his head. He had acne and he was sour smelling from his job on the dustbins and the fact that he was loath to jump in the shower, or submerge his skinny frame in a bath. He was the pinnacle of their clientele, and he stood before them like a dilapidated gladiator. He was sure of a warm welcome, after all, that was what he was paying for.

Imelda stood up then, and she stretched lazily, she was advertising herself, knew that she was the best merchandise he was going to ever get his grimy hands on. She saw the hope and desire in his eyes then, smiling broadly at the two girls she said gaily, 'It's all yours, ladies. I think I need to have a chat with this Basil person, don't you?'

As she left the room she heard the young bloke say peevishly, 'Now Cinderella's gone to the fucking ball, which one of you two ugly sisters wants to do the business on my knob?'

She could not help laughing as she heard Jacqueline's voice as she answered him loudly and with deep indignation, 'Oh, fucking charmed, I'm sure!'

Basil Payne was thirty-five years old, and he looked it. He was glad about that, because he looked fucking great for his age anyway, as far as he was concerned.

He was a big man, black enough for his needs, with a full head of dreadlocks that would put most real born and bred Jamaicans to shame, and a set of white teeth that made the Osmonds look almost poor.

He had a white mother named Nancy, and his father was, by all accounts, an African prince from the Gambia named, of all things, Gideon. Fucking Gideon. Those fucking Catholic missionaries had a lot to answer for, if you asked him. And, as for the African prince part of the equation, Basil was what was classed as seriously *sceptical* as to the truth of that. It was a recurring story that he had heard once too often from boys just like him. Boys in his position, half-breeds, with the same guarded disbelief as him. He had come out of his speculations on the subject with a deep sorrow for his mother, and also a deep anger at her eagerness to believe such utter shite. His father had bullshitted a child into the world, at least that was what Basil believed anyway. After all, he was that child.

Gideon had met up with his mother for one week, and

one week only, after promising the sixteen-year-old girl that he would marry her. He had loved her, and she had let him, believing that this was the man who was going to look after her for ever. But unfortunately, as often happened in these cases, he had done a bunk one morning, leaving Basil's poor old mum with a bellyful of arms and legs, and the unenviable task of telling her ex-army sergeant father that she was not only in the family way, but the culprit was as black as Nookie's knockers. She had finally told her father about the baby, but she had left the rest of the story until after the actual birth. One look at his grandson, however, and the need to explain had not been necessary after all.

Her mother had nearly dropped down dead with what she had called shame. Her father had never spoken to her again, and all her belongings were left at the hospital with a note saying that she was now dead in their eyes.

She had a ten-day lying-in, then she picked up her little boy and, just two months shy of her seventeenth birthday, she had somehow created a life for them both. She had stood by him at a time when having a black child was deemed so desperately bad, so wantonly brazen, most girls would have happily given their child up just to keep the peace where their families were concerned. Basil knew how hard it had been for his mum, his loving, kind and, at times, bewildered mum, because he had experienced the inbred racism of most of the people around him at first-hand on more than one occasion.

Consequently he loved his mum like he loved no other woman. He knew now that had she let him get taken away, she would have been welcomed back home with open arms. Would have been welcomed back into the fold that was her father's world. A world of bullying and of doing the right thing. Without him to care for, she might have been in with a chance with her parents.

But, as she had always said to him, how could she have walked away from her son, her own flesh and blood? The love of her life. Her only *real* family.

Basil knew better than anyone what she had gone through because of his colour and his illegitimacy. But his mum had weathered it, and he had been determined all his life to make sure that she would have a bit of a rest up, a bit of love and caring to repay her for every slight she had been given, for every insult she had endured. He knew that she had gone through hell to give him what she saw as a chance at life.

And he had succeeded in guaranteeing her a bit of the old rest and recuperation, had made sure she got the best that life could offer. He was as rich as Croesus, and he loved to see his old mum, who actually wasn't that old really, living the high life at his expense. She deserved it.

He was a pimp, but only by accident; he had a lot of fingers and he made sure that they were all buried right up to the knuckles in a lot of very lucrative and oftentimes very dodgy pies. But, like most over-achievers, he had been determined to make a name for himself so he could stamp out the labels pinned on him from early childhood.

As he sat in his office and monitored the calls coming in, he saw to it that his girls were well looked after, and looked smart. He insisted on that, he liked to think that he was delivering a service of sorts, and as the majority of the men who used him were quite well-to-do, and not frightened to weigh out a few quid for what they wanted, he made sure that the girls he provided were pretty, well dressed and immaculately presented. That included make-up, nails, etc. Once they had lost the first flush of youth, started to look like they were on the bash, he saw to it that they were relegated. Like West Ham, his home team, he loved them, but he knew they were not going to win any prizes.

Basil's main girls were big earners and, as such, he expected them to look the part. He believed that you got what you paid for, and he saw to it that his girls were paid very well.

He walked all the new girls through their first steps personally; he told them how to sit, how to smile, and how to get the cash first. After all, as well-to-do as the men might be, they were not above welshing on the deal once the dirty deed had been performed. Money upfront was a requisite for any brass worth her salt.

Basil also explained that if they ever got ambitious for the punters' watches, or had a terrible urge to get their pieces of shit, lowlife boyfriends round any houses they had visited to rob the men concerned, as was the norm for some of the women on the game, he assured them that, should that ever happen, he would burn their faces off with acid, and that he would then personally cripple the ugly fuckers they were trumping.

The threat was enough for the girls he employed. He already had his reputation as a person who held grudges, who paid out righteous retribution for any wrongs he saw against him, and he knew that was enough to guarantee their cooperation.

It was shit really, but the girls believed it, and he knew that there was now a little story that went the rounds about him burning a girl's face off many years ago.

As if. He knew that the story was embellished and told over and over again to every new girl he employed. It was a fucking joke; if he had done something like that it would not have been whispered about. The truth never was.

But it had made the girls in his employ wary of him, and the men that lived off them even warier. They were all terrified of him turning up at their houses with a bottle of acid, and a baseball bat. So he had learnt to live with it.

But he was not a bad bloke really, most of the girls liked him, and he played fair by them and, even though some of the women were now basically his property, he saw that as no more than an occupational hazard. Most of the toms in his employ were not happy unless they had a pimp they could turn to in times of trouble, and he was now that pimp. Unlike most men in his profession, he did not sleep with his employees. He would rather shag a table; who would want someone who had been bagged more times than a Hoover?

The girls were quite happy to go out and earn, but they were even happier that he was seen as their protector, and that was enough for the most of them. It ensured that no other pimp was about to come on the scene and take the girls as their own or, if he was being really pedantic, what he saw as his property. Not that he would ever say that out loud of course. But he knew that the inference was there. His girls needed to feel he was protection against other men. He was prepared to do that much for them.

Basil was sitting in his nice comfy chair, in his nice comfy world, when Imelda Dooley breezed into his office and, as he looked her over carefully, he knew before she had even opened her trap that he had just been the lucky recipient of a major earner. He knew who she was, as well, and even that knowledge didn't put him off.

'You're Basil I take it?'

Basil grinned then, and his large white teeth made him

look much more genial than he actually was. 'You can take what you like, darling.'

Imelda knew when she had scored a hit, and she also knew with her inbred gut instinct that this man was capable of giving her a really good earn. And that, as often happened, he was bowled over by her looks, by her body, and by her absolute disinterest in him as a man, even as a man who could further her career.

An hour later, after a short chat, and the unearthing of a mutual respect that astounded the both of them, Imelda was immediately on her way to a guaranteed hundred quid and, one hour and forty-five minutes after that, she was on her way to another hundred quid.

She was thrilled; Imelda liked money, she liked to be in possession of it, and she liked to know that she could score any time she felt like it. She knew that she was now in the real earning saddle, and she also knew that Bailey would be fucking gutted that she had gone on to bigger and better things than his poxy little penny arcade. She knew he would be fuming at her defection. At least, she hoped that he would, anyway.

Basil's set-up made Jimmy Bailey's cab rank look like fucking amateur night. Basil had the brains to make sure that the girls he used for his big-spending clients were all clean and well dressed. They could be mistaken for office workers, or as businesswomen in their own right. When they walked into a flat in Belgravia, or a large house in Kensington, they did not look out of place. They were primed by Basil to make sure they wore very good and very expensive underclothes. Imelda loved it, she loved the smart dressing and the nice surroundings, she loved the money she was earning and the ease with which it could be removed from the pockets of her very wealthy clients. She offered extras that the men involved had only ever dreamt of before she had come into their lives; she made their basest desires suddenly seem like no more than a reasonable request.

Imelda also liked Basil and his easy-going ways, and she liked that he was not impressed with Jimmy Bailey's set-up.

She was shrewd enough to know from the off that he was well aware of who she was, and she was also aware that he had since asked around and knew that Bailey had attempted to blackball her. She had eventually told him the truth of what had happened, and he had laughed with her at what he had called Bailey's provincial fucking mindset.

She knew that Basil watched her and that, like most men, he saw her as eminently fuckable. That had been her cross to bear all her life, and she had seen fit to use it for her own benefit when necessary. She also knew that as a brass he would see her as beneath him socially, and that suited her fine as well. She didn't want to marry the cunt, just earn off him.

Imelda wanted regular amounts of dough, and her gear as and when she desired it. Unlike most people, she was actually very happy with her life on the bash, it suited her, and she had no real ambition for anything different. She knew better than anyone that with her looks she could have married money, could have guaranteed herself an easy life. But she had no desire to be married to anyone, she *liked* her own company and her chosen lifestyle. It suited her, and she was happy as she was. She just lived for the chemical highs that she created for herself on a regular basis.

But Basil had great plans for her; she was unaware of

them as yet, but he knew that once he explained his ideas to her she would be receptive.

He saw her as someone delicate, feminine, so it was a shock to actually hear her talk. She still looked like a young girl, and yet he knew she was the mother of two children, and that she was the proud possessor of a temper that was by all accounts on a par with Vesuvius when it had erupted and decided to destroy Pompeii. Basil liked her, she had a strange honesty about her, and he also knew that she was not a fool in any way.

She knew how to pass herself off in good company. And she was his main earner within weeks. She was requested over and over again by his biggest clients, his wealthiest punters, and Basil knew that she was more than aware of her popularity. He wanted to expand his business, and he felt that she was the perfect person to help him to do just that. And, if it fucked off Jimmy Bailey in the meantime, then all the better. He wouldn't trust Imelda as far as he could throw her, but he knew that if he played fair by her, she would be more than willing to reciprocate.

Chapter Fourteen

Jordanna was laughing loudly at her brother's antics, and as they chased each other around the garden, Mary found herself laughing with them. If only life was always this simple how much easier it would all be. The sun was shining, the breeze was cool and the kids were genuinely relaxed for once. They were so happy with her, they had almost forgotten their mother's lunacy, her completely fucked-up existence. If only their mother was as interested in their welfare as she was, life would be much more pleasant for all involved. But she wasn't, all she saw was the next few hours, her next score, her next adventure. As she lit herself a cigarette, Mary pondered on this latest development in her family unit. A unit that was destroyed now, was devoid of anything even resembling care and affection.

Brendan's wife had recently birthed twin boys and, as expected, Mary had gone to see them at the hospital, thrilled at the new additions to her family. She had been received very coolly by the woman of the hour. Mary had felt the atmosphere almost immediately and knew that she was not as welcome as she would have expected, especially as she had been bankrolling the fuckers since day one.

She had not been invited to hold the new babies, or even to touch them in any way. The fucking treacherous whore had more or less mugged her off completely. She knew she was being set up, knew that they thought she would weigh out more for access to her new grandbabies.

No chance. She had just about been pushed to her limit by them all; at least with her daughter, as big a fucker as she might be, she knew that her kids were *actually* her kids. That Imelda had actually birthed them was never in any doubt. Unlike her parenting skills, of course. Mary herself had seen them both arrive, emerge from the child she had pushed into the world many years earlier. Daughters were a touch in that respect. With her sons, however, and allowing for their choice of wives, she was not so bloody sure about the parentage. And she knew that they were trying to force her into abandoning the children produced by Imelda in favour of theirs. As if that was ever going to happen! The fact they had no care or sorrow for the children in question spoke volumes as far as she was concerned anyway.

Well, she was well able for them in the future. The next time they were on the fucking borrow, on the want, she hoped they found a bank mug enough to entertain their stupid fucking ideas and their pathetic excuses for all their debts. Because she was finished with them all now. She had felt about as welcome as a nun on a stag weekend, she had been treated like an outsider, like the enemy. And this by the very people who expected her to see them all right for a few quid. She didn't even know the names of her grandsons.

Mary knew that Mel's kids were seen as the opposition,

were seen as the only people she seemed to care about, and she knew that, to an extent, that was probably very true. They thought that Mel being the cause of all the family's trauma should have guaranteed her and her children's exclusion. Mary understood that to an extent as well. But she also knew that she was open and willing for love from *any* of her children's offspring. She knew how important family was; after all, family had been her life for a long time. All she had cared about, or thought about. But the need of these two poor babies was like a canker with her sons and their respective spouses. They saw these children as standing in the way of any children they produced. They did not seem to understand that their sister's kids needed her, *needed* someone they could rely on. Needed their uncles as much as they needed their granny. They didn't understand that Jordanna and Kenneth needed the illusion of normality in a world where their mother's addiction guaranteed them a life of nothing more than abysmal betrayal, interspersed with their mother's haphazard affection, along with her blatant ignorance of them as people, of their lives, or of their welfare.

Poor Jordanna was already accused of being a murderer. Oh, they might dress it up as manslaughter, but it was still whispered about as murder when it was gossiped about. Like mother, like daughter, seemed to be the general consensus. And her sons had not even tried to help her out, had not shown any loyalty at all. In fact, they had distanced themselves so much that she had been surprised to find they were still in the same fucking country. That had hurt, that had really smarted.

Her Brendan was so weak and so childish he put her in mind of an old Irish shawlie. He was unable to even make a decent argument about why he had not attempted to help his sister's children out. Blanking Mel, she understood. But the children needed their uncles and yet they had acted as if they were the spawn of the devil. She had asked her sons for their help just once, and they had not even bothered to answer her calls. Her Brendan was completely manipulated by the ugly mare he had tied himself to, and by his misguided idea of loyalty. He was terrified of his wife, and so he should be, she was the size of a fucking all-in wrestler, and she had a face like a boiled shite. She was all scowls and unspoken insults, and that was when she was in a good mood. A seriously ugly bitch both inside and out, and a real bully as well. She had the art of the martyr off pat, and she played it for all it was worth.

Well, she could fuck her old man over with her constant carping till the cows came home, but where she was personally concerned, the ugly bitch could take a flying jump. Mary had told her as much on the quiet, with words of practised friendliness but determined insolence. She had told her that the twins were welcome, but as they had two parents her daughter's children would have to be her priority. She had been told in no uncertain terms that she had to choose, and she had chosen there and then. She had been advised that their children would be far better off if they did not have to mix with Mel's children, who they felt would be a bad influence. She had shaken her head slowly and sagely, and she had then told Brendan and his wife they were right. She was sorry that she would not see much of the boys but she understood their predicament, as they must understand hers. She had hinted that the money she was normally so liberal with could be much better spent elsewhere and had taken her leave from the hospital with her usual brusqueness.

She was willing to sit this all out, wait till the twins reached manhood if necessary, before she might finally manage a relationship of some kind with them, because then *they* would want to see her, would wonder about her, would be sick to death of the parents that God had seen fit to force on the poor little buggers in the first place. And that would be enough for her. That was all she could hope for in the future. Especially as it was so tough for her nowadays. She already had enough on her plate with Mel's brood, with the fact that she was now bringing up more children when she should be enjoying life as a granny, should be enjoying just seeing them periodically, not taking them on as her own.

She had not overstayed her very thin welcome at the hospital. She had swallowed the insults from her son's mother-in-law, who had acted as if she was an intruder, every word and look telling her that she was not welcome. Which obviously, she wasn't.

Mary knew that her son's mother-in-law saw her as a threat, even though she had been bankrolling the boys since day one. Well, *fuck* them all now, the new kids included. No one treated her like a mug; she was now so hurt and angry by their treatment of her that she was never again going to lend them a fucking halfpenny. She knew that Brendan would be round within weeks on the borrow, on the ponce, for money that they never had any intention of paying back anyway. She was just throwing good money after bad, and she knew that she had to make a stand at some point and now was as good a time as any. Let them get proper jobs now that the scrapyard had fizzled out. She was in a position to buy her grandsons' company, should she desire it, but she was not about to do that just yet.

She would not buy her sons' affection, or put up with their wives' contempt. She was far too shrewd, and far too busy with the children who genuinely needed her for all that crap.

She knew that Brendan and his brother Gerald Junior really believed that it was their *father's* money they were taking from her anyway, that she *personally* had no right to any of it. They were convinced that she wasted it all on their sister, the junkie, the whore, and her children. She was actually earning more than any of her boys would ever earn in their lives, and she was earning it on a regular basis. Her old mum had always said that everyone had their niche, something they were good at. They just had to find it. Well, she had found hers: ferreting out people's most private and personal agendas. This had made her a rich woman; her husband had provided, but she was making more money than he had ever done. She had a respect now from her new career, that she had never had when she had been no more than the wife of a repo man. People gave her the time of day, made a point of hailing her when she walked the streets. Yet she knew that she was still seen by her sons and their wives as a fool, as even worse than that, as the *enemy*.

She had brought up three fine children, or so she had believed for all those years, but what had she actually spawned? Two boys, sons who were chronically lazy, who were unable to grasp even the simplest of concepts. Who had been fed and cared for, firstly by herself, and secondly by their father. A man who had once described them to her as thick and thicker. She had laughed with him at that description, but deep down they had both known it was the truth, that there was not one ounce of real gumption in either of them. Gerry had known, as she had, that the boys' only real chance at any kind of life was if they worked alongside their old man. And they had, and they had convinced themselves that they were the dog's gonads. They still didn't have the sense to understand that without anyone to tell them what to do, they were useless. Which was why they had lumbered themselves with a pair of female bullies who, unfortunately, didn't understand the whole set-up either.

Her boys had both taken on complete arseholes and, as far as she was concerned, that was their prerogative, but they had alienated her and she was now quite happy to return the favour. Her disappointment in her children knew no bounds, and her sons' actions were not something she was prepared to dwell on. They were a pair of complete wasters and, as such, they were now beneath her contempt. She had needed them after the first of her tribulations, had expected the boys to stand by her and their little sister. But they had done what they had always done. Stepped back, and waited to be told what was the right thing to do, waited for someone to take over so they did not have to even think about anything, let alone make it all right. Her sons had turned out to be such a let-down, and she knew that their treatment of her had basically been the cause of her active dislike of them both.

Then there was her only daughter, the girl she had loved and cherished like no other. She had been the cause of her own father's death, and her lies had been believed by so many people that they were still assumed to be the gospel truth by hordes of people even to this day. Imelda had brought about so many heartaches, had been the instigator of so much pain and hurt. And now what had happened to her?

She had seemingly fallen on her feet once again, she

was earning fortunes, even though she was not on the bash any more, at least, not publicly. She had taken on the mantle of the pimp now instead, arranging for other people's daughters to go out on the bash instead. Her daughter actually saw this as a step-up in the world, as some kind of *promotion*. But all that aside, Mary guessed that her daughter probably still had a few private customers on the side, it was the nature of the beast that she would always put the earn first.

Imelda was so busy these days that her children did not see that much of her, and for that alone, Mary would be eternally grateful. She knew that could only be a good thing, for the kids anyway. Imelda was a strange entity: was a ponce, a leech, she would sell her kids for a wrap, and yet she could still come across as Marjorie Proops when the fancy took her. It was all about how you were perceived by the rest of the world, and it had taken Mel a long time before she had sussed that out.

As Mary watched the children growing up more each day, and wondered at how they would cope with their uneasy starts in life, she wished that she could keep them like this for ever, as innocents, as her babies. As she smoked her cigarette, she watched the two children as they sat together now, their heads close and their conversation obviously of a very confidential nature. They were so lovely, were such good kids, and she prayed every day that neither of them would inherit anything from their mother except maybe her good looks. She also prayed that they would not inherit anything from their uncles either, especially their cowardice.

The doorbell went, interrupting her thought. As she answered it she was shocked to see the two men that she had noticed hanging around and about, and as they smiled at her she felt a terrible feeling of foreboding. She had been expecting this to happen at some point, and she had assumed that it would be because of the car crash that masqueraded as her daughter's lifestyle. But even though she had convinced herself that she was more than ready for it, now the time had come, all she knew was that she was genuinely frightened and, worst of all, that she was without any real care for her only daughter's welfare. All she cared about were the children that she now felt were more her flesh and blood than the woman who had birthed them. And she was quite happy to fight the whole world if needs be, fight until she had nothing left inside her if it meant they would be all right. Would be safe.

'Basil, will you fuck off!'

He was laughing loudly at her anger, and she knew that he was not going to stop, no matter what she said, or how angry she became. And she could get really angry, she was even capable of frightening *him* when her anger finally became unmanageable. Basil sat on the edge of his desk, and looking at her seriously now, he said quietly and without any animosity, 'I know you don't like me mentioning this, but I feel that I have to, Mel. You are on the needle much more than is safe for you. Than is safe for anyone on the stitch as such. You are a skaghead, and that breaks my fucking heart. You are useless to me out of your box and you know that, darling. Just try and see the massive error of your ways. Listen to my advice, I am trying to help you.'

Imelda was not even smiling at him now, in fact she was outraged by his bare-faced cheek. He was a massive fucking dealer, and he relied on people like her for his livelihood. She paid his bills, and saw to it that he had a few quid on the outside.

But she also understood that it was much easier for people like him if they didn't personally know the people who bought his merchandise. That he actually tried to make sure that they were not in any way personally involved with him. She had tried to ensure that he did not feel any kind of responsibility for plying his trade to her and her friends. But he was still more than prepared to give his bad opinion of Mel and her lifestyle without a second's thought to the part he played in it. Now he was suddenly trying to tell her that she was a fool for her lifestyle, was no more than a mug for taking drugs. Drugs he had been providing for her on a regular basis. She was genuinely angry with him, at his hypocrisy.

This came across in her voice, and her physical demeanour. 'It's none of your business what I do or don't do, OK? Can you take that on board? Can you fucking keep your big conk out of my private business? Do you think you could manage that much, eh?' The sarcasm was evident to anyone who could hear them as they argued.

'Oh stop it, Mel, you are looking really rough lately, and you know it as well as I do. Now, I don't give a toss what anyone does in their spare time, but your fucking habit is affecting your work, and that means, Mel, that it has become *my* personal business. You are now no more than a fucking junkie in my eyes. You are the equivalent of one of those fucking idiots you see sleeping on benches. Basically that means you are on my personal shit list. Once I have to think about you as a real person, Mel, you are finished. You are over with.'

He shook his head in exaggerated sadness. 'You had better get it sorted and get it sorted sooner rather than later, all right? I have heard a whisper that you owe money, for your gear, and it ain't like you can't afford it, is it? You are on a decent earn so pay up, because if you bring trouble to my front door I'll bury you myself.'

Mel knew Basil meant what he said, and she also knew that without him she was probably finished. She was more than aware that her lifestyle was vital, was important for the punters she now serviced, was what guaranteed her all of her goodwill, such as it was. She not only sent the girls out to punters, she made a point of taking the more lucrative men for herself. She knew that Basil was more than aware of that, and she also knew that, as long as she ran everything smoothly, he would overlook anything that was not what he would class as a piss-take. After all, if they got a capture, she would be the one to take the main flak, it was her who would be put in prison.

She was the fall guy, that was the reason for the madams in the first place. The Filth didn't go after the main providers, they were happy enough with the middle management. She also knew that if something like that did ever happen, she would sell him up the river so fast he would not know what had happened to him until it was too late. She had been away before, and she was not about to let that happen to her ever again.

She had used her own daughter as a fall guy that time, so what made men so fucking stupid that they didn't think that they might be no more than a stepping stone for the woman involved? Especially when it concerned pimps, they should know better than anyone that they were the most despised people on the planet after rapists and paedophiles.

'I might be on the needle, but it does not interfere with my job, and you know that. You are more annoyed because I can earn, really earn, and you can't fucking get a touch near it. But by the same token, Basil, I earn you a wedge not just from me, but off of the girls in my charge.'

Basil was laughing now, really laughing at her. 'I am trying to help you, girl, but you are too fucking *dense* to see it. All I am saying is, don't skank at work. If *you* do it, the other girls will think that they can do it as well. And it's drugs that will eventually get us nicked, darling, that will eventually put us all in the clink. That'll be the reason for a police raid: drugs. Once they get their foot in the door for the Persian rugs, we will then be done for just about everything they can come up with, from procurement to living off immoral earnings, and that will all be down to you. So you either sort yourself out, or you can fuck off. But either way, you keep your lifestyle outside of this workplace, OK? This is your last chance, Mel. We had an incident last week where one of the girls was so out of it she started a fight with her punter, a very rich and very respectable banker. He was not a happy bunny, and neither was I. But, worse than that, Mel, you have been garnering debts all over the Smoke for your fucking habit and it's finally coming back to bite your arse. Get it sorted, and get it sorted soon. You are living on borrowed time; and you're being talked about as a loose lip. If I find out there's any truth in that, then I will have to sort you out personally, don't make the mistake of thinking that I am an easy target. You'd better get your act together, and you'd better start paying off your dealers.'

Imelda knew she was being given a serious warning, and that if she had any kind of brain she would heed it. And, for a few moments, she allowed Basil to have the upper hand, knew that she was on the wrong side of this argument. She knew that if she wanted to keep her position she had to go along with whatever he said, had to take it all with the minimum of fuss. So she did just that. After all, self-preservation was her middle name.

Imelda realised that Basil was not interested in her any more, that she was now classed as nothing more than an employee. She also knew that her use as a weapon against Bailey had backfired, and that she was now only worth the reputation that she had garnered as a brass and as a murderer. Basil had only been enamoured of her because of her reputation, and the fact that he had a real problem with Bailey, as did she. Bailey was the person who was calling in her debts, she knew that. It had to be him. It was how he was getting his own back on her. Well, let him. She owed him fuck all. In her mind she was blameless, she had nothing on her conscience where he was concerned. She would wait, and think, and then use whoever was weakest to ensure that she was all right, that she was safe from harm. And she would use anyone within her orbit to see that happened.

Smiling at Basil sadly, as if she was broken-hearted at his words, his threats, she saw him smiling back. He was not about to be had-over, and he was especially not going to be had-over by the likes of her. Of that much she was certain.

'I think you are after my daughter.'

The two men stepped inside her house. They were large, very intimidating and, in fairness, very respectful. So far.

Mary ushered them into the kitchen, she was sensible enough to know that they were not going to be fobbed off with excuses or threats of any kind.

These were men who would be heard, and they would be heard no matter what they had to do to ensure that.

She knew she was much better off letting them explain themselves in a calm and friendly manner, they were not the kind of people to be ignored. As she looked at the two men as they stood in her pristine clean kitchen, Mary felt the first real shudder of fear wash over her.

Shutting the kitchen door behind her, she smiled lazily at the two intruders and, taking a deep breath, she said with as much force as she could muster, 'You don't scare me, so let's cut the fucking crap and get down to the basics. What do you want?'

The elder of the two men smiled with a deep sadness, then he pulled out a chair and, motioning for her to sit down, he somehow took over as the head of her household.

She felt his strength, his arrogance and knew that he was there for something very serious, and very dangerous. For the first time in years, she was frightened.

She could hear the children as they chatted together in the next room, and the sound of their voices made her predicament even more terrifying. She was frightened they would use the children to make her tell them whatever it was they needed to know.

The older man seemed to read her mind because he said kindly, 'They are safe, Mary, we aren't fucking thugs.'

He watched as Mary Dooley physically relaxed at his words. He saw her body deflate, and her shoulders drop at his kind words. She was an old lady, he was not about to harm her unless he absolutely had to. Even then, he would not do anything to her personally. That was why he had his trained chimp with him. But, either way, he was determined to get what he wanted from her before he left.

He sat down opposite her. He liked the décor, liked the cleanliness of the place. She was old school, like his own mother. The kitchen smelt of use, of fresh vegetables, cooked meats, coffee and fried eggs. It was reminiscent of the home he had grown up in. It had the distinctive aroma of safety, of caring. It made him feel nostalgic for his boyhood, for his youth.

As he sat down opposite Mary, he really hoped that he would not have to force her to talk to him. He *liked* her, but he was not worried about any comebacks should he feel the need to put undue pressure on her to achieve his objective.

She was a feisty old bird: she had her own little reputation, and he knew all about her struggle to bring up her grandchildren. He liked that about her, respected her for her loyalty; he only wished his first wife had been so inclined. So, in his mind, he was only there as a formality. He had to make her understand that if he left empty-handed, which of course he wouldn't, someone else would come in his place, and that person would not be as friendly or as generous as he was. Fear was a great leveller, he had found that out at a very early age.

He made a point of not talking to Mary or even acknowledging her for a long while. Instead, he sat opposite her and watched her calmly as she waited for him to tell her what was going on, tell her why he was in her home. But he didn't say a word. He knew the longer he kept quiet, the sooner she would demand to know what was going on.

Denny Broadbent was leaning against the kitchen sink. His heavy body looked cumbersome in the small space. He had the face of an overblown cherub and the physique of a boxer. He looked like he could hurt someone, and the fact of the matter was that he was more than willing to hurt anybody for a price. He had large eyes, and a cruel mouth. He also had the nonchalance that Mary's husband had looked for in his workforce. So she was more than aware of the man's reason for being in her home. She knew he was the one she needed to watch. She knew that he was the paid muscle and, if asked, he would be quite happy to hurt the children if need be to get her to discuss whatever it was they wanted to discuss.

She also knew that her standing was such that these two would not be there unless they were in the employ of someone of serious renown. Someone who had no interest in anyone outside of their particular orbit unless they could be of some use to them.

Lighting another cigarette, Mary blew the smoke out slowly then, shrugging, she asked in a friendly manner, 'Well, tell me what you want, I ain't a fucking mind reader.'

Leaning forward in his chair, James Marler said sarcastically, 'I had actually worked that much out for myself.'

Chapter Fifteen

'Your daughter has upset a lot of people, and she has done so without any real care for the trouble she has caused.'

Mary shrugged. The man was not telling her anything she didn't know. Her attitude told them exactly how she felt about them as well as her daughter.

Once more Marler was impressed. Like his old mum, Mary was a game old bird. She would fight with the police until he had managed to escape through the back door. It was a loyalty thing, she had hated what he had done and that he was to be arrested, but she had still felt the need to protect him. It was inbred in the Irish and in the East End women. If they were a mixture of the two they were doubly loyal, and doubly argumentative.

'My daughter is nothing to do with me and, for the record, I think that is a given for most people in this locality. I bring up her children, I do the best I can, but she is not my responsibility. I don't need this shit. So say what you've got to say, and get yourselves off out of it.'

She was good. She was frightened all right, *terrified*, in fact, but she was still game enough to fight her end. She had not offered her daughter's address to them, even though they already had it; she was not to know that. Though he suspected she would assume they were up to spec with all her daughter's movements. It wasn't like Imelda was a wilting violet, she made her presence known. Yet this woman was still protecting a child who had been the cause of every ill that had befallen her. Nature had a wonderful way of making women into fools. Mothers, wives, daughters, they all seemed to possess a loyalty that the person in receipt of that said loyalty rarely deserved. This woman was still protecting a daughter who had used her and everyone around her like a Filth used a grass. With a deliberate and calculated dislike, and with no care whatsoever about her well-being. It was common knowledge that Imelda would sell her kids for an easy shoot, so her mother would not be on the top of her list where loyalty was concerned. Imelda was a junkie and, like all junkies, she had no soul. The skag took care of all that; once the drugs took over the user was lost. But James also knew that the majority of users had never been a hundred per cent anyway. All the dopers he had ever come across had been missing a vital ingredient; they were selfish, insular, horrible people. They were solely interested in themselves and their lifestyle. They were basically loners who only really mixed with other junkies, anyone outside of their manufactured reality was without any interest to them. If only this woman could understand that her daughter as she knew her was long gone, that the girl she hoped and prayed would one day return to her, was dead and buried this long time.

She was a nice lady, really nice. Marler liked her, as he had known that he would. Not that he would allow his feelings to interfere with his judgement, or with his job of work. He would get his henchman to bury his own mother alive if the price was right. Thankfully his mother had never upset anyone enough for them to call him in to put the hard word on her. The irony being, of course, that his reputation would guarantee his mother an easy pass, no matter what she did anyway.

Life was a bastard all right, he knew that better than anyone. He also knew that for this woman, her life would never be the same again.

'Your daughter has fucked over one too many people, and we are here to ask you if you would be so kind as to mention this fact to her. She is a user, in more ways than one, but then you know that. But she is also a fucking piss-taker. Tell her we want the money she owes. If we don't get it in the next few days, we will take it out on all her relatives. That includes you, by the way. We are also here to make sure that Louise Parks gets her fair crack of the whip where Jordanna's concerned. Her great-uncle, Davie Driscoll, has just come home after a rather lengthy stay at one of Her Majesty's holiday camps. Eighteen years on the block can give a man a seriously bad attitude, as I am sure you can understand. So we have been watching you for a long time, and we know *everything* about you. Tell your *cunt* of a daughter that if after all this, we still have to give her a tug, it will not be in a friendly way. Tell her we want the money she owes, but mostly we want her to understand that she needs to show a bit of respect for other people. Namely Louise Parks, who has been fucking outed from her granddaughter's life, and that is something that needs to be addressed. You explain to Imelda that now Davie Driscoll is back on the pavement, she had better start toeing the fucking line. Louise Parks has a brother whose gratitude for her constant loyalty towards him while banged up knows no bounds. She wrote to him, visited him, and she always made sure he had a few quid in his bin. I am here, Mary, as the good guy, I am trying to make you see just how perilous your position could be should you decide to ignore my advice. Davie wants to be a part of his great-niece's life, and what Davie wants, Davie gets. He has taken it on himself to see that Louise is given her due where her only grandchild is concerned. He wants his great-niece in his life, and he wants you to make sure that happens in a friendly and decorous manner. He also wants your fucking daughter to pay her dues and, by doing so promptly, she will show the world at large that he has made an impression on her. If he has to do that with violence, he will. Explain that to Imelda in words and syllables she might understand. There's no room for negotiation here, she has to do as she is told.'

Mary already knew that she was beaten, the fact they were on her doorstep, in her face, had told her that this was a serious matter. She knew it was not going to be something that could be sorted with a few words, or a few quid. She was too well connected to worry about trivia. So the news of her daughter's latest fuck-up was not entirely unexpected.

Mary had known in the deep recesses of her mind that whatever this was all about it was going to cost her emotionally or financially; she had accepted that much.

It was the knowledge that Davie Driscoll was once more out and about and mixing with normal people that was the real shocker. He had been a friend of her old man's, and she had grown up with him. They had gone to the same school, she had made her first Holy Communion with him. Davie was a seriously dangerous man, and he had done a seriously hefty lump inside. Like all the people in her world, she knew that money and property would always guarantee the big sentences; rob a bank and you were put away for the best part of fifteen years, rape or murder someone and you would be out within six. It was a fucking scandal.

Poor Davie had been unlucky enough to be caught at a time when the Filth were cracking down on the organised crime that was the staple of the London underworld. That the police involved had been the recipients of a large percentage of the money earned was neither here nor there, they had been under enormous pressure to put away the known criminals, had even leaked their arrests to the newspapers. Their double standards, and their acceptance of the way the world they were supposed to be policing was being run, had suddenly been questioned, their part in allowing it to exist in the first place had suddenly become common knowledge. Without the powers-that-be turning a blind eye to their blatant machinations, the known criminals would never have been capable of getting such a strong hold over the streets in the first place. It was like anything else: they needed each other to survive. Then it had all fallen out of bed in a spectacular fashion.

Like the Krays and the Richardsons before them, Davie Driscoll had suddenly become public enemy number one. The police and their counterparts, who had been lucky enough to benefit from the largesse of their criminal associates, were suddenly able to purchase nice properties, expensive holidays, a private education for their children and, more importantly, the goodwill of the men who paid their real wages. These were men who had no real loyalty to anyone or anything, they had taken the bribes and basked in the reflected glory of their friendships with the criminal involved. They loved the association that these men afforded them and had exploited their positions without a second's thought. They had taken, and they had used, and they had never understood that they would never have been accepted into the world of Faces, they were classed as scum from the second they took a few quid. From the moment they became bent Filth, they were despised by everyone involved.

These same men, who had sold out their mates, and their colleagues, were now only too happy to arrest the very people who had made their affluent lifestyles possible. The late sixties and early seventies had not been a good time for anyone involved in the criminal fraternity. Consequently, men like Driscoll, who had weighed out heavily to guarantee their freedom, and who had seen it snatched from them by people who were in their eyes far more bent than they could ever be, were now being rehabilitated back into polite society and were possessed of what they saw as genuine axes to grind. And grind the fuckers they would.

Davie Driscoll had been put away as a youngish man, he had been in his prime. He had lost his wife and his kids within two years of being sentenced. She had gone on the trot with a bloke she had met on Romford Market, and he had not heard from her or his children since. He had *not* held her treachery against her, he had understood her need to have someone at her side. He knew that she had been lonely, had been a young woman, had wanted a life of sorts. He was only sorry that she had been forced to take his kids from him and he wished she had been brave enough to tell him how she felt to his face. He *was* sorry he had to lose his kids. But he was a realist, and he had decided that he had not wanted them to see him once a month behind bars. He knew his wife had been forced to take them away with her, and he understood her reasoning. He understood the fear that an eighteen-year sentence would have on a young woman still in her twenties, still stupid enough to believe in romance and love. A young woman needed a man in her bed, and in her home. So she had left him, and Davie had accepted her desertion because, in a strange way, he had actually admired her for making a clean break.

He had not been allowed out of prison to bury his parents, had not been allowed out to bury his sister's child. He had not been allowed to shit, turn on a light switch or make a phone call without someone knowing about it. He was a very angry man, and he was also a very strong man. Both physically and emotionally. So he had come home at last, and he was determined to right a few of the wrongs he felt were well overdue for a large percentage of the population. He was without the kindness and the care that had once been a large part of his personality; prison had seen to that. A category prison, to be precise. He was the top of the prison food chain for all the good that had done him. He had been locked up for twenty-three hours a day, and he had seen the savageness that was needed to survive in the harsh world of the lifer.

The Davie Driscoll who had finally been released was a very different man to the one who had been put away all those years ago. He was now the proud possessor of patience, but he was also without mercy. He was only interested in getting what he saw as his due.

'You can tell Davie from me that I will make sure that everything is sorted out to his satisfaction, and you can also tell him that I would have preferred it if he had come and talked to me in person. I ain't exactly had it easy over the last few years meself. As for the kids, I have never stopped Louise from seeing them. You can tell Louise to pass that message on to her brother for me. I have to tread carefully where my daughter is concerned, as I am sure you know.'

James Marler grinned once more, he was not a bad man really, and Mary knew that. But if he had been keeping an eye on her for Driscoll, then her daughter was going to be caught up in trouble so perilous that she would be amazed if Imelda survived it. She was not known for her intelligence, or for her foresight. In fact, Davie Driscoll could end up being the making of her. Because, unlike everyone else she associated with, Davie would not let her daughter get away with anything.

Davie was helping out his sister, and so he should, but Mary knew he was also challenging Basil, and anyone else who might be fool enough to try and protect Mel. He was flexing his muscles, and Mary knew how dangerous that could turn out to be, for all of them.

Imelda was looking good, and she knew it. Her hair was freshly washed and set, her make-up was perfect, as always. And she was wearing a new suede outfit that had cost her a small fortune. She had picked up her children from her mother's house, ignored the dire warnings of terrible retribution she forecast for her only daughter at every available opportunity, and she also ignored the *sensible* advice that her mum spewed out so copiously to all and sundry. Especially to her.

The days when she listened to that fucking old bag were long gone. She did not need her mother, or anyone else for that matter. She was not going to let her mother make her feel like she was nothing ever again. She had buried her old self, the girl who had been destroyed overnight by her family, and she was now the person she wanted to be. The person she had always been, who she had tried to suppress all her life. She was happy with herself. She was happy with her way of life and she liked her independence.

Imelda was now strolling down Barking High Road pushing the buggy, and perusing the shop windows like any other young mum. She liked it around here, she knew everyone for a start, and she felt confident among the people she was mixing with. She knew that her reputation preceded her and that she was guaranteed a friendly and warm reception.

She was also meeting up with a dealer she had been introduced to by one of the girls she employed. He was a large Welshman with a killer smile and deep-green eyes that were without any kind of feeling or emotions, but which had attracted her all the same. He was named Jed, he was built like the proverbial brick kharzi, and he was the first man in years to garner any kind of interest from her. She was playing the mother today, the victim, and that was why she had insisted on taking the kids out with her in the first place. Jed had agreed without a second's hesitation.

She sensed that Jed was the type of man who would be bowled over by a woman with kids. He was that rare breed of man, a dealer who didn't indulge personally in his own product. He saw his dealing as no more than a job.

He had given her the once-over, as all men did on first meeting her. She was a looker, and she knew it. After a while, the same men who had eaten her with their eyes avoided her like the plague within weeks of actually being in her company. But Jed, she knew, was already hooked. She had sensed his need of her, knew he was hers for the taking. So she had taken him without a backward glance.

The Driscoll situation and her mother's fear of him *had* communicated itself to her, even though she pretended she wasn't bothered about it at all. She wasn't bloody stupid, even she had the brains to know that if her mother was *wary* of him, then he was obviously a man to be wary *of*. She had heeded the warnings and she had done what was expected of her. She had paid her debts in full. She wasn't a fucking moron, regardless of public opinion to the contrary. She had paid off everyone she owed money to, not that she had told her mother about that. Let her sweat for a while longer.

She had deliberately sourced a new contact for her chemicals because of all the aggravation. That was where Jed came in.

As Imelda walked along the pavement with the kids, she relished the power that she always felt when on her home turf. Here she was well known, was respected in her own way. She was in control of her environment, and she used that to her advantage. Barking High Road was a strange place in many respects, everyone she saw was on a mission. They all had a reason to be there; even the old dears with their shopping trolleys and their headscarves. They were all watching what was going on around them, were aware of what was going on in the real world, their world. The world that was their bread and butter, the world that was never really talked about to outsiders, but had given them and their families a livelihood that Ford at Dagenham could never have afforded them. It was all about keeping yourself to yourself, and understanding how it worked. Once you understood it, which most people did from a very early age, you slipped into the habit of it. You knew instinctively how to survive inside of it and knew that it was not a world that was understood by the majority of the people around you. It was a secret world of nods, winks and a very determined ignorance, that kept you safe and, more to the point, kept those close to you safe as well.

It was the ultimate in the black economy and it was not for outsiders, not for the people who had no standing in the world of real villainy, who were destined to spend their lives on the periphery of it all, those who would always be small-time: thieves, gas meter bandits, shoplifters. It was sad, really, they were the fucking mugs who deliberately attracted police interest. Whereas a real Face would be mortified to have brought that on themselves and, having done so, would be mortified to know that they had brought the same interest on to their friends, families and associates. It was a world where the real Faces were not that well known to the outside world; they relied on the ice creams to take the flak for them, knew that there would always be someone who was willing to become the local bully boy, become so notorious that they would be the first person accused of anything that happened in their vicinity.

It was the way of their world, it was how they survived. For Imelda, it was also all that she really understood. It made sense to her, and not much else did if she was honest. Like the fact that she was not bothered about who knew she had been on the bash. Why would she care about that?

Unlike the people around her, Imelda had no real sense of allegiance; she was without anything even remotely resembling loyalty. She would sell anyone up the river, unless it was a Driscoll or another serious Face, and she knew that better than anyone.

Imelda Dooley was a user, and that was not just where

the drugs were concerned. Everyone who came into her orbit was seen by her as a potential fall guy. Like all addicts, she was constantly looking for the easy option, the easy way out. She was also capable of selling out anyone around her to ensure that her habit and her way of life was not disrupted in any way.

Jordanna was wary of her mother, she knew how quickly she could change from happy and gay to angry and destructive. She sensed her mother was in some kind of trouble, she felt the change in the atmosphere when her mum came into the house. She also knew that poor Kenny was her mother's blue-eyed boy and, instead of being jealous of his place in her mother's affections, she was devastated for him, because she knew just what the woman who bought them sweets, who joked with them and hugged them when the fancy took her, was really capable of. She saw the lifeless body of the man her mother had shot every day of her life. If Jordanna was playing happily with her dolls, or with her brother, she would suddenly be overwhelmed with the vision of her brother's father lying back on her mother's filthy sofa, his face a mask of surprised bewilderment and half his head splattered all over the place, his life's blood pumping out of his body as he tried to understand what had happened to him.

As her mother shoved a couple of expensive shirts behind Kenny's back, pushing him down forcefully so the buggy hid them from view, Kenny tried to grasp what was going on, knowing it was something secret, some kind of skulduggery that was not to be mentioned until his mother saw fit. Jordanna knew Kenny was being used to hide the stolen items from the people who owned the shop, who were thrilled to see Imelda as always. Were all smiles and kind words. Who would never have believed that she was capable of stealing from them, from her own. Imelda chatted to them, asked after their families, their lives, and she left the shop with a smile and a wave, knowing she had stolen the stock that kept the people concerned's heads above water. She didn't care that she had just put a huge dent in their profits, in their livelihood. She had no thought about the people she had just stolen from.

Later, Jordanna watched her brother laughing at Imelda as she showed him her booty; he was already becoming a thief, a taker like her. He was not sensible enough as yet to understand just how dangerous and underhand what their mother did was. He did not understand that she was just using them, and that if they were caught, arrested, she would blame them without a second's thought. Kenneth did not yet understand that he was setting himself up for heartbreak, because Jordanna knew better than anybody that her mother was incapable of anything even resembling love or affection. She used them, as she used everyone. She was not trustworthy and, one day, poor Kenny would have to accept that. She hoped for his sake that it would come sooner rather than later.

As they were wheeled into the pub Jordanna saw a large man with green eyes and a suspect smile walk towards them all. She understood then her mother's sudden interest in her children. But she played the game expected of her, and she played it with a perfection born of desperation and necessity.

She saw her mother hand over the shirts she had hoisted to her latest paramour and she knew that, once more, she and her little brother had already been relegated to the back recesses of her mind. They had ceased to exist and, because of that, her brother was already heartbroken. She hated the woman who had birthed them both with a vengeance that would one day erupt and, literally, cause murders.

But until that day arrived, until she was old enough and strong enough to push her mother away from her once and for all, she did as she had been taught. She smiled and made herself amenable. She had sussed out what her mother wanted from her, what she expected from her. She had learnt that at a very early age, and she delivered. But as she made herself smile at Jed, as she allowed herself to be manhandled by him, placed on his lap and petted by him, as he attempted to use her to get into her mother's good books, she felt what it was to really *hate*. She felt how overpowering that emotion could be.

She also felt the overwhelming sense of desolation that her mother's haphazard affection always caused inside her frail little body. She knew she was incapable of fighting back, knew she was far too small and far too young to say what was really in her heart. So, like many a child before her, she took whatever was thrown her way, and she buried the feelings of anger and hatred at her plight.

At least Jed bought them both crisps and a cold drink, and at least he had the sense to realise that, where her daughter was concerned, Imelda had a problem. He had studiously ignored Jordanna once he had sussed that out, and she had breathed a heavy sigh of relief. Jed was shrewd and, where her mother was concerned, that was not a bad thing.

Jed was drunk, but not drunk enough to be a problem to anyone. In fact, he was one of the lucky few who could drink all day and night and still know what was going on around him. Not that he drank all the time. But since he had taken up with Imelda, he knew he was drinking more than usual. In the last six months he had come to the conclusion that if you couldn't beat her, your best bet was to join her. So he had done just that.

Now they were both the worse for wear, and Imelda was in fighting mode. She was the most awkward, miserable, vicious bitch that God had ever put on the earth when the fancy took her, and even though he knew all that, she still had the power to make him want her.

Jed knew that Basil was fed up with her, that most of the people in her world were fed up with her. Had been for a long time if truth were known.

He also knew that she was not impressed with Davie Driscoll's continued interest in her child, which was something she could not do anything about. Driscoll made the occasional visit and to add insult to injury, for some reason that Imelda could not fathom personally, he had also developed a deep regard for little Kenny Boy. Jed understood why Driscoll had taken to Jordanna like he had, she was a beauty, there was no mistaking that. But, more to the point, she was a real little brain-box. Bright as a button, and with a great sense of humour. She loved her younger brother, and she did the lion's share of caring for him when they were at their mum's. Kenny loved the bones of her, and he guessed, rightly, that it was mainly for that reason Imelda was once more on the poor child's case.

When Imelda was in her cups she would bully her daughter from morning to night, she would say things to the child that were hateful, vicious and demeaning. She would put her down, accuse her of all sorts, and she would enjoy every second of it.

'Leave the child alone, why do you have to pick on her all the time?' Jed would ask. He hated this side of her. As she sat opposite him with her wide-spaced blue eyes and glossy, well-styled hair, she was the antithesis of what most people perceived a drug addict as being. She had stages when she did look dog rough. Then, somehow, she would drag herself up and out of the mire, and she would once more embrace the wholesome, healthy look of a young girl in the first flush of sexual awakening. She was still a real looker, and even though he now knew everything about her, he still could not bring himself to walk away from her.

Jed's sensible head told him that he should run a mile, that he was a fool for wasting his time and energy on a skaghead. He knew that she was using him; he had known for some time that her initial attraction to him had not lasted very long, but his ability to procure drugs had lasted much longer. His attraction to her, however, didn't seem to be on the wane, nor would it, for the foreseeable future. Even her bruised and scabby legs, peppered with the vicious white, raised scars of her addiction, didn't put him off. The only thing that made him hate her was the jealousy she harboured towards her daughter, who was a sweet little thing.

Imelda was now looking at him with the absolute venom that she somehow kept in reserve, only to vent on her daughter. No one else got the same level of hatred as her eldest child. No one else could make her so angry, so furious. It was as if the child made her into a different person, an even worse person than she already was. She loathed her daughter, she hated her with an all-consuming passion that was terrible to behold. And Imelda hated with a passion, she hated a lot of people, and she hated them with a viciousness that was as shocking as it was generally unwarranted.

But her feeling was plain spiteful. Why this shocked Jed so much, he didn't know. He was more than aware of

Imelda's paranoia, her disregard for not only her own well-being and safety, but for others as well, and that included him he knew. He was also aware of her irrational belief that her daughter was somehow the catalyst for all the ills that had ever befallen her, that her jealousy of her daughter was so great it had almost taken over her life.

Jordanna was watching the pair of them from the corner of her eye. She knew that they mainly argued over her. They argued about Jed being too nice to her. They argued over her mother's treatment of her, yet she also knew that her mother would not have been capable of looking after Kenny if she did not come along as well. Jordanna did the majority of the hard work, and she was due to start school in the next few weeks. She was terrified of leaving her little brother alone with their mother without her to watch over him. She had a feeling though that her granny was not about to let Imelda get her hands on him without her there to keep a beady eye on the proceedings. She knew that her granny was as worried as she was about Imelda being alone with her son.

That knowledge depressed her, she knew that even her granny, who loved her, used her to make sure that Kenny Boy was well looked after. No one seemed to care about how she might be treated while all that was going on around her. She was already the recipient of her mother's warped lifestyle, and so everyone assumed she was immune to it all. They all assumed that even though she was nearly five years old, she was capable of looking after not only herself, but her little brother as well.

Jordanna sighed heavily. She felt as if she had the weight of the world on her shoulders.

She wished her granny would hurry up and take them home, take them to their real home. She hated being in this place, hated the dirt, and the stench of her mother's uselessness but, most of all, she hated her mother's complete indifference where she was concerned.

She wished that she could make everyone understand that she was fed up with being the sensible one, that she was desperate to be treated like the child she was. She wanted someone to notice her as a little girl, she wanted to play with her dolls in peace, go to the park, be taken to the zoo or play schools like other kids of her age. She wanted to stop feeling so angry inside, and so sad. She wanted to tell someone how awful her life was when they lived with Imelda because no one saw that she was only a child. She was never allowed to be a child, she was always expected to be the older sister.

Even though she loved Kenny Boy, she knew already that his birth had ensured her own childhood was lost, gone. She had been forgotten about so that Kenny could experience his childhood without too much trauma.

Jordanna watched her mother warily these days, she was never far from physical punishment, and she beat her daughter in a calm and calculated manner that was all the worse because there was no real anger in it. No real reason for it. She was only doing it because she *could*, and because she *wanted* to.

She knew that her mother only took them out to vex her granny, and because Jed asked her to. Jordanna wished she was back at her granny's house, and she wished she was grown up enough to be able to have some say in her own life.

Basil was fuming, and he knew that he had every right to feel as he did.

Even though Mel was good at her job, he knew how

important it was for the girls to be wary of the person who was controlling them all. He hated that she had already slipped back into her usual pattern of behaviour so soon. More to the point, she had also taken it on herself to recruit a lot of new girls.

Unfortunately, she had not bothered to talk to him about any of it, so she was skimming money off of girls he had no real knowledge of. She had not bothered to give him any of their details. Or, more to the point, she had not given him the details of their current client lists either. She had more or less been running a separate business, and the fact she had thought she could get away with it spoke fucking volumes.

Imelda Dooley was a shrewdie all right. He had to give her that much credit. She was a great girl in many respects, she made sure that everything ran smoothly and, even though she was a fucking junkie, she also knew how to function in the real world when it was necessary. She could be out of her tiny mind, but she was never so far gone that she didn't know what was going on around her. In many ways Basil admired her for that. She was the only person he had ever come across who could junk and still function. In fact, she functioned better on the needle than most people in their game did without it. She was the anomaly, the wild card. She was also having him over big time, and he had sussed that out only recently. It was his own stupidity that was really getting his goat up.

In reality he had never expected anything less from Mel. She was always up for the con, always up for the thieve. It was why she was so good at her job in the first place. But knowing that she had been skimming him royally for months still fucking rankled. She must have been laughing up her fucking sleeve at him, and she would pay for that. She would not walk away from this lot. Not this time, she needed a lesson in priorities, and he was just the man to give it to her.

A quiet tapping at his office door caused him to take a deep breath, and forcing himself to calm down he called out loudly, 'Come in.'

A young girl with deep-brown eyes and thick brown hair timidly popped her head around the door. He felt a sudden sorrow for her, knew that she was terrified at what she was going to be asked. He knew also that she would probably answer him truthfully. She was too young to have mastered the art of real lying. Brasses had a whole different approach to lying than the rest of the population. They were forced to learn to lie by the very nature of their profession. They pretended and lied from the moment they went to work to the moment they left. They were liars by nature.

This one, though, had been conned along with him. She was also a real little newey. She was also capable of getting them all banged up if she happened to get herself nicked. On closer inspection she looked about twelve. He felt the anger rise up inside him once more.

He beckoned her inside, and offered her a seat. When she was finally settled in the chair opposite him, he leant on the huge oak desk he had purchased on a whim and, smiling kindly, he said, 'How old are you, love?'

Amy Dart looked at the man who ensured she had a roof over her head and enough money to do pretty much what she wanted to, and she decided then and there to be as honest as needed. That alone told him how green she was.

'Fourteen.'

Basil digested that information and felt the heat of

shame wash over him. She looked younger than that. He knew that he had not spoken to her before now because he had not actually known of her existence. She, though, believed that she worked for *him*. She probably told people that. Bragged about it. Basil was finding it very difficult to keep a lid on his colossal anger.

'Where did Imelda get you from? Were you introduced by one of the other girls?'

Amy shook her head vigorously. Believing that she was doing all involved a favour with her honesty, she said proudly, 'I am the one who has brought in most of the other girls; Mel pays me a fee for every one I procure. I was in a children's home in Surrey, then I ran away to London. I met Mel at King's Cross station. She approached me, offered me somewhere to stay, and warned me about how dangerous London could be if you didn't have someone to look out for you. She was really nice. She helped me get on my feet. So I got in touch with some of the other girls I know, and they came here as well. We like it, and Mel is really good. She looks out for us.'

Amy believed that she was doing Imelda a favour by talking her up to the boss, telling him what a great girl she was. In fact, Amy actually harboured the secret hope that Basil would tell Mel how she had sung her praises.

Basil was seeing the girl as the punters must see her, the heavy make-up that she believed made her look older than her years, but which in reality only emphasised her extreme youth. The clothes, cheap and garish, that caressed her slim frame and made the illusion of childhood even more apparent. Made her seem vulnerable. Just what the nonces were looking for. Amy looked like she was dressed up in her mum's clothes, and Basil knew how alluring that could be to certain people. Basil had no interest in employing girls like Amy Dart though. Girls in their early teens who had been through the care system. He believed that the care homes were the hotbed for prostitution. Most of the girls he employed had been the products of children's homes, care facilities or fostering. He would not touch them until they were over the legal age of consent though, and looked it.

He had seen the young ones off, and he had made sure none of the girls he employed got under his skin. Only one had ever got his attention and he was determined not to let that happen again.

Basil had found out about Imelda's little sideline purely by accident. He had trusted her to run things for him, had known she was more than capable, and had immersed himself in his other businesses, happy to be away from her, and quite content with how she would be running things in his absence.

But then a regular client had mentioned to him that the girl he had requested had been a bit too young for his tastes, and so new to the game that she was still a bundle of nerves. The man in question had laughed it off, but Basil knew he was being told not to make the same mistake again. The man in question was very well-to-do; he wanted a woman, and he expected a woman. Also, if his pastime should ever become common knowledge, he might live down paying for sex, although that would be bad enough in itself. But if it was a little girl he was meeting once a week, that would destroy him completely. And so it should, as far as Basil was concerned. That was a market Basil had never wanted to explore, even though real money was there for the taking. He knew that there were a lot of men willing to pay a lot of poke for the chance to fuck a child. The thought of it going on was enough to make him feel sick with disgust and anger. After the chat with the client he had pondered the situation, as he pondered any decision he had ever made. He had asked around, and he had not been told what he wanted to hear.

Basil had then started his quest for the truth, and the truth had blown his mind. Thanks to Imelda, he now had a reputation as a peddler of children, and as such he had no real protection any more. The police he paid off would not look the other way if this ever became common knowledge. Imelda had dragged him into the sordid world that she loved, and such was her vileness, her baseness, she was willing to trade these little girls in his name. She was willing to hide behind him. Use his good name and his friendship, and earn herself a lot of money and, at the same time, destroy everything he had ever accomplished for himself. If anything had gone wrong, if the girls had been discovered, she would have said he was the boss and, as such, he would have had to take the flak. But he had taken her on and given her the opportunity to better herself. She had been his number two, she had been his stand-in, his namesake. She worked for him, and she had taken advantage of his good nature. Of his good name. Imelda Dooley was fucking scum. She was without any moral code whatsoever. But then, deep inside, he had always known that.

Amy Dart was watching the man before her with the fascination of all children who were worried because they did not know whether they were in trouble or not. She sensed that she was not telling him what he wanted to hear and was sick with fear that he might get rid of her. If he did, where was she to go?

'The house you share with the other girls, who pays for that?'

Amy grinned, her small, even teeth were coated in the yellow custard of heroin and cigarettes, and Basil wanted to scream in despair at what he had inadvertently stumbled into. The house turned out to be a squat in Brixton, and Basil knew it would not have been long before it was raided by the police and social services. He was a hair's breadth from a long sentence and permanent shame. He was only pleased he had found out Imelda's scam before it was too late.

He had trusted her, he had helped her. He had been good to her. She had found a niche with him that had given her a measure of respect. She had then mugged him off without a second's thought, had seen fit to put his whole operation in jeopardy for her own ends. She had not even thought of how her little sideline might have affected him. She was such a fucking junkie that she had not allowed for what would happen to her if he was closed down, what she would do if that ever occurred. She had jeopardised all their livelihoods, and he would not fucking let that one go. Now she was going to find out just how vindictive he could be. She was going to find out just how dangerous the world she inhabited actually was for the people who were foolish enough to take advantage of their betters. Imelda Dooley was going to be made aware of just how far she had pushed him, and shown just how far he was willing to push her back.

But first he had to make sure that Amy Dart and her little cohort were dismissed from his world, that they understood that the mentioning of his name by any of them would result in serious aggravation. In extreme cases, even death.

Chapter Sixteen

Jordanna was nervous, but then she spent the best part of her life being nervous. Her mother's sudden interest in her children would make anyone nervous, let alone a small child. Especially a child who had spent the best part of her life on the receiving end of her mother's whims, her paranoia, or her plain bloodymindedness. Jordanna knew that her mother only turned to her when the rest of the world was beyond her reach. She knew that her mother only needed her when everyone else within her orbit was fed up with her, were sick of her demands, and her mother needed to believe that she had someone who would always care for her, no matter what happened.

Jordanna played the game. She had played the game where her mother was concerned since she had been old enough to understand what hate was, had understood that the majority of people in her world were not capable of anything even remotely resembling love or caring. Although they did understand the power of usefulness, and they made a point of using it, accompanied with either fear or emotional blackmail. Depending on the circumstances.

Imelda's need to have Jordanna there beside her was also larger, for no other reason than that she needed her to watch over Kenny Boy; she was the only person for whom he would do as he was requested without a fight of some kind. Imelda also knew that Jordanna was the only person in the world who she could rely on to keep her son happy.

So Jordanna was seeing much more of her mother than usual. Since she had met Jed, Imelda had taken to playing at grown-ups, and it was not something she was any good at. In fact it was almost painful to watch her as she pretended an interest in her two children that was so forced it was traumatic for everyone concerned.

Kenny was still quite small, but he already knew that he had his mother's love, even if it was a haphazard only-when-it-suited-her kind of love. But it was there never-theless. Jordanna, on the other hand, had to make do with Kenny's adoration of her, and Jed's genuine kindness and gentleness. He was always ready with a hug or a kiss and he made her mother acknowledge her existence. So, for the first time in years, spending time in her mother's presence was almost tolerated.

As Jordanna curled up on her mother's sofa with her little brother cuddled into her arms, the usual stench of overflowing ashtrays and stale lager surrounding her, she made a point of not looking around her, made sure she didn't judge her mother or her lifestyle. She just kept her ears open and she ensured that the dirt and filth that denoted her mother's life didn't affect either of them too much.

Jordanna was used to her granny's spotless home and the cloying aromas of bleach, furniture polish and freshly cooked food simmering on the stove. So the dirtiness of her mother's flat and the absence of baths or even washes, made her feel dirty and unkempt. She was not used to the stickiness of her own sweat any more, nor the sweet smell of her brother's unchanged nappy. He was not even offered the opportunity to use a potty or the toilet. Imelda had no bother with such things. Like she had no bother with proper meals, they had to eat as and when food was available, and Jordanna had to keep in the forefront of her mind that whatever they were given might have to last them for days.

Jordanna had thick blond and lustrous hair that hung down her back like a curtain. She was used to it being brushed until it shone like spun gold, her granny loved it and said it was her crowning glory. Jordanna loved having her hair brushed by her granny, the action itself had proved to her that there was love involved. Jordanna also knew that her hair was really beautiful, was very unusual. People had been remarking on her locks since she could remember.

Yet here, at her mother's, it was tied up and left until she was once more relegated to her granny's house. She was always scratching her head when she stayed here, she felt cooty, as if something was crawling under her skin. She knew, even at her young age, that it was only because she hated being there and hated feeling dirty. As she watched TV with her little brother, she was listening with a growing nervousness to the argument that was erupting in the kitchen.

Jed was angry, but he was always angry about something lately. As young as she was, Jordanna knew that Jed's expectations where Imelda was concerned were so off the wall they were just about impossible. She was never going to be mother of the year, she found it hard to even talk to her kids for more than a few minutes at a time.

Even then she was only interested in getting them to say something to Jed that she thought was hilarious. She got poor Kenny to swear, to sing dirty songs for her. She just wanted them to repeat things parrot fashion and, in doing so, she was entertained for a few moments but, more to the point, Jed was being entertained. Imelda felt that Jed's interest in the kids was all that was needed to keep him interested in her.

He was sometimes a bit too interested in her, and Jordanna knew that her mother was more than aware of this. He would take her into the bedroom, and when it was over Imelda would give her sweets, and then at some point an argument would start and the episode would be forgotten about. She knew her mother felt jealousy at times when she was getting too much attention from Jed. Attention she didn't want, had never asked for. Jordanna knew that her granny didn't like them coming here so often, but was powerless to do anything about it. She kept quiet about Jed, as she did about everything else. It made life much easier for all concerned. Her mother had the edge where their futures were concerned. Imelda knew how to play the game, and she played it without any conscience, or care for her children's welfare.

Jordanna had already found out how important money and power were in her mother's world. She understood just how hard it was without any kind of real money, without anyone in the world to see that you were treated fairly, with decency, with respect. If you had nothing to use as leverage, then you were destined to spend your life doing what other people wanted. Jordanna knew how the world she inhabited worked, and she hated it. But she accepted the inevitable, telling herself that one day she would be grown, and then she would be in charge of her own life, her own destiny. Until then, she had to look out for her brother, and see that he was cared for. Her granny had to swallow her real feelings for her daughter too, and she had to wave her grandchildren off as if she was thrilled at their golden opportunity to be in their mother's care once again. She had to let them go to someone she knew was not fit to look after a dog, let alone two young children.

Kenny was restless, and lying with his head in her lap, he watched the film with bright eyes. It was very late and the film was about aliens who had come to earth and were now killing everyone they could lay their hands on. It was violent and bloody.

Jordanna didn't like it very much, but Kenny Boy was flushed with excitement; between the overload of sweets and fizzy drinks and the violence on the TV screen, he was where he loved to be. Up late, and without any boundaries or guidelines whatsoever. Jordanna was stroking his hair, trying to calm him down, knowing that until he dropped off to sleep she couldn't drop off herself. She would not allow him to be let loose in this flat without her to watch over him. He was too young, and he was also much too reckless. He had inherited his mother's disregard for rules or regulations of any kind. Like her, he felt that if he wanted to do something, anything, then that was his prerogative. He had the same selfish streak that Imelda had, only with little Kenny it was overlooked because he was a child. But Jordanna knew that it was not something he would ever grow out of, despite what her granny seemed to believe would one day be the case. Kenny was ruined already, had been since his birth. He was his mother's son but, unlike her, he had the ability to love back when it suited him.

As Jordanna heard the argument reaching its crescendo, heard the cursing and the viciousness of her mother's mouth, she turned the volume up a little more, trying to blot out the car crash that was her mother's life. But the voices were still audible, and still had the strident angriness that seemed to be the norm in this household.

Mary was like a ship without a rudder. She sat in her pristine home alone and wondered, as always, if the kids were all right without her to take care of them. That they were with their mother was not something she felt easy about; in fact, it was what was worrying her so much. Imelda was not what could be classed as a person in possession of maternal instincts. As she poured herself out yet another whisky and dry ginger, she told herself to relax and stop worrying so much. She reminded herself that Jordanna was there, and she would make sure that they were both safe. What she meant was that Kenny Boy would be safe with his sister to watch over him.

She knew that relying on a child of only four years old was wrong, but she really didn't know what else to do. If she brought in the authorities, she could lose the kids for ever. She knew that Imelda was capable of putting Jordanna up for adoption if the fancy took her. She would do it as well, just to prove a point. And, as she had the law on her side, Mary knew she had to keep her daughter sweet. She was stuck, as always, between a rock and a very hard place.

As Mary heard the loud knocking on her front door she assumed that it was Imelda bringing the kids back because they were getting on her nerves. So Mary plastered a wide smile on her face and opened the front door expecting to see her daughter's usual dark countenance. Instead, she was confronted by a very worried-looking and agitated Michael Hannon.

'Are the kids here, Mary?'

Michael was already inside the house, looking around him as if expecting the children to leap out of their hiding places in front of his eyes.

'No, they are with their mother, what's wrong? What's happened?'

Mary was already uptight as it was, she knew that Michael Hannon's arrival this late at night, out of the blue, could only herald bad news for her grandchildren. The fear was taking over now and she was finding it hard to breathe. She felt the terror that her daughter's lifestyle could bring in an instant. 'What has she done now? Tell me what's happened!'

Michael looked at the woman he had come to love as if she was his own flesh and blood and he said sadly, 'Mel has upset a lot of people again, heavy-duty people. But they have swallowed because of you, and because of me, and out of respect for her father and what he stood for. But now she has really crossed the line, Mary. Basil is going to fucking open her up, he's going to wipe her off the face of the earth.'

Mary was staring at Michael as if she had never seen him before in her life and had come home to find him naked in her bath, drinking her Scotch while listening to her Connie Francis LPs. It was not to be believed, yet she knew he was on the up and up. Michael Hannon would not lie to her.

'Did you say Basil? That Basil is going to open Imelda up? Are you off your fucking game? Imelda could wipe the floor with him with one hand tied behind her back.'

Michael nodded. 'Yeah, that is what everyone seems to

think, Mary, only he ain't as big a mug as people tend to think. He has a much bigger stake in the world than he lets on. Also, he is now in cahoots with Jimmy Bailey and the Driscolls. Mary, Basil has got to teach Imelda a lesson, it's a matter of pride now as well as everything else.'

Mary was half-pissed and wondering what had caused Michael Hannon to come to her home accusing all and sundry. 'Come and have a drink. You have it all wrong, Basil wouldn't hurt Mel. You know he is one of the good guys, he is a blinder.'

Michael was not in the mood for a government white paper on his news, he was only interested in making this woman understand the seriousness of what he was trying tell her. He pushed her in the chest, none too gently, his anger taking over.

'She's been running a fucking nonce-fest with that Jed by all accounts, Mary. They have been delivering young girls all over the Smoke and, as if that ain't enough, they have been using Basil's name to collect the earn. She has been using girls as young as twelve, Mary. Basil is like the Antichrist, I have never seen him so fucking worked up before. He is on his way over to hers now. He has the blessing of everyone; he is in the big time and no one realised that, especially not Imelda, by the sounds of it.'

Mary was shaking her head in denial, even Imelda was not capable of doing something like that. It was a misunderstanding, it had to be. If it was true, what was happening to her grandchildren?

'You are wrong. Imelda has her faults, and they are legion, I know that better than anyone. But she would never be involved in anything like that. No way . . .'

'Oh, Mary. She is scum, you know that. She is capable of anything, and as for this latest fucking debacle, I heard it from the horse's mouth. She is using everyone around her, as always. Well, I have given her the benefit of the doubt in the past, but not any more.'

Mary was shocked into silence. But a voice inside her head was screaming over and over. It was Jed who wanted the kids there. Jed who insisted that her daughter have the kids overnight. Jed who had convinced her that Imelda was only ever going to learn to love and care for her kids if she spent time with them. It was Jed who was to blame, it had to be.

Mary felt physically sick at what she knew was going to turn out to be the truth, no matter how much she hoped that it wouldn't. She knew that Hannon would not have come near her unless he had been convinced that what he had been told was gospel.

Jed was rolling a joint and Led Zeppelin was pounding out 'Black Dog' on the stereo as Jordanna tried to shout over the noise. It was deafening, and it was the norm for her and her brother. They were expected to sleep through it all, were expected to be immune to the racket. She actually liked Led Zeppelin, she only wished her mother and Jed did not feel that it was only relevant if it was played as loud as possible. She knew that this racket would go on for hours now. But she needed to attract their attention, and she knew it was not going to be easy.

Her mother was burning a spoonful of skag, and Jordanna knew she would not listen to her now even if she happened to be accompanied by the Holy Trinity. The hammering on the front door continued as Jordanna tried to attract the attention of her mother, or at least the attention of her mother's lover. The people trying to gain access to the house were now shouting through the letter box, and she could hear the annoyance in their voices even if she could not understand what they were saying.

She shouted once more as loudly as she could, 'There's someone at the door.' But the music was so loud, and so heavy, her little voice was completely lost. She could not compete with electric guitars and Robert Plant. Jordanna knew she was fighting a losing battle so she decided to answer the door herself. She assumed it was one of their friends, assumed it was another junkie who would flake out with her mum on the sofa, all smiles and silence. Or it could be a drinker who had nowhere to go, a pisshead who would eventually flake out with Jed. That was something Jordanna had sussed out a long time ago. No one came here through choice, it was the last resort for most people, the only place where they could be guaranteed some kind of welcome and, even then, that welcome depended on what they had brought with them. Jordanna knew her mother would want to see the people who had arrived in the middle of the night, would welcome them with open arms. And if she didn't answer the door her mother would accuse her of being lazy, of being a vindictive little bitch.

So Jordanna knew that answering the front door was her best bet and she did just that.

She was knocked off her feet by the three burly men who burst inside the small hallway, followed by a seriously irate Basil. Jordanna had only opened the door a fraction and, when it was slammed against the wall she found herself lying in the bedroom doorway, winded and frightened at what she might have caused by her actions.

She recognised Basil and wondered why he didn't even bother to acknowledge her. He had always said hello to her in the past but tonight he was not even looking in her direction; it was as if she was invisible.

He had three men with him, two huge black men with shaved heads and expensive leather jackets and a heavy-set white guy with a baseball bat, a really bad perm, and a mouth full of gold teeth, and they were already making their way into the front room.

Jordanna knew aggravation when she saw it. She had seen enough of it in her short but eventful life. She knew that she had done a wrong one, and that it would probably cost her dearly in the long run.

As she watched the commotion that erupted around her, Kenny came out of the bedroom and stood beside her, watching with wide eyes as Basil shut the front door once more, locked it firmly, and then stormed into the lounge where Imelda and Jed were standing like stuffed dummies, their faces white and frightened.

Jordanna noticed that neither of them even attempted to ask what they were being punished for. But a punishment was the only reason for something like this, was the only rational explanation for such a situation. As the baseball bat crunched heavily against her mother's head, Jordanna closed her eyes tightly and, pulling her little brother behind her, she went back inside the foetid-smelling bedroom they shared. She shut the door quietly, then proceeded to push anything she could move in front of it. She dragged the old dressing table with its water-stained mirrors and scuffed surfaces across the room, using all of her strength to push it in front of the door. She was determined to keep trouble out of this bedroom, whatever her mother had managed to cause this time. After all, she knew that there was a good chance they could be next in line for a beating.

Jordanna then prayed out loud that her brother would be spared from harm. She had already experienced so

333

much in her little life, but she was determined that Kenny Boy would not have to be a part of this. Imelda, her mother, seemed to court danger, seemed to attract violence and it was not fair that they were caught up in her crossfire. She knew how dangerous her mother's life could be, knew how easy it was to be caught up in the lunacy that surrounded her. Jordanna had been dragged into a nightmare once before and she was terrified of it happening to her again.

She could hear screams of pain and fear, hear the dull thudding sound of the baseball bat as it smashed against bone and skin. She heard the commotion of her mother and Jed trying to escape the fury of their attackers.

She could hear the absolute violence of the attack, the sounds of the beating, the terror and the anger. She knew that fists and feet were involved and also that it was not like anything they had experienced before. Jordanna knew that this was about something very serious, and very dangerous. The whole place was drenched with the stench of hatred and revenge.

She held on to her little brother, burying his face into her body as she tried to drown out the noise of the fracas. Her eyes were wide with fear, and they were almost glued to the door as she waited to see if the men involved were going to come after them, were going to make sure they did not have any kind of tale to tell about what had occurred this night. She knew that if this was as serious as it sounded, Kenny and herself were living on borrowed time.

Kenny was distraught now, sobbing with fear, terrified at the noises he could hear coming from behind their closed door. He had finally realised, even as little as he was, that this was a very serious situation, and that they were both in real danger. For the first time in his life, he understood how precarious their lives were when in the care of their mother. He had just realised how dangerous and perilous life could be, thanks to Imelda's lifestyle and her complete disregard for her own children's well-being or safety. Jordanna knew exactly how her brother felt, she had been through the same thing herself many times.

As she heard her mother howling in pain, heard the cursing and threats from Basil and his cohorts, Jordanna grabbed her brother roughly and forced him underneath the bed that they shared, pushing him against the wall, making sure he was as far away from the danger as was physically possible. She then lay beside him, holding him tightly against her and, whimpering in fear, she waited for Basil and his cronies to come for them as well.

Jordanna could taste the fright that had enveloped them, could feel the coldness of their terror and knew that Kenny would not be able to forget what had happened, knew that this time the situation would stay in his mind for a long time to come. She also realised that Imelda would finally lose the power she had over her beloved son, and Jordanna knew that could only be a good thing for all concerned. It would do Kenny the world of good to see his mother for what she really was. Jordanna knew that the fracas that was occurring this night would in effect make Kenny realise that they could never really be safe around Imelda, he would finally be able to understand that she was bad news, that when they were with her, they were always going to be exposed to this kind of violence.

As Jordanna lay beneath the bed, she could smell the filth that was ingrained in the carpet and feel the stickiness of her mother's life. She knew she was lying on years of dirt, stale urine from her mother and her cronies, when they had been so wasted they had not even been capable of using the bathroom, and she felt the loneliness of neglect. She knew how it felt to be dismissed by the person who should have loved you more than anyone, who had grown you from a seed, had kept you safe inside them for nine long months. She knew the loneliness of being ignored, of being invisible to the one person who should have been the mainstay of your life. She was due to start school soon, and she knew she was already more educated than anyone of her age had a right to be. She had not had a choice, she had spent her whole life seeing how the land lay, judging how best to act around her mother, and her mother's friends. She had sussed out, as a babe in arms, that her mother was not someone you antagonised. She hoped that if they both survived this, they would be allowed to stay at their granny's without having to keep on coming to their mother's house all the time. Jordanna knew that school would curtail her visits, and she hoped that her absence would curtail poor Kenny Boy's as well.

Kenny was shaking in abject terror, he was shivering with fear and shock, the sounds of his mother's beating were loud and Jordanna knew that her screams would stay with him for a long time after this was all finally over. She knew he could hear Imelda's voice as she begged for mercy, knew he could hear Basil's voice as he threatened and accused Imelda of all sorts. As he swore at her, called her names, he sounded so different to the man they had always known. The man who had been a friend to them all. It made this whole thing even more horrific because Basil was one of the only people who had ever been kind to them, and now he was the enemy. He was what was frightening them both out of their wits, he had become their biggest fear. If he decided to come after them, they were helpless and she knew that; they were only babies. Babies who were lying under a bed, terrified out of their minds, who already knew that life could be harsh, frightening and perilous. They clung tightly to each other and Jordanna whispered quietly into her brother's ear, telling him to keep silent so as not to draw any attention to them. She held him in her arms and calmed him with her words and with her love. She knew that he was shrewd enough to understand that they were not to advertise their presence in any way.

She wondered briefly if, when it all went quiet, her mother would be dead.

Basil was mortified at what he had done; he was also aware that he had been left with no other choice, Imelda had forced him into a corner. She had known that her actions would have had dire consequences. She was a bloody pulp, and that did not bother him. It was Jed, he was dying and he knew it. He was still trying to talk, trying to beg for his life. His lips were smashed beyond recognition, as was his face, but they were still moving, talking, he was still trying to justify his behaviour.

As the men looked at their prey without any kind of feelings whatsoever, Basil knew that he had stepped over the line. He was now blooded; he had said he was going to pay her out for her treachery, and he had done it.

He saw Imelda's eyes flicker, was amazed at his feeling; he wanted to finish her off. He felt the urge to start kicking her again, he wanted to wipe her off the face of the earth.

'Are you coming?'

Basil shook his head slowly. 'You lot go. I have something to do, I'll see you tomorrow.'

The men left quietly. They were not in a rush, they knew that no one was going to be coming here this night. That had been arranged beforehand. It had all been put in place and, if you planned well, you were pretty much guaranteed an easy shoot. It cost, but it was worth the initial lay-out. No one wanted a capture, especially not for a piece of shit like Imelda.

Basil sat down on the nearest chair, suddenly exhausted. He knew that Imelda would come away from this with her life intact, she was as strong as a fucking ox. But he knew that was for the best, he knew that he wanted her to remember what he had done to her. He wanted her to look at the scars every day, and be reminded of what she had done. He wanted her to remember that he had been the cause of them, had been the instigator of her demise. And now he would make sure that she never worked again, unless it was on the pavement.

She had been so good at running things; she was a cunt, if she had been content with her lot, she would have been under his protection for life, and on a decent earn. Now she was finished, she was destroyed, in more ways than one.

Imelda Dooley looked like a bloody lump of meat, there was nothing to remind anyone of how lovely she had been. She would heal, and she would get back on her feet, but she would never again look in the mirror and see a beauty, see a looker. She would have to mourn the good looks she had taken for granted all her life. She would finally know what it was like to have to rely on her personality and not her looks. Ergo, she was finished.

Basil heard Mary and Michael Hannon coming in the flat before he saw them. Mary stood in the doorway, her hand clutched over her mouth, her eyes wide with terror.

Michael was behind her, looking at the little tableau without any kind of expression on his face. He was not about to show his hand, and Basil respected that. Looking at Mary he said quietly, 'You knew the score and you knew that this was on the cards.'

Mary was looking at the carnage that had once been her daughter, who was only recognisable by her clothes. What was left of them anyway. She was a bloody pulp. She was still breathing but it was loud and laboured, it sounded raspy and painful, and she was sorry that it didn't move her in any way. She was sorry that she did not feel in the least bit protective of her child. She had come here through instinct, but not for Imelda; for her grand-children.

'Ain't you got nothing to say, Michael? I waited for you both. I wanted to see you here while it was still new. Fresh. So, what have you got to say for yourself?'

Michael Hannon stared warily at Basil, he had not expected this at all. He had known it would all come out on top, but not like this. Imelda and Jed had been beaten and tortured, they had known exactly what was happening to them, and why it was happening to them, no doubt. He knew that there would not be any kind of come-back. But looking round this room, at the blood splatters on the walls, and the destruction of the faces, he knew that this was a completely different Basil from the one he had known all these years.

The stench of blood was heavy in the room and Basil stood up, stretching as if he was tired out and ready for his bed. He said to Mary, 'The kids are in the bedroom. I don't know how much they heard, or how much they guessed, but they need to be taken away from here.'

Basil walked to the door, then turning around, he

looked at Michael Hannon and said in a low and penetrating voice, 'You looked down your fucking nose at me for years because of my business, but I could buy and sell you, boy. You blanked me over and over again, until it finally clicked, until you finally realised that this business was worth fucking fortunes. Then you wanted an in. You saw that Bailey was earning off the business, and you demanded your fucking slice from it. Well, you see her down there, and that cunt she thought would protect her from the likes of me; that is my message to anyone who tries to mug me off. I ain't fucking swallowing it any more.'

Basil left then, and Mary stood still, her hand still covering her mouth, and she said nothing. Neither did Michael Hannon.

Then Mary went to the bedroom, gathered up her grandchildren, and walked away from her daughter and her daughter's excuse for a life without a backward glance.

It was over.

Finally over.

Imelda was finished.

Book Three

Blessed are they that mourn:
For they shall be comforted.

– Matthew 5:4

Chapter Seventeen

1994

Imelda was tired, and she looked it.

She had recently been released from prison, and she had the yellowish pallor that was a dead giveaway to anyone in the know. She had been in and out of prison over the years. She had also moved about quite frequently, disappearing for months on end and then turning up again in her old haunts, acting as if she had never been gone. She was a real loner; as always, she only really needed her own company. She still liked her life in many respects, even though she knew it was not a life most people would want for themselves. But it suited her, suited her personality.

It was a really hot day and Imelda sat in the pub garden and enjoyed her drink. She sipped it slowly, savouring it; she was low on funds, and her need to score was uppermost in her mind. She knew that she was luckier than most of the people in her position; she had no one to lie to, no one to consider at all. She preferred it that way, it suited her. For most people being alone spelt failure; to her it just guaranteed contentment and the knowledge that she was able to do what she wanted, when she wanted, with who she wanted.

Imelda was watching the world go by, something she had acquired the knack of many years before. Like most junkies she had no interest in the world itself, the actual economics of the world were beyond her interest. For example, if the four-minute warning ever came, heralding a nuclear war, she would only be interested in getting herself an armful, it was her *only* interest. Her mind would then become focused on whether she would be able to walk into any chemist she wanted to and take what she needed, thanks to the decimation of the world and mankind. It was a junkie's dream. The world itself and the people who inhabited it were so far beneath her interest that she would never even consider their welfare over her own.

It was all she really cared about, drugs and money. All she had ever cared about. From her first hit, she had felt as if she had finally come home. It was all she ever thought about, her life was spent gathering the money to purchase it. Anything else was treated with disdain, with her usual disinterest.

As she watched the young girls around her, in their short skirts, heavy make-up and high-heeled shoes, she didn't even have the energy to envy them their youth and their freedom. They had their whole lives in front of them, and they didn't yet understand how fleeting their youth would turn out to be.

At the moment they could not even imagine being thirty or, God forbid, forty. She knew they were just at the age where drink, men and adventure were calling to them, and she knew by the looks of most of them, they were only too ready to start calling back. It was like a recurring circle of disappointment, it came around every year or so, the launch of a new batch of young girls who thought they were the first ones to know it all. Young girls who didn't have the brains to see that their mothers had thought that once too, and were now lumbered with kids, bills and the prospect of getting older on a budget, all while pondering how it all happened to them in the first place.

It was a bastard, life. It had the knack of throwing you a curve every now and then to keep you interested. To give you a reason to keep going. Then, just as you thought you had cracked it, you took delivery of a blow that was so severe you were amazed at how you could ever have survived it. But somehow you did, and somehow you carried on.

Imelda was not one of those people, she had given her life over to herself at a very early age. She had only ever had one love, and that was the needle and all it could offer her. She spied her dealer as he came into the pub. She could see him through the window, knew he would get himself a drink, say a few hellos to the regulars, and would then come outside to serve her up her usual chemical cosh. She smiled at the thought. Her life was already settling back into a pattern, and the pattern she chose was one that afforded her peace of mind and, occasionally, complete oblivion should she feel the need of it. Imelda knew the real value of oblivion, knew that it was what kept her on an even keel.

The girls at the table opposite her were getting noisier, she listened to them as they swore and cursed loudly at one another, determined to make sure that everyone heard them. They thought that their bad language made them seem sophisticated, clever even. They believed they were acting like adults instead of the little schoolies they so obviously were. She knew they were looking for trouble and that they were liable to get it, sooner rather than later. Especially in this pub, which was frequented by the lower echelons of society, and that was being kind.

She lit a cigarette, her hands were stiff; she had never regained the full use of them after Basil had finished with her. He had been angry enough to need personal retribution but, unlike him, she had never needed her own personal revenge, she knew it was a pointless exercise. She held no grudges; she had accepted her capture. In reality, she was amazed that it had taken so long to straighten her out. But then she was of the opinion that her family name had more than likely been a great help in many ways. Not any more though.

She glanced at the girls once more. They were not that bad looking, they were reminiscent of her at the same age. Although she had been much more sexually aware than these girls. They just wanted to be noticed, wanted to be part of the world that they knew was only a couple of sexual encounters away. They were fucking idiots, they believed that sex would automatically make them grown-ups, make them adults. Nature was a bastard in that way; they were physically ripe but mentally they were still so ignorant they would accept the first man to give them any attention.

Imelda was sore. Her body was aching, was reminding her that she needed her meds. She still had the long fingers and shapely wrists of her youth, the only difference now was that she sometimes had trouble doing up buttons or using zips. Her fingers were full of arthritis, but she was not about to let that spoil her day. It was over, it had happened. She had made a point of getting over it. She had not had any real choice in the matter, she had been battered so badly that the doctors had not expected her to survive.

Jed had died on the way to hospital, but who cared? He was never someone who you'd bet on to make old bones.

When Imelda finally left her hospital bed, she had been hooked on methadone; the people who had saved her life had also been the people who made sure she kept her habit alive and well. She had played them as she had played everyone who came within her eye line. She saw them all as jokes, saw their kindness and concern for her well-being as the ultimate idiocy. She knew she would use them, and that they would let her because they were too fucking stupid to see her for what she was.

Their kindness had only made her feel even more superior than usual because she knew that, deep inside, they saw her as nothing; ergo they felt guilt about it. They were so fucking blinkered to the real world, they actually believed that their education and their liberal beliefs would be enough to get them by. So she had played them, like she had played everyone else, and she had *loved* every second of it. She had told them what they wanted to hear, and she had sat with them and told them her life story. They had believed her, but then why wouldn't they? It never occurred to them that she was lying through her teeth. The more outrageous the story, the more they were interested in it. She knew they would dine out on her porks for weeks to come. And pork she had, she always made sure she was the victim in her tales of woe, made sure she was seen as someone who had been judged because of her lifestyle, not for the crime she had been accused of. She was dealing with people who had no real experience of the world or its filthy reality, who saw her as the underdog rather than the Queen Bitch.

She also knew that these same people would eventually move on, would run as far from her and her ilk as was physically possible once the real world they had craved suddenly became a little *too* real for them. When it started to scare them and that was generally when they suddenly became aware that they were being used, used by people who were experts at it. Once these people realised that they had been exploited by people who laughed up their sleeves at their complete readiness to believe their stories and, even worse, had let on where they lived and where they had grown up. Eventually though, they saw the error of their ways and left the social services for another government job, only next time, they made sure they had no contact with the masses on a personal level.

Imelda, of course, had not voiced her opinions outright, she had just enjoyed playing them for the fools they were. She laughed at them secretly, watching them as they used their power and influence to make her life easier.

Eventually she had been given a nice flat to live in and a Social Security book that guaranteed her a weekly wage. She had also been given furniture, clothes and other sundry items that were deemed important to her rehabilitation. She had taken all that they had offered her with a grateful smile, but a hidden anger at them for the condescension in their words and the way they had eventually seen her off with relief and, more to the point, a studied disinterest in how she would cope alone. She knew that there were a lot of women in her position who would need far more than the zealous, but short-term caring of these fucking imbeciles. They were only trying to make themselves feel better; the people they used to make themselves feel *useful* and *needed* were forgotten about almost overnight.

Imelda had sold almost everything they had given her at the first opportunity, apart from the bed and a chair. She had then taken the money offered and scored herself a decent bit of skag with the proceeds. After all the months on methadone, she felt like she had finally come home. She had then settled herself into a routine; she scored, she went out to earn, and she scored again. Not like she had in the old days, of course. She knew her limitations, she always had. She knew her market better than anyone. She was still in pretty good nick bodywise, but her face left a lot to be desired. She had good bone structure, and she looked as though she had once been a good-looking girl, but she was a realist and she knew that the scars and broken bones she had incurred had not exactly helped to make her look like she was worth more than a few quid. That had been the whole point, she had been destroyed by Basil because he had known that was what would bring her the most misery. She also wondered if her destruction had actually been for his personal benefit; after all, she knew he had always had a penchant for her, the same as Jimmy Bailey. She knew that had bothered him. Her looks had caused him to want her, and he had wanted her badly. Even knowing what she was and, in her defence, she had never pretended otherwise.

She was not that bothered about it though. Even at her best she had never turned down a trick, she would fuck anyone for any amount without any thought whatsoever. Imelda had never cared about the big bucks; she had only ever cared about covering her expenses. She had eventually made her way to Shepherd's Market, to the Cross, and she earned her crust so she could go out and score for herself in peace. Nothing had really changed in that department.

Imelda noticed one of the young girls on the table opposite her watching her closely but she was used to that kind of attention. The scar across her forehead was still livid enough to make people give her a second glance. She understood the curiosity, she would have done the same thing in their position. Plus she knew how deep and how noticeable it was. It was not going anywhere, she would never get rid of it. She didn't see it any more herself, she was used to it. But she knew that for some people it was still a shock. They assumed that she had been in a car crash, had gone through a windscreen. She had played up to that old chestnut on many occasions, had talked to the interested parties about her terrible accident, and they had bought her drinks in exchange for her tragic tale. She told them she had lost her family in the crash, and they would then regret asking her about it, would wish they had left her well alone. She would take their drinks and laugh to herself as they suddenly realised that other people's tragedies were much better if you read about them in the paper and did not have the person concerned sitting opposite you and, even scarier, they also realised that terrible things could happen to anyone, at any time, even *them*.

No one was immune to heartache, and if they wanted a sad story she would provide one for them. All they had to do was buy her a few drinks. They always left before she did, that was another thing she liked about them. Her scars were what had interested them in her initially, and eventually those same scars were what made them want to run a mile. She knew she looked scary on close inspection, knew that her face told the people who were interested in her misfortune that once she had been a real beauty. She still had a vestige of her former glory, and that was why people were so sorry for her. If she had been ugly to begin with they would not have given her a second glance. Human nature was a bastard, and so were most of the humans she had ever had the misfortune to come across.

The crowd of young girls were now dancing together, gyrating to the music blaring out of the pub with all the passion they could muster. Imelda watched them half-heartedly, her eye still on her dealer. He was engaged in a deep conversation with a redhead of indeterminate years who had a very well-developed bosom. She was drinking Guinness, which Imelda always found startling. She could never understand how women could drink pint after pint like men. She liked her drinks short and to the point, like her drugs. A double vodka could be downed in seconds, a pint of Guinness was not something you could neck quickly.

The young girls were all sitting back down at the table opposite her once more, the music had been turned down low for some reason, and she watched them lazily as they lay back in their chairs, their languid movements and newly developed bodies causing the men nearby to stare openly at them. She knew the girls wanted that to happen, knew they counted on it, were pleased at the reaction they were getting from the men. She wanted to warn them; they would waste their youth because they did not realise just how fleeting it was, and because most people did.

She saw one of the young girls stand up, she was walking towards her. Imelda looked away, her interest in them already waning. Then she saw that her dealer had finally extricated himself from the redhead, and was on his way out to her, at fucking last. The girls and their antics were forgotten now, she was only interested in the bit of business she was going to conduct.

Imelda watched him as he bought another pint for himself en route, willing him to get a move on; she was bored now, she wanted to make herself feel at one with the world again. She wanted her dealer to shift his fat arse and get out here to her.

Imelda was so engrossed in observing her dealer's movements that when the girl she had noticed earlier stood in front of her, she did not register her presence for a few moments. She was then forced to look at her, because she was standing right in front of her face, blocking her view of the bar, her dealer, and blocking out the sunlight as well. She looked up at the girl with her usual blank expression, wondering what she could possibly want from her.

She was pretty, she was not someone who would usually try and strike up a conversation with the likes of her. She wondered if the girl was going to ask her to purchase drinks for her and her friends, or cigarettes. She would do that for them, for a price, a few drinks for herself.

Out of all the people around her, Imelda could see why they might think she was a viable option for something like that. She was sitting alone, she was not threatening, and she was probably the only woman there who was not on the pull.

Imelda was amazed when the girl said to her quietly and with a certain rough dignity, 'You don't even recognise me do you, Imelda? I'm your daughter.'

Mary was worried, she knew that Kenny was up to no good, but she didn't know exactly *what* he was up to or how no good it might be. He was heading for serious trouble, and she knew that he was not geared up for it. He thought he was, they all did at that age. He had no experience of the world of skulduggery, he just thought he did.

But he had been given an easy ride, thanks to her, and he did not understand the way of the world. In fact, he did not understand that his name guaranteed him the respect and the interest that he got, that because of his name people gave him a few minutes of their time. He thought it was because he was a fucking interesting person. Which he was, if you liked overgrown schoolboys. He was a big lad for his age, and he looked much older than his years. He had not yet realised that petty thieving and the ability to throw a punch were not enough to get him through the rest of his life. He inhabited a small world and in that world he was a big fish. He still had a lot to learn about how big fishes could be swallowed up by even bigger and better fish if they were not careful.

Kenny was such a nice boy in many respects, but he was also a very arrogant and a very ignorant one. He would not listen to reason, had no time for advice, no matter who was offering it to him, and he was already of the opinion that only idiots went out to work each day. He saw paying tax as a mug's game, that was how green he was. Mary would save the lecture on how a legitimate business could be a blind for other, less lawful, enterprises for when he was sensible enough to listen to her advice, and take it on board. He was such a fucking *scratcher* even though, in fairness, he tried to scratch a living so that he could provide her with money, see that she was all right for a few quid. But if he had any brains at all he would have already sussed that she was a real fucking grafter in her own right.

Mary was not going to argue with him any more. She knew that she had to let him get on with it now. Like all young men his brain was not yet wired up to listen to reason. He needed to learn a lesson in his own good time, he needed a fright, and once he had experienced that he would be more amenable to her gentle persuasion, or her manic screaming, which all depended on what form his fright would take. She hoped it was not something she would not be able to smooth over. Knowing him though, that would be the case; he was a law unto himself.

Mary looked at the clock. It was nearly nine, and she knew he would eventually come home, if only to be fed and watered. Her worry had stemmed from the fact that he had not come home as usual, he had not been there for his food, and he liked his food. It was his main preoccupation while at home with her. So she poured another drink for herself, and settled down in the chair to wait for his arrival. Until he came home, and she saw him with her own two eyes, she would not rest. He was a little fucker, but he was her little fucker, and she loved him no matter what.

Jordanna was amazed at her mother's complete indifference to her words. She had not really expected anything else from her, she remembered her mother very well. She knew better than anyone just how easy Imelda found it to write people out of her life as if they had never existed. She erased people from her life within moments of deciding she was fed up with them.

Jordanna knew what her mother was capable of, she also knew that she did not even register on her mother's radar. She genuinely had not known who she was. She had not even been written out of her mother's life like everyone else; she had never been important enough to her for that to happen. But she had recognised her mother immediately. She had glanced over at her, and felt her breath leaving her body as the shock of recognition set in, as she felt the physical pain wash over her. It was the day she had dreaded all her life.

She had known her own flesh and blood within a second. She had braced herself for the inevitable approach, had waited for her mother to make the first move, had assumed she was probably as disturbed by the meeting as she was. After all, she *was* her mother. But that had not happened, in fact, it had taken a while before Jordanna had realised that the woman who had carried her inside her belly, who had birthed her, who had named her, did not even recognise her. That she had no recollection of her at all, until prompted.

That had really hurt. She had not forgotten how her mother had been, how selfish and vicious she was, she had not endowed her with pretend attributes or made-up stories about her as a lovely lady who did really love her kids, but had problems she needed to deal with. She had never made excuses for her, she had always understood that her mother was not like other mothers, knew that she was not capable of loving anyone. Even herself. She had always accepted that her mother had no real *interest* in anyone except herself and her habit. And she could cope with that. She had known the truth of it from a small child. She still remembered how nasty she could be, remembered how having to stay at her mother's house would terrify her, how her nerves would be on edge. She would always remember how much she hated her mother and her lifestyle. She knew that, and she had accepted it a long time ago. But still, to find out that her own mother had not even *recognised* her, that had really hurt. She was annoyed with herself for letting it bother her so much. But it did, and when she had realised that her mother had no idea who she was, she had felt angry enough to go over and force the woman to at least acknowledge her existence.

Even though when Jordanna had first seen her mother, had recognised her immediately, she had not wanted to make any kind of contact with her at all. She had been determined to say a brief hello and leave it at that. She wanted to let Imelda know that she did not need her, had never needed her. She wanted to let her know that she was all right, that her saying hello after all these years was not that big a deal to her. She wanted to be the one who broke the tenuous connection between them, who was strong enough to say, 'Well, we've said hello, so can you go because I am busy?' But it had not happened; how could it if her mother had no recollection of her at all?

She had expected her mother to come over to *her*, to want to see *her*, see how she had turned out, had expected her to at least initiate some kind of communication. She had expected her to have some kind of reaction at seeing her daughter for the first time in ten years.

But no, she had not even known who she was. She had not even recognised her own child. She knew that physically she was her double, but that just made it worse; she was her mother's clone.

It was eerie, even she could see it; she knew her granny had seen it as well. She also knew that her granny wouldn't mention the likeness between them if her life depended on it.

A short while ago she had been really enjoying herself, she was on the threshold of life: she was grown up enough to get served in a pub without a big song and dance, she was pretty, she was popular, and she was finally getting up the nerve she needed to see herself as a grown-up at last. As a young woman. Now she was reminded all over again that she had not been wanted by her own mother, that she had not even been of enough importance for the bitch to remember what she looked like.

She was catapulted back to her childhood and the fear, the hate and the guilt this woman commanded at her leisure.

'Did you not even notice the resemblance between us?'

Imelda was seeing it now, of course, but she shook her head and motioned for her dealer to join her, trying to indicate that she wanted an end to any further conversation with her daughter.

Her dealer sat down at the table happily, the lovely young girl was more than enough to keep him there for as long as needed.

Jordanna didn't walk away, even though she knew that her mother wanted her to go. Her mother wanted her to crawl back into her past, where she belonged. But she didn't. She couldn't.

Imelda had not allowed for this shit, and she was not going to start playing happy families at this late stage.

'This is Charley Buckman. Charley, this is my *daughter*, Jordanna.'

Charley was amazed at her words and it showed. Jordanna was suddenly gripped with the urge to get away from them. She knew that this slimy man with his ponytail and unironed shirt was her mother's dealer. He now knew who she was, and he was in possession of her name. She was sorry she had come over, sorry that her mother's indifference had bothered her so much, she had been a fool to force the issue. She had been a fool to let this woman and her associates into her life once again.

'I knew you had kids, Mel, but I didn't think you had anything to do with them.'

Imelda saw the changing expressions on her daughter's face; the disgust, the regret and she saw her daughter register Charley as her dealer. Then she said snidely, 'I don't have anything to do with them if I can help it, she came over to talk to me. I didn't even know who she was.'

Jordanna walked away then, and she knew that her friends were wondering who the woman she had spoken to was, and she wondered what lie she could fabricate to explain her actions away though she guessed the resemblance between them would tell them what they needed to know.

She was just about to say that she was a distant relative of her granny's when she heard Imelda shrieking at her vociferously, 'Oi, Jordanna, the least you could do is buy your old mum a drink.'

Jordanna felt the shame wash over her as her friends stared at her sadly. She knew that if any one of them had been in the same boat as she was, she would have wanted to curl up and die for them.

She sat down heavily and, swinging her heavy hair away from her face, she said loudly and with as much pride as she could muster, 'I thought she was dead. I only went over there to make sure it was her.' Picking up her drink she gulped at it, but she was mortified and they all knew it. They also knew the story of her mother, although Jordanna had never talked about it, ever, so they were only in possession of rumours and hearsay. Now they had seen Imelda Dooley with their own eyes, and they were not impressed.

Joanie Barker, her closest friend, said quietly, 'Fucking hell, what a turn-up for the books. Ignore her, Jorge, she ain't worth a wank.'

Jordanna smiled then, and she answered her loudly, 'You got that right anyway.'

But the night was ruined and everyone knew that. No one was sure what to say, or what to do, it was a really strange situation.

All they knew for sure was that Jordanna's mother, who they had heard about at some point, was even worse than they had expected, and that was saying something considering what had been said about her.

Imelda sat and scored as she had arranged, and then she watched her daughter warily until she finally left the premises with all her friends in tow.

Imelda waited to see if Jordanna would look back at her one more time, but she didn't and that annoyed her. After all, she had been the one who had dragged up their past lives, not her. She had been the one to fucking approach her, so why was she acting so fucking innocent? Imelda had been spooked by the encounter though, and she had not expected that. She rarely thought about the kids and, on the few occasions she had thought about them, it was her Kenny she had wondered about. Jordanna had never really been of any interest to her whatsoever.

Charley had watched her daughter with the look of a man on the want; the girl was a beauty. But although she might have inherited her mother's good looks, she had *not* inherited the spark that had set her apart from everyone else. Imelda still had it, still commanded people's attention, and she knew that it was what had been her downfall in the end. She left the pub and went back to work. Within the hour she had forgotten the meeting with her only daughter.

*

Joanie was shocked, and as a bona fide drama queen, she was determined to make the most of it. She had heard so much about Imelda Dooley and all the things she had been accused of, but to see her like that, it was unbelievable.

Jordanna wanted to slap her friend, but she knew it was a pointless exercise. Joanie loved the feel of tragedy, she felt the power of a story and would not be satisfied until she had got it out of her system. She needed the excitement of other people's misfortune, she would then throw herself right into the middle of their bad luck. Unlike the poor people who could not walk away from their tragedies, Joanie could do just that, and she did when she had had enough of it all.

Joanie had not felt confident about broaching the subject of Jordanna's mother until they were alone, knowing that Jordanna would not want to discuss her with all the others present. Now she had seen her mother up close and personal, she understood why. Joanie had occasionally been the sounding board for Jorge's rare wonderings about her mother, but even then it was only about the woman's whereabouts. Not about her as a person.

Joanie had a natural curiosity about the woman who had produced her best friend, and she would sometimes ask about her. She would be discussed briefly, and then dismissed by Jordanna as if she was not worthy of any further interest.

Jordanna had never had a mother to turn to, she had her granny but that was not the same. She was from a completely different generation, so Joanie had passed on all her mother's gems of wisdom to her friend. They had laughed themselves silly at most of them, but some of her mother's advice had made sense and they had heeded it, accepting that there were a lot of things they did not know.

But it had still hurt Jordanna, knowing that her mother was alive and well, and yet she had not even asked after her daughter, that was really destructive for anybody to experience. She had not wanted her mother in her life, but she still felt that her mother should have cared about her in some way. No birthday card, Christmas card, nothing. It was heart-breaking knowing that she was not even worth a stamp.

'Are you all right, Jorge?'

Jordanna nodded sadly. Her lovely face was resigned now, and that just made Joanie even more angry. She wanted some kind of a reaction from her friend, wanted her to finally open up and tell her about what her life was really like with her mother.

'How can you sit there so normal? Your mother has surfaced after all these years and you act like it means nothing. Don't you want to find out what she's been up to, what she's been doing?'

Jordanna shook her head. 'No, I don't. You saw her, Joanie, would you be interested in someone like that? She's a fucking junkie. She is only interested in one thing, her skag, everything else means nothing to her. It's how drugs work, well, heroin anyway. I only really remember her burning herself an armful, that and the trouble she would cause for us all.'

Joanie nodded sagely. Her thin lank hair was already sticking to her scalp in the summer heat, her eyes were grey, large and oval shaped, and they gave her a permanently startled look. She was pretty enough in her own way, but she knew that beside Jordanna she paled into insignificance. But she didn't care about that, she was not jealous of her friend's beauty, she had a feeling that her kind of looks eventually brought you nothing but trouble.

'Can I ask you something?'

Jordanna shrugged, hoping she was finally going to change the subject. ' 'Course. We are best friends, aren't we?'

She saw the way Joanie's eyes seemed to change. The dull grey was now the colour of steel and they looked as hard. She saw the way Joanie's body seemed to draw away from her as if she was tainted somehow, as if her mother coming back on the scene had made her less of a person, as if she was now without any kind of respect.

'Did *you* shoot Lance, Jorge? I know we have never talked about it, but now your mum's turned up, I can't help wondering . . .'

Jordanna went white at her friend's words, staring at Joanie as if she had never seen her before. As if she was a complete stranger.

She knew that the story of Lance's death would always be talked about, but until now no one had ever mentioned it to her face. She was nearly sixteen, and she had never discussed that night with anybody. She understood now that it had not stopped everyone else from discussing it behind her back. Especially her so-called friends. The realisation that she was basically no more than fodder for the gossips was another shock to her already depleted system. First her mother had appeared after all those years and hadn't been able to recognise her, and now her best friend wondered if she had killed Lance. She had asked her outright, 'Did you shoot Lance?' She had not asked her gently about what happened on that terrible night, had not tried to get her friend to open up to her, had not attempted to get her to unburden herself. Joanie wanted to be told that she was a murderer, and given all the gory details. She had asked a question that had obviously been on her mind for a long time. A question she had obviously answered for herself long ago.

Jordanna looked around the bedroom she loved, and she saw it as Joanie and everyone else must see it. She had a double bed, new mirrored wardrobes, fitted carpets and a TV. She had a state-of-the-art stereo system, and she knew that in comparison to her friends she was classed as rich. She had not really thought about it before, she just saw herself as a person; what she had and what she owned was always secondary in her mind. She liked people because they were nice, not because of what they had.

Now though, after the day's revelations, she knew that her lifestyle was probably another thing that was discussed in graphic detail by all and sundry, like her mother's departure and the shooting incident. She felt a fool, an idiot, wondered why it had never occurred to her before that her life might be the cause of so much speculation, even among her closest friends. People she would never have talked about behind their backs, no matter what might happen to them. She would not have discussed them with anyone, and she knew that was a fact. She had believed that Joanie was the same as her, was not capable of treachery, was only interested in friendship and loyalty. She had been wrong, so wrong.

Her mother, as always, ruined everything she touched. One meeting with her, and suddenly Jordanna's life was in tatters once more. It was almost as if Imelda deliberately set out to ruin everything for her.

Joanie knew she had just done a wrong one, had fucked up a good friendship with a few ill-chosen words. 'I'm sorry, Jorge . . . I wish I had not asked you about . . . I could fucking cut me tongue out. Please forgive me . . . Please don't hold it against me . . .'

Joanie was literally begging for forgiveness, she was genuinely sorry for probing into her friend's past life. All the years they had known each other, she had never once even referred to it, even in passing. Guessing that if Jorge wanted to tell her something so huge, she would do it in her own time. But she had not been averse to hearing other people's opinions on it, she had listened to the stories and wondered, like everyone else, what had really happened.

Now she knew that Jordanna would never, ever trust her again, and that she had ruined a friendship that was even more important to her than she had realised.

Jordanna took a deep breath, then, turning her back on Joanie, she said quietly, 'I think you had better go, don't you?'

'Please, Jorge, don't let's fall out over this. I wish I had never mentioned anything. You know how much I care about you.'

Jordanna could see the angst and remorse on Joanie's face as she watched her in the mirrored doors, unable to bring herself to turn and face her friend once more. She felt as if she was suddenly in a parallel universe where everyone and everything she had believed in was gone, replaced with distrust and deceit; it was like a physical pain it hurt her so much.

'Just go home, Joanie. I need to be by myself.'

Kenny came in late, and he knew he was in for a mouthful. As he stepped through the back door into the kitchen, he saw his sister kneeling beside his granny, her head in her lap, and her body shuddering with the strength of her sobs. She was in bits, and he had never before seen her crying like that.

Jordanna was not a crying type of person, and as he took in the scene before him a huge and black anger began to erupt inside him. He was a big lad, already over six foot. He was also handsome, and he knew it. He had a deep voice and a kind nature. He was also capable of great violence if he felt his family or his personal pride was being abused in any way.

Going to his sister's side, he put a huge hand on her head and asked loudly, 'What the fuck is going on? Has someone done something to you? If they have, you tell me who they are and I'll fucking annihilate them.'

Mary waved him quiet. 'Sit down, you bloody fool. She has had the misfortune to bump into your mother who, as usual, has caused fucking ructions. I curse the day I brought that whore into the world. If it wasn't for you two, her life would have been lived without any meaning whatsoever.'

Kenny was unsure what to say to that. He had never really known his mother, he had only vague memories of her and he knew they were always accompanied by a feeling of a terrible, crushing fear. Now he was grown, he did not think of her at all. Only sometimes, at Christmas, or on his birthday. But the thoughts were fleeting, and he didn't really know her well enough to say he missed her. Though from what he had heard over the years, she was not a person who would be missed by anyone who was in full possession of their faculties.

So his sister's reaction to meeting her was not something he was prepared for. 'Come on, Jorge, wipe your eyes. Don't let her fucking make you feel bad. She is a cunt and she ain't worth it. Tell her, Nan, she shouldn't waste anything on her.'

Mary nodded and sighed. She had been all set to launch her grandson into outer space when poor Jordanna had come home. She had known then something was wrong. When young Joanie had left without even saying goodbye to her, she had guessed something was in the offing. When Jorge had come down the stairs and told her that she had met her mother in a pub in South London Mary had nearly died. It had been a long time since she had even thought about her daughter. She had happily wiped her from her memory and her life, had been overjoyed at seeing the back of her.

Mary knew that the time was nearing to tell Kenneth about his father's demise and that, from what poor Jorge had told her about Joanie, she now knew for definite that if she didn't put him in the picture then someone else certainly would. He needed to hear that story from his family, not from friends, people who had told it so often it had been stretched and bent out of all recognition. People who had not been there and who actually knew fuck all about it except what they had heard through drunken gossip and speculation.

She hated Imelda for the trouble she had caused for everyone who had ever come into her orbit. Her father was dead and everyone she came into contact with she had destroyed one way or another. Now Mary was faced with how Kenny Boy was going to react once he was told the truth of his family history. Imelda was not a person who garnered sympathy, and she was not a person who had understood the power of it. She had once more taken her own child and destroyed her in a heartbeat without any real understanding of how her actions affected those around her.

She was good at that, always had been. But Mary was

determined that these children would be protected from her, and she would make sure it was done properly and with the required threats. That was all Mel understood, so she would make sure that is exactly what she got. Her old dad used to say God is good, and he was good, but he was also very busy. He just needed a bit of help now and again.

'Oh, leave it out, Mel.'

Imelda was laughing, and it was a pleasant sound. She was, as always, on the skank. On the ponce. She would try and get anything she could for free. A cigarette, a drink, a pair of tights. She saw it as her mission in life. The man was zipping up his trousers, and she carried on laughing at him as he fastidiously checked himself over. She had him a couple of times a week. He was a fucking earhole, but he really believed he was a ladies' man. He combed the remainder of his hair with a plastic comb that had more teeth missing than a gypsy wedding picture. He smelt of Boots shaving cream and American strong mints. He had a very overinflated opinion of himself and Imelda found him absolutely amusing when she was this stoned.

'I need another fiver, El, I hope you can see your way to helping me out. I have to see me daughter. I swear to you, she needs me. Lovely girl, real pretty.'

'No chance. I'll be back tomorrow or the next day, you can earn it. I ain't giving the money away, what am I, a fucking charity?'

Imelda grinned once more in her usual, easy-going way. She had already palmed his cigarettes and lighter so she was not going to push the issue, she knew when she was beaten. She slipped out of his car and sticking her head back in the warmth once more, she said gaily, 'See you soon then, eh? And do me a favour, El, have a fucking bath first next time, you smell worse than a dustbin outside a kebab shop.'

She slammed the door shut and he drove off. She gave him a wanker's sign once he was out of range. She knew he would be back, she was not only within his price range, she was also on his wavelength. She knew how to do the business afterwards, and that was something most of the girls never got the hang of. If you left them with a good bit of chat, decent banter, something to make them remember you, they always came back, over and over again. They felt safe, confident that you would make sure they were satisfied.

It was very dark, but it was still a nice warm night. The traffic was not even audible now, the roads being almost empty. The night was all hers. And she enjoyed it, she loved the night, always had. The night was for the people who knew that they were different to everyone else, who embraced the darkness and relished the anonymity it offered them. The night was all she ever wanted: she endured the days because she had the surety of the night to come and the ease it had always afforded her.

She settled herself down on a wooden box that had once contained cheap trinkets from Sri Lanka, her legs were still pretty good and she crossed them, showing them off to their full advantage. She knew that she would probably get another couple of goes tonight. A lot of the men she serviced liked the night. Like her, they wanted to use it as a cover for their activities.

She knew there were men working someplace near who cruised the market on their breaks. They would never normally have entertained the notion of a prostitute, but the night workers were often tempted by the proximity of the women who were not only cheap but were also available and especially welcoming.

She waved at another woman who was leaning against the wall nearby, she was a heavy blonde with thick lips and an over-abundance of varicose veins. She was nice enough though but, considering she was only in her late-thirties, she made Mel feel like a fucking Page Three girl beside her, and that was saying something, she knew.

A dark-blue Jaguar slid to a stop beside her. Pulling herself up slowly from her box, she was not surprised when the passenger door was pushed open for her. Imelda smiled at her good fortune, she was on another planet and her body was relaxed and comfortable for the moment. It was as if she was outside of herself, looking in. If she died, she would not care, would just enjoy the moment as a great way to go.

She slipped into the car's interior, smelt expensive leather and even more expensive aftershave. She liked the feel of the seat, knew it was built for comfort. She knew that the owner of such a fine vehicle would be worth a few quid, and would not be averse to paying out for services rendered. That happened occasionally on the Cross, a few quid would come looking for the thrill of the unknown fuck. It was what kept her sense of adventure alive.

So, smiling her professional smile, she finally looked at the man who had decided he wanted a quick fuck or an even quicker blow job.

'Hello, Mel, long time no see.' Basil looked good and he knew it. He also knew that whatever Imelda had taken to send her to the moon was now bringing her down faster than an anvil in a Tom and Jerry cartoon. He was pleased to note that she was frightened of him, and so she fucking should be. He was her worst nightmare, and he knew that, wanted to be that.

'What do you want, Basil?'

He looked her over as if she was so much dirt he had picked up on the bottom of his expensive, handmade shoes and said seriously, 'Not you, darling, that's for sure. If the bomb dropped and we were the only two people left on this earth, civilisation would have to die out.'

Chapter Eighteen

Imelda was crashing back down to earth with a vengeance. The high that she had been enjoying so much until now had turned into a paranoid nightmare within seconds of her recognition of the man who had nearly killed her, and who had taken great pleasure in it.

She had not held a grudge as such, she had taken her punishment and accepted that the general consensus was that she had deserved it. She knew that she was not the most popular of women, she also knew that her lifestyle would always be held against her. She had had no choice but to swallow and, in fairness, she had done just that.

Seeing him in the flesh, though, was a different ball game altogether. She knew Basil would always be her Achilles heel, he was the one person in the world who *could* frighten her, could make her feel nervous. She also noticed that he was looking really good, he had aged well. In fact, he looked better now than he had looked all those years ago. She was conscious of her own failings suddenly, was bothered by her scarred face and her broken body. He had done this to her, had made sure that she had suffered at his hands, not just physically but mentally, and she had accepted the former and disregarded the latter. She had never understood people who allowed their emotions to dictate their lives; it had happened, get over it.

Basil had wanted her desperately, she had always known that. Even though he was the opposite of her she had known that he was capable of deep and dangerous feelings. Like Jimmy Bailey he had not been able to resist her. He had hidden his feelings from the world, and when he had finally turned on her, she had known that it was personal. He had wanted to hurt her for a long time, all he had lacked was a reason. Once he had acquired that, he had really gone to town on her. She bore the scars to prove it. She knew that to feel that kind of hate, you needed to be able to feel that kind of love. There was a fine line between the two. Basil had not just hurt her, he had *maimed* her. However, he had killed Jed, so she felt she had come off lightly. She knew that if he had wanted it, she would have been dead.

The severity of his attack had told her that she was finished in their world. She had accepted that without a thought too, she'd had to, she had no choice in the matter.

Once something like that happened to you, there was no going back. She'd known then that, if she had any sense at all, she had to keep away from everyone and everything she had ever known. She had to keep a low profile for a while, and she had. She had played the fucking game to the letter.

In fact, she had not only needed to escape from Basil's disgust but, more importantly, from his angry bitterness and hatred. His beating had been delivered in a cold and calculated manner. He had enjoyed inflicting it.

She had eventually recovered from her physical

wounds, had been grateful to come out of it with her life intact.

He was more than capable of killing her himself, after all, he had not paid anyone else to do the dirty deed for him. It had been personal, and she had allowed for that. That he was in a position where he could call on any number of friends or associates to do the dirty deed for him had spoken volumes. She had been foolish enough to believe that she could have him over. She had believed that she had been capable of controlling him. At the time, she had really thought she could get away with it, had been willing to blame Jed for it all. It had simply never occurred to her until then that her dealings might be found out, might be misconstrued by the people she dealt with. The downside of the chemical cosh was that you did not know just how fucking cuntish you had been until it was too late. She knew better now, she understood that she had made a really big mistake. She had underestimated him, and he had shown her the error of her ways. Imelda could only hope that he was not here now for a return match of some sort.

Basil saw the scars she still carried upon her person and he felt every one of the blows he had delivered on to her face and body as if for the first time. He had made sure that she had been destroyed physically. And, God help him, he had enjoyed her demise, had loved every second of it.

Now though, after all this time, seeing the damage he had inflicted on her, and seeing the way she had overcome it, he felt a sneaking respect for her. She was one hard fuck when all was said and done. He knew men who could not have survived that level of violence and still had their balls intact.

Imelda Dooley had been in hospital for months, and that had assuaged his colossal anger towards her just a little, had caused the hate he felt for her to finally abate.

He saw her terror of what he might do to her this time, and he liked the feeling that gave him. He knew that he had finally shown her that no one was beyond retribution. Even her. Imelda had needed to fear someone. Until he had put her in her place, she had always been the person who had caused the fear. Until he had chastised her, hurt her, she had never quite understood the power that fear could produce.

She did now, though, he could see it in her eyes, in her body language. 'Are you going to hurt me again, Basil, is that what this is about?' Even her voice was different, she was still trying to play it cool, trying to act like she was not that scared. But she was not convincing him, or herself for that matter.

Basil saw the livid scars on her forehead, knew that they would not fade for many more years and he knew that every time she looked at them she thought of him.

She was like a parody of her former self. He knew she had not really changed, not internally anyway. She was still the same junkie piece of shit she had always been, only now she was frightened of someone. She was frightened of him, of his power, of his anger.

He lit another cigarette and, looking out of the windscreen, he said softly, 'If I wanted you hurt, Mel, you would be hurting by now, believe me.'

She nodded almost imperceptibly and relaxed a little, assuming he wanted her to tell him something, or find out something for him. She assumed he was after something from her, needed something from her.

'So, what do you want then, Basil? Why are you here?'

He saw the sweat that had enveloped her whole body, could smell it coming off her. It had a faint uric tang to it, and he knew she was not aware of it. Imelda was only aware of the desperate need to put more drugs inside her. He had a feeling that the drugs she craved would be in even greater demand than usual after this visit. He knew that his arrival into her useless fucking world had thrown her off course, she was so wrapped up in herself that she had given no real thought for why he might have encouraged her to get into his nice clean motor. She assumed, as always, that this was about *her*.

'You are drenched, Mel, do you sweat like this often?'

He was genuinely interested. She was now so wet that her clothes were sticking to her body, not that he was that interested in her body these days. She was like a fucking doughboy, and she was beginning to smell like one into the bargain.

'What do you want from me, Basil? Don't prolong the fucking agony, tell me what's going on. What I've done this time, or what you want from me, should that be the case.'

He laughed then, she was so fucking different. Gone was the arrogance and the need to fight her end, no matter what. Gone was the feisty girl who had no fear of anyone or anything, who believed that the fact she wanted something was reason enough for her to demand it. Take it. Who saw the world from her point of view only, didn't see it as something that was to be shared. Didn't see it as something that was also the domain of billions of other people, all living their lives quite happily without her interference. He had cowed her, so he had achieved something at least. He had done a good job on her. He had often wished he had finished her off, but seeing her like this, he was pleased that she had survived his anger and his hatred.

Seeing her like this was like a balm to him, seeing her so humble was worth all the money he had amassed, and he had a lot of money, even by so-called rich people's standards. He was worth a fucking fortune. She knew that, and he also knew that she did not give a flying fuck about it. He had always known that she had earned, but providing she had enough to score she was actually quite happy.

'I have always known where you were, Mel, I made it my business to know that. I am here to tell you that if you *ever* go near your fucking kids again, you will be hunted down like a fucking dog and, this time, lady, you will be disposed of permanently. That is a promise.'

Basil saw the bewilderment that his words had caused and he knew then that she had not even thought about her children at all.

Imelda laughed at his words, her whole body language telling him she was amazed to even hear her kids mentioned.

'What you on about? I don't want to fucking see them, either of them, why would I? If I had wanted to, I would have seen them long before now.'

Imelda was genuinely bewildered by his words. But she sussed out what was wrong in seconds and knew that she was being warned away. Like she needed to be told. She had no interest in her kids anyway.

'Is this about Jordanna? Only, I did not even know who she was. She came over to *me*, mate. I was not in the market for long-lost kids, I was after a bit of nifty, that was all. I would have been none the fucking wiser if she had not felt the urge to come over and reveal her identity. I half expected Jimmy Savile to turn up.'

Basil knew that this woman was a hard fuck, knew that she was without any scruples, was devoid of any kind of love or care. He had always known that about Mel, yet her complete absence of memories or even a mild interest in her kids, still had the power to blow his mind. He knew she was just being honest, knew she had no care or want of her children and that she was incapable of anything even remotely resembling love.

He was a second away from beating this woman to the ground once more. Imelda Dooley was a fucking nightmare, she was the only person on God's green earth who made him feel that murder was not a deadly sin. In her case it would be classed as a mercy killing, mainly for all the people she had ever been near or by. Especially her children.

'She don't want to see you, Mel. I am here for your mother and your kids, we want you to know that if you ever see any of them again, you had better walk away from them. You need to leave them alone. Jordanna was devastated that you did not even know who she was. Did you really not recognise her, your own daughter? Can you imagine what that feels like to a young girl? Her own mother doesn't even have the sense to know her own child? Then, when she finally gets up the nerve to approach you, you mug her off, treat her like a *cunt*. You shout at her in front of her mates. Do you think anyone is going to let you get away with that? Did you honestly think no one was going to give you a tug at some point?'

Imelda was angry herself now, she was being criticised and threatened for something she did not feel was in any way her fault. 'Look, Basil. I didn't know *who* she was. I am sorry for that, but it's the truth. She came over to *me*, and I was not expecting a fucking relation to jump out of the woodwork, know what I mean? I was as shocked as you are. I won't just run if I see her again, I'll fucking invest in a set of roller skates, but believe me, I do not want to see her again any more than she wants to see me.'

Basil knew Imelda was telling the truth, he knew that Jordanna was the person who had initiated contact and, God love her, she had expected her mother to have at least known who she was. How Imelda had not seen the likeness between the two of them was fucking outrageous. But then he knew that Imelda was never really interested in her surroundings. She looked, but she didn't really *see* anything. She was only interested in her own doings, in her own dramas. But poor Jordanna, the child who Imelda had used and abused as the fancy took her. To realise at such a young age that your own mother had no recollection of you, and still had no interest in you even when she was informed of who you were. That had to hurt, that had to really make you feel like you were nothing.

Basil faced Imelda then, saw the utter confusion in her eyes, and knew that as bad as she was, she had been honest when she said she had not recognised her own child. He also knew that she was unable to see what the problem was anyway. As far as she was concerned, it was over with, finished, it was done.

But then, Imelda had never understood the consequences of her actions. She had always believed that she could walk away from anything, that she could talk her way out of any situation. She had learnt the hard way that no one was beyond reproach. Especially where he was concerned. She had been made to see the error of her ways.

But he wondered now what had she really learnt from his beating. She was still without any kind of morality. She was still living the life of a junkie. Only, as usual, she was looking quite good on it, considering.

'Can you honestly sit there and tell me that you didn't even have an inkling that your own daughter was nearby? She is your fucking ringer, Mel, like the spit out of your mouth. She knew who you were from the off. Even after all this time.'

Mel shrugged nonchalantly, her whole countenance was without any kind of guile or pretence. She was being totally honest with him. Truthful. She was also being sarcastic now. Unable to comprehend what the big deal was.

'I am sorry, but *no*. I had no reason on earth to think that about her at all. I was only there to *score*, Basil, not to appear on This is Your Fucking Life. Fuck her, and fuck you. I couldn't give a fucking toss, she is me mother's property now, they both are. I have no interest, darling, and you can tell her that from me.'

Basil hated Imelda more at this moment than ever before. She was the most selfish, uncaring, disgusting person he had ever laid eyes on. Her honesty was all she had going for her at this moment in time. But even her honesty was not a given, she could lie like a politician if the need arose. It was all part of her job, lying, scheming, pretending. She was a natural at it, he knew that from bitter experience.

But this, her complete ignorance of her daughter's dilemma, of her daughter's feelings when she had made herself known to her, to her own mother, a mother who had then dismissed her like she was nothing? Who had *not* even had the decency to *pretend* that she cared about her child, who was quite happy to see her daughter crushed and demoralised? It was beyond him. He knew that Imelda was incapable of any feelings and he could live with that. After all, he knew her, knew what she was. But she could have pretended she cared, feigned an interest. She had to know how difficult it was for a child to introduce herself to her own *parent*, especially since that parent had been the cause of all her troubles and all the ills that had plagued her young life.

Jordanna had never once talked about the murder of Lance, or of Jed, come to that. Basil knew, as Mary knew, that Jordanna remembered everything that had ever happened around her, but she had never said a word to anyone. She had a loyalty that was amazing in someone so young. And this parody of a woman before him did not deserve to have such great kids. It was obscene to see her children growing up and know that she did not even give them a passing thought.

Basil side-swiped Imelda suddenly with his clenched fist, putting all his strength into the blow. Her lip split, and the blood spurted out immediately. She had been unprepared for his attack. He had not known that he was going to smack her either. In fact, the blow had shocked him almost as much as it had shocked her. But Imelda Dooley needed to be reminded of her responsibilities. She needed to remember that she was the mother of two children. Even though she would never get any access to them, she needed to remember that they existed.

Imelda wiped the blood from her face with a tissue she had retrieved from her jacket pocket. He noticed that, like her, it had seen better days. It was crumpled-up, dirty. Like her, it had been used once too often.

She did not flinch though, she just sat there quietly. Waiting for him to do whatever it was he felt the need to do.

He told himself that she was not worth his anger, or his hatred, that she was like a stranger to him now. But her complete disregard for her daughter, and her daughter's feelings, made him want to really hammer the fuck out of her. He smacked her across the face once more, his hatred overtaking his good sense. 'You *cunt*. You broke your daughter's heart and you are so fucking dense you can't even see it, can you? Do you know something, Mel, I would not want to be you for all the money in the world. You will die a lonely death like all junkies, probably of an overdose. One day you will finally score a decent bit of gear for once, and that last armful of shit will be your last fucking hurrah. Your body will probably not be found for weeks; after all, who would bother to visit you? Your kids will be left with the legacy of your fucking reputation, though. They will spend their lives living you down. They will spend their lives wondering what they had done to make you abandon them, leave them, and they will eventually understand why they were better off without you. Especially Jordanna, you used her, and you don't even feel that you did anything wrong, do you?'

Imelda didn't say a word, she was not going to antagonise him, give him another excuse to belt her one. He was so wound up that he was tighter than a watch spring. He would not need much of a push to go ballistic once again. She knew his words were meant to wound her, hurt her. But they didn't. She wished she could talk to him, explain to him that she really didn't care. He was a nice bloke was Basil. In fact, he knew her better than most people. But he didn't understand that she knew herself better than anyone ever could or would. She was a fucking *junkie*, and she actually *liked* being a fucking junkie. It suited her. It was enough for her. It was her life, her choice. Why were people always so quick to make out that their lifestyle was the only one that mattered? Why didn't they just leave people to do what they wanted with their own lives?

Her daughter had crossed paths with her by sheer accident, she had not gone looking for her, had not sought her out or tried to contact her by phone, letter or fucking pony express. She was without any curiosity about the girl or her life, she had no interest in her at all. She never had been afflicted with a conscience and she was not going to develop one now. That Basil had taken it upon himself to warn her, threaten her, chastise her even, was telling her to keep away from her daughter, suited her right down to the ground. She did not want to see her again, she had never intended to in the first place.

But she was bleeding and she was frightened and, quite frankly, she was bored out of her skull.

'Can I go now, Basil? There is nothing I can say that will resolve this, you know that as well as I do.'

Basil sighed heavily. Imelda was right in what she was saying, but that did not make it any better. She was like a robot, or one of those women who were destined to find work in doctors' surgeries. She was without a personality, without any scruples whatsoever, and she would make sure that no one ever got past her without a fight.

'Fuck off, Mel, you ain't worth a wank. But I'll tell you this before you go. Your daughter is a fucking star, and your son, remember him, do you? Your little boy, he is a real good kid. How that happened with you in the background like the spectre at the feast I do not know. But they are better off without you, and that is what I came here to say. Keep away from them in future, leave them alone. Even your own mother hates you, and who could blame her? You make Myra Hindley look like mother of the year.'

Imelda got out of the car then and closed the door gently. As Basil drove away she shook her head in baffled silence.

Her crony was walking towards her now, and giving her a lighted cigarette she said sagely, 'The bigger the car, the smaller the prick, and the more liable the bastards driving them are to try and get the price down or hurt you in some way. It's his problem, darling, not yours. Though it's probably his poor wife's as well. After all, unlike us, she has his company all the time.'

Imelda grinned at her, grateful for the woman's sympathy. That was the real bonus of the pavement, the girls looked out for each other. After all, no one else cared about them. Most of them didn't even care about themselves; if they did they would not have been there in the first place.

Her lip was swollen, but the bleeding had stopped now. She went back to her seat, settled herself down once more, and smoking her cigarette slowly, she started to ponder on what had happened to her.

But twenty minutes later she was ensconced inside a beaten-up Fiesta and as the man, an Asian guy with bad breath and dirty fingernails, fucked her hard, she was already getting herself psyched up to go and score some brown. The night's events were already gone from her mind, after all, Imelda never dwelt on anything for any length of time.

*

Kenny was sitting on his sister's bed, it was very late and they were keeping their voices as low as possible. If their granny heard them she would be in on top of them within nanoseconds. 'Was she really that bad, Jorge?'

Jordanna sighed heavily, her whole body seemed to deflate with the expulsion of her breath. 'She was *worse*, Kenny, I went over there to say hello. That was all. I *knew* her, *knew* who she was from the second I laid eyes on her.'

She sighed again, her whole body tense with anger and betrayal. 'She looks really battered these days. In fairness, she was a real beauty once. She is scary-looking now though, because of the scars all over her boat race, but then she was scary anyway when we were kids. I just wanted her to acknowledge me, that's all. I didn't want a fucking big reunion, I didn't even want to go and talk to her. I just wanted her to look over and see me. I wanted to see her reaction when she knew it was me. Her daughter. I mean, she was watching us for fuck's sake, me and me mates, and she had no concept of me as a person whatsoever. It was like I didn't exist, Kenny. Had never existed. That was how I felt, like I was nothing.'

Kenny was shaking his head in abject disbelief. 'That is fucking outrageous, how the fuck could she not know who you were? Maybe she was pretending . . . You know what she was like.'

Jordanna laughed then. But it was a wicked laugh, full of sarcasm and hate. 'I wish I could say that was true. Kenny, she was watching me and my mates for ages, we were making a bit of a stir you know, dancing, shouting, we were making sure we got attention from everyone. She really had *no* idea who I was. I could see it in her eyes. I was just a girl in the pub, nothing more.'

Kenny lit himself a joint, took a deep toke on it and

expelled the smoke slowly. The aroma of grass filled the room, sweet and cloying, the smoke hanging in the air like a fog. Jordanna waved her arms around to dispel it.

'She is a real piece of work, ain't she? I mean, once you told her who you were, she could have asked after us, asked if we were both all right. I mean, she didn't have to fucking start mothering us, did she? But a polite enquiry, I mean, it ain't fucking rocket science, is it? I ask after me mates' nans and that. It's just being nice, respectful. She fucking brought us into the world . . .'

Jordanna closed her eyes in distress. 'Don't remind me! Unlike you, Kenny, I actually remember her and all that went with her. I remember her hatred, her fucking bullying, I remember her habit as well, the stench of her burning it up, the soot-blackened spoons all over the place. I remember the neglect, the dirt we lived in. I could tell you things that would freak you out no end. I am glad of one thing though, you were too young to remember her. She only wanted us when she was after something, she used us as weapons with Nana. I hate her, I really fucking loathe her.'

Kenny was quiet for a few moments, digesting what she had said. 'I heard about her years ago, Jorge. I know she was accused of killing me dad and that she said you had shot him, even though you were only about three then. I also know that my so-called dad was a right fucking lemon. Poor Nan is worried out of her mind now. She wants to talk to me tomorrow and I know that it will be the story of Lance. I am just going to tell her that I have known the story since the Infants. I have never talked about it before because I never knew what to say. Now though, I think it's time for us to get it out in the open, don't you?'

For the second time in twenty-four hours the murder

of Lance was being dragged up and Jordanna was not comfortable with that subject. She would not talk about that day, no matter who wanted to know about it. Like Jed, Lance was filed away for future reference.

Jordanna's face had drained of colour and Kenny saw the fear that had crept into her eyes. He knew that whatever she had witnessed was not something she was going to talk to him about in the near future. She had never spoken about it to anyone, as far as he knew. She always closed up if it was mentioned.

He grabbed her hands, held them tight and, looking into her eyes, he said sadly, 'Please, sis, I don't care what happened, all I care about is you. Me and you, that is all I am interested in. Please don't be frightened. I think the world of you, I care about you more than anyone else in the world, even Nan.'

Jordanna did not answer him, he had not expected her to. She looked like she had been hit over the head with a blunt object.

'That is me last word on the subject, Jorge, I swear to you.'

She nodded gently. Her face was still a deathly white, and her palms were now sticky with her sweat. He let go of her hands and relighting his spliff he drew on it deeply once more, pulling the harsh smoke into his lungs and holding it there for a few seconds. As he exhaled, he smiled sadly at his older sister, sorry to the heart for all that she had been forced to endure.

'I love you, Kenny Boy.'

He grinned. 'Same same, sis. You have always looked after me, I know that. *Fuck* the old woman, who needs her anyway? We've done all right without her so far.'

Jordanna sighed at the suppressed anger and the

obvious bafflement behind her brother's words. 'Well, be fair, Kenny, we never had any choice in the matter, did we?'

Imelda was sitting in the pub in her usual place, well dressed as always. Her body was still slim and her hair was washed and styled as always. She was one of the few brasses who understood the importance of keeping her body clean. She might live in shit, and she did. Her flat looked like a squat after a bad weekend catering to squaddies. But she took care of herself. She was not in the first flush of youth and she was far away from her real earning days, but she still groomed herself as a matter of personal pride. She had the look of a woman who had seen better days, but she also knew that in her game that could often be a bonus. The men who trawled the streets were not expecting a fucking babe, if they somehow got one for themselves, the pressure would prove too much for them anyway. She was a woman who did not look like she expected satisfaction, she looked like a woman who had experienced enough satisfaction for *everyone*.

Young girls were often seen as frightening, intimidating, older men often wanted a woman they could use without any preliminaries. They wanted to rent a hole, no more and no less. If they wanted a big fucking song and dance they could go home and fuck their old ladies. The whole attraction of a prostitute was that the man concerned did not feel under any obligation to make the experience good for all concerned. And thank fuck for that much anyway!

Shove it in, shove it out, shove the money in her direction. That was Imelda Dooley's mantra. Although she had her regulars, of course, and she was willing to play whatever game they wanted her to.

Imelda was quietly rocking now. She could feel the buzz as it enveloped her. She was smiling, the real smile that only heroin could tempt her to produce. The dope had hit the spot, and she was now so relaxed and laid back that she would not have been surprised if her body had dissolved into the furniture around her. This was the feeling she spent her life trying to re-create. Since her first hit, she had been chasing that same high. Only it rarely saw fit for a return match. Today though, it had overwhelmed her, and she sat there enjoying the intense pleasure it brought with it. She was really enjoying the initial high and, once the euphoria wore off, she would get herself another drink.

As she gazed around her she saw a few of the girls that walked the market with her, and waving to them half-heartedly, she saw them raising their eyes heavenward at her drugged condition. But she didn't care, she was thrilled to be where she was, saw the dirty old pub as a place of wonderment. As she came down a few minutes later she began to concentrate once more on the earn.

Imelda had wraps all over the place, she was in possession of more wraps than Liz Taylor and Doris Day combined. Except her wraps were very small, easily hidden, and gave the owner of them a feeling of confidence and expectation. She would not be wearing them over an evening dress at any time in the near future.

The knowledge that she had more than enough brown to fulfil her needs gave her a real feeling of calmness, made her feel as if she could take on the world if she wanted to.

Imelda scored repeatedly every day; even though she had more than enough for her daily needs, she liked to know she had an overabundance of brown to hand.

Since the first time she had been detained at Her

Majesty's pleasure, she had learnt the value of methadone and had seen her addiction as a medical condition when she needed to. But methadone was not for her, she hated to be without the real thing. She loved the way she was now, at peace with the world around her.

The pub was getting busy now. It was filling up quickly, the men who were arriving were all out on the gatter, looking for cheap drinks, cheap conversation and even cheaper female company. None of the men around her would ever win any awards for good looks, but then again if they could pull a bird without the aid of paper money and alcohol they would not be of any use to her anyway. She liked the warmth that was enveloping her, liked the camaraderie she encountered. One day a week this place was rocking. Still, she always kept herself to herself, she liked her own company. Unlike a lot of the women she encountered on the bash, she did not feel the need to justify her existence by surrounding herself with women of her ilk. She liked her life as it was, a lot of the women on the pavement were there to subsidise their kids, a man, or a habit. And, in extreme cases, all three.

Imelda saw herself as far superior to them because she only ever worked by herself, for herself. She dressed well and when she ate, which was not always a regular occurrence, she ate well. When she blew the needle it was always with the best gear she could locate. She had read in a book once, while banged up in Holloway, that pure heroin was addictive, but not really that harmful. It was what the fucker was cut with that caused most of the damage. Sir Arthur Conan Doyle had been a skaghead, and he had done all right for himself. Sherlock Holmes was a cokehead in the books, she had read them in nick and had discussed them with her drug counsellor. But she did not see herself as a junkie as such. She did not use jellies, never had and never would. She knew that they were the cause of many an amputation and she liked to be in possession of her arms and legs, they suited her lifestyle.

A drink was placed on the table before her and she looked up expectantly. She was not surprised to see the pub landlord winking at her. He liked her; she knew that was because she was always alone, quiet and respectful, and he liked to get a quick feel when the opportunity arose. That was not often, however, his wife being a heavy-set lass from Lancashire with huge breasts and a stomach that was already determined to stroke her knees sooner rather than later. She kept one eye on her husband and the other eye on the tills, she didn't trust the barmaids either. But once a week she visited her sister in Islington, and her old man, along with the barmaids, made the most of her absence.

Imelda smiled at him, and picking up the large vodka and tonic he had delivered to her table, she took a large gulp.

'There's plenty more where that came from, Mel. You enjoy it, lass.'

'I intend to, Ronnie.'

He grinned once more, thrilled at the prospect of a bit of strange. She was a nice lass was Imelda, despite all the rumours about her being a murdering bastard.

She was a quiet sort, never caused any trouble for anybody as far as he had seen, and she plied her trade with a dignity that was lacking in the majority of the brasses who frequented his establishment on a Friday evening. She was a bit ragged round the edges, bless her, but then as his old mum always said, you got what you paid for in this life.

As Imelda drank her free drinks, she was pleased at how

the evening was panning out. She was not really someone who liked the limelight, she preferred to ply her trade in the anonymity of Shepherd's Market. But once in a while she liked to be in the warm, liked to be in company, and liked to know that she was still attractive enough to get a few perks. As she relaxed back into her chair she was unaware of the young man who had been observing her since she had arrived.

Kenny was fascinated by her, he had finally tracked his mother down, and he was enjoying seeing her in action. She was something to watch, from her false smile to her carefully painted fingernails, she looked the epitome of an old brass. She had covered her scars with foundation, but they were still evident to anyone who knew what they were looking for. Kenny thought she was definitely a bit weird, he could see that she had no kind of connection to the world around her. He almost felt sorry for her. She was sad really.

He had felt an urge to see her for himself after Jordanna had accidentally come across her because he had known that he would not be able to rest until he had gazed upon her in person. She was exactly how he had envisaged her, and he understood now why Jordanna had been so devastated. For Imelda it had to be like looking in a mirror, a mirror that showed her as she had looked twenty years earlier. Whereas, on Jordanna's part, it must have been fucking terrifying to see what could happen to you if you weren't careful. His mother looked like a fucking poor man's Diana Dors.

Kenny watched her as she looked around her once more, saw her give him the once-over but, unlike his sister, his mother's ignorance of his closeness, his identity, did not bother him. He was quite happy for the moment to be like David Attenborough, to just observe her in her natural habitat. He was amazed that, even though he recognised her, knew her, he did not remember her at all. Not now that she was in front of him anyway, the woman he remembered was nothing like the Real McCoy. He had a feeling that was probably a good thing. For all concerned. Especially him.

Chapter Nineteen

In the six months since Jordanna had seen her mother, she was a changed girl. Mary saw the difference in her granddaughter and she did not know how to make it better for her. She was like she had been all those years before, when her mother and her lifestyle had interrupted her life; she was distant, frightened, unable to relax for any length of time. She was also brasher, always on her dignity and argumentative.

It was as if her mother's complete disregard for her as a person, as her own flesh and blood, had made her realise that she had been born without any kind of real thought. She knew now that she had never been wanted by anyone. She knew that her mother had carried her inside her for all that time, and still had never once cared about her. Even her granny's love had only been incidental, she suspected that she had not relished her birth either.

It was as if her own mother's lack of recognition as to who she actually was, had destroyed her confidence overnight. She was not the same; she was harder, had lost her softness, her kindness. She was almost like her mother in some respects and she seemed determined not to let anyone get past the guard she had suddenly acquired. Apart from Kenny, she would not let anyone get close to her, it was as if the knowledge that her own mother didn't want her had convinced her that no one else ever would either.

For Mary it was soul-destroying to watch her granddaughter as, ironically, she turned into the person she hated most. Mary knew that Jordanna remembered what had happened the night Lance had died. She also knew that Jordanna had loved her mother unconditionally as a small child, even though she had been frightened of her, frightened of her lifestyle.

Unfortunately, Jordanna had never understood that heroin addicts didn't have feelings or emotions like everyone else around them. Junkies thought they did, at first, thought the way they acted was normal, thought they were still normal. But they weren't. They could never be normal again. It was the introduction to a new way of life, and if they embraced it, they would never be the same ever again. It was an illusion. They were slaves to a craving that nothing or no one could ever compete with.

Jordanna had been too small to understand that her mother had never cared about anyone in her orbit unless that person could be of some kind of use to her. Jordanna had only ever wanted her mother to love her, she had never understood that where Imelda was concerned, loving anyone had never been an option. Even Kenny had only ever been the recipient of his mother's interest because he was a male. A big, handsome boy, Mel had seen him as something to show off to people. She saw him as an achievement because he wasn't a girl.

Like a lot of women, Imelda saw the production of

masculine children as some kind of trophy. Proof of her womanhood, something to perpetuate her myth of being a good mother. But she had walked away from him without a second's thought when the need had arisen.

Imelda had always been strange, Mary could admit that to herself now. She had been tipped over the edge by Jordanna's father, and his treatment of her. She had known for a long time that Imelda had never been right in the head. She had caused so much heartbreak and trouble for so many people, and she had not cared about any of it.

Her daughter was the last person she wanted in her life, and that hurt Jordanna deeply. Seeing poor Jordanna's distress at her mother's indifference to her only made Mary dislike her daughter even more. She had walked away from everyone, even her own children, without a backward glance. She was glad that Basil had put the hard word on her, she didn't want her near the kids. In fact, if she could, she would be quite happy to erase her daughter from their life once and for all. But unfortunately she knew that her daughter would never really be out of her life, not until she was dead and buried and, unlike most junkies, that seemed to be a long time coming.

Imelda had a habit of turning up when you least expected it. Usually when she needed money; when she had come out of the big house and needed a sub. The worst of it was that when she had last seen her daughter, Imelda had not even enquired about how her own children were getting on. It was as if they didn't even exist to her. She had not asked after them once. Mary had secretly been glad about that at the time, if she was completely honest. It saved her having to deal with her. She had given her a few quid and promptly forgotten about her. She had certainly not mentioned her to the two children that she had produced and then used as weapons against her, her own mother. That was the hardest thing for Mary to come to terms with, that Imelda used her own children to get whatever she wanted, and she used them without any kind of guilt. She knew that her children were all her own mother had left in her life, were all she really cared about, and she had still seen her own babies as nothing more than a bargaining tool.

Mary had turned her back on her sons, and she knew inside that she could be a hard case when she needed to be. But at least she had been given another chance at motherhood; she had Jordanna and Kenny and they were all she cared about now. They were all she needed in her life if she was honest.

Now though, through Jordanna, Imelda had once again infiltrated their lives, and Mary knew that no good would ever come of it. Imelda tainted everything she came into contact with; she was a pariah, a Jonah, and all she could do was wait and see what trouble her daughter was going to bring to her own children's front door this time. Imelda had already brought them enough heartache, but it seemed that the avalanche of destruction had already begun and Mary did not know how to stop it. She was unable to prevent any of the usual destruction Imelda left in her path, because she didn't know what to expect from her this time. She had never encountered the kids as grown-ups, and that was something she felt was about to bring its own set of problems. Especially where Kenny was concerned, he seemed fascinated with his mother, he was like all men where women were concerned. Fucking stupid. Kenny thought that he could cope with her and all she would bring with her. He was too young to see that she was always on the look-out for a new mug to manipulate, use, and that he fit the criteria down to the proverbial ground. Kenny was an accident waiting to happen.

'You all right, mate?'

Kenny was grinning, and his huge, toothy smile just made him look even more sinister than usual. He was a natural Face, had criminal written all over him. He had an inborn love and understanding of skulduggery that would stand him in good stead throughout his life. He loved a scam but, more to the point, he *understood* a scam, and he had no qualms about perpetrating the said scam for his own ends. He was a natural-born villain and he had unconsciously known that from a very early age. He was not even sixteen but he already looked much older.

Basil grinned back at him. He liked the kid, he was a really big fucker. All biceps and bad man attitude. He had the natural ability to make people aware of him that was essential in their business. Just one glance told you he was not frightened of anything or, for that matter, anyone. It was a rare gift and, if nurtured, it really could be an asset to anyone who wanted to use it. Kenny had the rare gift of making people around him uneasy, even when he was being nice, being genuine. But Kenny Dooley was also possessed of real personality, he had it in abundance, he had a really nice way about him. He was also a right little tearaway when the need arose, and he would soon be ripe enough to enter the world of real villainy. He would embrace it, he would enjoy it and, more to the point, he would be bloody good at it. Basil wanted to harness that power before Bailey or Hannon got a look in.

'I am really feeling great, son, and yourself?' He was smiling once more at Kenny's complete and utter front.

The boy was like a fucking giant magnet, he attracted people to him. He was a real personality when he wanted to be. Though bipolar was probably the correct diagnosis for his lightning changes of mood, and his natural proficiency for violent retribution. But as far as Basil was concerned, why look a gift horse in the mouth, when said gift horse could become a good earner if reined in and trained properly? Plus, he liked the kid, always had, he possessed an overabundance of charm. What was there not to like?

'Personally, I am well kicking, Bas, me old china plate, and I am in the market for some information. Information I understand that only you can provide.'

Basil was sitting behind his desk. He always wore expensive bespoke suits, hand-made shoes and out-rageously noticeable silk ties. He made sure he not only looked the part of the influential businessman, but that he lived it. After all, in many ways that is exactly what he was; he was a businessman, and he was successful. It was about how you perceived it, how you perceived yourself. Basil understood that how you were seen by your contempor-aries was of paramount importance in his game. If you looked like you had a few quid, you would be treated like you had a few quid. That meant no one would bother him with deals that would only garner him with pennies and halfpennies, he would only be accosted if there was a real earn to be had. If it was considered to be worth his while. In their world that was all people really understood.

Even the Filth were wary of someone who was in receipt of the amount of money he was. Who could buy the best legal team available to them should the need arise, and who could guarantee a good drink, if necessary, for all concerned as and when it might be expected. He bought off a lot of people and, consequently, that meant he owned a lot of people.

Kenny was, as always, easy in Basil's company, he felt quite happy about asking him anything he felt he needed to know.

Basil knew that he was the nearest this boy would ever get to a father figure, and he liked that. Unlike his own kids, Basil actually *liked* this one, was interested in what he had to say. Kenny Boy asked sensible questions, and was genuinely interested in the answers. He listened to the advice given with a quiet respect and a shrewd intuition that meant he took the lesson on board within moments of hearing it.

'Fire away, mate, what do you want to know?'

Kenny was sitting opposite the man he now knew had hammered the fuck out of his mother, and he was not really sure how he felt about that. He gravitated from gratitude for him taking revenge on her to anger, because at the end of the day, she was still his old woman. He was not really sure how he was supposed to react to it. So, without any preamble, he said loudly, 'I have heard about me mum, and she interests me. I want to be properly introduced to her, and I think you should be the person to do it.'

Basil made sure that he did not let any kind of expression creep over his face. He was not pleased at the boy's request, he knew that Imelda would eat him up and spit him out without any qualms whatsoever. He had also told Imelda that she was to keep away from her kids, and she had been as amenable to his request as was physically possible, largely because seeing them was the last thing she wanted anyway. Her kids were practically non-existent as far as she was concerned. If she did think about them, which he doubted, it was not along the lines of a family reunion, he knew that much anyway.

Now though, here was Kenny Boy asking for a fucking personal introduction to a woman who was toxic. Who would see that as some kind of personal interference in her life. She would also enjoy the fact that he had warned her off already and would now be seen as backtracking.

'Why me? Why ask me to do it?'

Kenny grinned then and, opening his arms out wide in a gesture of friendliness, he said sarcastically and with barely concealed anger, 'Well, from what I gather, *Bas*, you are the only man she listens to. I want to meet me *mother*, Basil, and believe me when I say that if you fuck me about I will not be a happy bunny.'

Basil was suddenly unimpressed with Kenny's attitude, and he was not averse to letting his feelings about the boy's request show. He pointed his finger at him, trying to keep a lid on his temper. 'You would fucking dare to talk to me like this? You lairy little fucker.'

Basil was out of his seat now, his anger was such that he was more than willing to give this boy a lesson that he would not forget in a hurry. He was still a kid, and kids needed to be disciplined.

Kenny also knew that for all his bulk he was not yet in the same league as Basil. Kenny saw the way the man stood over him, saw that he had the determination needed to wipe out any kind of opposition. He also knew that this bravado of his would be filed away for future reference, and that he had been a mug to give it large where Basil was concerned. He was always willing to learn important lessons and, unlike most young men, he was also willing to take the said lessons on board. He was doing that just now, his temper was always going to be his downfall and he had to learn to contain it. He had to learn to use it constructively, and not let it get the better of him.

He had only turned on Basil because he was embarrassed at wanting to see his mother in the first place. He had known that his request would not be welcomed. He knew that his mother was not someone who most people saw as worth getting to know. He knew Basil had given her the face full of Mars Bars she still carried. The scars were really livid, but he had made a point of finding out about her anyway, years before all this. He had never felt the urge to see her though, not until now.

He saw how angry Basil was, and he was sorry for his arrogance. Basil was not a man you crossed lightly, and he was also the only man who had ever given him the time of day in his own right. Kenny felt the shame wash over him, Basil had always been there for him and he knew that loyalty was more important than anything else. Even if Basil's *was* tinged with guilt.

'I am sorry, Basil, I can't believe I just mugged you off. But I have been watching me mum, and knowing how everyone hates her, I didn't know how to bring the subject up without us having a tear-up of some description. I know I was out of order, and I sincerely apologise. But she is *still* my fucking mum, no matter what people say about her, true or otherwise, and I want to see her for meself. I want to know her. Surely you can understand that?'

Basil did understand, that was the trouble. He sat back down, forcing his face once more into a neutral expression. He saw that Kenny Boy was on the verge of tears and knew that he would have felt the same way if he had been in the same position.

People were always interested in where they came from,

at least, *who* they had evolved from anyway. That seemed to be something most people yearned for. It was why adopted children looked for parents who had given them away and didn't appreciate the people who had taken them in and brought them up like their own. Strange how *they* never felt the urge to tell the kids involved that they felt no real care for them, wished they had been their real flesh and blood and not some other fucker's cast-off, who would now be hunted down and treated like visiting royalty. Life was a joke really.

Basil was sorry for the boy, sorry for his extreme youth and his adolescent belief that he would find out something about his mother that would make him happy. No chance.

He knew that Imelda would fuck this boy up, and she would laugh while she was doing it. Her big, handsome son would appeal to her for a *while*, would make her feel like a valid person for a *while*. She would hold him up as a yardstick, use him to make herself feel better, look better. She would then devour him without a thought, and this boy would probably let her. He was ripe for her kind of manipulation.

Basil wasn't without feelings and he understood the boy's need to feel he belonged somewhere, knew that his initial contact with the woman who had brought him into the world would be exciting, would be of importance to him and his self-esteem. But, unlike Kenny, he also knew that at some point that same woman would *lose* her interest in him. One day she would not be able to fire up the enthusiasm for his company that he would demand as his right. Basil knew that eventually Imelda would destroy Kenny, just as she destroyed everyone else around her when they got too close. Probably when he started to suss her out.

But, on the other hand, the boy had apologised to him and Basil knew that the lad needed to find out about Imelda first-hand. Otherwise he would never understand how dangerous she actually was. If he saw through her now, as a young man, it could make it easier for him in the future. Sooner rather than later seemed like a good idea. After all, no one had ever wanted Imelda in their life for any real length of time. She saw to that herself.

'I assume you want me to keep this quiet?'

Kenny nodded. He really was a big lad and yet, for all his size, Basil knew that his mother would still chip away at him until he finally had to admit that she was no good. He only hoped that he was right, and it *would* be sooner rather than later.

'If you want to meet her I can arrange it. But I warn you now, Kenny, one day you will regret it. She is poison, she lives for skag, nothing else. Remember that she did not even offer to help pay for you and your sister's food or clothing. She is a dog, she's been in more hotel rooms than the Gideon Bible. She has no real care for anyone or anything. She'll fuck you up, believe me, I know that better than anyone. I know what she is capable of better than anyone. So, when she finally fucks you over, boy, and she will, promise me you will walk away and chalk it all up to experience?'

Kenny nodded. He didn't really trust himself to answer the man who he knew was only looking out for him. Who was only telling him the truth of the situation.

Basil looked long and hard at the young man, at his arrogant face and his nervous demeanour and, smiling sarcastically, he said with a real insight that Kenny had not expected from him, 'You've already seen her, haven't you? But you didn't have the fucking guts to talk to her? You were frightened you'd get an even worse reaction than your sister?'

Basil waited patiently for a reply, a retort of some kind that would give the boy an out if needed. Nothing happened though.

'You think that if I introduce you to her, she'll be forced to recognise you. That that way she can't blank you, deliberately or otherwise. You fucking idiot, she will not care about anything that is relevant to you and her. All she'll care about is how she can use you. It's what she does.'

Kenny didn't answer him, he had a feeling that what Basil was saying to him was true. But that aside, he still needed to know where he had come from, and he needed to know what his mother was really like. First-hand, not just what he had been told about her.

His sister remembered her, he did not. Now and again he felt a fleeting memory of her wash over him. A sound, a word could conjure up images he had long buried.

He remembered her smell though, but even that was not something he could truly rely on. He did not know if he had ever really known her, or if he had made her up. His whole life he had wanted to meet her, and Jordanna seeing her had just forced home to him how long he had been without her. After all, she was his mother, she had carried him inside her. She obviously had no care for him or his sister and, even though he knew that, he still wanted to meet her. Until he understood her, how the fuck could he ever understand himself?

'Will you do what I'm asking or not? I don't want a fucking big drama about it. I just want to see the woman who birthed me.'

Basil laughed then, a real belly laugh. 'There's an old

saying, you know, be careful what you ask for, you might just get it.'

'Oh, for fuck's sake, what do you want now? Are you stalking me or what?'

Basil looked into Imelda's eyes and, as always, he was sorry that he had never seen any kind of emotion in them. She was like a basilisk, all she saw was how things could be turned in her direction, could be made to work for her somehow. There was never any kind of care, or even real interest in them.

If, as someone had once said, the eyes were the window to the soul, then Imelda Dooley's eyes showed that there was nothing even remotely resembling a soul inside her body. She looked, but she did not see. It was impressive, she had fooled so many people over the years, and she would continue to do so for as long as she lived, he was sure.

People, it seemed to Basil, saw what they wanted to, what they needed to. Not what was there in front of their eyes. And it seemed that his theory had been proved by this woman's son. Only a child would still want to know someone with her reputation, and her knack for walking away from anyone who might even pretend to care about her.

Basil was here now because he believed in damage limitation. He knew that the boy would not welcome this much interference on his part, but he also knew that the boy was still far too young to understand that he was only doing this in his best possible interests.

'You make me laugh, Mel, I hammered the fuck out of you and yet you still think you can talk to me like I am a cunt. Like I am one of your punters. Your mother is right about you, never did learn when to keep your trap shut, did you?'

Imelda sighed. Basil knew she was irritated by his presence, knew she was more than willing to take another hiding if that was what it would take to get him off her back. She forced the admiration from him; he knew men who would be wary of a private visit like this.

Imelda shook her head, and he saw a flicker of the younger Mel, the feisty girl who had captured his imagination all those years ago.

'What can I say, Basil? In prison I was told by a shrink that I had a negative personality disorder. He also wanted me to wank him off. You tell me, who wouldn't be negative in a situation like that?'

'Did you do it?'

She grinned then, and it softened her whole face. 'What do *you* think?'

'You are scum, Mel, but then you know that, don't you?'

She shrugged nonchalantly. 'You say that as if I would care about your opinion. You should know me better than that by now. I might have to let you dictate to me, you are stronger these days, but I don't have to let you bother me as such. The shrink was right, Basil, I do not give a shit about anyone, it's part of my charm. I am a negative person, it's what gets me up in the afternoons.'

Imelda was satisfied to see that Basil was not smiling now. She had hit a nerve, as she had intended to. If she was going to get a hiding she was of the opinion that it was better to get beaten as a sheep than as a lamb.

'You ain't got anything charming about you, Mel. You're a dog, pure and simple. But I need you to do a favour for me.'

Imelda sat back in the car seat, relaxing her body now. Basil could smell the muskiness that always seemed to emanate from her. It was strange how she always managed to put him on his dignity. How, after a few minutes in her company, he felt the urge to obliterate her from the face of the earth. She had a way about her, she always seemed as if she was laughing at you even though you could not prove it in any way. She made sure the people around her could feel her utter contempt for them.

Imelda Dooley was more than capable of murder, Basil knew that and she knew that he knew that. His only real concern was that her son didn't seem to understand that about her. In fact, he wondered if her son had inherited the mutant lunacy gene he obviously carried from her. But whereas Imelda's ruthlessness was seen as something to be abhorred, in her son it could, one day, be seen as his greatest asset. Even for Basil, that was food for thought.

'So, who do you need tucked up?'

It was the way she said the words that caused Basil to sideswipe her; catching her on the side of her face with his fist as he put all his considerable strength behind the blow. The sound was loud in the darkness, he could almost hear the pain it caused and yet she didn't even whimper. Instead, she sat back in her seat once more and, as the blood dripped on to his nice leather upholstery once again, she didn't even attempt to use her tissue to stem it. She was bleeding profusely, and Basil knew she probably needed stitches.

As the blood found its own pathway, as it glistened and thickened all over her clothes, her skin, and the interior of his car, he knew she was pleased at his reaction. He knew he had done what she wanted. Imelda loved a violent reaction, if not from her then from the people around her.

It was what made her like she was, what set her apart from everyone else. It was why she was like she was; violence was the thing she craved once the high had dissolved, it was the same thing that had caused all her problems in life. She was an adrenaline junkie.

'Feel better now, do you? Feel like you're better than me?' She was looking directly at him now. In the half-light of the lamp-post he was parked under, she looked like something from a Hammer Horror film.

Not for the first time, Basil wondered if heroin killed not only emotions, but also pain. She seemed immune to pain of any kind. Mental or physical. He was convinced that even if she did feel real hurt like everyone else, she at least enjoyed the sensation of it. Or, at least, she enjoyed the guilt it caused in the perpetrator of the pain. She wanted to be the victim at times, it suited her. If she could not control the situation by her own force, she controlled it by letting the protagonist use their own force, their own anger, against her. Taking the passive stance gave her a strength that was in some ways more powerful. Mainly because, unlike *her*, the people she was dealing with were capable of guilt, disgust and shame at their actions.

Imelda was like a predatory animal, she sensed the weakness in her foe, and she exploited it without any kind of preamble whatsoever. She used, or she allowed herself to be used. Either way, it had kept her alive much longer than expected. She was a real piece of dirt, and he was about to inflict her and all she stood for on a young man who was completely without the strength needed to deal with her and everything that came with her.

His only regret was that he would need to wait until this animal showed her real self to the boy and, when that happened, he would be in a position to make her disappear once more. Only then would he be in a position to pick up the pieces. Because Imelda would shatter her son's life as completely as she had ruined everyone else's around her.

Basil pulled a pristine white handkerchief out of his jacket pocket and threw it at her. 'Wipe yourself, have you no fucking shame?'

Imelda shook her head, and he could see the puzzlement at his anger and his hatred. He knew that she was willing to take what he was going to give her, but that his actions had affected her for the wrong reasons.

'Have *you* no shame? You sought me out, not the other way round. I have the bruises to prove it.' She was laughing gently, as if it was an intimate moment they were sharing together.

'What is it with you, Mel, why do you make people so fucking angry with you? Why do you enjoy other people's hatred so much?' He was being honest with her, wanted to know the answer to his question.

Imelda knew that what he was really interested in was why he felt the need to hurt her so much, and she was confident that they both knew the answer to that one.

The blood was everywhere now, as she wanted it to be. She hoped it was sinking into every nook and cranny around her. The stitching would never be the same again, nor would the carpets. Blood was a fucker like that, it lingered longer than a bad fart.

She wanted him to see the damage he had caused her. Wanted him to know that his back-hander had caused a real wound once again. She did not really care about things like that, she never had. *He* was the one who cared about this crap. He cared far more than she did that he was once again guilty of opening up her face. She knew that his reaction to her simply proved that she had been right about him all along. He still felt something, and they both knew it.

Satisfied that he was not going to repeat his earlier action, she picked up the handkerchief from her lap and began to wipe away the blood from her face with gentle, feminine strokes. The action was almost sexual in its intensity. Looking at the blood that now soaked the white cotton, she looked towards him once again and said sadly, 'Is this about Kenny Boy? Only, he has been watching me for a while now. After Jordanna's histrionics and your fucking outrage, I had a feeling he might come around. I heard many moons ago that he was asking everyone about me. I know that you and my mother keep him close. So, what do you want from me, Basil? Only, I think I might need to see a quack, don't you?'

He realised then that she had known what he would want from the second she had laid eyes on him. She had been expecting something like this.

'How come you are saying all this to me now? If you knew what I wanted, why not save this aggro?'

Imelda grinned. Basil noticed that she had lost a few of her back teeth. All junkies lost them eventually, it was because they spent the best part of their lives gritting them. She was also missing clumps of her hair, another junkie trait. But she did what all functioning drugheads did, she backcombed the remaining hair and, in so doing, she managed to look normal.

'Why would I, Bas? I didn't know for certain what you wanted from me. I ain't a fucking mind-reader. You never gave me credit for what I am capable of. I junk because I *like* it. It's the same reason I gave my kids to my mother, because *she* wanted them. She needs them like I need the junk. Except, unlike her, I can only fuck meself up these days. Now, can we finally get to the point?'

Basil had a handgun underneath his seat. It was loaded, ready for action. He knew that he could retrieve it quick smart, then blow this skank's head off. He looked around him, the road was quiet; it was very late, two-forty in the morning. He would be able to dispose of her and the car within an hour. It would not be the first time he had felt the urge to take out trash on short notice. He was in possession of a scrapyard near Tilbury Docks where more than one belligerent fucker had been crushed and forgotten about. But he knew that this was not an option at this particular moment in time.

Kenny would not appreciate the favour he would be doing him until he had experienced the evil slag first-hand.

'You know the boy needs to see you; now, I want you to be nice to him. Not too nice, but I want you to make him understand that you have nothing personal against him or his sister. Let him down gently, and when the time's right, you can do one of your famous disappearing acts.'

'So you don't want me to fuck him off then, is that it?'

Basil shook his head slowly, and pointing his finger into her face he snarled, 'Just be yourself, Mel, that should do more than enough damage. But if you draw him into your shit, the drugs or the whoring, I will fucking decimate you and laugh while I do it. I mean it, Imelda, I'll torture you and watch as you die in fucking agony. Just give me a fucking excuse, that is all I ask. He is at an age where he needs to know who you are. He needs to know where he sprang from. He ain't a cunt either, naïve maybe, but he has a fucking built-in shit detector and I am relying on that to make him see you for what you are. But he would not survive you using him for money, drugs or just because you think you can. He cares about you, needs to understand you and why you left him.'

'So what am I supposed to do with him then? What if he decides to drag Jordanna into this family reunion or, God forbid, me fucking mother? What then?'

Basil grinned, his expensively capped teeth were bright in the muted light. 'You just be nice. No more and no less. Don't feign too much interest, just make him feel like you remember him. All he needs is a hello and a goodbye, that's it. He is a handful, Mel, and if you upset him, he'll let you know. He ain't got the intelligence yet to suss out the exact nature of the mind games you rely on to exist. But he will suss out if you take him for a mug. If that does happen, I will see to it that you end your days delirious with pain and regrets.'

She knew he meant every word he said. She was quiet for a long while, then, sighing with inevitability, she said, 'It's his birthday next week. Bring him round my place then.'

She never ceased to amaze him, he would have laid odds of a thousand to one that her children's dates of birth were something she had long forgotten. It was this kind of thing that reminded him just how dangerous she really was. Imelda forgot nothing of importance. It was another reason she had lasted so long in such a precarious occupation.

Chapter Twenty

Jordanna was drunk, dangerously drunk and seriously stoned. She knew she was not capable of cohesive rational thoughts, and the knowledge pleased her. She was with it enough to know she was out of it, and this was the feeling she liked. She was just broken enough to be able to blame any bad behaviour on her condition. As she listened to the noise of the people around her, heard the chatter, the laughter, she felt a sense of security. She needed to be in company, needed the anonymity that being part of a crowd afforded her. She was not aware of where she was, but that was something she was used to these days.

She glanced around the packed room, was aware that she had slept with the majority of the men in there and felt a wave of self-hatred. As always, when reality kicked in, she went in search of more alcohol, more cannabis, more disco biscuits. She knew she was letting herself down, but she didn't care any more. She was her mother's daughter and she had a reputation to live up to.

Jordanna remembered all the things that had happened to her as a child, they were inside her head day and night, and the only way to cancel them out was to get off her lovely little face. To blot everything out, and do it in a spectacular fashion. Her mother had taught her that much anyway.

Julie Parsons, a girl she had known from school and who she had once actively disliked, avoided like the plague, was now her new bosom buddy. All her old friends had been systematically alienated by her, they had all been witnesses to her shame. Joanie, the bitch, had made her disgust self-evident and she had never forgiven her for that. Never would, either. Her mother calling out for her to provide her with a drink had been the catalyst she needed for her hatred to take root inside her. If her mother had only left her alone that day, had not felt the urge to make her feel like an object of derision, of scorn, she knew she could have overcome everything once again. But her mother had gone out of her way to humiliate her, and she had more than succeeded.

She had kept quiet all her life about the night Lance had died, had believed that somehow her silence would make her mother realise how much she loved her. Would make her see that she was worthy of her love, loyalty.

Jordanna had harboured a secret hope for years that the woman who had given her life would one day seek her out and thank her for her loyalty. If not thank her, then at least acknowledge her. She knew her friends saw their mothers as the bane of their lives, and she had envied them the attention and love from the women they had spurned so easily, knowing that when they were ready those same women would be waiting to welcome them back with open arms. Jordanna had seen the hurt in their mothers' eyes, and the way they had pretended not to care about the shabby treatment they had received from the daughters they loved more than life itself. She had wanted that unconditional love so badly it had nearly broken her. She had appreciated her granny's love and care, knew she was loved by her, and always would be. But it was not the same thing. If your own mother couldn't find it in her heart to love you, who else would? She had been the victim of her mother's dislike since day one. Her mother had allowed her to be used and abused, and had not cared enough to remember what she looked like. She had not even known her own child. It didn't matter how much her granny told her that her mother was useless, because she had worked that out for herself. Many moons before. But to see her, to be on the receiving end of her mother's complete dismissal of her as a daughter was too much for her to endure.

Jordanna finally knew for sure that all she had been told about Imelda was the truth, she knew that she had not even scratched the surface where her mother's deceit and hate was concerned. She now knew that her need to be acknowledged by her mum had been not only foolish, but laughable in its naïvety. She still remembered how her mother had rarely bothered to acknowledge her existence as a child, unless it was to get something for herself. She remembered exactly how she had been used as a pawn in the war that raged between her mother and her granny. She was aware that she had been used, along with Kenny Boy, to manipulate the social workers and anyone else that her mother came into contact with.

But what really hurt her more than anything else was that she had been showing off for once, with her sexy dancing and her loud-mouthed antics, and she had somehow managed to find her mother's pub to do that in. She had paid the price for her youthful actions by her mother's public display of disinterest. She was a fucking fool, and fools were the grateful recipients of other people's humour. Her mother had quoted that more than once to her as a child and she had only just found out what it really meant. That she had instinctively gone to a place where her mother was comfortable, where she drank, had proved to Jordanna that blood will out in the end.

Now she had finally faced the truth of her life, she was sorry that she had not listened to the stories that she had been told all those years before. If she had understood and accepted her fate, she might not feel so distraught about it now. She really was growing up now, had always looked much older than she was. She knew that, had always known that.

And she knew now that her well-developed body would eventually be her downfall, as it had been her mother's before her. And it was, she offered it to anyone who wanted it. She basked in the few minutes of uninterrupted attention that it provided for her. For that short time she felt valued, needed. Because for that short while, she *was* valued, *was* needed.

It was strange, but men didn't see an actual age as such, they saw the age you *looked*. Not the age you *acted*, or the age you might insist that you were. It was as if her early development had wiped out all their common sense and decency. Men had been hitting on her since she was a kid. She had learnt how to ignore the sexual overtures, knew that her family name, along with her grandmother's association with Bailey and Co., had ensured her a security that most girls could only dream of once they hit their teens.

Then that casual meeting, that one might of humiliation in her mother's company, had wiped that out, had taken her confidence away. Now she raved as far away from home as possible. As long as she was drunk and stoned, she was all right. Then she could forget, even as she believed that she was only being her mother's daughter.

Jordanna loved her granny, and she loved her brother. But neither of them could help her now. Neither of them could understand the way she felt about herself, her loathing at what she had let happen to her. Her mother's murder of Lance, the father of her little brother, Jed's treatment of her, and his death, had been inside her all of these years. She had witnessed far too much, far too soon, and no one cared. She was Jordanna, the older sister, she was supposed to look after her brother. No one had ever looked out for her. Not really.

How she had ever been stupid enough to believe that her silence had been for the good of them all, she did not know. What she did know was how having been used and then promptly forgotten about had broken her both mentally and physically. Not that anyone would ever notice that, or care about it.

Jordanna always felt unwell now, always had a cold of some sort, she often complained of being under the weather. But the amount of drugs she took was bound to make her feel a little bit off her game, surely. No one had noticed that either, not her gran, her brother, Jimmy, Basil, no one in the world. So she took more and more. It was really just an excuse to distance herself from the people who wanted to get close to her. The people she now wished would leave her alone with her guilt and her shame.

Jordanna lay in her bed and played the scenario of

Lance's murder over and over again in her head and, each time, she felt the full force of what had eventually happened to all those concerned. Especially herself.

Then she would think about Jed, Jed and his whispered endearments, his wandering hands, and his eventual possession of her. She remembered the pain and the blood that had lasted for days, that had been the cause of her and her brother staying in that filthy flat for weeks until she had been capable of walking properly once more, until she was without any outward scars, was only left with the ones inside her brain.

She had suffered so much for her silence. In care, foster care, she had been the unlucky observer of just how vulnerable the parentless child really was, saw how predatory the people who were supposed to be caring for you really were. How, if you came from a family like hers, you were seen as fair game. How you were looked down on because of where you were born, and because of who you had the misfortune to be born to. It was a lottery, life. And bullies were the only people who prospered. Jordanna had known at a very young age that she had more savvy up top than all the so-called government agency workers put together. People who couldn't find their own arses with both hands if their lives depended on it. They needed people like her to make themselves feel better. Her granny had fought for her, and she shuddered to think what her life would have been like if she had not done just that, and won.

She had suffered in so many ways, but until her mother had been in front of her, until she had admitted the truth of her situation to herself once and for all, had seen the complete ignorance of who she actually was on her mother's face, she had not understood how worthless she really was. Not just to her mother, but to everyone else around her as well. If your own mother turned away from you without a backward glance, then there had to be a reason for it.

She had forgiven Imelda for causing her father's death, and even her grandfather's death, she knew it was because of her chosen lifestyle, and her selfishness. So why had she harboured dreams of her mother's love when she had destroyed everyone she had ever come into contact with? What had made her think she was any different, believed that somehow she deserved Imelda's love and gratitude?

It was that utter stupidity that was chipping away at her self-esteem now, eating away at her like a cancer. And, no matter how much people tried to tell her that she was not at fault, the more she felt the burden of her shame as it pressed down on her. It coloured her whole life, and she hated it. She hated her foolish belief that one day her mother would find her, would come looking for her. Would make it all right.

As Jordanna wandered away with yet another new male acquaintance, she felt the numbness inside her that was at the crux of her self-loathing. He was just using her, but then she was using him, so what was the difference really? The more she slept around, the worse she felt about herself, and the worse she felt about herself, the more susceptible she was to this kind of situation. She was in a vicious circle and she did not have any kind of idea how she was ever going to break free from it. Or even if she wanted to.

'Are you telling me she knew who he was, Bas?'

Basil shrugged then, his handsome face neutral as he felt Mary's annoyance at his interference in her life. He knew that her anger was also intermingled with her gratitude that, thanks to him, they were in a position to monitor her daughter's effect on her son. She would be happier if her daughter had kept her distance, well, so would everyone. But Mel, being Mel, had not seen fit to do the right thing. As always, they were expected to pick up the pieces and mend the broken people she would leave in her wake.

'She had seen him eyeballing her; I think she put two and two together, Mary. But she was wary of showing her hand until she was sure it was him. Unlike poor Jordanna, I think it was a bit too obvious if you get my drift. She saw him on a lot of occasions, and you know Mel, she is not a fucking idiot. Still, I was surprised that she sussed out who he was. I do know he hadn't got a fucking clue that she'd made him. Let's see how it pans out. Hopefully the fact he wanted me to arrange their first proper meet, and didn't want to chance a reception like Jordanna's, means he is just curious. Once he satisfies his curiosity the chances are he will lose interest in her. I mean, think about it, Mary, this is Imelda we are talking about. She is not known for her sparkling personality or her ability to form lifelong friendships, is she?'

'Kenny will appeal to her, he did as a baby. I know my daughter better than anyone and I can tell you now that he will appeal to her ego. His size, his demeanour, his fucking arrogance. He is all the things she thinks a man should be. He is all the things she tries to destroy in the men she decides she wants for herself. You should know the truth of that, Bas. I saw him tonight, he was like a dog with six lamp-posts. His excitement was almost palpable. He went out that door to meet up with you, and it was all I could do not to drag the silly little fucker back inside, tell him that he was making the biggest mistake of his life.'

Basil sighed heavily. He resented the amount of time and energy everyone seemed to use in keeping a piece of shit like Imelda on their radar. 'But the point is you didn't, did you, Mary? Look, London is a big place for most people. But for anyone born and bred here it's a fucking village. Eventually he would have come across her, he moves in our circles so it was inevitable. Same as it was with Jordanna. We didn't think it would happen so soon, but we knew it was on the cards. Only, at least this time, with Kenny Boy, we can control it to a certain extent. I am going to keep a close eye so stop worrying.'

Mary sipped at her mug of tea, she had laced it liberally with whisky. She had needed the burn of the alcohol, needed the feeling of relaxation it would give her.

'Basil, poor Jordanna is not the same girl since she met up with her mother. I am trying to do what you asked of me. Giving her a bit of space, whatever that really means. But I can see just how much damage has been done already because of her. Imelda has been the cause of more death and destruction than even *you* fucking realise. You would think twice before turning your back on her, same as I would. But not Kenny. He is still young, impressionable . . . and on his birthday, is that really a good day for them to meet up? If it goes wrong he will never forget it as long as he lives, will he?'

Basil was fed up already, he had been through all this earlier in the day. Looking at his expensive gold watch he jumped up, saying, 'All the better really, if you think about it. Look, I will be late meeting him if I ain't careful. Just chill out and let me deal with this, all right?'

Mary knew when she was beaten, and nodding sadly, she watched him leave the room. He had been a good friend to her, but she was not as cavalier as him about her daughter and the influence she might have on her grandson.

Her Jordanna had learnt to survive the gossip that had always followed her. The girl had been strong enough to push that away, she had been liked and respected for herself. She had understood at a very early age that her start in life was something she needed to take on board, knew that it would always cause people to wonder about her, and what she might be capable of. She had to live down her mother's reputation, and the deaths of not only her own father, but her brother's father too. A death that some people still attributed to her, even though she had just been a baby at that time.

One meeting with her mother though, and all Mary's hard work, all the love and affection she had showered on her granddaughter, had been erased within minutes. Imelda had seen to it that her own child had suffered for her curiosity and her misguided loyalty.

Mary had wiped her mouth so many times where Imelda was concerned, and she was not sure if she could swallow much more from her daughter. She was much stronger now, she had a decent few quid, and she was finally willing to use the connections she had forged over the years to ensure that her daughter disappeared one day and never returned.

She had lost so many people; even her own sons had been sacrificed because of Imelda's selfishness, her disregard for how her actions might affect those around her.

Mary knew that she could not allow her to get away with it any longer. If Imelda put one step out of line she would guarantee that, this time, her daughter would pay the full price for her treachery. Mary would not sit back and watch her hard work go to waste, or see her grandson start playing happy families with that bitch after everything she had caused. She had not even been afforded the pleasure of a decent night's sleep for years, and her daughter was to blame for that. She had guessed what had happened to Jordanna, had not felt the strength to confront it, had not been able to live with the guilt of the knowledge that she had sacrificed her for Kenny Boy. She was no better than Imelda really, they were both guilty of using Jordanna for their own ends; to make sure that Kenny was protected, that Kenny Boy stayed safe.

Mary pulled her rosary from her cardigan pocket and, kissing the Cross of Christ, she began to pray for the salvation of her family. What was left of it anyway.

Kenny was nervous. He was unsure if he was doing the right thing, but he knew that he needed to speak to his mother at least once in his lifetime. He knew all the talk about her, had heard all the stories. He knew she was a fucking muppet, but she was still his mother. No one could change that, no matter how much they might want to.

He had felt really bad earlier on, his poor granny had given him his birthday present and he had wanted to cry, weep, at the love and sorrow in her eyes. He was sixteen and he knew that Mary was sad because he was now his own man, was sad because he was now out of her jurisdiction.

She had given him a really expensive sound system, and he knew that he should have stayed in for a while with her, set it up, and played a few songs on it. She would have been expecting that much at least. Instead, he had thanked her profusely, kissed her and hugged her, then told her he was meeting his mates for a night out.

Now he was actually here, about to come face to face with the woman he only knew from newspaper cuttings and other people's memories. The woman he had watched, unable to approach her without a third party. It was almost surreal.

Her treatment of poor Jordanna had made him naturally wary of her, but his overriding emotion was not just curiosity, but also yearning. He yearned to know her personally, know her for himself. He wanted to understand her from his personal standpoint, not through the eyes of other people.

It was strange, but he hoped against hope that she liked him. Even if he didn't like her, he felt an overpowering need for her to like *him*.

He knew she was a liar, knew she stretched the truth to suit herself. She had told some people that she had killed his father, and told other people that his sister had done the dirty deed. In all honesty, he didn't really care who had done what. His old man had been a right cunt by all accounts, a real piece of dirt. All he wanted to know was the truth, the *real* truth behind his conception and his birth. From what he had gathered over the years, Lance was a convenient father for Imelda's baby at that particular time in her life.

He had a sudden memory of his first real fight. He saw the classroom as it had been that day. The steamed-up windows from the overly hot radiators, and the condensation that had pooled on the window sills and the floor. His sister had been cornered by a few boys in her classroom and as he had entered the doorway, he had seen her fright. He had seen her bewilderment as the rest of her classmates looked on expectantly, not even attempting to help her out. He knew then that she was bullied because of their situation.

She looked after the dinner money for them both, so he always went with her at first playtime every Monday to pay it into the office. That was why he was there.

He had realised straightaway that she was in difficulties and, even though the kids surrounding her were older than him, he was already aware that he was much bigger than them, as he was in his own peer group. In fact, he was already wearing the clothes of a ten year old, and he had just turned seven.

It was a few seconds before he understood what was being said about Jordanna, and such was his shock and his anger at what he was hearing, that he only became aware of his reaction to it when the teachers had removed him kicking and screaming from the room. They had calmed him down before informing him that he might have to see the police because he had nearly brained two of the boys in his sister's class.

He had heard the amazement in the men's voices, and also the grudging respect that he had defended his sister and his family name so ably. One of the teachers, a young priest called Father Patrick, had taken him into the room usually reserved for those who were sick and ill. He had smiled at him, shaking his head in disbelief. Then, after giving him a few sweets and allowing him to calm down, he had eventually asked him what the hell had happened to cause such anger and violence in a young fella like himself.

Kenny had told him the truth, you couldn't lie to a priest, everyone knew that. He was God's emissary on the earth, His go-between. As he told Father Patrick about them calling his lovely sister a murderer, that she had broken one of the main commandments, he had seen the look of real animosity that had clouded the man's face.

'You're a good boy, Kenny, you are a real fecking bruiser. What you need is somewhere to channel that aggression. I am the boxing coach for the older boys, but I think I can make an exception with you, as young as you are. Now, I'll have a chat with the powers-that-be and see what I can do. But never forget that your sister is your *blood*, and while what you did was wrong in some ways, you did it for the right reasons. Remember that our Lord Himself was put into prison, was treated like a common criminal by the Romans. He was accused without a fair trial and He had to withstand the mockery and accusations that were levelled at Him by the ignorant and the uninformed. You are a good lad to defend young Jordanna, and don't you ever forget that. Never let anyone destroy your good name or that of your closest kin. They're all you've got in the end.'

Kenny had understood then that he was in receipt of a big secret, knew that fighting was perfectly acceptable as long as you were fighting for a good cause. He had been punished for his outburst, but he had also been admired for it. He was suddenly popular, the bigger boys liked him and allowed him acccss to their gangs and their games. He had already made his name in his own right by the time he had reached the senior school, and the care of the Jesuit priests. He was also an accomplished boxer, but he had long lost any urge for an education. He wanted to get out earning, but he had always kept the respect for the clergy that Father Patrick had instilled in him that day.

Kenny Boy had defended Jordanna from her bullies and won. He had also developed a life-long hatred for anyone who preyed on those weaker than themselves. It was different if the people who needed punishment owed money, or had crossed over an imaginary line and therefore needed to be disciplined. But if Kenny saw anyone being bullied just for the sake of bullying, he could not countenance it. And that was something that stayed with him for his whole life.

Now though, as he waited for his mother's arrival, he knew that the memory had been brought to the fore because of her disappearance from their lives and because she had been the reason for that trouble in the first place.

He and Basil were in a drinking club Basil had opened up in Lewisham. It was frequented by the kind of people who needed a private place to conduct their business, and where they knew that they could talk without any worries that their conversation might be overheard and repeated. It was in a very prestigious location and Kenny was aware of that. He was out the back, in a small private room that smelt of furniture polish and cigarettes. He was feeling overdressed suddenly, and wished he had not suited and booted himself. He felt very formal, and very clumsy. His hair had been cut recently, and he had laid his brand-new cashmere overcoat, courtesy of Basil, carefully across the back of the settee. He knew that his look made him seem much older than he was, and he also knew it was what would be remembered about him for years to come. Basil had taught him well. If you looked the part, you were treated accordingly. Basil had also warned him that he had better make sure he lived up to it. More than lived up to it, in fact. Talk was cheap. That was what British Telecom were for.

Kenny heard the door opening and he stood up quickly.

He was sweating with nerves, and suddenly overcome with embarrassment.

As Imelda walked towards him she smiled widely, the same phoney smile she used on her punters. The smile that had made Basil want to smash her face in all over again; she was the only female in recorded history who had caused him to lash out at the opposite sex and not care that he had done it. She was so fucking annoying, especially now, as she treated her son like any fucking punter she might come across. He wanted to smack her one again, just for the way she was treating her only son. But Kenny Boy did not know any of that, so he smiled back quite happily.

Jordanna had awoken in agony, but she was unable to make any sound whatsoever. She was desperate to groan, to beg someone to make the pain go away, but she was powerless to make her lips form the appropriate words. She felt paralysed and disorientated.

Opening her eyes she felt a jolt of pain so intense it caused a wave of nausea to wash over her whole body. It was a sickening pain that told her she was in some kind of trouble. That she was really ill, needed help of some kind. She was trying to remember where she was, who she was with. But her mind was a blank. She was unaware of anything that might tell her where she was or how she had arrived there, and that realisation frightened her.

She heaved then, a dry heaving that she knew was pointless; she caught the stench of her own vomit and knew instinctively that she had nothing left inside her to expel. She tried to lift her head up but she couldn't. She was unable to even raise her arms, although she wanted to wipe the vomit from her face, wanted to clean herself up.

The feeling of panic at her sudden helplessness was bubbling up inside her now. She could feel the terror as it filled her head with silent screams, and as it caused her heart to beat so fast she wondered if she would survive it. She dropped back into unconsciousness once more, unaware that she was near to death.

She was smiling slightly when the ambulance crew restarted her heart and then sighed with relief as she opened her eyes and looked at them. She was finally lifted out of the dirty gutter, and it was only when she was inside the brightness of the ambulance and on her way to the hospital, that the paramedics realised that she was just a young girl. They also realised that she had been used roughly and discarded. Left to die in fact.

It was only the fact that a young couple had taken a short cut home from a family party and found her lying there, bloody and broken, that had saved her life.

Mary was distraught. She had listened quietly to the doctor as he told her, in no uncertain terms, that her lovely Jordanna had enough drink and drugs in her system to keep the Rolling Stones high until the new millennium. She knew then that she had to do something drastic, and she had to do it sooner rather than later. He had also hinted that she had been raped and beaten.

Jordanna had changed so much, and Mary had been frightened of trying to push it, had been scared of making the girl flee, run away from her. Jordanna had been broken within minutes of her mother's presence, and this was the upshot. And now the same bitch was with her grandson. It was so unfair, it was as if they were all being punished somehow, just because they were related to Imelda Dooley.

Well, she was not going to sit back any more, she would sort this if it killed her. Jordanna had needed to be taken in hand, and Mary's fear of telling the girl what to do, of causing her to run away, had led them to this. Why did people feel like this nowadays? Why were they so scared of chastising their kids, of making them listen to reason, explaining that what they were doing was wrong? Mary had not felt for a long time that she was in a position to offer her advice and she wondered when the children, the youngest members of the family, had suddenly acquired so much power that they were more or less laws unto themselves.

Now this was the upshot; her lovely Jordanna was in a hospital bed and pumped full of drink and drugs. Had been used like a fucking old pair of slippers. It was like Imelda all over again, except Imelda had gone into her life of drug-induced squalor with her eyes wide open. Jordanna, on the other hand, had only been attempting to blot out everything that had happened to her.

Mary remembered when Kenny Boy had started truanting, remembered the social worker's face when Mary told her she had caught him as bold as brass in a pub. She had explained that she had hit him across the face in anger and frustration. She saw then that *her* reaction had cancelled out *his* constant truanting, and had only caused them to question her 'anger management issues', as they insisted on calling them.

She had finally given up the day she had heard the social worker, a lovely girl with a weight problem and an overabundance of rank stupidity, ask Kenny Boy seriously, 'What days do you feel you would like to go to school?'

Mary had understood then that any parental rights she had thought she possessed were long gone. The children were now in the driving seat and even though Kenny's truancy could eventually bring her into court as his guardian, she could not use force of any kind to ensure he attended the fucking school in the first place.

Esther Rantzen and her ChildLine had inadvertently created a monster, because the kids now thought they were well able to flout the laws as and when the fancy took them. This was the final proof of it all.

Because of Imelda's actions all those years ago, these children had spent their lives being monitored by the different government agencies. Social workers, probation officers, family case-workers, to name but a few. Consequently, Mary's hands had been tied for years. She earned, and she did the best she could for them. But any real power she had over them had been gradually chipped away until the kids, being just that, kids, had understood the power was now theirs. It was laughable. Once the schools became involved as well, there was nothing left for the parents or guardians to do. The kids were responsible for their own downfall.

Well, she was finished with it. Jordanna was over eighteen and Kenny Boy was sixteen, she would see that the powers-that-be were aimed out the door once and for all, and her word in her house would become law again.

As she held Jordanna's hand, she swallowed down the tears that threatened to choke her. This girl was at the end of her tether, and it was up to her to make sure that nothing like this ever happened to her again.

Kenny was going to want to know who his sister had been out with, and who had supplied the drugs and drink that had put her in this hospital bed.

Well, he could wait till the morning, she did not want him here quite yet. It was his birthday and he would find out about this soon enough. Why meet trouble head-on?

Basil would also be a handful when he heard about this. So Mary decided to sit with her granddaughter quietly. She wanted to be the first person Jordanna saw and the first person to talk to her. She wanted to hear the whole sorry story in private so that she could edit it, if needs be, and stop another murder from being committed by one of her own family.

Imelda was amazed at how her son had turned out. Considering what her brothers were like, he was a right touch. But then they had her old man on their back as well, so she had to allow for that.

Kenny looked like a real good kid, and he was a kid, even though he was like the half side of a house. He was handsome, and as he chatted to her and Basil she saw that he had that extra little something about him, knew he would always be noticed by people. She had it, and she had wasted it. And anyway, women only had it as long as they had their youth and beauty. Men who possessed it were guaranteed it for life. She knew it was not the proud mother talking either, after all, she was only here because Basil had primed her. She had to admit, though, that Kenny was a live wire; funny and articulate. He was a strange mixture of grown man and immature teenager really.

Imelda was interested now to see if he used his natural shrewdness for his own ends, or did what she had done with hers, waste it, because she had been so convinced of her own immortality that she had lost sight of the main prize. She knew that her selfishness and arrogance had eventually caught up with her. But it was the heroin that had really been her downfall.

It had been inevitable really and, as everyone found out in the end, hindsight was a wonderful thing. Something she pondered on when she remembered how she had used people, how she had deliberately been nasty and dismissive of people who were now in positions where they could help her out, had she been sensible enough to give them the time of day when she had the chance.

So, this new-found friendship with her son would be made tolerable because she was interested in seeing how he would operate in the future. He had Basil in his corner, and that was a bonus in anyone's book. Plus her mother had pulled herself up through the ranks and forged a decent earn for herself as a paid gatherer of information and rumours with Jimmy Bailey. So, Kenny had a decent start in life.

As Imelda lit herself another cigarette, she saw that Basil and Kenny Boy were both looking at her expectantly. She had obviously been asked a question of some sort and, as she had not bothered to listen, she was in a quandary.

'Well, answer me?'

Kenny had not referred to her as 'Mum' once, and she was a bit peeved about that if she was completely honest. She had been bloody good to him when he was a baby.

'What do you want me to say?'

It was a trick question and Basil knew it but Imelda was not sure if Kenny Boy had sussed out that she was oblivious to what he had asked her. Her years on the bash had taught her how to look interested and alert even though she had tuned the punter out from the off. Now though, she knew she would have to be a little bit more on the ball.

Kenny was frowning at her, and she knew he had asked her something that he felt was of real import.

'I'm sorry, son, but I don't know what you want from me.'

He stared at her with those dark-blue eyes of his, eyes that he had inherited from her. The word 'son' had thrown him, as she knew it would.

Basil was impressed at Mel's deft handling of her son and, seeing the effect her words had on Kenny he said quickly, 'I think that what Kenny wants to know is why you didn't just pretend you knew Jordanna, why you had to make a snide remark and humiliate her in front of her mates?'

He had exaggerated the question, and they knew it. But Kenny also knew that it had to be asked at some point, so now was as good a time as any. He had worked out already that she had not even heard him ask her why she had more or less blanked her only daughter.

He saw the feral glint in Basil's eyes and then saw the same glint mirrored in his mother's. He knew that Basil was just waiting for an excuse to pounce on her and he understood that was because this woman was genuinely without any kind of feelings at all. It was a real eye-opener for him.

'In all honesty, I was embarrassed. I did not recognise her, and if that makes you both angry, so be it. I am trying to be honest here and, believe me, that is not something I tend to do very often, as Basil will tell you.'

Kenny nodded. He looked at her once more, at her tight clothes, heavy make-up and well-cut hair. She wore good shoes; she was obviously vain about her legs and, in fairness, she had good reason to be. She looked what she was though, a brass. A pro, an old tom. She was a user, a ponce. She was without any scruples or decency.

This woman had given birth to him and yet she felt no

connection to him whatsoever, even though that was not something most women did lightly. Labour was a long and painful experience from what Kenny could understand, and she had only gone through with his pregnancy and birth because she had hoped it might get her a reduced prison sentence if that became an issue. Otherwise he would probably have been scraped out and flushed down the bog long ago.

She was quiet now, watching him as he digested everything she had said. She knew then that he had made his mind up about her, and not in a good way either.

They looked at each other for long moments then, sizing each other up. He would keep an eye on her, he'd decided that she was someone it was better to keep tabs on. Now that he had finally spoken to her, the allure he had felt initially had vanished. But she was still his mum and, unfortunately, nothing or no one could ever change that.

Chapter Twenty-One

Jordanna was still not right and Mary was at a loss as to how she could make the girl she loved more than life itself feel happy once more. As Jordanna lay on the sofa softly sleeping, Mary wished she could make it right for her. In the months since the attack she had reverted back to how she had been as a child.

Jordanna had never been what you might call an ebullient kind of girl, well not since Lance's death anyway. Away from her mother's oppressive personality, and the foster home she had been forced to stay in, she had come home to her granny and brother and, after a while, she had started to emerge from her self-induced shell. Eventually, after a lot of hard work, she had become a child once more, albeit a child who knew too much, far too much than was good for her. But Mary didn't like to dwell on any of that.

She was a child who had silently watched the people around her, who waited to see how the people around her were going to react to the abrasive forces surrounding them, before ever allowing herself to interact with them. A child who, for a long time, had been nervous, without any kind of authentic emotions. For years she saw everyone around her as possible enemies, users.

The more they loved her, or tried to care about her, the more she seemed to mistrust them, believed they were only trying to use her for their own ends. It was all she had ever really known in her young life.

But Jordanna had one saving grace; she had always loved her granny, the only constant in her little life. She was the only person who she knew genuinely loved her, no matter what she had done, or what had happened to her. Jordanna needed someone in her life who did not judge her, or try to question her about the events of the fateful night when Lance had died, or about Jed and her mother. About the night when they had been bought to book and which she had heard in stunning clarity by all accounts.

Mary remembered now that Jordanna had pushed her little brother under the bed, had tried to protect him. It was a shame that no one had managed to protect her when she had needed it.

She had seen to it that the girl she adored had been given everything she needed, everything she asked for. She had loved them both, especially Jordanna, with a vengeance. She had also used her influence to guarantee that the girl had never had to answer to anyone about Lance's death, she had made sure that the girl had been allowed to live a relatively normal life.

Because of that, the children had managed to get over it in the end, and Mary had created a life of sorts for them all. In fact, she had eventually even managed to bring laughter and a sense of normality into their daily lives, something they had never known before. She had been determined that these children *would* be loved and wanted, would *feel* loved and wanted, and Mary knew that she had achieved that much.

Then, once again, Imelda had come into their lives and in a few minutes and with a few choice words she had destroyed everything they had built up together without a second's thought.

Now Kenny Boy had been determined to get in touch with her, and, having thought about it some more, she thought in all honesty that he was right, they were far better off if they knew where she was and what she was doing: in that way they could police her. Imelda had a habit of turning up like a bad penny so, in this case, forewarned *was* forearmed. Mary wanted to keep her as far from Jordanna as was physically possible, though. Imelda had been responsible for the girl's problems and Kenny knew the truth of that as well as she did, as did Basil and everyone else. Michael Hannon hated her with a vengeance and so did Jimmy Bailey. Imelda had managed to fall out with everyone who would have helped her out if she had used her loaf now and again.

But now, looking at Jordanna and seeing the toll the last months had taken on her, Mary wished, once again, that her daughter would just die. An accidental overdose, or she could fall under a train; anything to get her out of everyone's life once and for all. As long as she was alive, Mary knew that Jordanna would never know a day's peace.

Jordanna awoke at last. She looked terrible.

Smiling falsely, Mary asked, 'Are you all right, my darling? What did the doctor say this time?'

Jordanna smiled tremulously. She saw through it all as if she was looking through a pane of glass. But she played the game, she had no other choice.

'I'm all right, Nan. But he told me something, and I need to talk to you about it.'

She was suddenly on the verge of tears once more. Her huge blue eyes, so like her mother and her grandmother's, were filled with pain and sorrow.

Mary sat down on the sofa beside her granddaughter, and placing her arm around the girl's slim shoulders she said gently, 'What is it, my love? There's nothing you can't tell me, I have heard it all. I love you, and I always will.'

She was terrified inside, wondered if the girl was going to tell her she was HIV positive. It was all you seemed to hear about lately. On the TV, the news. Everyone seemed to have it. So she braced herself for whatever was coming. No matter what it was, they would cope somehow. It was all they could do.

'I'm pregnant, and I don't know who the father is. I have no real recollection of anything as you know . . .'

Jordanna was crying now, really sobbing. And Mary was so relieved that it wasn't a terminal disease that she was almost smiling with gratitude.

'Look, Jordanna, things happen in life. *We* know that better than most people, darling. All I can say to you now is that a life coming into the world is something to celebrate. A gift from God Himself. But if you don't want to have this baby, I will understand, and I'll even help you to arrange . . . whatever.'

Mary could not bring herself to say the word abortion. But she was quite willing to arrange just that if this child felt that was what she wanted to do.

Jordanna looked into her nana's face then. 'I am like her, ain't I? Pregnant and without any idea who the father is. I hate meself for that, hate that I have so much of her inside of me. But I can't have an abortion, I just couldn't.'

Mary was so sorry for this girl who was the antithesis of her mother if she could only see that. She had *acted* like her mother, she had been destroyed by her, but she had nothing of that bitch in her at all.

'Listen to me. You look like her, granted, but that is where the similarity between you ends, believe me. Now, you listen to me, and then let this be an end to it. You'll be all right, but you have to put her out of your mind as I had to. She is a canker that taints everything around her and if you let her colour the rest of your life, then she will have won. This little child you're carrying will be tainted by her, and so will anyone and everything that comes into your orbit. She is not right in the head, and you know that is true. Somehow she was born into this world with something missing, she has no kindness, no caring, no emotions like normal people. Once you accept that, as I have had to, and remember this is my daughter, my child, I am talking about, you will feel much better, believe me. I've watched you lose yourself because, somewhere in your silly fucking head, you thought you were like her, that she was your destiny. Well, she ain't. I am your mother, to all intents and purposes, not her, and this child will have you as its mother, and you are bursting with love and caring. So please, Jordanna, just try and forget about Imelda, she is not worth the time or the effort. But, if you can't do that, then don't drag a child into all this; your mother did that twice, and I had to pick up the pieces. I am too old to be doing that again.'

Jordanna knew that her granny was telling her the truth of the situation. She had already let her mother poison her life, and this pregnancy was the result of that. She had gone into a spiral of drink, drugs and casual sex until, finally, she had been left for dead in the gutter, beaten and used. She had allowed her mother's hatred and evilness to overtake her and become, for a while, the very person she had once loved and then, eventually, despised. When Imelda had humiliated her and laughed at her in front of her friends and when the stories had once more started to emerge about her childhood, she had suddenly believed that, no matter what she did, or what she achieved, she would never really be anything more than Imelda Dooley's daughter.

Now Jordanna knew it was time to take control of her own life. She hoped this child would help her to find the good in life, hoped that it would help her to find some kind of peace inside herself. A child was born with the knack of unconditional love, she had first-hand knowledge of that, and she knew she needed someone to love, someone who was capable of loving her back, no matter what. Her mother had never returned her love, and, in the end, she had killed it. She hoped that this child would be healthy and happy, because she needed it to wipe away the sadness she felt inside herself.

Kenny was like a tightly coiled spring; he was ready to explode at any minute of the day or night. As much as he had thought he was on the ball where life was concerned, his sister's dilemma had made him realise that he had no personal knowledge of the real world. Not when it pertained to women anyway.

He now understood that experience was of paramount importance in the world he inhabited. It was why old lags were still on the payroll well past their sell-by dates, and why the likes of Basil needed youngsters like him. He had the nous of his peer group and Basil had the experience to use it to its full advantage.

That his sister, his Jordanna, had been out and about with geezers of somewhat dubious characters was bad enough, but that they had to have known who she was, had known that she was his sister, was beyond his belief. He might only be young and on the first rung of the ladder, but he was already known well enough to garner respect. He was a *fighter*, and he knew that was what gave him the edge over his contemporaries. He was already working for some real Faces, and they were pleased as Punch with him and how he conducted himself. He was confident enough in his ability as a tear-up merchant to happily go up against anyone at all. Maybe not Roy Shaw, but then who would be that fucking suicidal? But anyone else, anyone who wasn't a professional fighter, he would happily take on in a second.

So this drama with his sister was even more outrageous than it should have been. He felt it showed him in a bad light, it made him look like he was of a negligent nature. And he should have had his eye on the ball; if he had done that, then Jordanna would have been shown the error of her ways long before it had gone too far.

Poor Basil was in the same boat as him. Although Basil did insist that she had taken herself away from her manor and had not given anyone she met her family history so, in fairness, he blamed Imelda for that, as was his right. After all, it made sense that she would not want her relationship with her mother broadcast to all and sundry. The association had never enhanced her life up till then, and that was not going to change at any time in the near future, he was sure.

Jordanna had systematically dropped all her friends and all her usual pursuits, and Kenny had not even taken the time to wonder why. He had been heart-sorry for what had happened to her, but he did not feel the same way as Jordanna about their mother. She did not affect him so much, and he understood now that was because, unlike Jordanna, he had never known her. She was a fucking fleeting memory, she meant nothing to him.

Kenny felt that his sister being found nearly dead, used and battered in the gutter, was something that needed to be addressed, and addressed sooner rather than later. It reflected badly on him, and that bothered him. It was personal now. This was not just about his sister's fucking predicament. It was about his pride.

So that was why he had been so busy the last few months. Jordanna had been found in Ilford, she had been dumped in the gutter just off Green Lane. The road itself was private and quiet, used only by the residents who lived nearby. It was not somewhere that was ever really busy, so it seemed logical to him that Jordanna had actually been left there to die. Another few hours and that is exactly what would have happened. He also knew that, whoever had dumped her had wanted her demise, had known that if she lived to tell the tale then her story would have guaranteed their complete annihilation.

He knew that she had fooled them, telling them she was staying at a friend's house, and that she was going away for a few days. He had not even cared enough to ask her about anything, but then he had trusted her. He had no reason not to.

His granny had an inkling that Jordanna was not right, he knew that, as she seemed to think that telling him about her worries now would somehow help the situation. If she had told him about her worries at the start, he would have sorted it out then and there.

But, in his heart of hearts, he knew that he had just

assumed that she was OK. He had believed that she was safe and sound. He also knew that he had failed her, that, after the run-in with Imelda, she had changed drastically, almost overnight. He should have kept his eye on the ball, and he hadn't. He had been so busy making a name for himself that he had neglected to take care of the main business, the business that should have come before anything else, should have taken priority over everything else. The family and their welfare.

But he had snooped and he had finagled and he had passed out large sums of wonga, along with threats of violence and torture, so he could ensure that the people involved would be discreet about him, and about his enquiries.

Finally, he had collated all the stories he had been told, and through sheer hard graft, even more threats, and some promises of future business dealings, he had finally found out where Jordanna had been on that fateful night. And, more importantly, who had seen fit to take such a personal interest in her. She had refused to talk to the Old Bill, and he had agreed with her decision about that much anyway. He knew Jordanna was not that sure of the circumstances herself, and she did not want what had happened to her to become another talking point when her name was mentioned. He understood that, as his gran had.

Now though, after a lot of money, and a lot of terrorising, he was outside a terraced house in Vauxhall. The tenants were two brothers from Grenada who thought they were Yardies because they had sold a bit of puff, and bought a gun from a fucking schoolboy in a pub on the Old Kent Road.

Well, they were about to get smashed all over their own back Yardie, and Kenny was already feeling a deep sense of satisfaction as he contemplated his revenge. He knew they were the prime culprits, and as he saw the two minders Basil had promised him pull up in a dark-coloured Range Rover, he rubbed his hands together with gleeful anticipation. He loved a fight, always had. He loved the rush of adrenaline beforehand, the excitement that overwhelmed him as he contemplated his enemy's total fucking destruction at his hands.

It suddenly occurred to him that his sister's baby would, in all likelihood, be black; *well*, that didn't bother him at all. He had no feelings about anything like that.

What did bother him, though, was that the child would also be fatherless; it seemed that in the Dooley family that was now a common trait. It was starting to feel like none of them was going to be blessed with a father worth their fucking salt. Well, this pair would not be fathering any more children in the near future, not if he had anything to do with it anyway.

He was raring to go now, and motioning to the two men standing idly by, he kicked the front door in. He strode into the house, his anger physical in its immensity, and shouted at the top of his voice with an affability that made his friendliness seem almost believable, 'I'll have a consonant please, Carol.'

The men accompanying him were still laughing about his entrance years later. It was yet another story that would be told about the Dooley family. As far as his minders knew, the men inside the house had tried to have Kenny over for a few quid. Afterwards, they had both privately felt he had gone overboard with the amount of violence he had used. A lesson was one thing, leaving the two men almost dead was something else entirely. Kenny knew that his liberal use of knuckle dusters, mixed with breaking open the men's heads with a length of lead piping, would eventually become just another story about him and his colossal temper. And it would be used in the future to explain why he was not a man to be crossed.

That was what Kenny hinted, he wanted his reputation to be such that no one of his age or generation would feel the urge or the nerve needed to try and usurp him from his chosen position in life. He felt his hatred for the two men overwhelm him, knew that it was this ability to hate so viciously that gave him his almost superhuman strength, gave him the edge in many respects.

He knew he was going to be talked about a lot after this little debacle, and that was exactly what he was depending on. This was Kenny Boy's way of cancelling out the negative stories that had haunted his poor sister since she had been a baby, and he was going to spend his life creating newer, more interesting stories for people to tell about them all. He would also make sure that if anyone talked about his sister out of his earshot, he would not be best pleased. Careless talk cost lives.

The two men with him were going to talk anyway, so why not give them something to talk about? If he used his loaf properly, the new stories would far outweigh the old ones.

He was a man now and he had to protect his family. He could never again let them be hurt or used. It was down to him to make sure they were safe. Safe from harm and safe from hurt and, more to the point, safe from the truth.

Imelda heard about Kenny Boy's latest stunt through the grapevine. By the time it was relayed to her, the two men he had taken on had seen their reps exaggerated out of all proportion; they were now a real pair of titans, top-of-the-range Yard boys with a house full of shotguns and a fridge full of Red Stripe. Stories always got stretched in the telling and this one was no different. Imelda smiled as she listened to her son's latest escapade, she was proud of him, liked that her son had already made a name for himself. Reflected glory and all that, she was not averse to it.

Imelda wondered, as she often did lately, who Kenny Boy's father could have been. She knew the children didn't have anything to do with their paternal grandparents any more; as the years had gone on her mother had seen to that. She guessed that Mary was jealous of the children being near other people. In fact, Louise Parks had met a man through David Driscoll and had moved to Spain, though she still kept in contact with Jordanna. But Imelda knew nothing about that, she only listened to bad gossip, never the good.

As her friend, a fellow brass, finished the story about Kenny Boy for the second time, Imelda opened her arms wide as if she had already heard the story long before, and laughed as she said, 'That's my boy.'

Danielle Clunes laughed with her. Danny, as she was affectionately known, was very tall, extremely thin, and she wore heavy make-up and even heavier jewellery.

Imelda called her Big Bird behind her back; as she often wore yellow dresses the name was quite apt. She had a lovely nature, though, and was well liked by her fellow brasses and the regular punters alike.

'So, Mel, I bet you can't believe you are going to be a granny at last, can you?'

Imelda was unaware of her daughter's condition, and guessed that it would have been hidden from her until Jordanna's condition could not be denied. That no one had seemed fit to enlighten her annoyed her. After all, she was the grandmother, she had a *right* to know about it.

She recovered her equilibrium within seconds. 'Well, Jordanna wanted it kept quiet, so what can you do?'

Danny smiled, but she was not fooled. She could see it had been news to Imelda, that her daughter and son had not seen fit to inform her. And why would they? She was hardly mother of the year, everyone knew that. But she would play the game.

'What would you prefer, Mel, a grandson, or a grand-daughter?'

Imelda shrugged. 'Couldn't give a fuck, to be honest. It ain't like I am going to be babysitting is it?'

They both laughed at the truth of that statement.

Imelda turned away from Danny then, grateful for an excuse to leave that conversation behind and walked towards a battered Renault that had pulled up at the kerb. She knew the man, he was a regular, all oily hair and ointments. He was also the proud possessor of a repeat prescription for sleeping pills, which he gave to her every month for a freebie. She leant provocatively into the open window as always. 'Hello, George, you got anything nice for me?'

George nodded, the grin as wide as ever, the stench of his aftershave hanging on the night air. It never quite masked the stench of Germolene mixed with Deep Heat, treatment for his so-called bad back.

She slipped into his passenger seat, and he gave her the pills almost immediately. 'Look, Mel, if it's all right with you, love, we'll keep this on the once-a-month basis from now on. There's a new girl, she's only twenty and very athletic, if you know what I mean? So, in future, I'll be going to her for me twice weeklies.'

Imelda nodded and, placing the pills in her handbag, she felt the first fingers of fear that all brasses eventually experienced as they started to understand that they were going over the hill. For someone like her, who was already about as low as she could go, the knowledge that she was being overlooked by such as Georgie Boy was a real learning curve. She had known that her volume of punters had been steadily decreasing of late, but she had assured herself that her regulars were the real bread and butter anyway. Once they deserted her though, she was finished.

She needed to get herself an alternative income, and she needed to do it sooner rather than later. She had never been a saver, never thought about the rainy day, because every day was a fucking thunderstorm to addicts. As always, she was only concerned about herself, and feeding her habit. She now needed to make some kind of provision for the future.

'Come on, Jordanna, smile for fuck's sake.'

She smiled, despite herself. Kenny Boy was like a big kid, and his good humour was infectious. He took the photo of her and saw that she was really genuinely smiling at him for once. She was getting heavy with her child, and he knew she was looking forward to its arrival. He was looking forward to it coming as well if he was honest. He liked babies, and he liked the thought of the family getting larger. He also liked that they were starting to expand the name.

When he got himself a decent bird he would make it his business to slip her a child a year for six or seven years on the trot. He wanted a big family, but he also wanted all his children to be with the same woman. He was not enamoured of those men who splashed their sperm about all over the place. Kids here, there and everywhere. He wanted to know his kids, see them grow up, be there for them when they needed him. He had it planned out. Nice wife, nice house, nice cars, good schools and decent holidays every year. His kids would have all the things he never had. The stability of a father figure was the most essential requirement, as far as he was concerned. His kids would never know what it was to wonder what each day would bring, they would be loved and cared for from the moment they arrived. As would Jordanna's little baby. He had made a solemn promise to himself that he would take on the role of father figure, and see that the child never wanted for nothing. It was the least he could do for Jordanna.

'Is it true that you are already being groomed to be Basil's number two?'

Kenny grinned, his open face, as always, unable to hide his true feelings. 'Yeah! I like it, I like the people I am involved with, the lifestyle. We'll be rolling it in before you know it, girl.'

Jordanna grinned. 'We ain't doing too bad, Granny is coining it in. You must get that from her, your shrewd-ness.'

The doorbell rang and Kenny Boy sighed. 'I bet that's Timmy B, for me, he's fucking early for once.'

Jordanna lay back on the sofa, she was tired out with her pregnancy. She heard the familiar voice of her mother then, seconds later, she saw the woman she dreaded pushing her way into the room.

'I want to see me daughter, I hear I am to be a granny at last.'

'Well, Jordanna does not want to see you. Now, stop all this, Mum, leave her alone, eh?'

Imelda was on a roll now, she actually believed her own story.

'Please, Kenny. I want to see her, she is having a baby and, whether you two like it or not, it's my grandchild. All I want is to see that my daughter is all right.'

Imelda looked down at her daughter's body with its bump and saw the tiredness in her eyes, the pallor of her skin. She knew Jordanna was about as low as she was ever going to get. Like a hyena Imelda could sense weakness in people, it was something she had been born with, had developed over the years, and that she used when the need arose.

'Please, Jordanna, just let me see you one time. I know I ain't been the greatest of mothers, but I still care about you.'

Kenny shook his head sadly. 'Out. You know the score, Mother. You've seen her now, let that be enough.'

He turned her round then so that she was once more facing the front door.

'If me gran comes home and finds you here there will be fucking ructions, now go. Just go, will you?' He was trying to keep his voice neutral, didn't want to cause a fight, wanted Imelda to just leave them both to it.

Imelda turned to face her daughter once more, and, pushing her son away from her abruptly, she said softly, 'I just want to wish you well, darling. That's all. I know what you're going through. After all, how do you think you two got here?'

She shrugged then, her thin body almost welcoming, her eyes seemed almost sparkling at the thought of a grandchild, a new member of the family she had never even pretended to care about. It was odd, it was unnerving. Imelda had hoped for this reaction, she knew that kids were like any other mark. If you knew how to press the correct buttons, they were guaranteed to act in the appropriate manner. Her two had not disappointed her so far. She knew they were stuffed full of guilt, her mother would have made sure of that much, and because of that she knew she was already a few inches into the front door of their lives. She smiled again, aware that she could not strong it just yet. She needed to gain their trust and their affection before she started to bleed them for money.

'Look, I am going, so don't worry. I just wanted to see you for meself. Needed to see that you were all right.'

Imelda seemed so sincere that they were both unable to find anything to latch on to, could find no real argument against her being there.

'I won't outstay me welcome, but Jordanna, make sure you eat properly, and get enough rest. OK? You have my future grandchild in there. Bye, mate.'

Then, smiling sadly at them both once more, she allowed herself to be walked off the premises.

Outside the house Kenny was at a loss as to how he was supposed to deal with his mother now. She was being nice, calm, friendly, and that meant she was obviously up to something. But until she said anything detrimental he was not in any position to cause any real aggravation. So he decided to play her at her own game. 'Leave her alone, Mum, don't fuck this up for her.'

Imelda stood before him, her shoulders slumped, her face looking pained, and her whole demeanour one of hurt, hurt and bewilderment. 'I swear, Kenny, on your father's grave, I am not here for any other reason than my daughter, she is about to produce my first grandchild. Even I can see how important that is. I ain't completely fucking heartless. I might not be the babysitting type, but

I still care about you both. I ain't asking to be its fucking mentor, I just want to know it's all right, that's all.'

Kenny saw how dilapidated Imelda looked, how scrawny and underweight she was. Even with her perfect make-up and well-cared-for clothes, she looked rough to the trained eye. Unlike most junkies, his mother had a kink in her nature; she managed to function, managed to see that she kept on top of her addiction. He knew that was not an easy thing to do, knew that if that strength and that determination to keep herself like she was, had been channelled into something constructive, she would have been capable of almost anything. Would have been enough to take on the world if need be.

He also knew that her personality was the reason she had chosen the paths that she had. It was also the reason she did not dwell on her mistakes like normal people. She was such a fuck-up she did not care about her own failings or disasters, let alone anyone else's. Like Jordanna, he was terrified that he would become just like her one day, that he would wake up to discover that he ceased to care about the people around him.

He was scared that he would forget to keep his eye on them all, would, without realising it, become a vicious, uncaring loner, and eventually lose the people closest to him.

As if she was reading his mind, Imelda grabbed his arm and, squeezing it tightly, she said simply, 'You will never turn into me, Kenny, so stop worrying about it. I am a one-off, a person like me is thrown up in a family once every other generation. I still care for you though, in me own way.'

Kenny pulled out his wallet and, taking out a thick wad of cash, he thrust it into her hand.

She was stepping away suddenly. 'I don't want your money . . . I didn't come here for that, son . . .'

'Oh, Mum, please. By that criteria the Pope is *not* a Catholic and Fidel Castro was all for a democratic state.'

He shrugged in irritation. 'Take it. You know you want to, it's why you came here.' But, as she had known he would offer it, she knew she would take it. He forced the cash into her hands as she had known he would. One, to get shot of her, and two, to assuage his guilt.

It was at least two hundred quid, she could see that with her practised glance.

'You're a good boy, Kenny. I can go home now and have a rest. I am getting too old for the pavement, boy.' She grinned as if she had just made the greatest joke of all time.

He grinned back at her then. 'That was what you came here for, ain't it?'

She was silent now, unwilling to say anything that might queer her pitch for the future. Then, suddenly, she was offering him his cash back with an outraged expression, and a choked-up voice. 'Take it back, son. If that is what you think of me, have it.'

She threw it to the ground then, and even though he knew that it was an act on her part, the guilt overwhelmed him as always.

'I won't deny that I need it, son, but I would rather not have it if you think that is what I came here for. Remember that I have not had the easiest of lives meself. I have a face full of Mars Bars, courtesy of Basil, and I lost a really good earn. I have swallowed all that, accepted the blame, and left you both alone, as my mother and Basil insisted. I don't want fuck all from you two, and you remember that . . .'

He picked the money up and gave it to her once again; this time she snatched it from him.

'Thanks, son. Tell your sister I wish her well . . . I really do.'

She walked away from him then. He watched her until she was finally out of sight. At last he went back into the house. Jordanna was still lying on the sofa, only now she looked even worse than before.

'I feel really bad . . . Has she gone?'

He laughed then, unsure if he had been had, or if his mother had been genuine about them all at last. 'She's gone, Jorge, because I gave her a wedge. Now, let's forget about her and get you to the hospital, shall we? You look a bit iffy, girl.'

Jordanna nodded, but he knew that she was unnerved by Imelda's sudden appearance, and even more unnerved at her interest in the child she was carrying. They were both quiet as they left for the hospital.

Chapter Twenty-Two

'Come on, Jorge, or we'll be late.'

Jordanna was laughing at him. They were actually early, very early. And he knew that as well as she did. Kenny Boy was the guest of honour at his own pub opening. Tonight was the culmination of everything he had worked for. He knew it was a real achievement, and he understood better than anybody how unusual he was to have even managed it so quickly. But he had, and it was because he never did anything without thinking it through from every possible angle beforehand. He had always watched and learnt, and he had made a point of finding the weaknesses in everything. Unlike everyone else, he knew that if you could pinpoint what could potentially be your downfall, you were guaranteed to succeed. It was the little things that eventually let you down. If you looked properly, you could find them and eradicate them. It was no more than basic economics.

'Nearly done, Kenny. Just one minute.'

Kenny was a stickler for punctuality, in fact, he was renowned for it. If Kenny said he would be somewhere by seven o'clock, he would actually be at the designated meeting place by six-twenty at the latest. Ready and able to conduct the business in hand with anyone involved with it. He made a point of knowing everything about the deal he would be discussing, and he would also know everything about the people concerned. As he often joked, he knew his game from head to toe. Backwards and forwards and inside out.

He could answer any questions that might need answering, and he would be so knowledgeable about the subject in hand, that the person who had arranged the meeting with him would walk away confident that the money they had agreed to invest would be more than safe in his capable hands.

Kenny Boy, however, expected the same courtesy in return. If he arranged to meet up with somebody, and the person was tardy, late, by even a few minutes, Kenny would refuse to deal with them ever again. He argued that if the person involved didn't have the brain capacity to watch the time and therefore arrive as previously arranged, then anything else that might be reasonably expected of them was now in grave doubt.

Kenny Boy was always on the lookout for the hidden insult or the clever riposte. He was so determined to make sure he was never disrespected by anybody that he had made a point from day one of ensuring that anyone within his orbit knew he was not to be taken lightly. Not ever. Not even once.

He had been completely on the ball from the off, and his foibles, his natural eccentricities, had worked *for* him. People respected him for his organisational skills, even saw his refusal to do business with anyone who did not have the manners to arrive on time, as a strong point. As his right. Kenny Boy had made his reputation by being *different*. It had worked for him. The real Faces appreciated him, they wanted to deal with Kenny Boy, with someone who insisted on complete privacy, who insisted that they met up without women or hangers-on in the mix. Kenny Boy saw business as being something very personal and he always conducted it in complete privacy. One to one.

What had been seen at the beginning as Kenny Boy's paranoia, had been laughed at as him being over-cautious, was now seen as his personal signature. No one who had ever dealt with him had even been questioned about their investments, let alone captured. What Kenny saw as nothing more than precautionary measures, others now saw as a guaranteed swerve where Old Bill were concerned. This, coupled with Kenny's insistence that he would only deal with the people who mattered, also worked for everyone involved. So he had inadvertently managed to give himself a certain mystique, and therefore his natural distrust of people was now seen as his greatest asset. He did still have a healthy distrust for the people he dealt with, and it was this that had made sure no one would ever get a tug. He knew somewhere inside that his behaviour was not really normal, but he also knew it was working in his favour, so he didn't bother about it too much.

Mary looked around at the gathering. Gerald Junior and Brendan, and their pug-ugly wives, were sniffing around. She turned her back to them and looked for Kenny Boy and Jordanna. The brother and sister were standing together and Mary wondered at how two such beautiful people had been produced by her daughter. It was beyond her comprehension. She saw Imelda off and on, and she saw that the drugs had finally started to take their toll on her. Unlike most junkies, Imelda had somehow been immune to their lasting effects for a long time. Her skin had stayed good, the hair and body had not deteriorated within months as normally happened; her daughter had looked good for far longer than was expected. Far longer than was good for anyone, herself included.

Mary knew that she came here for money, and only then if she was rock-bottom; she dressed it up as an excuse to see the kids. Consequently, if possible, Mary tried to be out when Imelda deigned to visit them.

A large part of her was angry about that, but the sensible part of her knew that the kids had to see Imelda as she really was, for themselves.

At the moment, Imelda was once more on her best behaviour, she had no choice but to try and become a part of their lives. She was well past her sell-by date, and all that was left to her now were the children she had abandoned. But Mary was not going to let her daughter cause any more upsets than absolutely necessary.

But if she kicked off about her daughter's reputation, she knew she would only make Imelda seem even more alone, even more unwanted in their eyes, and they both felt guilty about her, about their feelings towards her. Jordanna loathed her, but she felt guilty for those feelings, which was something Imelda played on, as she did anything that would get her what she wanted.

Since Jordanna had given birth to a tiny premature son, and then buried him within the week, she had not been right. She was like a pretend person now, like a marionette. She laughed and talked, but inside she was dead. It was evident in her eyes, in her smile.

Mary saw the devastation eating her away, and yet there was nothing she could do about it. She had always said that Imelda was a fucking Jonah, and she was. Everything she touched disintegrated, was somehow spoilt by her presence. She carried sorrow and heartbreak around with her like other people carried a handbag.

It was not that noticeable at first, it was such an intrinsic part of her personality. But she caused trouble wherever she went. And Kenny was determined to overlook that for the time being. He wanted to believe his mother really *had* changed, was a different person. He believed that she could be reached if only they would give her a chance. A last chance.

Well, *she* had given Imelda more chances than the Chinese lottery, and it had been a futile exercise. She knew her daughter was incapable of making something good happen in her own life, let alone her family's. Imelda needed only one thing; her stash. If she had enough drugs to last her for a few days, she would be in a happy frame of mind. She would also be on the lookout for the next stash, and the one after that. If she had concentrated her efforts on getting herself heroin into getting an education or running a business, she would have topped the tree.

She had done well at running the girls all those years ago, and what had she done then? She had let the self-destructiveness that was such a large part of her overtake everything else. She had taken up with another piece of shit, and she had sat back and waited for it to explode. And, as usual, the explosion when it came had caused dire problems for everyone concerned. Imelda knew she looked good, but she still had no real confidence in herself. Her natural beauty was fading rapidly and her panic at her future was now all-encompassing.

Imelda needed the kids to survive, and that was all she needed them for. One day Mary knew they would see that for themselves. Until then, she had to let them do whatever they felt was necessary to ease their troubled minds.

But Mary was determined to watch, wait and, when the time came, step between them all. She was going to make sure that, this time, the kids were not going to become no more than collateral damage in the abortion that passed for their mother's life.

Jordanna was pretty, very pretty, she had the look of an older girl but that was put down to her tiny baby's death. Everyone knew that it had broken her in some way.

The fact that Kenny Boy had been quite vocal in private, had certainly not gone amiss. He had been seen as a bigger, better person by the people he dealt with because of his care for his sister and her unfortunate predicament. In fact, his loyalty had endeared him to the people he had dealt with. His care for his sister, and his disregard for how it might be construed by outsiders was seen as just another of his foibles. Once more, his absolute resolve where a big problem was concerned was seen as another one of his strengths. That he was willing to kill anyone who even remarked on Jordanna and her problems was to his benefit. After all, if *he* didn't look out for his sister, who the fuck would? So he had inadvertently been seen as a young man of principles, a young man of decency and rectitude. In short, Kenny Boy was the young man they all hoped would one day marry their daughters. He had an old-world morality that struck a chord in the most jaded of men; he was the epitome of what they believed in.

Kenny Boy was like the old-time Faces, all decent beliefs and caring retributions. For the majority, it was a real privilege to be in his company. And he was the biggest fucking annoyance for the minority, for the people who saw the dinosaurs once more emerging against the odds, because he was already seen as a fucking rising star and as someone to emulate and see as a role model. It was like he was re-writing the book of villainy and everyone but him was coming up wanting.

Kenny Boy had systematically brought back every old-style value and belief, and it had worked for him. The other young guns, who saw their elders as muppets, saw them as people to walk over and away from, were now having to regroup and rethink. Basically, Kenny Boy had cornered the market and, to make things worse, he had not even tried to do that. It had come naturally, it was just his way of doing his business.

Imelda was looking around her nervously, she knew she was not about to be welcomed with open arms. The majority of the people here had an axe of some kind to grind, and if they could grind it by giving her a permanent parting she knew that they would do just that. She had made a lot of enemies over the years and, at the time, she had not understood just how foolish she had been. Like all bullies, while on the top of their game, she had never allowed for how hard her life might be should her star begin to wane. Well, her star had not only waned, it had imploded, and in a spectacular fashion. All the people she had blanked without a second's thought when she had reached her heyday were now, through hard work or, in some cases, good marriages, the same people she needed to accept her so she could once more be a part of normal society. Imelda was having to eat enough humble pie to make Uriah Heep look like Fanny Cradock.

But she was willing to do just that, after all, she was the mistress of illusion, she had even been known to fool herself when absolutely necessary. As she waited on the sidelines, she was impressed, despite herself, at the people who had arrived to give their blessing to her son's new enterprise.

She was in the bar, mixed in with the other no-necks, all watching the door in the hope of seeing a real Face or two. That she was waiting like the other plebs had not gone unnoticed by the people around her. She was a well-known name, and her son's new status as a man of importance had not gone unnoticed, either. That she was waiting in line like everyone else was more shocking than anything. After all, Kenny spent his life making sure he was respected, why would he be so resolute about that if not for this woman who had birthed him? Her name and reputation had been the reason why he was so stroppy and pedantic; he was the antithesis of his mother and he was proud of that fact. He was so strong-minded and so resolute in everything he did because, unlike his mother, he was never about to let anyone ever get the better of him. He would kill before he would ever be seen as a waster, as someone without self-respect. He was so frightened of being seen as a cunt by his peers that he had created a whole persona to counteract her negative influences. He knew how quick people were to judge, and he also knew how quickly people reassessed their opinions when faced with someone who was willing to destroy them if they did not decide to take on a new, more enlightened opinion of the person concerned. He had, without any thought for the people around him, or their hangers-on, made a point of erasing his mother's reputation, and he had replaced it with one of his own. He was happy to acknowledge that he had single-handedly wiped out the bastardy his mother had caused in her life. And, as she had caused more fuck-ups than the whole of the West Midlands police force, he felt he had done a really good job.

Tonight he was opening his new premises and he was being fêted by the best of the best, and he finally felt that he had shrugged off the shame of his birth, of his beginnings.

Most of the men here this night had done the same thing: had been born poor, had been forced to make their way in a world that was not really attuned to the uneducated, the permanent poor. That was the expression the Irish used to describe the men who were unable to better themselves because of politics and governments. The men who were left with no other course in life but villainy.

The men here, though, who had come to pay their respects to a young lad who was making it against all the odds, were all aware that they had never had to live down a mother like Imelda. She was the cause of so much death, so much hate, and so much destruction. She was a byword for everything that was to be despised in the female species. Yet, somehow, this boy had proved to everyone that you really could overcome the biggest of handicaps, the hugest of embarrassments.

Kenny Boy had lived her down and, more to the point, he had ensured that no one ever said a bad word about her. She was off-limits where he was concerned and, on the rare occasions he mentioned her, he spoke of her with the utmost respect, thereby ensuring that everyone else did too. It was another reason why he was so liked, why he was seen as a good bloke by all and sundry.

Anyone else would have turned their back on her, but his loyalty towards her, especially as she did not warrant it, only made him look even more like a viable option where they were concerned. He was possessed of a loyalty unsurpassed in their world; his determination and forceful- ness where his mother was concerned had caused people to take a step back and remember who they were talking about and had struck more than a few chords with the people he had become part of.

Coupled with his zealous care for his sister and for his grandmother, he had become a person of real interest to those in the know. Now he was about to reap the benefits of his labours, and there was not one person who felt he was undeserving of that. He was a real little dynamo, well, a big dynamo in reality. But although his youth still saw him referred to as the new boy, his innate shrewdness and business acumen already had him marked down as a permanent player.

As Jordanna sipped her drink, Kenny Boy watched the men who were already eyeballing her; he knew she was a looker, and he also knew that as his sister she would now be seen as a bit more than a decent-looking bird. Jordanna was unaware that, even with her track record, she would soon be in demand. He also knew that she could never be told that, her confidence was almost zero as it was. He knew that he would have to steer her in the direction of someone he could trust, someone he could manipulate. Jordanna would fuck anyone who was nice to her, she was still very fragile and he knew he needed to keep her close and safe.

She was good tonight though, he saw her smiling and

chatting with the other women around her and he sighed in relief. He was thrilled at the turn-out for him, saw the rows and rows of Faces who were there. He knew that even as young as he was, he had somehow managed to command this kind of respect from his betters. All because he was not willing ever to compromise, because he had never once gone back on his word. He was proud of that fact. He was proud that he was already on the verge of joining the pantheons of the big boys, was already being hailed as the new Face on the pavement. He was proud that he was seen as the perfect person to run the new businesses that were emerging all over the Smoke. He was more than willing to be a trailblazer and, as such, open up a whole new set of businesses through which everyone could benefit in some way.

Kenny Boy had an almost encyclopaedic knowledge of the drug business, and he was more than willing to share it with people who were willing to utilise and exploit that knowledge for their own personal gain. Kenny Boy had made sure he was the future for these people, and that is exactly what he was. It was as simple as that.

Jimmy Bailey was impressed. This was a real good night by anyone's standards. Kenny Boy had laid on a great spread. Good food, plenty of drink, no drugs that were obvious to the untrained eye, but plenty of good-natured banter and camaraderie.

Kenny Boy was where he wanted to be, among the people he liked to mix with and, as an added bonus, he was also the centre of attention. That was his main forte; being in the middle of everything; being the instigator of whatever was happening around him. Kenny was a mass of contradictions. Like his mother, he had the knack of sussing any situation out within seconds and, like his mother, he would then use that knowledge for his own ends. As he looked around him at Bailey, Driscoll, Hannon and Basil and saw their enjoyment and pleasure at his accomplishments, Kenny knew he had made it. After this night, he was set. He would always be remembered for this one outrageous evening. His youth, coupled with his natural friendliness, would always be remembered. He knew that this night was his entrance into the world of men, real men. He felt that he belonged here, and he knew that feeling would never leave him. Then, just as he was really enjoying the night for what it was, he saw his sister talking to a large West Indian man with overly white teeth and a very suspect sense of fashion.

The man was Jamsie O'Loughlin, a very well-known pimp and a drug dealer. That he was talking to his sister with a smile that was as bright as a hundred-watt bulb and had an arm around her shoulders, and that she seemed to find it enchanting, rang his alarm bells; Kenny Boy knew she was ready for any old shit that might be fed her. He knew she was vulnerable and naïve, she only needed someone to give her a load of old cods and she would swallow it hook, line and sinker. Jordanna was an accident that had already happened, and he was not about to let it happen to her again, not on his watch anyway.

Jamsie, for his part, was genuinely thrilled with Jordanna; like most pimps he could actually distinguish between his earners and his love life. He would never be faithful to any woman; as far as he was concerned that was not something to even be discussed. He was, however, capable of loving and, as far as he was concerned, that was far more important, even though it had never happened to him before.

This lovely girl with her huge blue eyes and thick blond hair had attracted him from the moment he had clapped eyes on her. She had a deep sadness inside, a desperate need for care and attention that had hit him full-on from his first glance in her direction. He had wanted to protect her from the world, wanted to protect her from everything that she was terrified of, from that split second of seeing her standing alone. He had never felt like this before in his life, he wanted to make sure she was safe, get to know her, talk to her. He wanted to become a big part of her life and, from the way she was smiling back at him, he had a feeling she was of a similar mindset.

Jamsie did not know Jordanna was Kenny's sister, he was not aware of her history at that time; all he knew was, for the first time ever, he was bowled over by a female, and not because of her earning potential.

As Jamsie chatted to her he was amazed to realise that she was all he had thought she was, and much more.

Jordanna for her part was thrilled at his attention; Jamsie was handsome and he had the gift of the gab but mainly because it stopped her from thinking about her mother and studiously avoiding making eye contact with her. Once that happened, she would be forced to acknowledge her and, worse than that, she would be honourbound to invite her into her company.

She had no intention of doing that, her mother was still someone she was wary of. Kenny might think she was rehabilitated, but Jordanna knew that people like Imelda were immune to real life, real situations. They used everything for their own ends, to ensure they got what they wanted from any situation.

Jamsie was just what she needed; he was big, strong and funny. He was making her laugh and making her feel special, and that was just what the doctor had ordered.

'Are you all right, girl?'

Jordanna nodded, her huge blue eyes, as always, expressing her innermost feelings. 'I am feeling pretty good actually, better than I have for a long time.'

Jamsie didn't question her answer, he felt the truth of it and he also felt pleased that he was the reason she was feeling so good about herself. He didn't know how, but he knew instinctively that she had not felt happy for a very long time. The sadness was all over her, the hurt was almost tangible, and he promised himself then and there that he would be a staunch supporter of this girl in whatever she wanted to do.

Jordanna was totally enamoured with him, from his dreads to his killer smile he was sex on legs. She felt a connection with him, and knew it was more than reciprocated.

She could feel her mother's eyes burning into her and she refused to meet her stare, this was Kenny's night and it was up to him to make their mother a part of it all. She was only a by-stander these days, and that suited her. Jordanna Dooley had no interest in becoming a part of Kenny's world, or her mother's, for that fact. It frightened her. Been there, done that, and she had the scars to prove it.

Basil could hear the conversation that was going on nearby and he was impressed with Kenny's acumen. He was a real man's man and, more than that, he was a fucking personality in his own right. That he was suddenly a good friend and confidant of Jamsie O'Loughlin had not gone unnoticed. Well, he was determined to point out a few of

Jamsie's less edifying qualities to young Kenny Boy when the opportunity arose. Especially as his own mother was a real watchword where hard drugs and Jamsie were concerned.

Jamsie O'Loughlin was not a mug, he was the real deal in many respects, and he was the general spokesman for the local West Indian population. He ruled his empire with fear and humour – he was not someone to be taken lightly in any way, shape or form. That Basil was in throes of a tear-up with him was neither here nor there this night. It was Kenny's night, and he was not about to rock his boat in any way. He would never ever ruin anyone's night. Trouble could wait, it came soon enough as it was. Why bring it into the open when there was no need to, when it was the kind of trouble that was not going anywhere, could wait a few days.

Basil had heard from what he classed as very good contacts that Jamsie was treating his girls to the needle, and very young girls at that. Juveniles who were unable to make an informed decision about anything; not that most junkies chose to become skagheads, an informed decision about anything was usually beyond them by the time the drug took hold.

Once on the needle the girls were no better than captive prisoners, when the brown took over, they were its slave. Junkies would fight, steal, lie and even kill, for the next high. It was not their fault, not really. They were at the mercy of a need that transcended love, loyalty, family, basically anything that stood in the way of the next score. The girls were very young, and they would now do anything to get the money for an armful. Most of them would be destroyed completely by twenty-five. Most of them would look thirty before they hit their nineteenth birthday. They would lie about everything and anything, always wondering if they could con their way to another few quid. They would forget what it was like to be cared about, what it was like to care about other people, about themselves. They would forget about everyday things like cleanliness, regular eating, and they would not only stop bathing and eating, they would also stop interacting with other people. Junkies might needle up together, but that was as far as their interaction went. They might jack up in a flat somewhere, but their high was a very personal moment. Heroin was not a social drug, although it might have seemed it at first. In the initial stages people skanked and laughed as they watched the drug being burnt on a spoon, might even have chased it the first few times. Then the lure of the intravenous high would be spoken of, explained in all its Technicolor glory by people who either had a hidden agenda or were still in the first flush of the skag love affair. Amphetamines, cocaine, grass, none of them had the same resonance as the brown. Heroin was a drug that was more often than not introduced to a body by someone with an alternative agenda. A man could have total control over a girl once she was introduced to the opiate benefits of the heroin high. He would then make a point of procuring the drug for them and, in extreme cases, taking the fucker alongside of them, to prove it was not as dangerous as they might have heard. But it was always a scam. It was a form of social control that most of the political philosophers had never thought to investigate thoroughly. After all, like politicians and judges, they were, as always, unaware of what was really going on underneath their noses. It was a win-win situation for the dealer. No one liked junkies and, more to the point, no one wanted them either. As society's outcasts, they were dropped into a nightmare of supply and demand, with nowhere to turn.

Once on the brown, the person involved gradually lost their free will, along with their kindness, their decency, their whole personality. Coupled with the instigator's total control over them. Then came the paranoia, the belief that everyone who was trying to help them were parasites, were liars and cheats.

It was not long until the girls involved found themselves without family, friends or morals. Within a few weeks they were totally dependent not only on the drug, but also on the supplier of the drug. That most wraps bought on the streets often contained so little heroin it would not get a puppy dog high was neither here nor there. It was a physical and psychological addiction that lasted the person concerned their whole life. It was, in most cases, a death sentence, and it went unnoticed because once a person got on the H, they were immediately classed as the lowest of the low.

Basil could see Jordanna eyeing up Jamsie, and that the fucker was eyeing her up back. Kenny was watching Jordanna too, and Basil decided to wait and see how it panned out before offering his opinion about it. Kenny walked over to the pair.

Jamsie O'Loughlin was about to find that he was in the unenviable position of trying to explain to Kenny that his intentions towards his sister were honourable, not an easy feat when you were the pimp extraordinaire of your generation.

A pimp was someone who was looked on with a certain respect while, at the same time, the very nature of his business automatically made him a second-class citizen to most of the men he dealt with. It was like anything else. A pecking order existed in all walks of life and, until it affected him personally, it was never an issue. Once it became an issue, it was all-out war. Like any war, its cause was the inability of others to see things from a like-minded point of view.

Now, outside the venue and confronted about his intentions towards Jordanna Dooley, Jamsie had a decision to make. He could fight this, or walk away. He decided he felt a strong enough attraction to Jordanna to fight his case.

'Look, Kenny, I didn't know she was your sister, and I understand that you might have certain reservations where I am concerned. I understand that. But I can assure you now, I met her tonight and I liked her, a *lot*. There is no hidden fucking agenda, I just want to take her out. If I did want to put her on the pavement I think we can both assume that idea would now be what is commonly known as moot, don't you? She is lovely. I saw her and I got hit by a fucking thunderbolt.'

Jamsie laughed in complete disbelief at his own words, knowing how fucking silly they sounded to him, let alone Kenny Boy.

Kenny looked into his dark eyes, searching for the lie he knew was not there. Jamsie was a mate, he had always looked out for him. When Kenny's mum had been on the bash he had sometimes looked out for her too. He would track her down and pass on the information to Kenny Boy. That he had been requested to do so beforehand by Basil or Jimmy Bailey was neither here nor there. He had always given Kenny the info with a quiet and dignified demeanour. Jamsie's attitude was that if *his* mother had been flogging her arse he would not have wanted the whole world to know about it either.

Although, in Kenny's case, the whole world did know;

at least the world they inhabited anyway. Kenny's life had been blighted by his mother's fucking lifestyle, she was a mother who would have been better off drowning her kids at birth to save them the aggravation or, better still, someone, somewhere, should have drowned *her*.

Still, Jamsie had always given the boy the benefit of the doubt and respected him for keeping his eye on his mother. Imelda was a cunt and, like all cunts, she did not deserve this boy's care or attention. That she had it was more in his favour than hers.

Jordanna, who he had heard of, but never met, was a different kettle of fish altogether. She was a real good girl, and he felt a deep want of her that was so powerful it guaranteed him all this fucking old fanny. He was being questioned, and he was swallowing; that alone spoke fucking volumes.

'You fuck my sister up and I will hunt you down like a fucking dog, and I *will* kill you, Jamsie. I will rip your fucking heart out. She has had enough hurt in her life without you waltzing in like Steve Stunning and sweeping her off her feet. Unless you are serious about her, you leave her alone.'

Jamsie grinned, and his large white teeth and easygoing friendliness were very much in evidence as he said seriously, 'I understand your reservations about me, I would be the same if I was you. But I swear to you, I have never felt like this before in my life. I just want to take her out, get to know her, that's all.'

Kenny was inclined to believe him; he liked Jamsie, he always had. But he was a dealer and a fucking pimp, and that meant he used women. It was the nature of that particular beast. All women were beneath them, beneath their contempt. They saw the female sex as paper money, saw them as less than animals. Pimps could not afford to be nice, it defeated the object.

His mother had been a real learning curve where most men were concerned. The average bloke would shag a fence given the opportunity, and Kenny did not want Jordanna stuck in another nightmare of her own making. He had not looked out for her the last time, and he was not about to let that happen again. He would fucking cut the next bastard up with a smile and a cheery song. Jordanna would never know pain like that again. Not while he was capable of drawing a breath.

'You had better treat her with the respect she deserves. If I find out any different, there will be fucking ambulances arriving.'

Kenny saw Jamsie relax at his words. 'All I want is the chance to get to know her. If it turns out we don't get on, then we'll both chalk it up to experience. But let it go now, Kenny, you've made your fucking point, no need to labour it.'

Kenny knew he had gone over the top, but what else could he do? She was his sister, his flesh and blood and he had left her to her own devices once and look where that had got her. He forced himself to smile then. He knew that Jamsie was not about to mug him off in any way, Jamsie being more than aware of his penchant for hurting people who disappointed him in any way. Jamsie knew that if he fucked up he would be living on borrowed time. Plus, he liked Jamsie. Always had, he had done him a few favours over the years where his ponce of a mother had been concerned. He hoped that his sister did fall for the bloke big time, he wanted to see her settled with someone who could look after her. Better the devil you knew, he had learnt that old fucking chestnut the hard way. His sister needed to be loved and cared for, more than anyone realised.

Imelda was over the moon. Her son had finally invited her to join him at the bar and she understood the significance of his offer as much as the people around her. By publicly recognising her, he had given her a new-found acceptance that she could now use to her advantage as and when the opportunity arose.

Until then, she had been shrewd enough to keep her head down and her trap shut. She knew that she needed to keep this son of hers onside for the foreseeable future.

With his public acknowledgement of her, she was once more on the cusp of public acceptance. She would be welcomed back into the bosom of the local drinking establishments, and would be seen as a viable borrower of money; she would now be in a position to run up debts, debts that she had no intention of paying.

Jordanna was still a loose cannon in many ways, but Imelda would work on her. She would ensure that her daughter came around to her way of thinking in the end. She was rocking, standing there in full view of everyone, being treated like a queen; she felt she was finally where she should be. Her son, against all the odds, had made it, and because of him, she was now ready to take her rightful place in the not-so-polite society she craved. Jamsie O'Loughlin was a dealer of platinum standards, as she knew better than most. They went back a long time. But she would keep that bit of information to herself. He sourced brown that was so pure it was dangerous until it was cut at least three times. If her Jordanna managed to hook him, Imelda was basically set for life where the drugs were concerned. After all, he would be honourbound to serve up his bird's mother, it stood to reason.

As she looked around her, she saw the sceptical glances that were coming her way. She knew that she was the only fly in her son's otherwise exemplary ointment. He was a real player now and he would go on and on until he became the *only* player. He got that single-mindedness from her.

Basil was watching her closely, but Imelda didn't react in any way. She was hated, and she knew that. But she could apologise for England when it was demanded of her. She could grovel with the best of them.

As Kenny winked at her, she smiled widely, she knew he was only making a point where she was concerned. She knew that he only wanted her in his life so he could keep an eye on her while, at the same time, forcing the people around him to accept her. If they did that, then it would prove to *him*, once and for all, that he was finally a Face.

She could write the fucking script for him, but she had to pretend she was ignorant to his ulterior motives, though she did wonder if he realised what was going down himself. He got his sneakiness from her, though. His natural desire to keep everything to himself, no matter how trivial, was an inbred thing she felt.

She was genuinely sorry though, because she had admitted to herself a long time ago, that she didn't really like her son that much. He was a stranger to her in many respects, and as he didn't really like her either, she felt that made them even somehow. He was a user like her, but he dressed it up and convinced himself that it was for the good of other people.

She did not like him, no more than she did her

daughter. She saw Jordanna as weak; she was like a fucking albatross hanging around everyone's neck.

A real party pooper, even now she was devoid of anything that even resembled interesting. She was a good-looking girl, she had to be, she was her double. But she had nothing that could be seen as individualism. She was a fucking wet blanket. A fucking poor-me merchant, and that was all her mother's doing. Mary had fucked up both her kids, big time. But then, she had not expected anything else. The girl was a complete washout, if only she had inherited *her* shrewdness, her mother's nous, then she might have had something about her. Something going on.

As it was, she was a boring bastard, and that was proved by her daughter's obvious interest in Jamsie O'Loughlin. Imelda knew him well, but then she would, he was her kind of guy. Jordanna was hanging on his every word and, more to the point, Jamsie seemed to be hanging on to hers in return. It was sick-making.

That her daughter had already buried a child, and lived through her mother's lunacy did not even register with Imelda. As far as she could see, her daughter was a weakling, a wimp who was incapable of seeing the main chance as and when it presented itself. With Kenny's new-found notoriety, Jordanna should have the brains to be using it to its full advantage; instead she was like a fucking moron, frightened of her own shadow. It was a crying shame. She should be at home watching *Countdown* with all the other anoraks, not here among the movers and shakers. This was wasted on her, and that really annoyed Imelda.

But she would keep her head down and her arse up, and wait for the chance to further herself. If she played a blinder she would not have to do another blow job ever again, unless she wanted to, of course. At this stage in her life, her son's new-found notoriety was a real touch. Imelda raised her glass at Jamsie in an imaginary toast; she was not surprised when he did not bother to reciprocate.

Chapter Twenty-Three

'You are a fucking imbecile, and as such you need a fucking serious livener, boy. You think you can take me for a cunt and I wouldn't fucking notice?'

Kenny Boy was livid, his face was bright red and his hands were clenched into fists of rage. He was breathing in short, staccato bursts, his heart was beating faster than an alarm clock, and he was swallowing down the urge to kill.

He was more than aware that he had not yet struck the object of his anger, and that pleased him because he knew he needed to rein in his anger. His rage was never far from the surface, and it was always his first reaction to anything that happened to him or his. Smash it, crush it, hurt someone. His rage was a natural part of his life. It was there when he awoke in the morning, and it was still there when he went to sleep at night.

He fought a daily battle to keep it contained. He knew he was often outrageously over the top where his anger and his personal feelings of retribution were concerned. He could quite happily kill someone on the slightest of pretexts. Wiping out anyone who he saw as a rival or as a piss-taker was par for the course. He fantasised about killing his enemies, he had done since he was a little child. It was how he coped with the day to day, how he coped with living down being his mother's son and all that entailed.

He knew inside himself that his anger often far outweighed the reasoning for it. But he also knew that his single-mindedness was seen as an asset by the people he worked alongside. He liked Harry, and he really didn't want to hurt him, but he couldn't see what else he could do. The man had fucked him over, big time.

'I'll sort you right out, Harry. A fucking hammering is just what you need and is exactly what you are going to get.'

Harold Carter was literally shaking in his brand-new, expensive boots. He had dropped a serious bollock and he knew he deserved what was coming to him. It still didn't help though, knowing that he had asked for it. If it was anyone else but Kenny Boy he would have swallowed. But Kenny was not known for his sympathetic nature. Kenny Boy would administer a punishment far exceeding the crime committed, it was nothing personal, it was just his nature. When Harold Carter had helped himself to the takings he had not felt he had gone over the top as such. He had only spiked a few quid, a fifty here, a twenty there. It was not as if he was creaming off the hundreds, or the thousands. At worst, he was guilty of giving himself a well-deserved drink, no more and no less. But he should have known that Kenny Dooley would know what he was owed down to the last fucking penny. It was a foible of his; he made a fucking point, apparently, of knowing how much he was owed by everyone and anyone.

Like that should be a big surprise, the general consensus was that Kenny Boy was a fucking weirdo. Of course he would be interested in the pennies and the halfpennies. It was what he did best. Everyone knew that Kenny could glance over a column of figures and work out the total in seconds without breaking a sweat. He needed nothing: no paper, pens, or calculator, he did it all in his head.

But this also didn't allow for the fact that everyone else in their world, other than him of course, were amenable to a little bit of skimming by their workforce, it was what made their world go round, what kept people on the payroll. Kenny was not the only criminal in town and, by the very nature of his business, he was honourbound to employ other criminals, who he, for some reason known only to himself, expected to act like choir boys. Harry was shitting it, and he knew deep down that all this was very wrong. But he was not about to point that fact out, he was not on a death wish.

'Look, Kenny, all I did was take the extra, it's not unheard of to extract a drink . . .'

Kenny didn't let him finish his sentence, he was already punching him to the ground. He saw the theft of his money as a personal affront, saw it as a mark of disrespect towards him personally. *That* was something that was never going to happen. Not in his lifetime anyway.

As Harry Carter lost consciousness he wondered briefly if he would ever open his eyes again. Kenny Boy was quite capable of finishing him off for this.

Kenny was still kicking at the prone body when Jack Carling dragged him away. Kenny was so incensed at Harry's audacity that he wanted to kill him, wanted to erase him from the planet once and for all.

'Come on, Kenny, he had a small skim. Get over it, for fuck's sake.'

Jack was having trouble keeping Kenny away from the prostrate form; he was holding him against the wall, forcing him to calm down and let his sensible head prevail once more.

Kenny knew that if he really wanted to, he could take on Jack Carling, and Jack's minions as well, without even breaking a sweat. His edge was that, unlike everyone else he dealt with, he did not really need an excuse to hurt people. He could hurt anyone at any time and, when he felt the urge, he did just that. He would use the slightest pretext to unleash his anger on an unsuspecting public. It was another thing that worked in his favour. If Kenny Boy gave someone a good hiding they must have deserved it; he was not known for being a bully, or for just flexing his muscles. Kenny had a violent streak, and that was common knowledge. What was not known by all and sundry was that he had to control himself from day to day, that he understood that his temper would be his downfall if he didn't learn to control it. But he knew he had to calm himself down, especially now. Harry had been a good worker, and most people would not feel the need to chastise him for his little scam. But then he was not like other people, he saw the theft of his poke as fucking disgraceful. He saw it as a challenge to him and his authority, as a fucking complete and utter piss-take.

'You tell that cunt he is finished with me now, he is gone, over with, and you make sure that anyone who takes a wage from me understands that if even a fucking fiver goes on the trot, I will personally hunt down the cunt who palmed it myself. I pay enough out in wages, I don't expect to be fucking robbed by me own.'

Jack was nodding in agreement, he knew *he* was getting a warning and he also knew that he would have to pass that warning on, and pass it on very vocally so this man could be placated. He was a real giant in his field was Kenny, he had the goodwill of every major Face in the Smoke. But he was a real weirdo in other respects. Jack pushed him towards the door, he wanted him away from Harry's prostrate form.

Kenny was not the easiest of bosses, but then who was? He was a real earner though, he earned fucking serious amounts of brass. But, in all fairness, he paid well, and so Harry Carter's little mistake was not to be overlooked from Kenny's rather narrow point of view.

'Come on, Kenny, let's get you out of here.'

Kenny followed him quietly now. He was a big lad, and he was also a very intimidating lad, especially when the fancy took him. Seeing him attack Harry like that had been a real eye-opener. Kenny was certainly not an easy man to placate, in fact he was a fucking handful. A big, paranoid and overly strong handful.

As they walked out of the warehouse into the weak January sunlight Jack said seriously, 'He did not deserve that, Kenny Boy. He was taking pennies, it ain't like it was fucking fortunes.'

Jack was a name in his own right; Kenny had specifically requested him from his last employer. Jack came with a fucking gold-plated guarantee, and that was the only reason he was being allowed to offer his opinion now.

Kenny laughed, his even white teeth and youthful good looks made him seem like a candidate for a boy band. He was a real handsome fucker, and he knew it. But he was also a nasty fucker, and anyone who chose to forget that, did so at their peril.

'The fact that fucking ponce skimmed *quids* off me is why I am so fucking annoyed with him. It's an even bigger insult than if he had tried to scam me for fortunes. Can't you fucking see that? He was tanking me for fucking *fag* money, so what the fuck does that make him and, more to the point, what does that make me? You tell him, if I see him again I will fucking hammer him all over again.'

Jack saw the logic in his argument. The bloke had a valid point. But he had still gone over the top. Kenny had delivered a beating that would have been given to a supergrass. The punishment had to fit the crime. After all, they were not the Filth.

As he turned away from Kenny, Jack was surprised to be grabbed physically by his hair and then violently forced back inside the warehouse by Kenny Boy. He was thrown unceremoniously on to the filthy concrete flooring and Kenny then kicked him over and over again, putting his considerable weight behind each blow. But this time the kicking was delivered with a viciousness that was all the more sinister because it was also very controlled. Jack curled up into a foetal position and waited for him to stop. He was bleeding already, and he knew his mouth would need to be stitched. He felt every blow as it landed strategically on his prone body. When the beating finally stopped, he waited a few seconds before carefully rolling on to his back. He was hurting badly, bleeding like a stuck pig. It was monstrous that this had even happened. As he looked up at Kenny Boy he could see the undisguised hatred in his eyes.

'You ever see fit to question me about any of my fucking dealings again, and I'll fucking kill you. You arrogant *cunt*. Should I want your fucking opinion in the future, I will request it from you in a civil and interested manner. I will ask you a series of probing questions, and I will then listen carefully to your well-thought-out and hopefully, your very enlightening answers. Until then, you keep your fucking conk out of my affairs. Do you get my fucking drift? Or would you like me to put it in writing so you can peruse it at your leisure?'

Jack understood then just why this young fellow was so well thought of, he was a real *bona fide* nut-job. He had no fear of anyone, and he had a rough dignity that was very difficult to ignore. Seeing him now Jack was frightened of what he could be capable of should he feel the need. Should he feel that he had been disrespected.

Pulling himself upright, Jack Carling knew when he was beaten. He spat out a mouthful of blood and, wiping a hand across his face, he felt the lumps and swellings that were already forming. He would look like a fucking accident victim for weeks. His ribs were broken, and he had trouble taking a deep breath. The shock of the attack was overwhelming him. He had never experienced anything like it before in his life.

'I am sorry, Kenny, I was trying to diffuse the situation, that's all.'

Kenny was smiling widely now, as if the earlier contretemps had never happened. He was the amiable friend, the joker. He was the big-hearted mate. He seemed unaware of Jack's condition, didn't seem to see the blood or the bruising.

'I know that, Jackie Boy. All I am saying is, I am more than capable of diffusing a situation as and when I see fit and, for the record, I will reiterate once again, when I want *your* fucking opinion, I'll ask you for it. Now, dump that cunt and let's get back to the job in hand.'

Jack knew then that what he had heard was basically the

tip of the iceberg where Kenny was concerned. He could see the absence of real emotion in his handsome face, in his deep-blue eyes. Someone had once said Kenny Dooley was a psycho, and he was. The big worry for Jack was that Kenny himself didn't seem to know that.

'Come on, Jordanna, I just want to have a coffee with you. Why are you so bloody against me? I am really trying here.' Imelda was angry and irritated with her daughter and this came across in her voice.

Jordanna sighed. She was in a hurry, she was meeting Jamsie and she wanted to tell him her good news. But her mother accosting her in the street had thrown her off-kilter. Jordanna was a much more confident person since Jamsie had come into her life. She also knew, thanks to her brother, that he had handed the pimping side of his business over to his cousin Dexter. It was his way of showing that he was serious about her. He just dealt now, and he was more or less the main dealer in London. That was also thanks to her brother, as she knew. But Jordanna did not see that as a negative, all she was interested in was Jamsie O'Loughlin as a person. And that person was the love of her life. He made her feel good about herself. He made her feel like a valid person.

Now her mother was once more trying to inveigle herself into her daughter's company and she didn't want that. She didn't appreciate her mother forcing her to spend time in her company. She had Kenny, why did she still think she needed Imelda as well?

'I am late as it is, Mum. Maybe we can meet next week.'

She was already walking away from her. But, as she knew, Imelda was not going to be brushed off so easily.

'Relax, will you? All I want is to know how you are.

Surely you can spare five minutes for your own mother. Jamsie will keep. Christ knows, he would wait months for you if you asked him to.' This was said in jest, but the underlying jealousy was evident to them both.

As Jordanna walked back towards her house she was annoyed with herself for her weakness where her mother was concerned. Where everyone was concerned. She always tried to keep the peace and old habits died hard.

Opening the front door, she heard her mother's heels as she clattered down the hallway behind her. It was just like when she was a kid, the feeling of dread that noise could still evoke inside her. The hollow click-clack of her mother's stilettos brought forth another memory. She saw herself in her mother's shoes, four-inch black leather courts, wearing a pink-and-lemon nightdress and, as she clattered up the hallway, she remembered being picked up by her mother's bloke and taken into the bedroom, her little body protesting, screaming in distress at what she knew would happen to her, and her mother turning away. Her mother pretending she didn't know the significance of the event, deliberately ignoring her daughter's cries.

She was still nervous around her even now, she remembered far too much to ever feel comfortable in her presence. 'How much do you want, Mum?'

She was standing in the kitchen now, her lovely face as always deeply troubled when her mother was nearby. Her figure was still good, tight. Like her mother she was high-breasted and slim of waist. She had also inherited her long legs and the knack of wearing clothes so they looked as if they had been handmade for her. She was opening her purse, ready to pay her off. Get rid of her.

Imelda was now acting the outraged mother. It did not

sit well on her broad and very aggressive shoulders. It was an act that even a child would have sussed out.

'I don't want anything, Jorge. I have plenty of poke, your brother sees to that. I just want to talk to you, see if you're OK. I care about you.'

Jordanna had put the kettle on now, and she was nervously waiting for it to boil. Her mother was watching her closely. It put Jordanna in mind of a stoat watching a rabbit, waiting for its chance to spring, its chance to kill. She knew that her mother had no real interest in her, she never had. She just wanted her onside, she had Kenny Boy but that wasn't enough for her. She needed her daughter as well, needed her to pretend that her mother was once more an integral part of her life. It was all about pretence with Imelda. That was all her life had ever been.

'I am fine . . . and you, how are you?'

She had a hard time saying 'Mum', it was not a word she found easy. When she said it, she knew it sounded forced, sounded all wrong. She knew it sounded more like an accusation than a term of endearment.

Imelda sat down on a kitchen chair, her body was fluid, still with the illusion of youth about it. For Imelda, her daughter was the equivalent of looking in a mirror. It was uncanny, she saw her own eyes, her own features. Only, her daughter was a much younger and softer version, of course. Too soft for her own good, if truth be told.

'I am OK, I suppose. Are you pregnant again by any chance, Jorge?'

The question caught Jordanna off guard. She had not told anybody yet, she had been holding the knowledge inside her, enjoying it for a short while, hugging it to herself and allowing herself to daydream. She saw a child who would be a scholar, a child who would be so intelligent they would confound everyone around them. She imagined a little boy, or little girl, tremendously good-looking, so stunningly beautiful that people would remark on their handsomeness on a daily basis. She had dreamt up a child whose life would be perfect in every way. Who would be so loved that they would never know the pain of insecurity, the pain of knowing they were not wanted by anyone who really mattered.

But now that was spoilt. Ruined. Her mother knowing about anything was like a poison, it was now no more than a guaranteed bad deal. How she had known she was pregnant, she didn't know. She couldn't even start to imagine. But Imelda did know, and the worst thing of all was that her knowing just convinced Jordanna that, as always, she was doomed. Her baby was doomed, and her mother was the cause of it all. She hated Imelda for that, hated her for knowing her secrets and for speaking them out loud as if she had some kind of right to discuss her daughter's life, had been a valid participant in it, thereby entitling her to have any kind of opinion about her. Her mother's arrival at this particular moment, her assumption that she would be able to talk her way into her life, was absolutely outrageous. Her mother's arrogance in thinking that she was so weak and stupid she would be thrilled at her sudden interest in her and her life made Jordanna absolutely livid. Her mother acting like she really cared about her when they both knew that *she* was the only reason Imelda had not been locked up and forgotten about made her feel so full of resentment and so full of anger she was finding it hard to breathe. 'How do you know I am pregnant?'

Imelda smiled widely, her face for once showing what

could be termed genuine happiness. Not because of her daughter's condition, but because she had guessed it so rightly. It had been a shot in the dark, but her daughter was such a fucking moron that her having a baby was to be expected. She had a bloke, so a baby would be the next step. It was hardly rocket science. Jordanna was a fucking walking cliché and, in all fairness, that only made it easier for her to manipulate the situation.

'A mother knows these things, Jorge. Have you told anyone yet?'

Jordanna shook her head vehemently. 'No.'

Imelda started getting irritated with this daughter of hers. Trying to get any information from her was like getting blood from the proverbial stone. The girl was two fags short of a full packet. It was also obvious to Imelda that her daughter was a holder of grudges; life was shit, big deal, she should get over it. She was tempted to give this little whore her side of the story, but she knew she wouldn't be interested in that. She was already determined to play the victim, well, so be it. She had nothing on her conscience where her kids were concerned. But the urge to slap this little mare's face was really tempting. 'Well, when are you going to tell people, love? It's hardly something spectacular, it's not like no one in the world has never done it before. How do you think everyone on the planet got here? Someone pushed them out of their body. You're *only* pregnant, Jorge. I did it twice meself, for fuck's sake, and I'm still here to tell the tale.'

Her mother had just dismissed Jordanna's baby and her need to keep it a secret for a while as if none of that mattered at all. And, in fairness, it probably didn't matter to her. Nothing ever did. Ever had, for that matter. Least of all her own babies; she had never really cared about them. Even Kenny, her golden boy, had only been a diversion for her.

Jordanna felt a black, filthy anger rising up inside her at her mother's cruel disregard for her and her wants. She was suddenly overcome with all the feelings she had tried so hard to suppress for years. They were the reason she was so nervous all the time, was so worried and scared of ever really letting herself go. She had never once allowed herself to give free rein to her deepest feelings, and she knew it was because she always tried to keep the peace, tried to do what was best for everyone around her. She felt it was her responsibility to keep everybody happy, even if that meant she was buried under the weight of it all. And, looking at her mother now, it finally hit her that she had wasted her time trying to do the right thing. She knew now that she had not ever even made this woman think of her, let alone understand the sacrifices she had made. Her whole life had been one bad dream after another.

'Do you really want to know *why* I ain't told anyone yet?'

Imelda felt the tension in the air suddenly; she knew this was a loaded question, and she also knew that she had to answer it. There was a subtle change in this daughter of hers, she was now almost confronting her. It was as if she had grown up before her very eyes. Imelda knew she had to diffuse this situation, knew she had to keep this girl on board. There was a naked dislike in her daughter's eyes now, it was as if she was challenging her to contradict her in some way. Jordanna had become the alpha female, she was angry enough to finally confront her mother for every wrongdoing, real or imagined. Imelda was high, she had bumped herself up before coming to the house and she was more than aware that there had been a subtle shifting in their positions, knew she had to reclaim that ground if she was to make any kind of life with her kids, could guarantee herself an easy pass for the foreseeable future.

'Why, why ain't you told no one your good news, darling?'

Jordanna saw her mother's fake smile. She was suddenly a little kid again, she was once more at the mercy of this selfish, self-serving bully. Only she wasn't a child any more, and this cunt of a woman couldn't hurt her.

Imelda was really on the defensive now, her daughter was not scared of her any more. She knew, without a shadow of a doubt, that she was about to hear some things she didn't want to admit as truth. She was going to be reminded of her failings as a mother, would be blamed as *usual* for all the things that had gone wrong in her daughter's life.

'Are you fucking *kidding* me, Mother? Are you taking the fucking piss?'

Imelda shrugged. She was wary of this girl now, saw the strength in her young body. She was depending on the girl's pregnancy now to stop this conversation from becoming violent.

'How am I supposed to know what's going on, Jorge? I ain't a fucking mind reader.'

Jordanna was so shocked at her mother's clumsy attempt at dignity, at her childish attempt at playing the innocent, that she was almost tempted to laugh. She was, for the first time ever in her life, unafraid; she could see her mother for the sad, disgusting bully she actually was. As a child she had been terrified of this person and that terror had followed her all her life. She could see the fear in her mother's eyes at her retaliation and, knowing that she was carrying a child of her own, she realised that she had to find the strength to repel this woman once and for all, get her out of her life, and out of her head. She knew she had to get everything out into the open. If she didn't do that now, she knew she never would.

'I am all busted up inside, *Mum*, but then I expect you know that, don't you? From when I was a kid. The baby that died, *Mum*, oh, I *can* call you Mum after all this time, can't I?'

Imelda was quiet as her daughter slaughtered her, she knew she had to let her say what she wanted to say. Needed to say.

'The doctors were amazed that I had managed to carry that baby for as long as I did. But they have explained to me that the chances of that ever happening again are remote. Funny word that, *remote*. So, now you know why I ain't shouting it from the rooftops. You took everything away from me, Mum, and I hate you for it. Kenny Boy might fucking see you as some kind of mascot, but I don't. You managed to destroy any happiness I ever had, and any happiness I might have had. So, let's stop this fucking charade now, once and for all. I knew even then, *Mum*, that you were aware of what was happening to me, with the men you brought to your flat, I know you condoned it. You did not give a flying fuck about it. I was so messed up inside I couldn't pee properly for months. Even now I wake up and I can smell my own degradation, just as I can smell your brown as you burnt it on a spoon. I can still see the look of euphoria on your face as the needle delivered your only happiness. You junkie fucking *whore*, you killed not only the people around you, and I saw you in action, lady, you also killed me and Kenny Boy. You killed any chance we might have had of real happiness, of normality, you and your fucking addiction poisoned everyone you came into contact with. Your own mother loathes you, your kids have wished you dead on a daily basis, and the manufactured world you inhabit is going to collapse around your ears one day soon. You look *old*, *haggard*, you know you're over the hill. Well, God pays back debts without money, and you owe big time. So, don't you *dare* come here and try and push your way into my life again. If I told Kenny Boy the truth about his so-called *mum*, he would string you up. I have done my best to keep the peace, but then I always did, didn't I? So, do me a favour, and leave me *alone*.'

Jordanna had forced the words out through gritted teeth, and her pale complexion and haunted eyes told her mother all she needed to know.

Imelda knew that this was why she had forced herself into Jordanna's life. She had needed to know just how much the girl remembered, just how much she was aware of. It seemed she had not forgotten anything. She needed to make sure that Kenny Boy was kept in the dark about it all though. He might forgive her a lot, but even he would draw the line at this kind of information. She was now on a damage limitation exercise. Her daughter's words had not even scratched the surface. As always, the drugs were all she cared about, the drugs and her ability to procure them.

'I swear to you, Jorge, it was the drugs. I can't remember fuck all about those days. I was well gone, I was out of me box . . . you must know that I wasn't with it. That I would have to be stoned off me crust to let that happen. I know I fucked up, but I just want the chance to put things right.'

Jordanna wanted to really hurt this woman, knew that her words, her pain, her loyalty had gone unnoticed by her. Her mother still couldn't find it inside herself to understand how her actions had affected everyone around her. Her addiction had taken over her life many years before. She had put her need for drugs before everything and everyone, she had caused so much death and hate. She had pursued the skag with a single-mindedness that had left no time for her family or her children. She sat there now, looking at her first-born child, and Jordanna knew that she had no feelings for her at all. She had wasted so much time and energy trying to make this piece of shit care for her that it was now almost unbelievable. She no longer needed this woman's approbation, in fact, this woman could now get *fucked*, as far as she was concerned. And she was going to tell her that, she only wished she had done it years ago. She saw that Imelda was still rocking, knew that she was too out of it to ever care about anything of importance.

'You are still stoned out of your nut, aren't you, *Mother*? It's all you care about. All you ever cared about. Anyone else would be dead by now. But not you, oh no, that would be too easy, wouldn't it? Janis Joplin, Jimi Hendrix, all those talented junkies died young. But not *you*, somehow you manage to go from year to year. You manage to dodge the bullet every day of your fucking useless life. Well I hope you get a fucking hot armful. You served me up to anyone who wanted me, and I remember it all. One word from me and you're dead. I want you to leave me alone.'

'Please, Jorge, I can't remember anything. I can't even begin to make you see . . .'

Jordanna sighed with a heavy tiredness and a sudden boredom. '*Stop* it, how stupid do you think I am? Just leave me alone, that's all I want. I had my fill of you a long time ago. I remember *everything*. I have a real party trick, you know. I can read something and remember it word for word. I know you think I am a retard, but in reality I am actually quite a fucking brain-box. I learnt very young how to play the *game*, your game. And I played it well, but I can't do it any more. My baby is dead and I know this child I am carrying now will more than likely never reach fruition. But I can still hope and dream. If I didn't have that then I would have stopped getting up in the morning a long time ago. I tried my hardest to make you love me, and it was a fucking waste of time. I can't be arsed any more. I don't *want* you to care about me, I know that if you did start to care, that would be even worse than your practised indifference. I *hate* you with a vengeance, I despise you and all you stand for. I hope you finally get what you want, Mum. Kenny Boy wants to show the world that he can forgive you, he thinks that will make the shame of you being his mother go away. But it won't, and I will give you a piece of advice, and you should take it on board. Kenny will kill you if he ever thinks you are mugging him off. If he knew the real truth, he would erase you off the face of the earth and smile while he was doing it. Kenny is a wild card, and you can't control him. You might think you can, but he is one dangerous fuck. Now, fuck off and leave me alone.'

Jordanna knew that she had the power now. The truth was *finally* out. It was a great feeling. Knowing that she was now the one with the power.

But Jordanna might have looked like the woman who had birthed her, but that was where the similarity ended. Jordanna didn't have the hate inside her that was necessary to keep the anger going. She would never use the information she had for her own ends. Not unless she was really pushed, and her anger was already losing its potency.

Imelda was shocked at her daughter's harangue, but she also knew that Jordanna wouldn't hurt Kenny Boy by telling him the score. He was her little brother, and she would do anything to see that he wasn't hurt in any way. She still carried the guilt of his father's death. He was too young to remember the bad things that had happened. He did not really remember her as his mother, all he really remembered was his granny Mary, and Jordanna and her love and care.

Imelda soon sussed out that this girl was beyond her use now. The only thing they had in common was the desire to make sure Kenny Boy never knew the truth of his life. It would destroy him if he knew his sister's secrets. Jordanna wouldn't tell him, because she knew that the consequences would be far too brutal and vicious and she would never be able to live with herself if she caused something like that. Unlike her mother, Jordanna didn't feel the need to create situations, she had spent the best part of her young life trying to avoid them.

At this particular moment in time, Imelda was panicking. For the first time in her life, she was not in control of the situation. She had come here in the mistaken belief that she could bring her daughter back into her orbit; had been convinced that she could have talked her round as she had done in the past. She had been wrong, very wrong. Her daughter had seen right through her and, for the first time ever, Jordanna had really let go. Had allowed herself to say what she wanted to. She had finally retaliated.

Now they were both quiet, were shell-shocked, and the silence was crashing down on them.

'So I can't make you believe that I am a changed

person, that I need you to forgive me, for you to please remember that I can't help how I am?'

Jordanna closed her eyes tightly. Shaking her head in angry frustration she said slowly, 'Get the fuck away from me. I ain't Kenny Boy, I see through you like a pane of glass.'

The kettle had boiled and Jordanna turned it off. As she eyed the steam and heard the sound of the water bubbling she felt an overwhelming urge to empty the contents over her mother's head. She wanted to make her hurt, really hurt, like she had made everyone else hurt who had been unlucky enough to come into her orbit. 'Get out, Mum, I mean it. Go now or I won't be responsible for my actions.'

Imelda nodded her head slowly. 'Jamsie is a good bloke, I know that better than you ever will. He's been good to me in his own way but I won't bore you with all that. What I will say is that no one is ever what they seem, and that includes you. Remember that in the future.'

Jordanna didn't answer her, she just stood there and stared at her mother coldly. Her hatred was threatening to boil over and Imelda knew then that, like her mother, Jordanna was capable of great violence if pushed too far.

She left a few minutes later, and her daughter breathed a heavy sigh of relief. Close proximity with her mother always made her feel as if she was slowly being suffocated. Once out of her presence she could breathe easily once more.

Basil was thrilled with his latest acquisition. He had gone into partnership with young Kenny and was now the proud owner of a nightclub. Michael Hannon was gutted, and that only made Basil enjoy the place more. That it was a front for drugs, for money-laundering, was neither here nor there. It was packed to capacity every night and the drugs were dealt out of the toilets as per usual. Providing they were never seen to be personally involved in the dealing, they were as safe as houses.

Young Kenny had his own workforce who all knew how to sell and, more importantly, how to hold their hands up if necessary. As long as they never let on that the club was aware of their dealings, they would be royally taken care of. As would their families, but they were too shrewd to ever be captured in the first place. It was like printing money, that's how easy it was.

Kenny was young, and he was in tune with what the young people wanted. He seemed to pre-empt them and knew before they did what they would want next. He then provided whatever that might be, in abundance, and with his natural paranoia and discretion he managed to keep beneath the radar of not only the regular Old Bill, but also the drug squad. He paid off a lot of bodies, but he kept their names and their job titles to himself. He was a one-man army in many respects.

Better than that though, was the fact that Kenny Boy was already seen as the eventual Face who would one day run the whole town. He was well liked, and he was trusted. He was also someone to be wary of. He was capable of great violence if the occasion called for it, and great compassion for anyone he saw as being the underdog.

He saw his mother as an underdog; despite all he knew about her, she was still his mother. He felt that if he could be seen to forgive her, then her public abandonment of him and his sister would somehow be negated. After all, if he wasn't bothered about it, why should anyone else be?

That logic made perfect sense to him. How he was perceived was everything to him. Since he was a little kid he had felt the stigma attached to them all. He knew now it was to do with his birth and his father's death, but even then he had understood how much harder he would have to work for people's respect. He knew that his start in life had not been what most people would call auspicious. He had felt people's disrespect because of his mother and her behaviour even as a small child. It had been a long time before he had been able to understand that, but he would never forget how people had made him feel. He had been determined to make his name mean something, make those people who looked down on him rethink their opinion of him. He had been determined to force the respect from them, and he had done just that. He worked his arse off and made sure that he was never seen as anything other than in control. He had always known that he would have to live down his heritage, and he felt he had finally accomplished that.

As he saw Jamsie walking over to him, he signalled for another couple of drinks. He knew his sister had got herself a real diamond. Jamsie was all over Jordanna like a cheap suit and that suited everyone perfectly. Providing he never hurt her in any way he was safe; Kenny saw his sister's well-being as being of the utmost importance, especially after the last fiasco. But he genuinely liked Jamsie, he knew he was a ducker and diver but then, in their world, who wasn't? What he did know was that he made Jorge happier than she had ever been before.

'Where is she, then?'

Kenny Boy was laughing as usual. He made a point of being seen in what he classed as a jovial frame of mind at all times. It was part of his master plan. He was never without the easy grin then, when he stopped smiling, people knew there was serious trouble ahead.

Jamsie looked, as always, as if he had just stepped out of a wind tunnel. It was his hair that did it, his dreadlocks were long, thick and, in his own words, very unruly. He looked like the wild man from Borneo first thing in the morning, and it was only by lunchtime that his hair had calmed down enough for him to look almost normal. But his face was his fortune; he was a handsome fuck as most men pointed out in exasperation. And he *was* a seriously handsome man; unlike Kenny Boy, who was in possession of serious youth, Jamsie's looks crept up on you. After a while, you realised that he was a real babe magnet. In fact, he was like a young Cassius Clay; he had the same chiselled cheekbones and clear skin, and he also had a set of perfect teeth, that although overly large, suited him, the gap in between the front two only making him look even sexier where the women were concerned. The fucker was a good-looking rude boy and he knew it better than anyone.

As they shook hands and hugged in greeting, Basil joined them. That Basil had a problem with Jamsie was more than evident. So his decision to join them for a drink was unusual, to say the least. Jamsie, being a very easy-going person until people made him otherwise, held out his huge hand and Basil shook it with about as much enthusiasm as a Northern Ireland Catholic shaking the hand of the Archbishop of Canterbury during the Orange marches. It wasn't what could be termed a friendly meeting.

'All right?'

It was a form of greeting, and both Jamsie and Kenny smiled in reply. Basil was full of himself, and that did not go down as well as he thought it would. He had a big problem with Jamsie, and he did not try to hide it. He did not think he was good enough for Jordanna, in fact, he knew that Jamsie was already slipping a portion to a few of his old flames. Basil could swallow that, he was a man. In their game, spare was all over the place; a name guaranteed an abundance of pussy, it was an accepted part of the job. However, Jamsie had apparently handed over his women to Dexter and everyone seemed to think that was fucking marvellous. Basil half expected him to be beatified by the Pope at any moment, wondered if Jamsie was on the first rung of the ladder to sainthood. Fuck Mother Teresa, Jamsie O'Loughlin was in town.

But what really bothered Basil was that he had found out that Jamsie *was* still involved with his girls; little girls, fucking schoolies, in fact. Children, and they were all getting lessons in how to deliver the ultimate high.

Worse than all that though, was that he had heard a whisper that the teacher of these girls was none other than Imelda Dooley. She and Jamsie went back a long time. He dealt her a good wrap, and she made sure his little girls were more than equipped for the trials and tribulations of a young tom's daily life.

Jamsie was watching him closely, he knew Basil was suspicious of him, knew he had some kind of information that could be used against him. Jamsie was a fool in that way; greed would get him every time. Greed was a bastard, people would chance all sorts for the big jackpot. Jamsie, it seemed, was no different.

'Have you heard the news?'

Basil shook his head and shrugged. 'What news, Kenny?'

Jamsie grinned, that easy grin that made Basil want to break his face open with his bare hands.

'Jorge is in the club, I am going to be an uncle.'

Basil congratulated them both, saw the closeness

between them and knew he had to tread warily because of Jamsie's association with Jordanna. Kenny Boy had a vested interest in his sister's happiness, would ensure that, no matter what it might take to secure it, she would be allowed any happiness she chose for herself.

But he could wait, he was a master of the waiting game. Jamsie thought he was living in a protective bubble with Kenny Boy, but people like Kenny Boy should never be underestimated. Basil would wait, and would gather his information and, when he had enough to ensure Jamsie's complete annihilation, he would pounce.

But he had to have it sewn up before he opened his trap and queered this cunt's pitch once and for all. Then Jamsie would realise that Kenny Boy would even take out Jordanna if he thought she was having him over, so what chance did anyone else have? Oh, he could wait, all right, it was what he did best.

Chapter Twenty-Four

'I've lost the baby, Jamsie, I'm sorry.'

Jamsie nodded, he didn't trust himself to speak. It wasn't until Jordanna's first miscarriage that he had realised just how much he wanted a child with her. Until then, he had given women children without a second's thought. He had kids all over the Smoke; he visited them when the fancy took him, shoved a few quid in the mother's hands and then, when they got on his nerves, walked away without any real emotion. They were his kids, allegedly, and he loved them, but they had been produced by women he had no respect for. Anyone could have given them the kids, eventually someone else would have. Jamsie had given them the children because, deep down, he had wanted to leave his mark on them. Make them remember him, it had amused him. He had seen their swollen bellies and secretly enjoyed the knowledge that, no matter what happened to them in the future, they would always have his baby, his mark, that would be there for the rest of their lives. Every man who came after him had the proof that he had been there first. Women were like Mount Everest; he climbed them because they were there.

It had been like a game; knock them up, then move on to the next one. He had enjoyed their insecurity when they realised that he had done this before, that they were not the first women to be planted by him. He had always seen them through the pregnancy, always made sure they wanted for nothing. But the actual connection between them had never materialised. He had made the appropriate noises, held his kids, but none of them had ever really registered. He had a certain pride in them, but not the urge to keep them close by. He knew he should have felt that, especially about his daughters.

Now he finally had a woman who he wanted to have his baby, and she couldn't do it. She had lost two babies already, and he knew that was not going to change. Jordanna could fall pregnant in a heartbeat, that was not the problem. It was keeping the child inside her for any length of time that was the bugbear. Within three months the child would be expelled from her womb, and with its departure it would take another slice of Jordanna's happiness.

As he held her in his arms he felt the overpowering sorrow that was not only for the loss of his child, but more so because he knew this woman felt that loss a thousand times worse than he did. She was a real diamond. He could see the deep sadness in her eyes, and it occurred to him that this was her attraction. It was her vulnerability that he needed. If she had produced a child, he had a feeling that she would have lost her allure overnight. Jamsie struggled with that knowledge for a few moments, knew he had just been the recipient of a devastating truth, and it had really thrown him off-kilter.

She was trembling in his arms, and he held her tighter, felt her heartbeat against his body. He wondered how he was going to look her in the face after this. She was a real heart, and she was desperate to give him a child. She wanted a child, she *needed* a child.

He hated himself for his brutal honesty, but he had always prided himself on that. He still loved her, he had never in his life felt like this about anybody before. He knew though, that it was her inability to grant him what he wanted that kept him interested in her. He knew he was beyond disgusting, he also knew that the truth needed to be faced. He had felt the consequence of abandonment, knew that was how Jordanna often felt; like her he had suffered at the hands of the one person who should have been the staple throughout her life. He didn't trust mothers, they were overrated.

His own mother had left him with a neighbour when he was four years old. She had laughed and joked with him that day, and the neighbour, a very prim and proper white lady who was prematurely grey, and spent the majority of her time at Mass, or shaking her head at the young women around her, had produced a bag of plain crisps and a glass of lemonade as per usual. She had watched him a few times before, and his mother had picked him up after a few hours, paid her a few quid, and carried the sleeping child back to their flat; he had always woken up in his own bed.

That night he had finally fallen asleep on the sofa and he had enjoyed a boiled egg and soldiers for the first time in his life the very next morning. By the second night of his mum's no-show, he had already sussed out that his mother was not coming back, but he had a shrewd feeling that Mrs White had not been as quick on the uptake as he had. She had brought him to church with her and he had quite enjoyed the feel of it. She had let him clasp her hand tightly for the duration of the Mass and had not let his hand go even after they had arrived back at her flat. Even she had worked out by then that no one was coming for him. His mother was a very pretty girl from Edmonton; she had given birth to him like she had done everything else in her life, without thinking it through. All these years later he had a sneaking suspicion that she had no idea who his father might have been; she was a very friendly type of person and men were always coming round to see her. It was two weeks before Mrs White contacted the social services about him, and by then they had fallen into a pattern of sorts. She would not let them take him to a home, arguing that he was all right where he was. She had eventually fought for him tooth and nail, and she had been really shocked when she had got him. When they were legal, they had sized each other up; he liked her, and she seemed to like him. They had an understanding; she was willing to let him live with her and, for his part, he was willing to live there. It worked out perfectly.

He had started school in September, had become a Catholic overnight. He had, for the first time in his life, eaten regularly, and eaten food that was not fried or been purchased already cooked and dripping with grease. He was suddenly living in the world of routines and he thrived on it. He had called her Mrs White for months then, one day, she had told him to call her Aunt Bee. Her name was Beverley, and he had done as she requested. Within two years they were tighter than a duck's arse. He had found out many years later that the Mrs was an honorary title, she had never been married. They had made an incongruous couple, the big black boy and the tiny, birdlike spinster of the parish. Her sister, a large, robust woman with red cheeks and mottled legs, had never really come to terms with her sister's charge, or the eventual adoption that had been celebrated with a rare visit to a Wimpy Bar. But Jamsie had loved her, and she had loved him in her own way. He had done very well at school, gaining seven O-levels, and he knew she wanted him to go on to higher education. Unfortunately, he had already begun his higher education; he was dealing by fifteen, and had walked his first brass out by twenty-one. Aunt Bee had chosen to believe that her Jamsie was in possession of a good job and a good legal income even though she had to have known that was complete shite. But he had admired her for choosing to believe the best of him.

He had paid her back a thousandfold for her kindness and her love, and he had held her hand as she gasped her last breath; breast cancer had stolen her away from him before any of them had even had the time to digest the news.

He was twenty-two and alone in the world, but Aunt Bee had been his main yardstick for women. His mother had been a good-time girl, and he knew that she had walked away from him without a second's thought for what might happen to him. She had dumped him on Mrs White and walked out of his life. Jordanna was precious to him because she was like Aunt Bee, she would always be there for him, no matter what.

People were complicated, and he was the most complicated of them all. He didn't really want any babies with Jorge, he liked it most when it was just them. Just the two of them, happy together. She cooked for him, she cleaned for him, she was happy just to be near him. He would give her the world on a plate if he could, but he knew she wouldn't want it. All she wanted was a baby, and that was not going to happen, not that he was going to air that opinion out loud.

He wasn't faithful to her, that was beyond him, but he loved her. That, as far as he could see, should be enough. He knew he was a treacherous bastard in many ways; he would use anyone for his own ends. He saw every situation from 'a what's in it for me' point of view. He had been determined from the day his mother had dumped him, never to let himself be that vulnerable and that broken again. Life itself, for most people, was a crock of steaming shit. He had no real loyalty to anyone, but Jordanna had somehow given him his first inkling of how love could change a person.

He had also heard rumours that he was seen as being softer than a virgin's pussy, and he knew the rumours were very much going in his favour. He had a real earner going for him although he knew that some people might not see the situation in quite the same light as he did. Well, he had always been a law unto himself, and that was not about to change now.

Imelda was feeling wonderful, she had the languorous feeling that always followed a good hit. She could feel her whole body relaxing, knew it would not last for very long, but it was heaven while it was washing over her. She yawned widely, and settling back in her chair, she enjoyed the moment. This was what she lived for. This feeling of ease, of being at peace with the world. Enjoying her own company, feeling the temporary relief that the skag always gave to her. It was a pyrrhic victory; she knew it wouldn't last long enough. She won and she lost every time. But that was the whole idea of it. Heroin was a loner's dream. Eventually all heroin addicts craved being by themselves, it was the only way they could justify their existence. If they had to interact with others it ruined the buzz, it was much easier to be by yourself. That way you only had yourself to think about. Eventually no one mattered: not your family, especially not your kids, they were far too needy, not friends, nor personal hygiene, nothing. It was all about the moment.

She could see the mess around her, the place was rotten. But she had never cared about things like that. Why would she? She kept herself clean and tidy and she took good care of her clothes and her hair. Her scars had faded over the years, and the wrinkles that had arrived also helped to mask them. It was amazing really, though her face was older and harder, she still got a few second glances from men. Certain types of men anyway. For her, that was a real ego boost.

She knew she had to start getting herself together, the day was wearing on, and she had to get to her job. She liked her job, it was what made her feel that she was still useful. She was out of the business in a personal way, but she was now paid very well to introduce others to the business. It was a good feeling knowing she was doing something she was very good at. And, at the same time, she was paying back a few debts that were well overdue as far as she was concerned.

Jamsie was nervous about her being involved in it, but he was like a fucking old woman. She had made him employ her, and made him keep her on. Her daughter would not be impressed if she knew the score about her old man. But the earn was what really interested Jamsie, he would sell his own fucking cock if the price was right. He was a pimp by nature, and a ponce by trade.

Young Dexter was about as much use as Karl Marx on

Family Fortunes. He had no idea at all, he was a fucking idiot. He looked good and he dressed well, better than Jamsie, but then so did most of the male population. But Dexter had no interest in what he was doing. To run a business with any degree of success, you needed to be *interested* in what you were doing. It was a given, if you knew the game you automatically knew the pitfalls. You were tuned in to the people you were dealing with and you could see trouble before it arrived. Dexter was a fucking earhole. A complete twonk; he didn't care what was going on, the girls could be dressed in gorilla suits and he wouldn't notice, he just turned up to collect the poke. Other than that, he didn't give a toss. Well, she knew, after all her years in the business, that if your protector didn't give a monkey's, then no one else would. It was bad for morale, and the girls on the bash were not big on self-worth anyway. If they were, they would not be doing the job in the first place.

She was the only person who bothered to keep the girls in check. She was enjoying her status; after all, no one knew the business like she did. She was now running it single-handedly, and it felt good, like the old days when she had run a much bigger outfit than this one, and she had done it without even thinking about it too much. Which had also been her downfall, she had not thought anything through in those days. She had believed she was beyond anyone's reach, whether it was the Old Bill, or the enemies she had made through her own arrogance. Imelda Dooley had finally learnt her lesson, and she had learnt it the hard way.

The game could be a real earner; it was also a business that you either understood from the first day, or you ran from as fast as you could because, after all, it was also a fucking dangerous occupation. Every punter was a prospective nut-bag, and there were plenty of those about. You had to have a built-in shit detector, and that was not something you could acquire overnight. You either had it from the off, and used it to your own benefit, or you sank without trace. Imelda had seen real lookers fuck up because they couldn't work out the real Looney Tunes from the general riff-raff. Imelda helped her girls to understand the business and taught them to look after themselves. Dexter was very appreciative of her help and her acumen, he was quite happy to let her do it, and she was skimming the take like nobody's business. She was back on the earn and loving it. She was back where she liked to be: in charge, on the take, and without anyone to oversee what she was doing. The girls were a little young, but they were game, and although they were not what she would describe as the cream of the crop, they were grafters, and they were quick learners. She had helped them get into the needle, it enabled them to settle into the life. They were at the lower end of the food chain so the needle was a fucking big bonus when you had to walk the pavement night after night. They had been given a set amount to bring to the table and they stayed there, on the street, until they had that money for her. She knew how to encourage them when the need arose, and how to frighten the crap out of them so they did as they were requested.

It was late summer and the nights were just starting to draw in; it was the best time of year for the girls. Men who had to pay did not like broad daylight, darkness was their forte. In fairness, the majority of the girls looked better in the twilight anyway. They were young, but not exactly raving beauties. She had drummed into their heads the importance of not fighting amongst themselves. It was most brasses' biggest failing, after a while they became very aggressive and started to see another girl's earner as theirs by right. They would convince themselves that they had a priority of sorts, that they were more entitled to the punters available than the other girls. That was not just a working girl's natural instinct, it was exacerbated by the needle. The girls embraced the needle to get a false courage to go on the pavement in the first place. Eventually they would pound the kerb to pay for the drugs. It was a win-win situation for someone like Imelda. And the younger you got them, the easier it was. There was a new batch of girls arriving in the Smoke every day, and that made them all the more indispensable.

She had always turned up for work on time, she knew her son had an obsession with timekeeping. He was a bastard for punctuality, bless him. She loved that about him. He was a right little Face and she was proud of him for that. His burgeoning reputation also helped her get a swerve when she wanted it. He treated her like family and that meant everyone else had to as well.

The knock at her door was a welcome sound, it was the start of her working day. She opened the door happily to three of her newest girls. All three of them were on the wrong side of legality, and between them they had more blackheads than a school disco. But they were very new to the business, and she was still pretending she had their best interests at heart. She welcomed them inside with her usual fake smile, and the promise of a spectacular high. She always had her kit on show, after all, she lived alone, and actual *bona fide* visitors were few and far between.

The girls clattered inside, their overly made-up faces and eager expressions were something she had come to expect. They were all the same, and she knew that if she played it just right, she could have them for life.

Kenny Boy was a bit drunk, he had allowed himself a few brandies to celebrate his latest deal. He had just negotiated a good take from a fleet of hire car companies. They gave him a drink, and he made sure that any aggro concerning their drivers disappeared; whether it was being drunk while in control of a motor vehicle, to dangerous or careless driving resulting in an accident of some sort, he had the market sewn up. He also had an endless fleet of motors to drop his packages around town. As he lay in the bed, he could feel the fluttering of the girl's heart as she lay against him. She was warm and friendly, and he knew she was with him because of his name. He had met her and bedded her within hours. But she had been a game little bird, not averse to a few of the more exotic moves he required. She had a very pretty face and good legs. He had a thing about legs. They were the first thing he noticed on a bird; he clocked the legs first, then the boat race. If the legs were spectacular enough, the bird could be pug-ugly. He only wanted to fuck them, not marry them. If they were a bit fucking rancid he did not entertain them to a few drinks beforehand in a public place; he would do them in the back of a motor and drop them off with a wave and a smile. But the legs were the thing for him, and this girl had killer legs. They were long and slim, and she wore clothes that showed them off to their full advantage.

Lisa Marks was in her element; she had fancied Kenny Boy Dooley since she was thirteen and had seen him out and about in the local pubs. He had the dangerousness that she required to warrant her interest.

She liked a good bounce round the mattress, and he had given her a decent seeing-to. As she lay there beside him, she was happy; she had achieved her objective and, if she played her cards right, he would maybe see her again and she could have her name linked with his. It would afford her a bit of kudos and the guarantee of five minutes of fame. She understood the way her world worked, and she was quite happy to use whatever she had in order to get what she wanted from life. She also had a great sense of humour, and she was already known for her ability to tell a joke and tell it well.

'Can I get you a drink or anything, Kenny?'

She had a nice little flat, clean and well furnished and he knew he would become the next man to provide a piece of furniture or pay a few bills. He was happy to do that, it was part of the game.

He hugged her close. 'I'm all right, mate. Relax for five minutes.'

He was ready to go to sleep, a few hours' kip was just what he could do with now; she was a real nice little thing and he could think of worse things than waking up beside her and getting a repeat performance a few hours down the line. She snuggled into him, her long legs entangled with his, the softness of her skin felt good against his and he squeezed her tightly once more.

Lisa loved this bit, the knowledge that for these few hours she was the only thing on the man in question's mind. Kenny Boy was a real feather in her cap as far as she was concerned; she would be bragging about this for weeks. She would exaggerate it with a few well-chosen phrases, and her ebullient praise for his sexual prowess would make it sound like a real relationship.

As she was basking in the afterglow of their encounter

her phone rang, its shrillness breaking the cosiness of their embrace. Lisa answered it quickly, she was half angry at the intrusion, and half pleased at the opportunity to name-drop Kenny Boy and prove he was there with her. It was a double-edged sword, though, he was quite capable of getting up and leaving while she was on the blower. It had happened to her before.

'Hello?' She was sitting up in the bed, her nakedness fully exposed; she had a good body and she was not shy about letting it be seen. She was also hoping her provocative stance would keep Kenny Boy there for another bout.

Kenny yawned and lay back on the pillows. The mood was broken now, real life had just forced its way in. He was about to pull the sheets back and go for a well-deserved piss when he caught the tailend of her conversation.

Lisa was now overjoyed at the call, she felt it was like destiny or something. This call could actually make Kenny see that they had a lot more in common than he realised. She turned around and lay on her back, her heavy breasts and tight belly were evident as she feigned a stretch to keep his attention. She winked at him saucily as she said with as much guile as she could muster, 'Tell Jamsie I can't, I'm busy. I know Dexter has the numbers, he got them from Imelda. She deals with that anyway. I only know Cassie's number because she sometimes works the bar in Soho.'

She put the phone down a few seconds later and, grinning at Kenny Boy, she said huskily, 'We have more in common than you think.'

Kenny Boy was still digesting her words, and he was not impressed with any of them. 'Who's Cassie?'

He was calm, he sounded just interested enough to not

make her suspicious. Lisa shrugged, as if bored by his question, thinking it would make her look sophisticated. 'She's one of your mum's girls. I used to work for Jamsie in his bar, not as a brass obviously, but actually *behind* the bar. I would often have to help him keep a tab on the girls he was running. Cassie was a nice little thing, and she would often be there; let's just say her and Jamsie were close.'

Lisa was smiling still, talking to what she assumed was a man of the world, unaware that his sister was actually Jamsie's other half, and had been for a long time.

He laughed then. 'Jamsie is a bit of a lad, I understand. I often wonder if he is all talk, to be honest.'

Lisa flicked her long black hair over her slim shoulders and, lighting a Benson & Hedges cigarette, she took a deep draw on it before saying, 'He is a fucking nightmare, if it has a pulse he will poke it. I've had to fight him off enough times meself.'

Kenny knew that meant she had slept with Jamsie at some point herself; she would sleep with any man who had the name or the money to boost her ego. It wasn't something he would hold against her, it was the only reason he was with her now.

'Cassie was a real little schoolie though, but you know Jamsie, he likes the babies, don't he? He's only a half-inch from a nonce, as your mum says.'

'She still looks out for his girls, does she?'

Kenny Boy was finding it very hard to contain the anger that was building up inside him. He knew he had been taken for a right fucking dimlo, and that was not something he was prepared to overlook.

'From what I saw, she just gets them acquainted with the life. She gives them the rules and regulations needed to make sure they don't fuck up. Jamsie knows that Dexter is useless, and Dexter hates the job anyway, so your mum basically does all the graft for him.'

Kenny was afraid to speak for a few moments, the girl really thought she was a fucking player by telling him this in such a light-hearted tone. He wanted to smash her face in now, wanted to make her understand that she was not endearing herself to him with her fucking banter. She only made him want to hurt her, want to see her pay for her treachery. Like Jamsie and that whore of a mother would when he got his hands on them.

'How old is this Cassie then?'

Lisa shrugged once more, her lightly tanned skin was almost translucent in the lamplight. She knew she looked good.

'About fifteen or sixteen now, she's been on the scene for about a year or so. Your mum picked her up at the Cross, like most of her girls. She would bring them to the bar sometimes and we used to chat a bit, you know. Jamsie thinks the world of your mum, Kenny Boy. She even puts the new girls up for a while when they first get involved, they need a stabilising influence at first, I suppose.'

Kenny was nodding once more, unsure if he was capable of coherent conversation. He also knew that Lisa was willing to keep talking if he kept quiet. She was trying to establish a common bond between them, and he let her think she was succeeding. He knew the girl was a dangerous fuck because this was knowledge she should have had the sense to keep to herself. As if she was determined to prove this point she asked him archly and with maximum emphasis, 'Is everything all right with him and old Basil now? I heard they had a bit of a tear-up.'

Kenny snapped his head around to look at her and Lisa

felt the first shivers of apprehension. Kenny was breathing in short, sharp pants. He could feel his heart as it raced inside his chest, knew that he was beyond any kind of pretence now.

'Over what? Why did they fall out?'

She knew then, without a doubt, that she was going to be the cause of something very big, and something very dangerous.

'Well, answer me, you fucking scab.' He was bellowing at her now and kneeling on the bed, he grabbed her by her throat and, holding her down so she couldn't move, he said nastily, 'Answer me or I will fucking take your face off! I will punch you until you look like a fucking piece of raw beef. I'll break every bone in your fucking face, and I'll rip your fucking lips off. When I am finished with you fucking Baby Jane Hudson will pull more blokes than you will.'

Lisa was choking, and he heard the sound of her absolute terror. It finally penetrated through his anger and his hate that she was near death. He loosened his grip on her throat and watched her as she coughed and spluttered, as she drew a long, deep breath into her lungs. He had nearly finished her off, and they both knew that.

Lisa was red eyed, and she was already crying. She was huddled against the bed now; bereft of her former confidence she looked what she was, a frightened young girl who had opened her mouth once too often. She knew that even if she walked away from this lot, she would still have to deal with Jamsie when he found out that she was the cause of his latest problem. And that was without this man's mother; she was already well known as being five cards short of a full deck. How this had happened so quickly was the real frightener though, this man had gone from tender lover to a psychotic animal in minutes. The danger she had always been attracted to was now being shown to her in all its terrifying reality.

Lisa Marks had just learnt a very valuable lesson; in the world she was so determined to become a major part of, you keep your trap shut no matter who you might be talking to. If they knew what you knew, then why bother to enlighten them about it all over again? If they didn't know what you knew, however, then there was probably a fucking good reason for that. Idle chatter could get innocent people banged up, beaten up or, in extreme cases, murdered. Talking for effect was a sin that was not to be tolerated by the likes of Kenny Boy or his peers.

They only survived because they kept a tightly closed mouth, and a healthy suspicion of everyone around them. That this little tart knew something he didn't told Kenny Boy that his friendship with Jamsie had blocked people's willingness to confide in him about anything that might pertain to his nearest and dearest.

That Jamsie was fucking around on his sister was bad enough, but he could swallow that. Men were men after all, but Jamsie's collusion with their mother was another ball game entirely. That was something else again. And, as Lisa spewed out everything she knew, Kenny Boy listened with growing disgust. He had to sort this lot out, and sooner rather than later.

Chapter Twenty-Five

'Look, Kenny. I *have* got the hump with Jamsie, but you can't come here all fucking hellfire and threats; you should have fucking had your eye on the ball. He has been in cahoots with that skank of a mother of yours for a long time. They go back fucking years them two. He was trumping her at one time, I heard that one *yonks* ago. Dexter is his front; Jamsie just can't resist the poke that can be earned off the young girls. He gets them on the pipe or the needle, depending on what the poor whores prefer, and then he outs them on the pavement. If they last five years they have had a result. I work in the flesh game, but I deal with fucking adults. I don't want the skaggers, they fuck up, and when they finally fuck up big time, they tend to take you down with them.'

Basil poured himself a large brandy and, gulping it down quickly, he said sarcastically, 'You made a rod for your own back there; you brought your mother back into fashion, and Jamsie was safe because of your sister's association with him. Who the fuck was going to come and tell *you* that you were being fucking scammed by your own nearest and dearest?'

Kenny was still trying to control himself. He wanted to hurt Basil now, he knew that even though he was telling him the truth, his humiliation was such that he would happily knife him just to shut the fucker up. 'Who else knew about it?'

Basil sighed. His heart went out to the boy, but this was a long time coming, and now it had finally happened, all they could do was get it sorted out and then put it behind them. 'A lot of people I should imagine, Kenny, you made your mark, and you made it well. A bit too well, in many respects. No one wanted to be the one to bring you the bad news. You have a fucking habit of going Greek on people. You want to kill the bearer of the news, and in our world that is a fucking big no-no. Even I was wary of putting you wise; me and Jamsie have been at each other's throats for a long time. I knew the score with him, but to everyone it looked like you were countenancing it all. No one likes the little girls being pumped out, and pimping isn't the most respected of professions anyway. But if you keep to the rules you are all right. Once you step over the line you lose all your goodwill, your respect and your credibility. Jamsie has only been able to get away with it because of you. Because of Jordanna. He brought your mother in and she is the one who finds them, grooms them, and disables them. She ensures they are dependent on her and him, it ain't like she would find something so despicable beyond her capabilities, is it? We all know she is fucking without anything even resembling morals or decency. She sees those girls without any compassion or guilt, they're paper money to her, nothing more. I can't believe she's had the fucking front to do it all again. Not after last time. I thought I had taught her a fucking lesson. But she never changes. And what you need to do now is decide how you are going to sort this out. You have no need to feel any allegiance to your mother, she is a fucking hard old bird. But you know that Jamsie has Jordanna onside. And, whatever else I might think of him, he cares about her. He genuinely cares about that girl. Even he couldn't fake that. I wonder if Jordanna will still swallow him, even if she finds out about this.'

Kenny had never felt like this before. He knew now what it was to be *too* revered, and he saw that his reputation for violent retaliation was such that even the powers-that-be were loath to bring such terrible skulduggery to his ears. They saw it as his problem, not theirs, so it was up to him to find out about it, and eventually do something about it. And he would, but he had to sort it out in such a way that he kept his self-respect along with his sister's affection.

Mary Dooley was astounded at what she had heard. She knew there was something snidey going on with Imelda but she couldn't prove it. But then there was always something snidey going on with her, it was what she was. Imelda was capable of literally anything, as she had proved over and over again.

Kenny was a broken man; he was still too young to have the experience that something of this enormity needed so that it could be dealt with properly.

'She killed your father and she blamed poor Jordanna; she destroyed her own daughter without a thought. She's caused more death and hate than anyone else since Hitler decided to grow a moustache and give himself a fucking comb-over. She has ruined my life, both of your lives. She is now ruining other lives. Jamsie and her in cahoots, well, you know what they say don't you? Show me the company you keep and I'll tell you what you are. My husband used to say that, and never a truer word was spoken. Jorge will have to be told and you'll have to do it. She will believe it if it comes from you. But it will destroy her all over again.'

Kenny Boy was not saying anything, and that alone told Mary how serious this situation actually was. He was sitting there in her lovely comfortable armchair just staring into space. He looked strange, he looked as mad as people said he was once they were away from him, and behind closed doors. Kenny Boy was the product of his mother's life, as was poor Jordanna.

Kenny Boy had that same coldness about him that Imelda possessed. But, unlike her, he was capable of deep feelings for the people he cherished whereas Imelda had been gone from them all the day she had been delivered of her first armful.

It was always about the drugs with her, and the people who gravitated to the addict's lifestyle. She was drawn to the filth and the scum of society; people who were like her. Whose whole existence was about nothing more than getting enough money to bankroll their habit, to keep themselves on the right side of chemical numbness.

Mary felt old suddenly. Her sons had been in her mind a lot recently, she knew their renewed interest in her was because they wanted to cash in on Kenny Boy's notoriety. She remembered the way she had been held over a barrel time and time again by her daughter, and how she had been forced to sit back and wait for her to get fed up with her kids before she would once more leave them with her. Then she would have the unenviable task of trying to undo all the damage their sojourn with their mother had caused them. Now, after all these years, Imelda had managed to do it again; she had destroyed her children's lives without even trying.

Mary went out to the kitchen to get some more tea, it was all she could think of to do. The fear was already upon her, and she knew that, this time, there would be no going back for any of them.

Jordanna was watching Jamsie closely; he was like a nervous schoolgirl and she knew instinctively that whatever was wrong with him also affected her somehow. His skin was almost grey and he looked like a man with the weight of the world on his shoulders.

He was slumped over somehow, his shoulders drooped, and he looked beaten. She was frightened to question him about it, she knew that whatever he said would only break her heart. She was still recovering from the loss of the latest foetus. She always thought of them as a foetus, the term baby had far too much resonance for her. 'Baby' conjured up images of prams and cots, of crying and love. A baby had the capacity to become a person and engendered hope and dreams; It was far too emotive a word. So, foetus was the lesser of two evils where she was concerned. It was no more than a bunch of cells that *could* become a baby, but wasn't one quite yet.

'Are you all right, Jamsie?' She was sorry for asking him, she didn't want to hear what he answered her. But she knew he was waiting for her to open up the lines of communication, he was looking at her as if he had never met her before, as if she was a complete stranger to him.

'Are you going to answer me, Jamsie?'

He nodded his head and she noticed that even his

dreads, that normally looked so alive, so unruly, were suddenly looking very lank and sorry for themselves. 'I've fucked up, Jorge. I've fucked up big time.'

Jamsie saw the beauty of her eyes, and knew just how much he really did care for her. He knew he should have guessed that his greed would be uncovered eventually. Imelda had always had the power of the gab, but he couldn't blame her for his predicament. He had seen the arrangement as a subtle dig at Kenny Boy and everyone around him. He had ruined everything himself, and now he knew he had to pay the price. Kenny Boy had beaten little Lisa to a pulp, and her friend had been good enough to call him from the hospital and fill him in on the details.

Lisa would live, but she would not be out clubbing for a good while; he had arranged a few quid for her since she would be out of circulation for at least six months. He also knew that her friend was as loose-lipped as Lisa, so she would be telling all and sundry, in strictest confidence of course, exactly what had happened to her friend; who had done the dirty deed, and why it had been done to her in the first place. It was a complete abortion, and the worst thing of all was that it was an abortion of his own making.

'What have you done, Jamsie?'

Jordanna had guessed he was not the faithful type and she had accepted that. She wondered briefly if Kenny had found out about one of his extra-curricular activities. Kenny Boy was capable of causing the Third World War if the fancy took him. But she knew that Kenny Boy would have spoken to Jamsie on the quiet, would not have brought that hurt to her front door. Then a fear gripped her heart as she asked him quietly, 'Have you got someone else pregnant, Jamsie? Is that what this is all about?'

Jamsie went to her then, his heart sorry for what she

had felt compelled to ask him. 'No, never in a million years, Jorge.'

She believed him, convinced herself in those few minutes that nothing else could be that bad, could hurt her as much. She was to find out that she was wrong about that assumption, so very, very wrong.

Paula Derby was sixteen but she looked about twelve. It was the heavy make-up, it made her look even younger than she was. She was built like a boy, much to her own consternation, and she had been a runaway for just over two years. Until she had been introduced to Imelda she had lived on the streets and survived by begging.

Her babyish looks, and her pleasing smile, had made that quite a lucrative enterprise. But she had found the first winter on the pavement very hard. As a minor who *looked* like a minor, she had not been able to use a lot of the hostels or homeless shelters. She had found out just how dangerous the streets could be; she had been raped within the first three weeks by two city boys overloaded on drink and drugs. She had suffered two muggings by other homeless women, losing her boots the second time. She had developed a hacking cough, and a penchant for letting her body be used in return for food, drink or drugs. Imelda had been like a saviour when she had been brought to her house by another runaway she had met while begging in Covent Garden.

Imelda had put her up, fed her food and the brown. She had scrubbed her, supplied her with new clothes, and helped her get a regular stint on the pavements at Kings Cross.

Like many of the girls, she was now almost totally dependent on Imelda, and looked to her for her every move. That Imelda took a cut for her trouble was expected; in reality Paula had never had it so good.

Imelda also passed on the brown to her, and she depended on her for that as well as everything else. So, sitting in Imelda's filthy flat, drinking a large vodka and Diet Coke, watching her as she expertly burnt them both a nice little bit of forgetfulness, she felt quite relaxed and at ease with herself. Two minutes after she first felt the hit of the drug, the front door was kicked off the hinges.

Mary arrived at Jordanna's within twenty minutes of her phone call. She let herself inside the house with trepidation; her granddaughter had been hysterical on the phone, and she assumed Jordanna had been told about the latest developments. What she was unprepared for was the blood. It was everywhere; all over the ceiling in the lounge, the walls, all over the furniture and the floors. It was all over her granddaughter. What really frightened Mary though was the man lying on the floor. Jamsie had been stabbed over and over and the weapon, a large bread knife, was sticking out of his back. It was obvious, even to the uninitiated, that he had been dead long before that final thrust.

Mary half expected to see Kenny Boy standing there; this was his kind of reaction, his kind of act. Jordanna was sitting on the white leather sofa. She was quiet now, her hands were folded in her lap and her legs crossed. If she had not been dripping in blood she could have been waiting for her appointment in the doctor's surgery.

Mary immediately went onto autopilot; she was all about getting her granddaughter to walk away from this. She was already plotting how to sort this out in her head.

Kneeling down, she took Jordanna's hands in hers and said softly, 'Did you do this, lovey?'

Jordanna nodded slowly. 'I'm like me mum, ain't I?' She started to laugh loudly, her whole body was suddenly shaking with mirth. Her head was thrown back and her laughter filled the room with its intensity.

'I listened to him telling me how he was in league with me mother, about the young girls they had put on the game, and look what I done, Nan. I didn't even let him finish what he was saying. You see, she warned me about him, and I didn't listen. She warned me that people weren't always what you thought they were.'

She was laughing again, her lovely face strained and white with sorrow. 'Like her, my mother, I just fucking killed him. I went to the kitchen and I came back with the bread knife and I killed him.'

She was laughing uproariously once more. 'Murderers, that's what we are, me and me mum. When people don't do what we want them to, we kill them. I remember the blood from Lance, his head was nearly gone. His brains were everywhere, all over my nightie. I remember nothing but blood from my childhood. Thick, sticky blood. I still wake up in the night and smell the heavy stench of fresh blood. I feel the fear that paralyses me, I have to lie there in terror until I am able to move my arms and legs once more, until I can feel the constriction leave my throat so I can talk or scream once again. Except, I never do. I try and keep it all inside me. Why upset you, or anyone else with it all? No one can help me, no one can ever help me *now*, can they?'

Jordanna sighed heavily, and she said quietly and very sensibly, 'I just wanted to stop him talking, Nan, that was all. As soon as he mentioned *her*, I knew I had to make him stop. She poisons everything she touches, and she does it without a second's thought for who she might destroy along the way.'

Mary was distraught. That this poor girl had ended up like this was a crying shame. Born to anyone else but Imelda, she would have had a chance. But for Imelda the drugs and all they entailed had always taken priority over everyone and everything. Mary often wondered if Kenny Boy was a victim of her drug taking; she had dropped anything she could lay her hands on through her pregnancy with him. That had to have taken a toll on him of some kind. But Mary loved these kids, more than she had ever loved her own. She hated her daughter with a vengeance that was so powerful it was almost tangible in the quiet of the room.

A few minutes later, Mary opened the door to her grandson. The blood didn't bother him, or the body, but his sister's tears did. He held her to him tightly, whispering endearments, and promising her that everything would be fine.

Mary wondered at what was going to be the upshot of this latest madness to have overtaken her family. She was trying to figure out how they were going to walk away from this lunacy in one piece and she just couldn't see how they were going to sort it out. It was far too complicated.

Basil chased Paula out of the flat with his loud cursing and his obvious anger. She had understood immediately that there was serious trouble afoot; the front door coming off its hinges had been the main clue for her, and snatching the nearest wrap to her, she had left Imelda to face the music alone.

Imelda waited silently for the beating she expected, but it had not arrived. Instead she had been amazed as Basil said to her angrily, 'Get your coat, and move your arse. Kenny Boy is looking for you and he'll kill you if he finds you.'

'Why? What's happened?'

Basil looked at Imelda then, she was finally bloating, and her beautiful hair, that had once shone like spun gold, was now lank and thinning. Her eyes had bags big enough to hold the weekly shop and her teeth had been ground away over the years so they now looked too small for her face. The heroin had finally caught up with her, she finally looked like what she was. A filthy skagger, she lived in filth and was happy to do just that. All she ever cared about was making sure she had the next dose of chemicals to put inside her once luscious body. She looked like a parody of the girl he had once lusted after. No man had been immune to her charms and yet she had found her only real love in a needle.

Because of that, she spent Christmas alone with only her kit to keep her company. Easter, even her birthdays, had been celebrated with an extra armful. She had dedicated her life to the needle and, somewhere along the line, she had lost the knack of actually living. Of being a part of real life, of the real world. Imelda existed in the twilight zone, and her actions over the years had caused so much hurt and hatred because of that.

Well, her son was not going to be captured and caged for the likes of her, and that is what would happen should he get his hands on this woman. Basil had sent him over to join Mary at Jordanna's, had told him he would be better off seeing how his sister was, and deciding how he was going to deal with Jamsie before he turned his attention to his mother. She was going nowhere, and that had been his mantra for years about Imelda.

Now Basil was here, attempting to save this woman from being obliterated by her own son, and she had the cheek to ask him what was going on as if she was unaware of anything untoward.

'You know what, Mel, you are thirty minutes from meeting your fucking maker. You and Jamsie have finally gone too far. Now, move yourself before Kenny Boy gets here with a sawn-off shotgun or his tool kit. You'd be surprised what he can do with a pair of pliers and a cordless drill.'

The fear of being found out was now enveloping her and Imelda realised then just how precarious her position actually was. Kenny would rip her apart with his bare hands if the anger he had nurtured so carefully was allowed a free rein. She owed her life to Basil.

'Thanks, Basil, thanks for warning me . . .'

'I am doing this for Kenny Boy and Jordanna, not for you. You ain't worth doing time for, Mel, you ain't worth *nothing*. Your son might go down one day, but it won't be because he beat a piece of shit like you to death. He needs you gone, once and for all, and I will make sure that happens.'

'But where am I going to go?'

It was always about her, she had not even asked how much Kenny Boy knew, how much her daughter knew, or what might be happening to Jamsie at this very moment in time. She had not enquired about her daughter's reaction to the latest aggro, but then that was par for the course with her.

'Well, my advice would be fucking Mars or, failing that, South America, but I can't see you going there, can you?

Just come with me and I'll hide you out for a few days. When I can, I'll get you shifted somewhere. But get moving before he lands up here looking for you.'

Imelda ran into her bedroom and started throwing things into a black bin bag. She was terrified now, she knew it was all over for her. She would have to earn for herself once more and she wouldn't even be able to sign on. Kenny Boy would find her in a heartbeat if she did that, any registered court bailiff would be able to find her in minutes. And, as most of them moonlighted as bouncers, it was easy enough to get a favour like that done. She would have to move as far away as possible from Kenny Boy, maybe Scotland or even Ireland, and as she had no real life to speak of now, how was she supposed to create another one somewhere else? Her habit would suffer; she knew she would have to stay on the outside of the criminal world. Her world, the only one she knew. She would be an outcast, and without anyone to give her a boost she would be forced back into the rough trade just to survive. She looked around her flat, saw it as others must. It was like a squat, but it was warm and comfortable enough for her. The thought of leaving it terrified her. She knew deep down that she couldn't survive on the streets, not at her age. She would also have to change her name, her looks. She'd have to dye her hair and hope no one recognised her; there was bound to be a bounty on her head. It was becoming more and more daunting for her by the second. Fuck Jamsie and his fucking schoolie scam. She had already convinced herself it was his fault; as always, she was the innocent victim.

Imelda Dooley left the flat twenty minutes later. She would never return. She was placed in a small house in Peckham, and she was watched over by a large West Indian man called, of all things, Nebuchadnezzar Arnold. He was known as Arnie for short, but he was better known for his famously short temper, and his absence of anything even resembling an inquisitive nature. He looked after people for a large amount of money, and he never asked any questions concerning them. It was a very lucrative profession and it suited his rather solitary nature. He fed them, he ignored them, and he forgot about them. Locked in a back bedroom with a small portable TV and her stash, Imelda's dilemma became very clear to her as the days crept by. She had blown it, and this time there was no going back.

Basil waited three days before he finally felt he could talk to Kenny Boy without him losing his mind. He spoke to him for a long time, and explained in graphic detail why he had done what he had. Kenny Boy had thanked him courteously and hugged him in gratitude. He had then smiled gently, and asked, politely, to be taken to see her.

'I mean it, Mum, if you don't do this one thing for me I will kill you.'

Imelda looked at her son's face and saw the determination there, saw the truth of his words. She knew she was being given a second chance and, even though she was still on her usual opiate high, she was sensible enough to know this was not something she could refuse.

She looked into her son's eyes; they were her eyes, deep blue and thick lashed. He was a really handsome man. He was also a vicious, dangerous man, and he was so disgusted at her, was so revolted by her and her life, and what he felt she had caused because of her addiction and the selfishness it had caused, she knew she had to do what he asked. She nodded, afraid to speak, knew her voice could cause him to lose control.

'You have to finally pay for your fucking mistakes, and you have to make things right for your daughter. You ruined her, you left her unable to ever know a really happy day. You saw her as your property, as your fucking own personal whipping girl. Well, it stops now. You will do this one thing for her, and you will do it with a good heart and you will let her think it was all your idea.'

Imelda nodded once more, afraid of this young man she had bred, afraid of the same lad she had believed was her saviour. He had offered her a lifeline of sorts; if she did as he requested, she would one day be welcomed back into the fold. It was that which made her know she would do as he requested. She knew it would give her some small measure of respect, and stop her son from having to hunt her down, because he would do just that. She had no doubts on that score.

'When do I have to do it?' Her voice was gentle, almost a whisper. It was drenched with fear and trepidation at what he wanted her to do. But it was preferable to the alternative; she was too old to go on the trot, and too lazy to start over at her time of life.

'Tonight, and you make sure you don't fuck it up.'

Detective Inspector Ralph Myers was an old friend of Michael Hannon and Jimmy Bailey. He was well known around the West End of London for his amazing capacity for alcohol consumption and his very liberal views regarding certain criminals and their business dealings. His large frame and his thick head of grey hair were instantly recognisable to everyone in the know, and his penchant for the company of Faces was seen by other policemen as their pension scheme. He was a fixer, and he was very good at it. He could fix almost anything, from getting a change of court venue or judge, to making sure evidence was accidentally lost or spoilt. He could guarantee a reduced sentence for certain drug dealers; he would tell the judge in chambers that the person convicted had been of enormous help to them by serving up their friends and relatives and the judge, for a good drink, would use that in his summing up. That way, everyone would go away happy, especially the person convicted to a five-stretch instead of a fifteen. So he was the man who was chosen to oversee the investigation into the murder of Jamsie O'Loughlin. His body had been found in Imelda Dooley's flat, he had been stabbed to death. He made sure that Imelda Dooley was charged as expected, and that her statement of guilt was worded correctly. It was all done with the usual decorum and haste he was renowned for.

Imelda was sentenced to eight years, and her long-time addiction to heroin was used as a motive.

Jamsie O'Loughlin's association with the accused's daughter was never mentioned. Imelda's incarceration caused more than just her close family to breathe a sigh of relief. She was finally gone from their lives and, for once, she was seen as doing something altruistic. Only a few people knew the truth and they were not talking.

Jordanna looked out at the rolling mountains and deeply breathed in the clean air. She loved this time of day, when the sun was just setting and the sky was stained orange and purple. It made her feel glad to be alive, and she had not thought she would ever feel like that again. Though she wondered if she had ever truly experienced that feeling anyway.

She caressed the soft leather binding of her Bible. She had found great comfort in her religion since the breakdown. She had needed something to make her feel whole again, make her feel part of something. Her faith had helped her to heal, along with the therapists and the prescription drugs she took daily. But gradually she had begun to feel better inside, and that was very important to her, she knew that now.

She was drinking cold lemonade and she could feel the warmth of the evening wind as it touched her lightly browned skin. She knew she looked good, and she liked that she knew that. She felt a tiny glimmer of happiness inside herself, and that was more than she had ever hoped for.

'Hello, sis, how are you?'

She turned to see Kenny smiling the wide smile that made him look so handsome and so gentle. All the nurses loved him, and he flirted with them shamelessly. He liked dark-haired women, and it seemed that they liked him back. He leant down and kissed her on the forehead. He could see how much better she was; he flew out to see her every weekend and every weekend she seemed happier inside herself. Even a little contented.

Jordanna's eventual breakdown had been as expected as it was explosive. She had been in a private facility in northern Spain for over a year. The doctors were discreet, and had been known to harbour more than a few criminals who needed to disappear for a few months. It had been a difficult time, and Kenny had been beside her every step of the way.

She was finally on the mend though, and she looked and sounded like a different person. Her problems had been buried deep, and her acceptance of her eventual violent outburst was imperative to her finally being on the mend.

She would never have a child, she accepted that now, realised that her need for one had become almost irrational in the end. She had wanted a child so she could wipe out her own childhood, make up for her own unhappiness. That was no reason to bring a baby into the world. People did it every day and a small percentage of them should not have been allowed to keep a pet, let alone a defenceless little human being.

She knew she would never be like normal people who had been blessed with normal lives. Her mother had seen to it that she would never be able to know the real happiness that other people took for granted. But she was now able to relax and enjoy the little things that pleased her. She took each day as it came, and she knew that was all she could do. Healing took its own time, and she was learning slowly and surely how to accept herself and even how to like herself a little. She finally knew a measure of peace, and for that alone she would be eternally grateful. For Jordanna Dooley that was enough to be going on with. As long as her mother kept out of her life she knew she could cope. Her mother's addiction had blighted everyone around her and they had all paid a terrible price.

'Granny will be here tomorrow, she is mad to get her hands on you.'

Jordanna laughed then, and it sounded so natural, and so happy, that Kenny Boy felt the urge to cry.

'I'll be home next week, then we can get our lives back.' She grinned then and said quickly, 'I'll rephrase that, shall I? We can have some kind of life together at last. Without *her* in the background.'

Kenny nodded happily, and they were quiet then as

they watched the sun disappear behind the mountains. But Kenny knew that Imelda would be out within two years and she felt she was entitled to some kind of recompense for what she saw as her selfless sacrifice in doing her daughter's time. Once more she had rewritten history to suit herself, and she would come out expecting everyone to be grateful and welcoming.

His granny was visiting her, he knew; every few weeks she made the journey out to Cookham Wood and tried to have a conversation with her only daughter. He guessed from the little she said that it was not an easy couple of hours. One thing was sure though, Imelda was off the skag, and that alone was something to be glad about. But suffice until the time thereof, as his old priest used to say, he had no intentions of meeting trouble until he had to. Then he would do whatever was necessary to get it sorted as quickly and cleanly as possible.

Epilogue

'Why don't you let me get you a decent gaff, Jorge? Just because you caught religion don't mean you can't live in a nice drum.'

Jordanna shook her head slowly, smiling that half-hearted smile as always. 'I like it here, Kenny, and now, thanks to her, I'll have to move again.'

Kenny sighed in exasperation. 'No one knows better than me how fucking aggravating she can be, but she is hurting. She done the time for you and, in fairness, mad as she is, and she is fucking madder than a box of frogs, all she wants is for you to acknowledge that. She just wants to make things right.'

Jordanna hated her brother when he tried to talk her round like this. She had to force herself to calm down, make sure she didn't say things she knew they would all regret. Kenny Boy was her heart, in many ways he was all she really had left of her old life. He was a Face, and she knew that. Even with her new-found religion, she still understood that he was the best of the best in many ways. He loved her more than anybody else ever would. She respected that, and she would never hear a bad word about him. She knew that he was a little fucker, knew he was dangerous, could be vindictive and, more to the point, that he was devoid of anything even resembling a conscience or guilt. Well, she had accepted that about him, and she had found a way to live with that. What she was not able to countenance was her mother's influence over him, her mother's determination to influence her, her life, and her beliefs through her love for her brother.

Kenny had the knack of wiping away the hate and the lunacy that Imelda had wrought on them both. Unlike her, Kenny Boy was capable of deep forgiveness. Whereas she, on the other hand, the born-again Catholic, couldn't do that. She could not let her mother walk away from the abortion she called a life and act as if nothing had happened. She was strong now, strong enough to refuse her mother's attempts at reconciliation, even though she knew she should be capable of forgiveness. She now saw her mother's life for what it really was, saw how damaging her mother's addiction to drugs, drink and the pursuit of anything dangerous or disgusting had moulded her and her brother into what they now were. Both were incapable of anything even resembling normal behaviour; like Imelda, Kenny Boy believed that money and prestige were more important than anything else. But, unlike Kenny Boy, she had suffered at her mother's hands. She had suffered the consequences of her mother's complete disregard for her, and just because she suddenly wanted to be her best friend, felt that her sacrifice entitled her to some kind of reward, meant nothing. She had experienced a breakdown of Olympian standards, had eventually been reduced to her mother's level, and that was what she could not, and would not ever forgive.

Kenny might see the violence and the disarray of their mother's daily life as a joke, as something to laugh about. But, unlike him, she had taken the brunt of it, and she knew she could never let her back into her life. Jordanna knew that if she weakened, her mother would do what she had always done, she would inveigle her way in, and then, when it suited her, she would destroy them all without a backward glance. Imelda Dooley was without even a smidgeon of humility, anything that even remotely resembled real caring or genuine human emotion. She also accepted that Kenny Boy had inherited that same coldness and the same ability to forget anything that was deemed too awful or too shaming to remember. Her mother had the gall to stand on her doorstep and berate her, threaten her, and all because she didn't want to play happy families. Even Kenny saw Imelda's imprisonment as something to respect, saw it as something that cancelled out all the other bad things Imelda was responsible for. He had trouble understanding why she couldn't just let bygones be bygones. But then, he didn't know the whole truth about anything, really.

Kenny watched his sister as she stared into space as usual. He loved her, but he felt that her sojourn in the Spanish nut-house had left her a few paving slabs short of a patio. He wanted his sister back, wanted her to stop being so fucking determined to blame their mother for everything. In short, he wanted to play happy families and, where this family was concerned, that was not exactly a viable option.

He felt the distance between them, and he worried that it was because of him, worried that she secretly blamed him for her problems. For her breakdown. He knew she resented his defence of Imelda, unlike him, she could not find it in her heart to forgive or forget, and she was supposed to be the fucking big Catholic, the church-goer. And now he just wanted her to live decently, to appreciate his largesse.

'Come on, sis, let me move you out of this dump, somewhere you can feel safe.'

Jordanna shook her head sadly, sorry that Kenny didn't understand her or her wants.

'I like this little house, Kenny, and I don't need a good address to make me feel like a valid person. I spent my life trying to prove something to people who had no real interest in me or my life. So, thank you for the offer, but *no* thanks, Kenny. I can live quite happily as I am, without the big-screen TVs or the top-of-the-range motors. I do not need the clothes or the hairstyles. I don't need the fucking pretence that *you* need. I don't need money, I don't need anything. All I want is to be left in relative peace. I don't think that's a lot to ask for, do you?'

Kenny knew his sister was being honest and, if *he* was honest, that was what annoyed him so much. She was his closest blood, but her fucking smugness, her absolute denial of his way of life really aggravated him. He had worked long and hard to make their lives easier, and she took great pleasure in refusing his help, in refusing to become a part of what he saw as his success story. She was like a fucking hermit with her dowdy clothes and her constant praying. He went to Mass, he loved the whole concept of his religion. As Christ Himself said, I was in prison and you visited me. Jesus knew what it was like to be on the threshold of life, to be involved in something that most people didn't understand. He knew how emotive the Mass could be, how it was something that was shared by many, but was still a very personal experience.

Jordanna's religiousness was not as alien to him as she believed. He also knew how far she had come, knew how difficult her life had been. Even knowing all that though, Kenny still felt an anger at what he saw as her complete dismissal of him and all he tried to do for her.

Since she had come home from Spain, she was a different person. She was a religious nut-case for a start but, worse than that, she had gradually stepped back from him, and everything he stood for. In some ways he could understand her actions but, in his heart, he felt that her dismissal of him and all he had achieved was like a slap in the face. He felt that her refusal to be a part of his world was the equivalent of her saying that she repudiated it. He was at the top of his game, and everyone around him made a point of letting him know that, except for Jordanna: she never mentioned his accomplishments, it was as if they never existed. He knew it was churlish, knew he shouldn't care so much, but it really bothered him. It was as if she was looking down her nose at him, and that was something he could not bear. Kenny needed to believe that he had wiped out their childhood, wiped out the stigma they had been born into. As Imelda's children they had not really had a chance, and he had made sure that they were respected, that they were not ostracised because she had given birth to them. He had made a point of doing that for them, had made their names mean something. He also knew that his sister understood that better than anyone else around them. Her complete indifference to his achievements really bothered him. Her decision to turn her back on all that he could offer her was an insult. But he knew she was still in the thrall of her religious mania.

Kenny took a deep breath. He was determined not to

let his anger get the better of him. He knew from experience it was pointless where his sister was concerned. Unlike everyone else in his orbit, she had no fear of him, or of what he was capable of.

'Look at how you live, Jorge, all you do is fucking wallow in your own self-pity. I love you dearly, and you know that. But I hate to see you living like this. Hate to see you grateful for a kind word from the fucking same priest who has no qualms about cornering me for a few grand when the fancy takes him, even though he knows where it all comes from. I hate to see you old before your time, dressed like a demented social worker, and talking like one and all. I want you to accept that you had a breakdown: it *happens*, even in the best of families, get over it.'

Jordanna went to a drawer in her kitchen and opened it. Taking out a pack of Benson & Hedges cigarettes, she lit one slowly. Drawing the smoke into her lungs she waited until the crashing of her heart subsided, and the trembling in her hands quietened. Then turning back towards her brother she said quietly, 'Why do you always think this is personal, Kenny? What makes you so convinced that if only I would live my life as you want me to, I will automatically be happy? I like my life, I like living here, I like the fact that I don't *care* about other people's opinions. I like to feel that God is near me, that He can understand my suffering. I love you, Kenny Boy, but I cannot let her back into my life. You know I lost my baby after her last visit. You have to let me get on with my life as I see fit, you have to stop trying to justify her existence. I know you think that because she gave birth to us she can't be all bad, well, do you know something? You're wrong, she would sell you down the river for a fucking

Happy Meal from McDonald's if it suited her. Now, I know you don't want to hear that, but it's the truth. And I would sooner hang myself from the nearest fucking tree before I let you talk me round, so either let it drop, or walk away from me once and for all.'

Kenny was distressed at his sister's obvious bitterness and anger. He knew that she had good reason for her antipathy towards her mother, he also knew that, until she faced her one to one, she would never be completely free. He felt that Jordanna needed to see their mother for the broken and nondescript person she really was. If she saw her properly, as she was now, saw how completely devoid of anything even remotely resembling her old self, he felt Jordanna would finally be able to move on. He had forgiven his mother when she had gone away to save her daughter's arse. He was a realist: he knew that Imelda had not really had any choice in the matter. But he chose to overlook that. He felt that whatever she was, she was still their mother. And, as such, they were honourbound to accept her. He also knew that Jordanna had always taken the brunt of Imelda's madness, had been the thorn in her side. He had guessed, early on, that every time she looked at her daughter, she saw herself, saw the person she should have been had she not chosen the needle over everyone and everything else in her life. But she had, and that was tough shit for all concerned.

'Look, Jorge, all I want is for you to make your peace with her. I have and, believe me, it wasn't easy. But, at the end of the day, she *is* our mother. And, as such, we have a fucking duty towards her. I forced her to go away for you, we all know that. It ain't like no one ever worked that one out for themselves, is it? She might still get on the big train; drugs are her lifeline after all, but she just wants you to accept that she done your time for you. That's all. And I think if you are *so* fucking religious, then you should see her, let her make her peace. If you did that, she wouldn't keep hunting you down, and she wouldn't keep starting fights with you. *You* know what she's like, she will cause a big fucking row just to get a reaction. If you really want shot, then *talk* to her, let her say her piece. She *needs* to talk to you and I think you need to hear what she has to say.'

Jordanna looked into Kenny Boy's handsome face and knew he was the victim of his own success. He saw his acceptance of his mother as him being the big, benevolent Face. If *he* could accept her, then so should everyone else. They had to, because she was *his* mother and, as such, she could *not* be disrespected. He saw that as a reflection on him, saw that as a personal affront. Even though the people concerned might not see Imelda in quite the same light. He chose to forget a lot and only then because he was more interested in his own fucking personal reputation, his own fucking standing in the community. Jordanna understood that to an extent, she knew better than anybody how hard it was to be related to Imelda Dooley. But Kenny Boy's sudden fucking desire to defend his mother's actions and then to try and justify them to *her*, of all people, really rankled.

Kenny didn't remember Imelda, not really. He had been her golden boy, her little man and the only reason she had cared for him was because he had been a big lump, a heavy-boned child who was obviously big for his age, and Imelda had basked in his reflected glory. Everyone had remarked on his *size*, on his *strength*, on his good looks. Imelda had seen him as a reflection of herself.

Imelda had killed his father, and she had conveniently

put the blame for that on her little daughter. What *he* didn't know, or anyone else for that matter, was that there had been a second shot fired that night, fired from her little hands, and that her so-called mother had shot the gun into the big double mattress Lance had shared with her, while holding the gun in her daughter's hands. She remembered the pain from the gun's report. How its powerful kickback had hurt her all over. How it had *jarred* her shoulders, and made her teeth rattle inside her head. She had remembered her mother threatening her that if she spoke about it to anyone she would be taken away and she would never see anyone she knew again. Her own mother had forced her to look at Lance's corpse and had assured her that she would be blamed. She had to promise that she would never say a word about it to anyone. It had been easy, really, she had lived with lies and secrets ever since she could remember. Her mother and her granny had seen to that.

She had lived with the images of that night her entire life, and she had still kept her own counsel, even when she had finally understood what had really happened. She had spent such a large part of her life trying to make her mother care for her, make her mother acknowledge her in some way. She had hoped and prayed that her continued silence for so many years would make her mother finally accept her. But it had never happened and, finally, she had accepted that it was never going to happen. She had suddenly understood that she was so far beneath her mother's radar that her involvement in anything pertaining to her mother was negligible as far as Imelda was concerned. In short, she knew that she just didn't exist for her. She also knew, even then, as young as she was, that that would never change. It was another thing that she had pushed down inside of her, another thing she had tried to blot out. To bully a child was a terrible thing, but to ignore them and their desperate attempts for attention, was far more wicked.

Kenny Boy had *never* been on the receiving end of his mother's hate, or her spite. He still didn't understand, all these years later, how she had used her own flesh and blood for her own ends. He wouldn't understand, even now, that he had been protected, had been sheltered from his own mother's self-destructive lifestyle. And that was only because of how Imelda had used her own daughter. Kenny Boy didn't realise that, if it wasn't for *her* taking the brunt of Imelda's lunacy, he would have eventually been used by her as a scapegoat as well.

Jordanna knew that her brother was only arguing their mother's case because she, his sister, had in effect turned her back on him, and all he stood for. But that wasn't anything personal, it wasn't about him. It was about *her*, and her *need* to make her life mean something. She had realised after her breakdown just how useless and vacuous her life had been. She had been bundled off to Spain, money had been thrown about in huge amounts, and she had once more been expected to digest, to accept, and to forget what had happened to her. Even her granny, God love her, had expected her to just wipe it all away. Forget about it, pretend it had never happened. Kenny Boy, like Granny Mary, had managed to do just that. Like Mary Dooley, Kenny had the knack of deleting from his psyche anything that he saw as troublesome. Well, Jordanna didn't have that knack, and she had always known that. Imelda could do it, she did it unconsciously; she could edit anything that happened in her life to suit her own ends.

Imelda took after her mother for that and, as much as

Jordanna loved her granny, she knew better than anybody just how easy Mary found rewriting history for her own ends. This, after all, was a woman who had buried her husband amid serious accusations and violence, and who had then turned her back on her own sons. This was the same woman who had regularly visited her only daughter in prison, knowing all the while that she had been the cause of *her* granddaughter's complete mental breakdown. The same granddaughter that she had taken great pleasure in removing from her only daughter's orbit all those years before. Jordanna had believed, for all those years, that she had done all that to save *her* from her mother's car crash of a life but she now knew that she had actually done it to ensure that she had another family to raise. She had allowed her husband free rein with her first batch of babies, had walked away from her sons and made sure that her daughter's children were wholly hers. Her granny had her love, she always would, but she had lost her from the day that she had learnt of her granny's new-found interest in her daughter.

Jordanna couldn't pretend that things had not happened, couldn't pretend that she didn't care: unlike Kenny Boy, whose attitude was if you don't think about it then it never happened. Her breakdown proved that she *did* care, that all the things she had pushed aside, that she had forced away, that she had tried to forget, could *never* be erased, forgotten about. She had been forced to confront them, had been forced to accept them, and she had finally understood that her breakdown had culminated in an act of violence so shocking and so devastating that she would never get over it. She would never again know a day's real peace, or experience a full night's sleep.

Unlike her brother, Jordanna wasn't capable of

conveniently forgetting the things that she didn't want to remember any more. Her trouble was that she remembered them too well, in stunning clarity, and they were the reason that she would never again know a truly happy day.

Kenny Boy was genuinely heartbroken at his sister's sorrow, he could feel the deep sadness that he knew would always be a part of her. In fact, had always been a part of her since he could remember.

Jordanna had always been there for him, all his life she had been the one person he had known he could rely on. She had been the only person who had never been scared of him, who had never had a hidden agenda. He knew how terrifying he could be, he knew that, like his mother, he was incapable of really caring for anyone, except this woman before him. Jordanna was the only person he had ever loved. His granny Mary had his care, she had his loyalty but, like his mother, she was only really important to him because she was his flesh and blood. Other than Jorge, there was nobody.

Her breakdown had affected him far more than he had ever let on. He had seen it as a personal affront, seen it as something he could not control, that he couldn't mend, couldn't make better. He had understood, for the first time in his life, that money and prestige were worthless when you were faced with genuine grief. He had been forced to accept that some things in life were far too important for money to make a difference. Kenny had watched his sister live quite happily in her little house, and saw her try to heal herself with prayer and a belief in a God who he felt, in his darker moments, had abandoned his sister from a very young age.

'Please, Jordanna, don't make me feel like I failed you,

all I have ever wanted is what was best for you. I still want that.'

Jordanna smiled sadly, and Kenny saw the evenness of her teeth, the kindness in her face that her smile always portrayed. He saw the dark blue of her eyes that, even without make-up, made the person looking into them see the beauty inside her. She had high cheekbones and thick, blond hair that needed a good cut, but still shone with a burnished gold coveted by the majority of women. Jordanna was a real beauty, but the saddest thing of all was that she genuinely didn't know that. She honestly had no idea just how lovely she really was.

Jordanna had wandered through her life and she had never once realised her true worth, she had stumbled from one fucking disaster to another. Kenny knew that he had turned a blind eye to her problems, had been more than happy to pretend that they had not even existed. He had removed his mother from her orbit, and that had assuaged his guilt for a while. But, deep down, he had known that one day he would have to deal with all of this. Why was it that he only admitted that to himself now?

'I hate her, Kenny, and I pray every day for that to change. But it doesn't. In fact, my antipathy for her just seems to deepen, and my capacity for hatred towards her seems to grow stronger by the second. Every time I move away, she tracks me down, and I have to subdue the urge to physically attack her. Destroy her once and for all, because until she is dead and gone, I know I will never experience even one day of real peace. So *stop* trying to buy me happiness, *stop* trying to purchase my peace of mind, and please *stop* believing that one day I will finally let her come back into my life. It will *never* happen. Unlike *you*, Kenny, I remember the *real* Imelda and, unlike you, I know what she is really capable of. I'll move house again if I have to. I really don't want to do that, but if that is what it takes, then that is what I am willing to do. You want her, *you* can have her, but don't try and palm her off on me. I've had just about enough of her to last me a lifetime.'

Kenny saw the distress and the anger in his sister's face, he felt the hurt as she instinctively stepped away from him, distanced herself from him both physically as well as mentally.

'She went away for you, and because of that I will be eternally grateful to her. Nan pointed that out to me, Jorge, and she was right.'

Jordanna nodded her head slowly and Kenny knew that she'd had just about enough for one day.

'Read my lips, Kenny, I really don't give a flying fuck.'

Imelda was stoned out of her brains; she was unaware of how out of it she actually was, but that was nothing unusual for her. As Imelda cut herself a line of coke, she silently thanked God for her son's generosity. He knew she had done them a favour and, Imelda being Imelda, she now felt that her selfless act could never really be repaid by her children. As she snorted the large, fluffy white line of cocaine, she allowed herself to dwell on her children's disrespectful behaviour and their gross ungratefulness. Although her son saw her all right for money and her other sundries, knowing that he was in receipt of serious amounts of wedge, had started to bother her.

Imelda's sensible head reminded her that she was not to be trusted with money; she admitted that if she had twenty quid, she would spend twenty-*one* quid. But, all the same, she had come out of nick expecting her children to welcome her with open arms. She had kicked the needle, though she still used occasionally when the urge came over her. In Holloway she had been introduced to the wonders of cocaine. A drug she felt was far more suited to her particular personality. There, heroin users were seen as being below even child killers, and Imelda had understood that from the off. As a murderer, she knew that she would be kept as A-category for a while. So she had weaned herself off the habit with the help of methadone and a social worker from the Gambia who had a sketchy command of the English language and a rather unhealthy habit of believing everything he was told. Consequently, Imelda had had a field day. She had been weaned off the needle, but still maintained the availability of her methadone, and had sold it on in good faith for a tidy profit. Her son's name had guaranteed her an easy ride, and that was why she now felt confident enough to push her luck as and when the fancy came over her. She had gone inside because she had not had any other options available to her; she had fucked up big time with everyone around her. But she had also come to realise that she was doing a dirty great big favour for her kids at the same time.

Once she had settled in, her fear of her actions and their consequences had faded away. She had realised just what a big favour she had done for them both, after all, her son and daughter were very close, closer than a junkie and their dealer. It didn't come much closer than that. She had expected her daughter to have at least thanked her for her lost years. She had expected her to appreciate exactly what she had done for her. Instead, she had been on the receiving end of her daughter's absolute contempt.

Now, her daughter's constant refusal to even acknowledge her was really rankling. She had conveniently forgotten the past, as was her wont. Imelda had always been capable of editing her life to suit her own purposes. Jordanna's impudence and repeated rudeness had struck a chord inside her somewhere. Imelda accepted that she might not have been mother of the year, but she felt that her selfless act should have cancelled all those bad feelings out. She *owed* her mother; Jordanna fucking *owed* her. And she owed her big time, if not for her, she would have been banged up and forgotten about. After all, it was only her addiction that had helped her get a reduced sentence.

None of her kids had tried to help her with that. She had been left to sort it all out on her own, and as she told herself on a daily basis, that had been the story of her life. Her kids had been like a pair of fucking albatrosses hanging around her neck, dragging her down. At least Kenny Boy had afforded her a measure of entertainment, had grown up to make her proud of him. She prided herself on that much anyway.

In all honesty she had always loathed her daughter, had seen her as the reason for all her bad luck, had blamed her for everything that had ever gone wrong in her life. Yet now she decided Jordanna should recognise her, appreciate what she had done for her. She had done a lot for that ungrateful little whore, and she was determined to see that she was given the credit for it. She would hunt her down, and force the respect from her, if it was the last thing she ever did. She had Kenny Boy onside, so it was only a matter of time before that stuck-up little mare was forced to bend her knee, and finally accept her mother into her life. Because, for all her new-found faith, Jordanna would always be nothing more than the shit on her mother's shoes. Jordanna thought she was better than everyone else, well, she wasn't. As Imelda cut herself another line of coke, she couldn't help smiling; she was now welcome everywhere. She knew that was because of her son and she milked it for all it was worth. It was a matter of principle now, making her daughter come around to her way of thinking, she felt strongly that whatever might have happened in the past, she had cancelled it out.

She needed her daughter's approbation, because she knew that without it, her precious son would eventually be forced to choose between them, and she also knew that should that scenario ever happen, he was not about to choose her.

'Nan, she is driving me up the fucking wall. She sits in that fucking little house praying and reading her Bible. I don't know what she wants from me, I don't know what I am supposed to do.'

Mary Dooley sighed, she was too old for all this and they both knew it. 'That girl has had to put up with a lot and, unlike you, she has not been in a position to shrug it off. She *killed* somebody, someone she loved dearly. Now, I know you might not think that is something important, but she does. So, leave her be, will you?'

Kenny was angry, he knew that his sister had problems, but he also felt that she should be sane enough to let him help her with them. His granny suddenly acting like she was in the know annoyed him: she was the one who had decided that their mother should be brought back into the fold. As far as he was concerned, she should either shit or get off the fucking pot, and he said as much, his anger making him vindictive.

'*You* are the one who insisted me mother be treated like visiting royalty; if it was left to me I would have given her a drink and waved her on her way. She is an old brass, she spent her life on her back, pursuing the business, and she was very good at it by all accounts. She thinks that Jorge is a fucking nut-job and she is, she is a fucking Looney Tunes with her praying and her fucking ramblings about the Book of Revelations. I know she flipped her lid, but that was years ago. I think it's time Jordanna pulled herself together and stopped blaming everyone else for her problems.'

Kenny had finally said what he really thought out loud, and the words didn't make him feel relieved: they made him feel like a snide, like a grass. He was ashamed of her, knew that she was looked on with disdain, knew that people who saw her and listened to her felt she was a few sandwiches short of a picnic. He loved her, but he hated her for how she was, he resented her for not getting over her depression and making a life for herself.

'She does nothing, Nan. She looks like the Wreck of the fucking Hesperus, she talks bollocks and she won't move on. She's had a few bad breaks but, as you and I know, that's fucking life. If she doesn't get a grip soon she never will.'

Mary sat at the kitchen table and watched her grandson as he tried to understand his sister and her way of life. She knew he was incapable of even scratching the surface where Jordanna was concerned, and she was sorry for that. She knew that he was the kind of person who was classed as a doer. He didn't have the patience for anyone who wasn't like him, who wasn't capable enough.

Kenny opened his arms wide in a gesture of defeat. 'I think we should get her put away again, make her get better this time . . .'

Mary laughed at his audacity. 'You can't just put her

away because she doesn't fit into your world, she is happy enough. She is marvellous if you consider what she had to contend with all her life.'

Kenny dismissed her words with a wave of his huge arm, and Mary was reminded of how dangerous this young man actually was. 'I know she had a bad time, but she has to sort herself out now. Have you seen her lately, Nan? She looks like a fucking immigrant. She goes to Mass three times a day, takes communion three times a day. Look, Nan, I have tried to help her, but she won't let me. If she would face me mother I think she would be halfway home, but she just fights her. And, in fairness, Mum came up trumps for her. I know I might have *made* her take the can, but she did her time without letting on about the truth . . .'

Mary was now getting sick and tired of her grandson's constant insistence that his mother was some kind of fucking saint: she had been the cause of every ill that had befallen this family. She might have been grateful to her for taking the pressure off Jordanna but, considering she should have been banged up years ago it was what she now deemed a moot point.

Standing up with difficulty, Mary walked to her pantry. Opening the door, she removed a bottle of Teachers whisky, poured herself a large tot into a tea cup and swallowed it down quickly. Then, pouring herself out another hefty measure she looked at her grandson who was watching her in awe and she said softly, 'You don't know the half of it, Kenny, we all protected you from the truth. Jordanna has the right to do whatever she wants. Leave her be.'

Kenny laughed incredulously, his granny was supposed to be agreeing with him, she was supposed to tell him that he was right, that Jorge needed to be sorted out properly.

'So I should stand back and let her move again, should I? Watch her find another shithole to rent, and stand by while me mother tracks her down once more? Jordanna needs help, she is still not the full shilling. You know what I am saying is the truth.'

Mary looked at her grandson. He was the love of her life, and because of that she had forgiven him everything. He had been protected all his life from the harsh reality that was his mother's addiction, and his sister's destruction. His arrogance and his assumption that his opinion of his sister and her mental state was accurate annoyed her. That he had not understood the reason why his sister had finally exploded made her want to shake him, grab his shoulders and shake him until his teeth rattled in his head.

'Your sister was used and abused by your father, and many others. Your mother passed Jordanna out to anyone who wanted her; that's why she can't keep a child inside her, you stupid bloody fool. Your mother might have been good at the business, as you so joyfully pointed out, but she tortured that girl and her breakdown was a long time coming. So I am sorry if you think she is a bit too *strange* for you, and I am sorry if you are *ashamed* of her, but next time your mother turns up on her doorstep shouting the odds, remember that Jordanna, God love her, has never opened her trap about what she went through as a child. I had to sit back and wait for the opportunity to get you two away from her. Jordanna looked after you because your mother, Saint *fucking* Imelda, only cared about her drugs. So, the next time you see your sister, try and remember that she has been used and abused nearly all her life, and your mother is the culprit. Your fucking mother might have gone away for her but, in my opinion, it wasn't before fucking time. If I had my way I'd put her away for good.'

Kenny Boy had lost his usual ruddy complexion, he was almost grey. His deep-blue eyes, framed by long dark lashes, were almost closed as his grandmother's words penetrated his brain. He knew she was telling the truth, he knew that somewhere inside he had known about this all along. He knew that his sister's weakness bothered him because she had always been so strong in his eyes. As children, she had been the one to look out for him, he had *depended* on her to look after him. She had been the only constant in his life.

Mary knew she had spoken out of turn, knew that she should have kept the truth inside herself; after all, if Jordanna had not mentioned it then she had no right to broadcast it. But Kenny had needed to know why his sister had been broken like she had. He had needed to understand that she had actually survived her mother's ministrations and that his sister had actually overcome more than he realised, that Jordanna was actually proof of how faith and self-belief could bring a measure of peace to even the most persecuted of people.

Kenny had needed to understand that he should be applauding her for the way Jordanna had clawed her way back from the abyss, not trying to force her to be happy because her chosen lifestyle irritated him. Because he felt she should want the same things as he did, need the same things as he did. Mary gulped at the whisky once more, and watched her grandson as he digested all the information she had just given him.

It was only as her grandson stormed out of her house a few minutes later, that the enormity of what she had done finally hit her.

*

Jordanna knelt at the altar of her local church. She looked better than she had in years. Her hair was brushed to a silky sheen and her slim frame had filled out so that she once more had a figure of sorts. She was dressed smartly, and she looked a shadow of her old self. She had lost her permanent frown, was much more ready to smile and her eyes had lost the dullness that had become a fixture. She looked almost happy, she was looser somehow, had a softness to her features that reminded people of how lovely she actually was.

As Jordanna accepted the Eucharist she prayed silently and, bowing her head, she walked slowly back to her pew. Kneeling once more, she prayed with all the energy she could muster. As her brother slipped into the seat beside her, she blessed herself quickly then, pulling herself up slowly, she sat beside him. They enjoyed the rest of the Mass together, and as the weak November sun forced itself through the stained-glass windows, Jordanna prayed for a final end to her sadness. She knew she was finally emerging from the darkness that had enveloped her for so many years, and she felt lighter, felt more involved with the world around her. She was once more in accord with her brother, and that alone was something she was grateful for. They were close again, and he had even professed to an understanding of her love for the church, and had helped her to assuage her guilt at her relief when she had been told of her mother's death. She had tried to forgive her mother, had tried to tell herself that her mother's addiction had been the cause of everything that had happened. But she knew that wasn't true; her mother's addiction had been something she had *chosen*, her addiction had been the only thing her mother had ever really cared about.

The sins of the fathers, Jordanna understood those words now. They didn't mean that the sins a parent might commit would be visited on their offspring. The words actually meant that the *mistakes* a parent made while they were bringing up their children would be visited on the second, the third, even the fourth generation.

She was destined to be an auntie, her mother had seen to that. But she was also destined to find her own happiness where she could. She had recently met a widower with three children and she knew that he had been sent to her, that she had been looking for someone like him. It was early days yet, but she knew instinctively that he was her second chance at happiness.

Her mother had been found in an alley. She had been beaten to death and had choked on her own blood at some point during the attack. She had been there, scoring as usual, and the police believed that she had become involved in an argument with her dealer. Her mother had died as she had lived, pursuing the only thing that had ever mattered to her. She had been buried without any pomp or ceremony and with no mourners at her graveside. Even her own mother had declined to attend the service. The news had brought a measure of peace to Jordanna; knowing that she would never have to deal with her again had lifted her spirits, had brought her a measure of peace she had not known in her life before.

Her mother would never again turn up on her doorstop demanding attention, causing her daughter to relive the terror and the disgust that had made up her childhood and had eventually destroyed her chance of having any kind of real life. Her mother had eventually broken her both mentally and physically, and the worst thing of all was, Jordanna knew that the damage had been inflicted without any thought whatsoever. Whoever had come up with the idea that a child was better off with a parent, even an addicted parent, had a lot to answer for. Addicts' children should be removed from their influence, and placed as far away from the offender as was humanly possible.

She had watched silently as her mother's coffin had been lowered into the damp ground, had needed to see her mother finally entombed once and for all.

Kenny Boy had held her hand, had made sure she had not let the news get her down. As if. She had silently rejoiced at her new-found freedom. Kenny Boy had watched over her until the funeral was finished and life had resumed once more. In fact, he had been the *one* person who seemed to understand her relief at the terrible news, and appreciate her new-found lust for life. Jordanna guessed that Kenny Boy knew far more about Imelda's death than the police did, but that was only her gut instinct. Her granny knew far more about it than she ever would, and that suited her down to the ground. If her mother had died at the hands of her beloved son, then that was God's will. As long as that could not be proved in a court of law, she didn't really care. He was even more damaged than she was but, unlike her, he really had no concept of that. Kenny had inherited Imelda's knack for disregarding anything that might cause him a sleepless night, or make him feel a real emotion. He saw everything from his own unique point of view and, unlike her, he didn't allow regret to colour his life in any way. All she knew for sure was that her mother's death had somehow brought an end to her own suffering. She and Kenny Boy had lived with their mother's shadow looming over them since she could remember.

Now, at last, it seemed that they were both free.

Now you can buy any of these other bestselling books by **Martina Cole** from your bookshop or *direct from the publisher*.

FREE P&P AND UK DELIVERY
(Overseas and Ireland £3.50 per book)

Dangerous Lady	£7.99
The Ladykiller	£7.99
Goodnight Lady	£7.99
The Jump	£7.99
The Runaway	£7.99
Two Women	£7.99
Broken	£7.99
Faceless	£7.99
Maura's Game	£7.99
The Know	£7.99
The Graft	£7.99
The Take	£7.99
Close	£7.99
Faces	£7.99

TO ORDER SIMPLY CALL THIS NUMBER

01235 400 414

or visit our website: www.headline.co.uk

Prices and availability subject to change without notice.